# HOUR OF THE CAT

# HOUR OF

# THE CAT

## PETER QUINN

THE OVERLOOK PRESS
Woodstock & New York

First published in the United States in 2005 by
The Overlook Press, Peter Mayer Publishers, Inc.
Woodstock & New York

Woodstock:
One Overlook Drive
Woodstock, NY 12498
www.overlookpress.com
[for individual orders, bulk and special sales, contact our Woodstock office]

New York:
141 Wooster Street
New York, NY 10012

Library of Congress Cataloging-in-Publication Data

Quinn, Peter.
Hour of the cat / Peter Quinn.
p. cm.
1. Private investigators—New York (State)—New York—Fiction.
2. Germans—New York (State)—Fiction. 3. Nurses—Crimes
against—Fiction. 4. Intelligence officers—Fiction. 5. Death
row inmates—Fiction. 6. Conspiracies—Fiction. 7. New
York (N.Y.)—Fiction. I. Title. II. Author

PS3617.U584 H68 2005          813/.54 22          2005040602

*Book design and type formatting by Bernard Schleifer*
Printed in the United States of America
ISBN 1-58567-597-0
1 3 5 7 9 8 6 4 2

To Genevieve and Daniel
*A chuisle mo chroí*
*L'chaim*

# HOUR OF THE CAT

# August 1936

## PROLOGUE

Eugenics was a science that ruled that some forms of life were undeserving of life. The regime at hand merely had to draw the practical conclusions and carry out the death sentences. National Socialism, which harped incessantly on notions of purity of race, would have been the laughingstock of Germany had its scientists shown the imbecility of this idea. Instead, it was the scientists who gave an academic garb to racism or, rather, invented scientific racism as a modern version of pure and simple prejudice and fear of the other.

Finally, the Holocaust, the systematic "extermination" of human beings, would have been unthinkable without the medical profession's "detached" evaluation of these human beings as not only inferior and therefore unworthy of life, but as positively dangerous to the national Aryan body and therefore doomed to quick and efficient, yet of course wholly unemotional elimination. This is what makes the Holocaust central to our era, for it was founded on a scientifically sanctioned, indeed ordered, brutality.

—OMER BARTOV, *Murder in Our Midst*

### THE EXCELSIOR HOTEL, BERLIN

IAN ANDERSON TOOK a copy of the *Völkischer Beobachter* from the racks of newspapers lining the hotel café's walls. As soon as he returned to his corner booth, a waiter served the coffee and pastry he had ordered. At the sight of the German newspaper, the waiter checked the single letter that the maître d' had written in the corner of the seating card, a reminder of the Excelsior Hotel's commitment, for the duration of the Olympic Games, to address guests in their own language. Yes, *E for Englisch*, as he had thought. "Will there be anything else?" the waiter asked.

"Not for the moment," Anderson said. *"Danke."*

The waiter tapped his heels together, lightly, making an almost imperceptible sound, then moved into the room's cavernous center, beneath the immense electric chandeliers, through the closely placed tables, in search of more orders. Advertised as the largest hotel in Europe, the Excelsior had recently added "the most cosmopolitan," a claim given credence by the crowd eagerly availing itself of the international selection of over 200 newspapers and magazines provided gratis. Most of the patrons were engrossed in their newspapers, the front page headlines in seemingly every language on the continent—German, French, Spanish, Hungarian—announcing the success of the previous day's opening ceremonies at the Berlin Olympiad.

Anderson looked up from the *Völkischer Beobachter*, its gushing account of yesterday's event nothing less than what he expected from the Nazi Party's official newspaper. A paper flag bearing the rising sun held over his head, a Japanese guide led a straggly line of his countrymen to a table on the far side of the room. The maître d' approached. "Herr Anderson, your guest has arrived," he said in barely accented English. "Should I show him to your table?"

"Please, if you don't mind." Anderson folded the paper and laid it beside him. He stood and brushed the pastry crumbs from his pants. The maître d' was almost at the table when the person behind popped in front. "Ian Anderson, right?" He held out his hand without waiting for an answer. "I'm Chuck Weber, and I appreciate your taking time to meet with me."

"It's quite all right, Mr. Weber," Anderson said. "Won't you have a seat?"

"Call me Chuck, please." Weber sat in the booth, across from Anderson, who artfully slipped several marks into the hand of the slighted and scowling maître d'. The maître d' bowed in gratitude, whispering, this time in German, "Herr Anderson, I can only hope the manners of an English gentleman will rub off on your American guest."

Weber watched the maître d' as he returned to his station at the café's entrance. "What'd he say?"

"That it seems as though the whole world has come to see the Berlin Games."

"He's got that right." A waiter came to take his order. "Cognac, make it a double," Weber said. He had a pudgy, round face, topped by thick, slicked-back hair the color of dirty straw. He was significantly younger than he'd sounded on the phone, in his early thirties, not late forties, as Anderson had guessed.

Fumbling for a moment in the inside breast pocket of his tan hounds-tooth-check jacket, Weber finally found what he was looking for. He took out an alligator case not much larger than a cigarette lighter, extracted a business card and handed it to Anderson. "As I said on the phone, I'm with Holcomb & Belknap. We're headquartered in New York but, as you see from the card, we have offices in Chicago, London, and now Berlin."

"Yes, I see, 'Charles R. Weber, vice president.' An impressive title."

"Doesn't say so on the card, but I'm the youngest v.p. in the history of the firm."

"And your firm's specialty, it says here, is public relations. It's not a profession I know a lot about."

"P.R. is a bigger deal in the States than over here, but it's catching on. It's not complicated, really. In a nutshell, when an individual or business needs to deal with the press, we make sure it's done to their advantage. If you've got a good story to tell, we get it covered. If it's not so good, we help frame it in a favorable way or keep it out of the spotlight altogether."

The waiter delivered Weber's cognac. He lifted his glass. "Cheers," he said. "I'm interested in the book you're writing."

"Yes, you said so on the phone. What do you know about my book?"

"Well, Ian—you don't mind me calling you Ian, do you?"

"Go right ahead."

"It's this way, Ian. Mr. Holcomb, founder and managing director of our firm, was at a dinner party in New York also attended by your American publisher. His ears pricked up when he heard the title, *My Journey in Nazi Germany.*"

"*Travels in the New Germany* is the correct title."

"Sure, that's it. As Mr. Holcomb told your publisher, we've got clients with a standing interest in what gets written about Germany, especially given all the propaganda and emotions that get mixed in and passed off for facts."

"Do you have the German government for a client?"

Weber chuckled. "Not that I'd feel obliged to tell you if we did, but no, we're not on Hitler's payroll." He finished his drink. "Quite the opposite, we work with a number of American firms whose interests in Germany are purely commercial or philanthropic. They are very concerned about steering clear of politics."

"American interests in Germany aren't a subject of my book."

"A lot of times it hardly matters what's written. What counts is the interpretation put on it. Today, in the U.S., there are those whose only interest is in painting everything that happens in Germany as intended either to harm certain ethnic groups or to start another war. Here, in Berlin, you can see for yourself how wrong they are. Does it look to you as though a new version of the Spanish Inquisition is under way? Or that another war is on tap?" Weber gestured with his empty glass at the room filled with happy tourists and relaxed patrons.

"Germany encompasses more than this room," Anderson said.

"Exactly right. It's impossible to sum up all that's happening in Germany by looking exclusively at a small piece, good or bad. Think about it! A country flattened by defeat and depression is on its feet. Business is booming. Millions are back to work. Yet some only want to see the negative. I've been working with firms such as International Business Machines, Ford, and Texaco. You'd think they'd win praise for building bridges of peace through international commerce. Instead, they're attacked and pilloried for not joining a boycott of trade with Germany."

"It's absurd when you think about it," Weber continued. I mean, look at Avery Brundage and the American Olympic Committee, and the heat they took over the decision not to boycott these Games. In the face of every kind or pressure and threat, he stood his ground, so that today the United States is here, alongside the rest of the world, ready to compete, and with a team that includes Jews and colored as well as regular Americans."

"The issue was the treatment of Jews here in Germany and their exclusion from amateur sports."

"Sure, and then what do we in the States say when people turn around and point fingers at us for not letting the colored play in our professional baseball leagues? And you English aren't exactly pure as driven snow when it comes to the treatment of other races. I mean, 'Let the one without sin cast the first stone,' right?"

"What happens in America or Britain doesn't excuse what happens in Germany, and vice versa."

"Of course, I'm sorry for getting us sidetracked. I'll get right to the point. I've been told that you've been looking into the eugenic program underway in Germany, and without intending in any way to tell you what to write, I'd like to see to it that my client is left out of the discussion. Not praised, not criticized, left out."

"I told you, my interest isn't in any specific American involvement in Germany. My focus is on the people of this country and the direction in which they're being led."

"There are those in the p.r. business who think you have to be subtle and coy, insinuating your message rather than stating it. Not me. 'Give it to 'em straight,' that's the Chuck Weber philosophy. Just so you know that I've got nothing to hide, I'll tell you up front who my client is. It's the Rockefeller Foundation. Are you familiar with it?"

"Yes."

"Mind if I ask how?"

"I presume you already know or you wouldn't have sought me out," Anderson said.

Without mentioning names, Anderson told Weber that he'd spoken with a number of doctors and researchers at the Kaiser Wilhelm Institute for Anthropology, Human Heredity, and Eugenics. Anderson turned the last word over in his mind. *Eugenics:* A happy sound and a benevolent, if condescending, intent on the part of Francis Galton, Charles Darwin's cousin and the upper-class gentleman who coined the word—from the Greek for "wellborn"—and the concept. Encourage only the fit (the rich, the successful, the already blessed) to breed; discourage the unfit (the infirm, the poor, those devoid of pedigree.) A not-so-harmless concept in the hands of social engineers, racial theorists, and medical scientists, for whom eugenics was the key to ridding the world of the weak and securing the future for a master race.

"It's no secret," Anderson concluded, "that racial hygiene is a basic goal of the National Socialist regime or that the foundation has been a long-standing supporter of the institute's work, particularly its eugenic research."

"The foundation's interest is purely scientific, not political."

"The two aren't as easy to separate as some wish to believe. Scientists aren't without political views. Research doesn't occur in a social vacuum. Someone must decide what is worth researching, which projects should be funded, and to what end."

Weber turned and thrust his glass at a passing waiter. "Another," he said. He faced Anderson again "That's my point, Ian. In the U.S., for instance, most people came to accept the fact that idiots and morons shouldn't be allowed to reproduce. A decade ago, when our highest court affirmed the practice of compulsory sterilization, it proceeded on the principle that 'three generations of imbeciles is enough.' But under the present circumstances, with the bleeding hearts in the political driver's seat, the momentum is in the other direction. Hysteria replaces reason. Politics interferes with science. Radicals denounce anything to do with racial improvement as 'fascist.'"

"Do you think the science that's practiced here in Germany is pure and unbiased?"

The waiter delivered Weber's drink. Two tall, well-built officers in black SS uniforms passed the table. They were accompanied by identical twin sisters, blonde, svelte, clear-complexioned, each in a tight sheath dress fitted to her athletic form. The whole room seemed to watch as they crossed to their table.

"Nice scenery, eh?" Weber said. "That's the future Germany is trying to build for itself, a race of healthy specimens. They believe it can't be left to chance. Science must show the way by encouraging the strong to breed."

"And eliminating the weak and the sick?" Anderson said.

Weber wagged his finger, as if to scold Anderson for telling a fib. He recounted several visits he'd paid to Germany's eugenic courts, which had been instituted by the racial hygiene laws passed several years before. Each case, he said, was heard before a judge, a doctor and a social worker. No distinction was made among classes or religious creeds. The laws were equally applied to one purpose: using compulsory sterilization to reduce Germany's burden of hereditary diseases, mental as well as physical, and allow the fit to thrive. He stressed once more that any assistance by the foundation to the eugenics movement was based solely on the pursuit of "scientific truth."

Anderson let Weber's brief sermon on scientific truth pass without comment. "My book is about individuals, not institutions," he said.

Weber finished his drink and stood. "Thanks for being straight with me." He placed two tickets on the table. "Here's a couple of press passes to the track and field competition. It should be quite a show, given the quality of the American and German athletes."

The waiter came with a bill, which Weber plucked from the tray. "It's on me," he said, "and I'll keep you in mind, Ian. I started as a reporter. It's a good way to stay poor. There's a lot more money in p.r., believe me. My firm is always looking for good writers, and we pay the highest rates in the business."

"I won't give you any guarantee the foundation won't be the subject of further scrutiny. Though I never intended to look at the funding behind the Kaiser Wilhelm Institute, I won't discourage others from doing so."

"You know that, and now I know it. But my client doesn't. Far as they know, I've helped them dodge a bullet. That's p.r., Ian. It's not just what you do for your clients, but what they *think* you do."

June 1938

# 1

It's often been said that New York isn't a city in which to grow old. The truth of this bit of folk wisdom instantly impresses itself on the casual visitor. New York is a nervous place, a raw city, unpolished, unfinished, uncivil, more like Berlin in the days of the Weimar Republic than present-day Boston or Baltimore. The grandeur that was Rome and the hauteur that is Paris are utterly missing. If the visitor will linger here a while, however, he will discover that in its wanton disregard for rank or station, in its mongrel disdain for all that is ancient and outdated, in its restless lust for fun, fashion, and the future, New York is the man-made equivalent of the fountain of youth. New York might try your patience and test your wits. It might lift you to the heights of stardom or expel you to the provinces. But it will not let you grow old.            —IAN ANDERSON,
"New York, Home to the Next World's Fair,"
*World Traveler Magazine*

## PARK AVENUE, NEW YORK

THE GREEN, LEAFY SEA of Central Park's treetops framed in the window behind her, Mrs. Prudence Addison Babcock stood with one hand on a baby grand piano. Her other hand raised a cigarette to her mouth. She had a pretty face, except when she sucked on the cigarette. Her cheeks became sunken pits, the sharp, bony points seemingly ready to poke through her skin. Her eyes narrowed into slits. The embittered eyes of a woman with a hubby who'd been fingered before. Fingered and forgiven. Not this time. "I want the son of a bitch caught in the act. *In the act.* I want pictures."

She sat across from Fintan Dunne. A maid delivered scotch and sodas on a silver tray, set them down noiselessly on the taboret between their chairs, each glass with its own small, immaculate linen napkin. "He's a rat, Mr. Dunne, a lying, scheming rat. I want him destroyed. *Ruined.*"

Dunne rested his hand on hers for just a moment. She seemed neither to notice nor to be reassured. No six-week stay in Reno for Prudence Addison Babcock; no out-of-state settlement that set her husband free and rewarded his infidelity. She wanted him caught in flagrante delicto, with the corpus delectable. Pop open the door, photographer in tow, flash the Speed Graphic, send the photos to the *Mirror* and the *Standard*. He let her rant. Get the venom out. Like milking a cobra.

The next time Dunne met with her his retainer had been paid. Morning, pre-Scotch, the maid poured coffee from a silver pot, cream from a silver pitcher. He drew his chair in close for a heart-to-heart and tried to make her understand. In some cases the husband and wife arrange a "handshake shot." Hubby rents a room and a woman. They strip to their underwear and get beneath the sheets. The wife's witness and a photographer enter through a conveniently unlocked door. Take half a roll of film to be sure there'll be some usable snaps. Incontrovertible proof of adultery, the only grounds for divorce in the State of New York. Case quietly adjudicated. A mutually agreed-upon parting of the ways.

"This isn't one of those cases, Mrs. Babcock. Not an easy thing to get two people to stand still to have their picture taken in that sort of circumstance. And unnecessary. A carefully detailed record of his infidelity is what will stand up in court. Times, dates, witnesses, affidavits. Besides, once the circus gets started, the press won't stop with your husband. Drag everybody in, kids, folks. They'll be parked outside your door."

"Very well, Mr. Dunne. You're the expert in these matters." She dabbed at her eyes with a delicate lace hankie embroidered with violets.

He lit a cigarette and handed it to her. "I'll deliver an airtight case to your lawyers, Mrs. Babcock. You'll get what you want, I promise."

"Yes, you're right." She puffed softly on the cigarette. Her eyes stayed wide, her cheeks soft. "I just want it over and done, that's all."

Over and done. Turned out, she was a woman of her word.

Noontime, six weeks later, a cop gave Dunne the bad news. His face was glaringly familiar, a vice-squad detective for sure, *but his name?* They were buying cigarettes in the Liggetts on Broadway and Duane, and the detective punched him lightly on the shoulder. He had that tight, irrepressible grin a cop wears when he's got the pleasure of giving a private dick an item of information he should know, but doesn't.

"Hey, Dunne," he said, "I just seen the Professor."

His name rhymed with crimes: *Grimes? Symes? Pines?*

The detective tore the cellophane off the cigarette pack with his teeth. "He's just back from the Commodore. Some society dame plugged her hubby, and the Professor's fresh from covering it. You know him, always first on the scene." He spit the cellophane out of his mouth and it fluttered to the floor. "And you know what, Dunne?"

*Is his first name Tim? Or Jim?*

"What?"

"The Professor says to me, 'What a shame. The one who done the shootin' happens to be a client of Fintan Dunne's.'" The detective pulled off the tinfoil on top of the pack the same way as the cellophane, ripping it with his teeth and spitting it to the floor. "Who'd a thought in a million years I'd bump into you right after him? But that's the way life is, don't you know? Full of happy coincidences, even in a city as big and sloppy as New York." He delivered another, harder, punch to the shoulder. His grin got bigger. "Chief Brannigan is lookin' for you," he said. "Wouldn't make him wait too long I was you." He went out the revolving door without looking back.

A puff of carbon-colored exhaust from a Broadway bus made Dunne's cigarette taste like a blend of tobacco and coal. The detective's name popped into his head. *Tommy Hines.* Nephew of Jimmy Hines, Tammany bigwig, freshly indicted for running the Harlem numbers racket, an activity Uncle Jimmy had been richly successful at since the days of Dutch Schultz. Uncle Jimmy was the only reason Tommy Hines got to carry a gold badge in the first place. If Tommy was nervous about his uncle's fate, he'd given no sign of it.

As cocksure as ever. And as dumb. Never be clever enough to invent a story just to tease a former cop who'd gone out on his own. Unfortunately, the roster of society-types Dunne had to search had only one name on it: Mrs. Prudence Addison Babcock, wife (and now self-made widow) of Mr. Clement Babcock.

By the time he reached Police Headquarters, Centre Street was awash in blue with hungry cops on the prowl for lunch. He skirted the south side of the building and went around the corner into a ramshackle building on Centre Market. Inside was as cluttered and dingy as a sweatshop: crumpled paper on the floor, figures hunched over tables, typewriters' incessant metal chatter. The Professor was on the phone. He stood by the first desk on the right, a spot ceded by consent to the longest-serving tenant of the Shack, home of the hard-shells who crawled Manhattan's crime beat, scavenging for whatever morsels they could use to turn the latest rendition of Cain and Abel into a screaming headline and a two-day follow-up.

A few reporters looked up at the clock over the door. The low-hanging pall of gray-blue tobacco smoke grew more dense; the banging on the machines, keys, carriages, bells louder and more frenetic.

Dunne slumped into a rickety chair. The Professor put the receiver down with a slightly trembling hand.

"Babcock in the Commodore?" Dunne lit a cigarette and offered one to the Professor.

The Professor shook his head. "No to the cigarette. Yes, I'm afraid, to Mr. Babcock. Room 328. Five times in the epicardium, at such close range there were scorch marks on the silk pajamas. A sartorial as well as human tragedy."

"Who did it?"

"The police arrived to find a distraught but defiant Mrs. Prudence Addison Babcock, wife and now widow of the deceased, cradling the smoking weapon, while Mr. Babcock's nubile bedmate was whimpering behind the locked door of the bathroom. The perpetratorix was instantly pinched. Be the lead story in this evening's *New York Standard*, a well-crafted piece by the city's most seasoned chronicler of murder and mayhem, yours truly, John Lockwood."

"The woman in the bathroom, who was she?"

"A stenographer in the Babcock Publishing Company named Linda Sexton, a bosomy oread from the wilds of Washington Heights, not much older than eighteen." He looked questioningly at Dunne. "May I infer from your question that trysts of this sort were a usual part of Mr. Babcock's routine?"

"Hey, quit yappin'. I'm tryin' to file a story." The heavyset, crimson-faced man at the next desk clapped his hand over the receiver.

"Good God, Corrigan, had I suspected I was in any way cramping the literary efforts of the senior crime correspondent of Gotham's august morning journal, *The Daily Mirror*, I'd have stifled the urge to speak."

"Shove it, Lockwood."

"I return your gracious sentiments, *in perpetuum*." The Professor removed his homburg from the desk and put it on his head, adjusting it in the small, grime-ridden mirror tacked to the wall beside his chair. He framed his droopy-eyed reflection in the gray glass, stretched his long, thin neck, and straightened his collar, the old-fashioned winged variety. "*Mais où sont les neiges d'antan?*" he said. "Know what that means?"

Corrigan shook his head. "Buzz off," he said and went back to filing his story.

"Close enough. Wherever 'the snows of yesteryear' may be, they aren't here. Come, Dunne, why don't we retire to McGloin's for some lunch? It's a rule of mine to always work on an empty stomach."


"Your tab is ready to be settled. Goin' on three weeks." McGloin wiped the bar with a tattered gray rag. Except for an old man sitting in the corner, who was either blind or had his eyes closed, the barroom was deserted.

"I'll meet my obligation Thursday, when my wages are paid," the Professor said.

"Be nothin' in your glass 'less you do." McGloin poured two shots and put a beer next to each. The Professor slouched close to the bar, lifted the shot with a practiced swoop and threw the whiskey in his mouth before his shaking hand spilled a drop. He shivered slightly. "Encore," he said. McGloin poured another and walked away.

"I began as a patron here in the reign of McGloin the Elder," the Professor said, "a man whose great girth was equaled by his conviviality. The shrunken stature and squeezed sentiments of the present proprietor make me wonder how he could have been sired by such a colossus."

Dunne took a sip of beer, left the whiskey untouched. "You were in the room at the Commodore?"

"There hasn't been a noteworthy murder in this borough since the mayoralty of William Gaynor where I haven't been on the scene. I wrote the Babcock story on the train to Park Row, filed it at the *Standard*'s office and was back to the Shack whilst my hapless competitors still lumbered to the scene. Been at this as long as I, you develop a certain knack."

The Professor grasped Dunne's shot glass with a hand almost free of tremors. "I'll find a use for this if you can't."

"Be my guest."

He downed the whiskey and wiped his mustache with steady fingers. "The widow Babcock invoked your name with the police. A client, I presume?"

"Was."

"Our own beloved Chief of Homicide, Inspector Robert I. Brannigan, was there to take credit for the arrest. A blowhard who exaggerates his own exploits and expropriates those of others, often, in Melville's phrase, 'spending funds of reminiscences not his own.' He uses Corrigan as his personal press agent but knows better than to expect such sycophantic treatment from me."

McGloin filled their glasses. Dunne said, "I had this tied up. Now, I'm in a hole. Except for a retainer, I haven't been paid."

"I'll let you know what I hear from the sinkholes of matrimonial misconduct. Always played it on the up and up with me when you were a cop. One of the few." He held his glass high in an unwavering grip. "To better times."

McGloin poured another round. The Professor began a recitation of murders that echoed the circumstances of the Babcock case: a familiar burrow of whiskey, history, and stories in which to bury his head. After a few minutes, Dunne took his leave and stepped outside. A green-and-white NYPD patrol car moved slowly up the street. Brannigan was in the passenger seat, head turned to the side studying a row of storefronts. For a moment Dunne imagined that the sight might be a mirage, a mental mix of McGloin's 100-proof rotgut and undiluted sunlight. The instant he saw it wasn't, he ducked around the corner onto Broome, into the small Italian church nestled unobtrusively in the middle of the block.

The incense-sweetened church was packed with statues of saints. Most looked as though they were relatives of the little ladies in black who knelt before them fingering their rosary beads. Dunne walked halfway down the aisle, to a semi-darkened niche that held a statue of St. Anthony, who cradled the Christ child in one arm and held out a loaf of bread with the other. He crouched on the kneeler before the statue, took the change from his pocket, and dropped it in the offering box. He cringed at the racket it made. He lit a candle and listened for the tread of cops' shoes on the linoleum floor. There was only the low rattle of rosary beads, murmur of *Aves*.

*Pray for what?*

The repose of the soul of Mr. Babcock? Eternal damnation for his trigger-happy wife? An increase in marital infidelities among the well-to-do? The divorce business had suffered from the Depression along with everything else. Pray for a quick and not-so-happy death for Inspector Brannigan? God hears every prayer uttered with a sincere heart, his mother always told him. In the trenches, all the Catholic doughboys prayed or made some gesture of divine petition, rosaries around their necks, Miraculous Medals, holy cards in their helmets, prayer books in their pockets. Some filled canteens with holy water. They got hit the same as Protestants, Jews, and agnostics. Francis Sheehy was as devout as you could get, so quiet and kind no one mocked him when he knelt each night to say his prayers. He had his legs blown off and lay bleeding to death, in the same smoking hole as Major Donovan, crying, *O shit, O shit!* A prayer of sorts.

*Hail Mary*, Dunne prayed. The words came automatically, without having to think about them. *Full of grace.* He prayed for his father. Big Mike Dunne, lungs full of phlegm, half a skeleton before he died. *The Lord is with thee.* And Francis Sheehy, late of East 11th Street, now a permanent resident of a military cemetery in France. *Blessed art thou amongst women.* His mother. Knocked down by a delivery wagon on Houston Street. Broke her leg. Died the next week from a blood clot. Maura, his sister, wherever she was. *The fruit of thy womb.* And Jack, his kid brother, dead from diphtheria within days of his mother. *Now and at the hour of our death.*

St. Anthony sported a faintly sympathetic smile. It reminded Dunne of the kind a bartender (although not McGloin) might wear when he tried to look interested in a story he's heard a thousand times before. *"Blessed are they who cry in their beer for they shall be comforted."* How'd the Professor once put it? *"The short and simple annals of the poor."* His line or someone else's? Whose ever line it was, they were annals to avoid. Aunt Margaret took in Dunne and his sister Maura after their mother died. She already had eight of her own and a recently absconded husband, but she gave it a go. At first, Maura cried a lot but after a week or so she stopped. A week later she went silent as a mute. Nobody could get a word out of her. A month after that, she had her first fit. Rolled on the floor, eyes wide and fearful, pupils back so far, his Aunt Margaret said, you could barely see them. Diagnosed as a "feeble-minded epileptic," she was sent to the State Hospital in Buffalo and, after her discharge, never heard from again.

Aunt Margaret's twins had mastered the art of stealing fruit from pushcarts, an art in which they were schooling their cousin Fintan Dunne when he got nabbed and sent to the Catholic Protectory in the Bronx. "You're in for it now," the twins whispered to Dunne as they leaned across the railing in court to bid their cousin goodbye. "Nobody ever comes back from the Bronx."

First night there, kid in the next bed coughed till dawn. A veteran of Mount Loretto orphanage on Staten Island, he had his own craps, handmade in the orphanage's machine shop, expertly weighted, nothing left to chance. He'd been in and out of orphanages since he was five, when his old man walked out on the wife and five brats and headed to points unknown. "I got 'em fooled," he said to Fintan Dunne that first morning when his coughing subsided. "They think I'm twelve and I'm only nine."

Fintan Dunne stood with the kid beneath a statue of the Virgin, blue cloak draped over a white gown, her head encircled by a halo of stars, her foot crushing the head of a serpent. The kid shot a stream of spit through the gap in his front teeth onto the bed of marigolds around the pedestal. His eyes were as blue as the Virgin's cape; hooded eyes, lids half drawn, eyes that could have been eight or eighteen or eighty, nothing to give away their age: a timeless menace, ancient as the stars. "My name is Vinnie Coll," he said. "Don't fuck with me."

"Cowboy Coll" is the name they put on him because of his fierce, lonesome style. The moniker stuck through his early days as an independent gunman, until he earned himself the label of "Mad Dog," shooting five kids and killing one in an attempt to rub out an associate of Dutch Schultz. He grabbed Owney Madden's partner and held him for ransom, inventing the business of gangland kidnappings, which soon grew into an industry. They said he'd learned his trade as a gunman for the IRA. But he was a Protectory brat who'd never been east of Rockaway. Met his end in a phone booth in the London Pharmacy on 23rd Street, two bursts of a machine gun that blew his stomach open and let his intestines ooze across the floor: Mad Dog Coll dead at the ripe old age of twenty-three. There was no doubt he was fingered, maybe by a friend, maybe by the cops.

*Wonder who?*

Brannigan "happened" to be nearby. He had that kind of luck, especially during the Tommy-gun era, the glory days of Prohibition, twilight time for the squabbling gangs of guineas, micks, and kikes, gangs galore, the Candy Kids, the Bon-Bon Brigade, the Prince Street Boys, the Laughing Gang. They raided each other's garages, clubhouses, card games, fought for control of booze, bets, girls, muscled in on legit businesses, clothes, coal, garbage, kosher chickens. Cowboys like Coll were admired and in demand. But wiser, cooler heads could see the future and it didn't include penny-ante operations, crazed gunmen, and shoot-'em-ups in the streets. Consolidation was the order of the day. Organization. Syndication. Get with it. Or get lost. Or find yourself dead.

The Police eventually claimed they brought the mayhem under control. Brave boys in blue and their Gunman's Squad, with scores of heavily armed, ask-no-questions cops, supposedly busted up the gangs and returned order to the streets. That's what they told the papers, and what the papers printed, but all the while the Syndicate worked with quiet purpose to impose order and end the warfare and the unwanted attention it brought. The independent gunsels joined the fold or followed Coll to the grave. Force was used selectively; the demand for sex, liquor, drugs satisfied with efficiency; public opinion served, not outraged. Lawyers and accountants occupied the Syndicate's front offices. Police and politicians joined the payroll. Reporters, too.

The day finally came when a cadre of incorruptible prosecutors and investigators busted up the rackets. The Syndicate found itself under the scrutiny of the government and was punished for its success in replacing chaos with order. But while the Syndicate had the tide of history on its side, there were plenty of those with the right mix of ambition and greed to make sure they were aboard for the ride. Among the cops, Brannigan was anointed the fair-haired boy.

A small bell tinkled. An altar boy emerged from the sacristy. Behind him, the priest in white vestments carried the veiled chalice. The clatter of rosaries against the wooden pews subsided. The server knelt beside the priest at the bottom of the three steps before the altar.

They began the ancient exchange.

*Introibo ad altare Dei.*

*Ad Deum qui laetificat juventutem meam.*

Dunne walked back to where he'd been sitting, lay his forearm on the pew in front, and rested his head on it. His knees were stiff from kneeling. Out of practice. "Offer it up for the poor souls in purgatory," had been his mother's response to every emotional or physical complaint. The Church's cure-all for everything from colds to cancer. He decided to offer up the ache in his joints for himself, as penance for wasting the whole morning staking out Roberta Dee's place in Brooklyn.

Babcock visited Roberta Dee with such regularity it made shadowing him about as complicated as a shoeshine. She must have had the whole performance choreographed, *one, two, clothes off, three, four, once more, five, six, we've had our kicks.* The woman was a pro, the kind who apparently had Babcock running back and forth according to her clock, which made it seem unlikely he'd be bothering with a teenage stenographer. Mrs. Babcock was right about that much: her husband couldn't keep his fly buttoned. She made sure the SOB was DOA. Too bad it had to be today.

That morning, after leaving the BMT at Grand Army Plaza, Dunne had gone directly to Roberta Dee's and sat across the street. Babcock's routine never seemed to change. He always looked both ways as he left the taxi and entered her building, as though he might see someone he knew. In Newport or Palm Beach, maybe. In Brooklyn, not likely.

Fifteen minutes passed, still no Babcock. A nattily dressed gent hurried out of the building. Late for something. An appointment. A client. Maybe a girl of his own. The doorman stepped into the street and blew his whistle. The flummoxed pigeons loitering near Dunne's bench rose into the sky. The gent stood under the canopy that stretched from the building to the curb. Dunne had seen him before. A garden-variety specimen of the type that had taken root in the buildings this side of Prospect Park, a doctor maybe or a lawyer in the service of the Brooklyn Democratic machine. Two bull markets that never went away: pain and politics. The perennials.

The doorman blew again, emptying his lungs into the whistle. A cab appeared and screeched to a halt. Dunne half-expected Babcock to pop out. But when the doorman swung the door open, it was empty. The gent slipped him a coin, entered the cab and sped away. Dunne tossed the newspapers he was carrying into a trashcan and crossed the street. Was it possible Babcock had caught on to being tailed? More probable that he was just delayed or forced to change his plans.

Dunne unfolded the wrapper from a stick of chewing gum and stuck the gum in his mouth. He took a bill from his pocket that he'd already folded into a square, put the wrapper around it, and handed it to the doorman. "Can you get rid of this for me?"

"Sure bet," the doorman said.

"Mind if I take a look around."

"Be my guest."

The lobby was dim and cool. The only light spread from brass wall sconces beneath japanned, parchment-like shades. Dunne pressed for the elevator. A moment later, the gate rolled back with a thud.

"Well, well," the elevator man said, "if it ain't my favorite Sherlock. How'd I know you'd be here? Think I'm clairvoyant?"

"Let's see."

They'd been through the same routine several times before. Dunne held out his hand with another folded bill. The elevator man stuck it in his pocket and stared at Dunne's empty palm, squinting, as if struggling to see. "Can just make it out, Apartment 4C, a name right below the doorbell. Roberta Dee."

"All that's right there on my palm?"

"Better than a crystal ball."

"See anybody go in?"

"Not today."

Nor tomorrow, in Babcock's case. Dunne left there thinking how odd it is for Babcock to break his routine. But not to worry, these things happen all the time. At that same moment, the double-dealer was getting pumped five times by his wife.

*Amen, amen, I say unto you: Beware the sure thing.*

The priest stood at the right side of the altar, dipped his fingers in the small glass bowl held by the altar boy, who poured water from a cruet over them. He took the linen napkin draped over the boy's wrist, dried his fingers, and murmured the words of the *Lavabo*. The washing away of sins. Hold the starch.

Dunne left the church, stopped at a little place on the corner of Prince Street and ordered spaghetti and a glass of dago red. He took a cab back to his office. A faint smirk greeted him as he passed Marlene, the combination PBX operator and receptionist who sat in the building's lobby behind a low, dirt-streaked glass partition. A career in that box, along with a divorce and the loss of all her savings when the Bank of the United States folded, soured a once-attractive woman into a wrinkled killjoy.

"Had two visitors, Dunne." Marlene worked the phone lines as she spoke. "One was a cop." The smirk reworked itself into a sneer. "He said if you know what's good, you'll come see him pronto."

"Who else was here?"

"*Still* here."

There wasn't another soul in sight, unless he was hiding in the janitor closet. "Let me guess. The Invisible Man."

"*Woman*. Went up with Jerroff five minutes ago. Said she could sit in his office till you showed. Better be on the up and up. This ain't no cathouse."

The elevator, which had been on the fritz, was back in service. Its slow upward grind ascended into a keen for the fallen state of the Hackett Building. Nice digs, Dunne told himself, the day he rented space, in July 1929. Brokers and stockjobbers peddling day and night on the telephone, hum of people in the process of getting rich, happiest of human sounds. He'd quit the Police Department the month before, the end of a ten-year career, last of it with the homicide squad. *Enough cadavers for a lifetime, thank you.* Took up the work of tracking wayward husbands and adulterous wives. The supply of nuptial transgressions seemed to move with the country's booming prosperity. No more department politics. No more corrupt asshole chiefs like Brannigan. That October the Crash came. Seven billion dollars down the sewers of Wall Street in a single week. The Dow Jones plummeted, and with it, the divorce rate.

The hum in the Hackett Building sank, rose, then sank for good. Dunne was hard pressed to remember when he knew that neither prosperity nor the corner it was supposedly waiting just around was anywhere in sight. The awareness came to him gradually, like a bad cold or a case of the grippe. "For Rent" signs proliferated in vacant storefronts. Groups of working men stood idly on street corners. In the fall of 1930, the International Apple

Shippers Association got rid of its unsold reserves by letting the job-bers have them on credit. Within a few weeks there were 6,000 apple sellers on the streets of New York, some still wearing velvet-collared overcoats from Brooks Brothers.

The temporary cloud became a permanent gloom. Week after week, it invaded the flickering illusions of the movie house. Amid newsreels of starlets and athletes, statesmen and royalty, the chris-tenings of battleships and voyages of zeppelins, the mounting pres-ence of the unemployed and homeless spun into an epic of disasters. It was as though nature and the stock market were controlled by the same hand. The deluge poured out of the canyons of lower Manhattan, swelled the Mississippi, the Ohio, the Tennessee, a tor-rent of dark moiled water, sweeping away homes, factories, towns. People paddled down Main Street, dog, radio, lamp in their laps, whatever little they could salvage. From a distance they seemed almost cheerful, until the Movietone camera drew closer and revealed their bewilderment in a shrug of shoulders, a pathetic smile, eyes water-filled, like their lives, the illusion of security washed away.

One way or another, rain or shine, flood or drought, the ruin spread, biblical-style, across the country. Dunne was in the Hackett Building a few years when he bumped into Fuzzy Whalen, an old pal from the regiment, in the lobby. It must have been '31 or '32, before Repeal. They walked to Danny Cassidy's speakeasy on 28th Street and Seventh Avenue and had a few drinks. They came out to a bruised and threatening sky. A thunderstorm seemed about to hit. But there wasn't a hint of moisture anywhere. The dryness coated tongue and throat. A few drops fell. Hard as sand. A minute later, the storm arrived. A shower of grit, the blown-away fields of dry, exhausted earth from a thousand miles away, from the busted farms of Oklahoma and Texas, descended on New York in a blinding swirl.


Dunne drew back the gate and exited into the gloom. All the floors—two above and four below—had the same shadowy hallways, peeling walls, small-time salesmen peddling insurance, prostheses, elixirs, gadgets, cheap cutlery, nudist magazines. The titles stenciled on the frosted glass changed, but the faces didn't. Fail at one flimflam, try another. *Try, try, try again. Hack it as long as they can.* On warm summer days, when the doors were opened a crack, honeyed, desperate phone spiels spilled into the hallways: *Good morning Mr./Mrs. Jones, and congratulations, today's your lucky day!*

*Whatever you're sellin', I ain't interested. Click.*

The glass on the door next to Dunne's office had freshly painted lettering on it. EMILE JERROFF. ACCOUNTANT AND NOTARY PUBLIC. A month before, Jerroff's legend was "Toys & Novelties." Something else before that. Dunne couldn't remember what. The door was ajar. Inside, Jerroff perched Humpty-Dumpty fashion on the edge of his desk, short, sausage-shaped legs dangling above the floor. A lacquered black panama hid the head of the person sitting in front of him.

Jerroff hopped off the desk. "Ah, Dunne, at last. I was playing host until you arrived."

The broad-rimmed hat turned to reveal the guest's face, olive-complexioned, fine-boned, young.

"We were discussing the war in Spain," Jerroff said. "Miss Corado feels as I do. Defeat for the Republic will inspire new aggressions by the Fascists."

Miss Corado stood. A head taller than Jerroff, she extended her gloved hand. The touch of kid. A nice feel. She smiled. "I'm Elba Corado, Mr. Dunne. I apologize for not calling to make an appointment. I thought I'd try my luck and drop in. My luck didn't fail. Mr. Jerroff has been most patient and charming."

"*Emile*," Jerroff said, "please call me Emile."

"Of course, Emile."

"Remember, Miss Corado, whenever you're in the Hackett Building, you must stop by. Promise?"

She laughed. "Yes, I promise."

Next door, in his office, Dunne pulled up a chair for her in front of his desk. Miss Corado put her purse beside her and smoothed her dress with her hands, a white silk dress splashed with big red and black flowers. She took the cigarette he offered, leaned forward and put it into the flame of his lighter. Her black bra was visible, breasts firm and buoyant.

"Mr. Jerroff was very gracious."

"*Emile,*" Dunne said. Another smile from Miss Corado, more of her straight, pearly teeth. He couldn't place her name, but if he'd seen the face, he'd remember, for sure. "But you didn't come here to talk about Spain."

"No." The smile vanished. Eyes closed, she sighed.

They always had trouble getting started. Beat around it. *Oh, my wounded heart.* Tears first, then rage. Young, old, pretty, plain, they stumbled over the pain, shock, anger of betrayal, adultery. "Miss Corado, I think I know why you're here."

Her tropical eyes, brown pupils shaded by lashes lush as palm leaves, open wide. "You do?"

"It's my business."

"You know about Wilfredo?"

"Your husband?"

"My brother, actually my half brother. The papers used the English name he took for himself when he came here from Cuba, *Walter.* Walter Grillo."

Dunne lit a cigarette for himself. "Your brother is the one with the problem?"

"Mr. Dunne, they're sending him to the electric chair for a crime he didn't commit. They said he raped and murdered a nurse. The trial was a travesty."

A memory of it stirred in Dunne's head. Brannigan did his best to make it look as if it took real brains to solve. A chimp could have done it as quick.

"Wilfredo *couldn't* have done it. He's incapable of such an act." She rattled off a litany of Wilfredo's attributes. Courteous, kind, loyal. A real Boy Scout.

Dunne leaned back. The loud creak of his chair sounded almost like a moan. One of those things you don't notice until a visitor shows up. Like the holes in the linoleum, or the water stains on the walls, or the jagged puncture in the green leather couch. He opened his top drawer, lifted out a business card and placed it in front of her.

She glanced at it but didn't pick it up. "Mr. Dunne, please, I need your help."

He tapped the card with his finger. "There," he said, "underneath 'Private Investigator,' see? 'Matrimonial and Divorce.'"

"My brother is innocent. He came to America as a political exile. He loved freedom so much that even though he was raised to be a gentleman in Cuba, he worked as a janitor here. He is a hero, not a criminal."

*Not my boy:* The abiding faith of sisters and mothers, no matter what kind of bum they have for a sibling or son. It took a special kind of a shark to make a living off them. Devour their savings. Sometimes more than that: their trust, their love. Dunne wouldn't use a sermon word to describe the reason for not joining private eyes and lawyers who made a living off such fish. Just didn't want to be surprised by a passing reflection in a mirror or store window: The Judas gaze. His own.

"Sorry, but I don't handle criminal cases. That's a whole other line of work, 'specially homicides."

"You did. You were a cop."

"*Were*, Miss Corado."

"I was told you were one of the best."

A sister's persistence. The litany in honor of Saint Wilfredo continued: Lawyer, university professor, scholar, father of the poor, good shepherd, true light, you name it. Feeding time for the sharks.

"Whoever told you that should've also told you I'm now in a different kind of business. Sorry if they didn't."

"I hoped you wouldn't be indifferent to the execution of an innocent man."

"I'm not indifferent, Miss Corado." Dunne said. "It's just that I don't handle murder investigations." What he didn't say: *especially today, with Babcock in the morgue, his wife in custody, Brannigan on the warpath.*

Her brown eyes widened with the look of a child who'd been slapped, same combo of hurt and indignation. She got up abruptly. The end of her cigarette was a curve of gray ash. "Is there an ashtray?"

He pointed at the floor. She dropped the cigarette, covered it with the toe of her black high heels, ground it with a slow, deliberate twist of her thin, silk-hosed ankle. "Saving an innocent life, I suppose, is too much trouble when you can make more money peeping into people's bedrooms."

"If you want people to take your money, that's easy. You want results? That's another matter."

"But not something you care to rise to." She continued to grind the cigarette.

"Your brother have a trial?"

"The prosecution was on a crusade. Mr. Dewey wanted my brother's head so he could wave it about in a campaign. He even came in person to hear the summation."

"Mr. Dewey has plenty of heads already." Everybody's from Lucky Luciano's, the Syndicate's kingpin who'd ascended from the Lower East Side, to Richard Whitney's, the Wall Street titan and descendant of the Mayflower crowd. In his career as Assistant U.S. Attorney, special prosecutor, and D.A., Dewey had amassed a *Who's Who* of heads. The head of Miss Corado's brother would be only a secondary addition, a small but pointed reminder of Mr. Racket Buster's unremitting war on evildoers. "Your brother had his own lawyer, didn't he?"

"The lawyer for my brother? He might as well have worked for the prosecution. He never believed in Wilfredo's innocence. *Never.* He told Wilfredo to plead guilty and throw himself on the mercy of the court."

"Lawyers have given a lot worse advice, believe me."

"I can see I'm wasting my time. But to be truthful, the coldness and meanness of this city no longer surprise me. Roberta Dee may be surprised about you, but I'm not." She walked toward the door. "You are not the man she thinks you are."

Once in the war, at the start of the battle of the Ourcq, in 1918, soon before their position was almost overrun and Major Donovan was wounded, a German shell came out of nowhere and hit the rim of his foxhole, one of those 77 millimeter shells the Americans call a "whiz bang" because it exploded almost at the same time you heard it finish its descent. It would have been an instantaneously fatal explosion if Dunne hadn't been leaning down to pick up his canteen. He didn't so much remember the deafening concussion as the stunned quiet that followed, the paralyzed surprise.

A moment like this. "Who?"

"She was certain you'd take the case. She *insisted* I come."

"Roberta Dee is a friend of yours?" Dunne's chair moaned as he leaned back;  and again as he rocked forward.

"A friend and a customer. Although she could afford to go elsewhere, Miss Dee buys most of her clothes at my dress shop. She's been through the whole ordeal of the trial with me. She convinced me to stay away from the courtroom. She said the press would only use my presence to make an even greater sensation."

"Roberta Dee who lives on Grand Army Plaza?" Dunne half expected her to smile or laugh.

"Of course," she said. She seemed to be choking back tears. "I'll show myself out." She didn't bother to close the door.

Jerroff poked his head into the office. "If there's a divorce involved, and Miss Corado should seek advice on financial matters, I'll give her my special rate."

"Keep your special rate, Emile. I don't think she'll be back." Dunne put on his hat and stepped into the hallway. When he reached the lobby, he stood beside the revolving door and studied the street. The voice from behind the glass partition called out, "Better call that cop 'cause I won't lie for any of the momsers inhabit this dump. I don't get paid enough."

"Ask for a raise."

In the luncheonette across the street, back to the counter, an elbow to support him, Dunne sucked a chocolate egg cream through a straw. The racks next to the window were filled with magazines, an entire shelf devoted to detective and mystery pulp. He picked up *Real Detective: Secrets of the World's Most Thrilling Profession*. The cover had a nighttime scene, the moon barely visible, a blonde in a low-cut red dress clinging to a man in a gray trench coat holding a flashlight. They were on a beach. Just beyond the reach of the torch's beam, two menacing figures approached from a boat they'd dragged ashore. *Thrills galore*. Like trying to pay the rent after a client blows several holes in her husband and puts you in a hole of your own.

A coupe pulled up outside. The two men in it eyed the door of the Hackett Building. They might as well mount an on-duty sign on the car roof. Dunne left the luncheonette and passed them on the passenger side. He didn't recognize either one, but Brannigan discarded detectives like Kleenex. Don't do it his way, you're gone before he's finished blowing his nose.

The afternoon had become a rehearsal for high summer, hot and still, a taste of worse to come. BEAT THE HEAT read the top line of the marquee on the second-run movie house next to the corner. ALL NEW AIR CONDITIONING! Beneath, in smaller letters were the features, a double bill, *Charlie Chan's Secret* and *Charlie Chan at the Opera*. Dunne glanced back at the detectives as he bought a ticket. Still studying the front of the Hackett Building, they practiced one of the less well kept secrets of the world's most thrilling profession: spending all afternoon cooped up in a stuffy automobile waiting for a mark who'd already flown.


It was as hot in the theater as out. The few patrons, most asleep, didn't seem to notice. Dunne stayed awake through the newsreels: *A grinning Mr. Chamberlain, the British Prime Minister, comes out of 10 Downing Street. He bears a strong resemblance to the Professor, same ostrich neck and drooping mustache. Legions of German troops march past Adolf Hitler who returns their straight-armed salute.* By the time the young heir had been murdered in the first movie, Dunne was asleep. No need to worry about Charlie, no long, empty days for him, clients who take matters into their own hands, a chief of homicide looking for an excuse to rub his nose in the dirt. Chan always gets his man.

The usher poked Dunne with a flashlight. "Bub, wake up, you're snoring." The newsreel was on again, Chamberlain smiling, Hitler saluting. It was almost dark when Dunne went outside, cooler than before. The coupe was gone. No use going home. Be staked out, at least for the night. Dunne took the train to 23rd Street and walked the rest of the way to Cassidy's Bar & Grill. Cassidy kept the backroom as a flop for his buddies from the regiment. Four cots, first come, first served. A lifesaver for those laying low on account of bill collectors, wives, girlfriends, bookies, cops. Dunne had a drink with Cassidy and rehashed the Babcock murder. He didn't mention he'd been sitting on a bench in Brooklyn when Mrs. Babcock shot her husband five times in a Manhattan hotel room. A dick's got his reputation to uphold.

Cassidy laid the evening papers on the bar. Dunne had already seen the headline on the newsstand next to the subway: Society Hubby Shot Dead. Cops Have Wife In Custody. Beneath the fold was the picture of Mrs. Babcock being led out of the Commodore in cuffs, stylish, smiling. Brannigan had her by the arm. He was wearing his official police face, grim and serious, but it was easy to see how pleased he was. Cassidy put on his glasses to read the front-page account. "You've got no reason to hide, Fin. Wasn't you shot nobody."

"Brannigan will try to make it seem I did. Bet on it."

"You'll only make it worse if you try to avoid him."

"Have a loose end to tie up. Once I do, I'll set things straight."

Dunne waited for the backroom to clear out. It was being used by Red Doyle for a meeting of the maintenance crew from the Fifth Avenue Coach Company, which ran the main bus lines in Manhattan and the Bronx. Doyle was regularly dispatched from the uptown headquarters of the Transit Workers Union to encourage the men in their demand for a six-day week and an end to the shape-up system that forced them to report at the beginning of each shift to see who'd be hired, who wouldn't. He used a chair as his soapbox, pushed his fingers through his dense tangle of red hair and ranted against "the plethora of plutocrats" who ran the bus company.

A trucker in a worn leather jacket, who'd sat silent and alone drinking boilermakers, slammed his shot glass down so hard on the bar that it cracked. "Shut that sheenie communist up, will you!" he yelled at Cassidy.

Cassidy picked up the bat he kept beneath the bar. "First, pay me for the glass, then get out."

"My pleasure." The trucker tossed a dollar at Cassidy. "Bad enough the Jews run the White House, now they're taking over the bars." He jammed his newspaper under his arm and left.

When the meeting was over, Doyle came to the bar. "Do you

have to be such a rabble-rouser?" Cassidy said. "Can't you tone it down a bit?"

"You've only heard my sweet talk. Wait till I get fired up."

In the days when Big Mike, Dunne's old man, had been a well-known union organizer, Doyle had been an up-and-comer in labor circles. Later on, during the Red Scare when Attorney General Palmer rounded up alien radicals, Dunne read in the papers how Doyle's reputation for fiery left-wing rhetoric led to his detention. But, despite his convincing brogue, it turned out that Doyle had been born and bred in Butte, Montana, and wasn't entitled to a one-way ticket to the land of his origin. After a brief stint in federal prison, he returned to organizing, eventually joining the vanquished IRA irreconcilables who—their dream of a socialist republic smashed to smithereens by the Irish Free State—took up the cause of New York's heavily Irish transit workers.

Cassidy served Doyle a beer. "What I can't figure out about you," he said, "is whether you're called 'Red' on account of your politics or your hair."

"Neither." Doyle downed his beer in one long gulp and wiped his mouth with the back of his hand. "First place I worked in New York was Coney Island. Nobody bothered to tell me about the bad blood between Irish skin and the sun. Turned the color of a lobster. Italians I worked with had a good laugh. Dubbed me Red. After that I worked in sunless places, but the label of Red stuck."

By the time the crowd cleared out and Dunne was able to get to sleep, it was after one o'clock. When he awoke, the morning light was already leaking through the blinds on the front window, tiding across the floor. Cassidy was behind the bar washing glasses. Two stubble-face men rapped on the window. Cassidy shook his head. They grumbled for a moment before they left in search of another bar, fresh pack of smokes, some way to tell one day from the next.

Cassidy looked over the papers, offering a running commentary on the growing tensions between the Germans in the Sudetenland and the Czechoslovakian Republic, to which they'd been annexed by the peace the Allies imposed in 1919. He read aloud the accusations of Konrad Henlen, the leader of the Sudeten Germans—the Czechs labeled him a "a Nazi mouthpiece"—who denounced "the perfidy of the Czechs and the arrogance of the British, the world's premier practitioners of imperial oppression."

"Well, he's got that right," Cassidy said. "Look at the way the Brits treated the Irish and what they did to America in the wars we fought, hangin' our patriots, burnin' the capitol and encouragin' the Indians in their savagery. 'Arrogant,' for sure, that's the way the Brits will always be. But if they think they're gonna get us to pull their chestnuts outta the fire a second time, like we did in 1917, they're in for a nasty surprise."

After a few more minutes of Cassidy's commentary and a cup of his watery coffee, Dunne went next door to Rostoff's Cafeteria for some bacon and eggs. Old Jules Rostoff was on the stool by the cash register, where he always was, scowling across the room. According to Cassidy, Rostoff had been a member of the original Bolshevik government in Russia but had gone sour on the Revolution and fled to New York, a conversion seemingly affirmed by the yellowed hand-made sign above the cash register:

NO BUMS

NO CREDIT

NO LOITERING

"Rostoff's Commandments" is how Cassidy described them. "They should be added to the original ten." Dunne finished his eggs and smoked a cigarette. A patrol car pulled up outside. One of the patrolmen entered and looked around offhandedly, his casual saunter immediately giving away his mission. The counterman handed him a bag of coffee and doughnuts, and he left without paying.

At the Turkish bath on 14th Street, the fez-wearing proprietor was slumped in an armchair, sucking a narghile. His wife handed out towels as the sons cleaned up the lockers. Dunne paid extra for a shave, which the proprietor administered in a slow, careful manner while his wife ironed Dunne's shirt and pants for free.

The morning had already gone from warm to hot when Dunne exited the IRT at Grand Army Plaza in Brooklyn. Yet after the rank, sweltering subway, the air was gentle and refreshing. Around the great arch in the center of the Plaza, a contingent of slow-moving WPA men in green-gray coveralls tended the flowerbeds. Above, on the monument, the patinated copper soldiers brandished sabers, swords, bayonets.

The doorman let Dunne into the building without a question. If he'd connected the picture of Babcock in the papers with the lady in apartment 4C, he showed no sign of it. Expecting the elevator man might be more inquisitive, Dunne ducked into the staircase and walked the four flights. Miss Dee's apartment was at the end of the hall. He waited to catch his breath before ringing her bell. Nothing. He rang again. The peephole stayed shut, but a voice came from behind the door: "Who is it?"

"Friend of a friend, Miss Dee. Like a word with you." Dunne turned his ear to the door and bent close. Suddenly, it swung open.

"My friends know better than to bother me unannounced." She had the words out before Dunne could unbend from his eavesdropping.

He straightened up and removed his hat. "Miss Dee?"

"Only two types would come here unannounced. Either a detective or a dimwit."

"I believe you know who I am, Miss Dee."

"Let me guess." Her lips, full and pouty, were a deep carmine, the same color as her fingernails. "Too good looking to be a detective. You must be a dimwit."

"Unless you want your neighbors to hear, I'd suggest you invite me in."

"You already invited yourself." She led the way down a short hallway into a spacious living room that had the feel of a showroom in a suave department store, elegant but not really lived in. In the corner, next to a table with a lavish arrangement of rose and lavender centaurea, was a small bar. "Drink?"

"Little early, don't you think?"

"It's evening in Rome."

"When in Rome, I guess. Scotch, a jerk of soda."

She filled two glasses with ice, poured Scotch in one, and squirted soda from a blue syphon in both.

The image he'd had of her was from the photos Sniffles Ott had taken. A part-time snap shooter for the *Brooklyn Eagle*, Sniffles sat alone in his car waiting for Babcock. The way Sniffles liked it: A three-hundred-pound man nursing his eternal cold, nobody to complain about the incessant wheezing and snorting, rasp of phlegm being dragged up his throat. Charged twenty bucks for the job. Additional offer of snaps featuring women in black silk stockings and nothing else.

*Special price for you, Fin.*

*Sorry, Sniff, no sale.* A peek. Not bad. *Only what I asked for.*

Along with the pictures of Babcock were three that Sniff had taken from a distance of the lovebird herself: Miss Roberta Dee. The thing to keep in mind about cameras, Dunne reminded himself, was how often they lied, how they can make an average face seem exquisite or turn extraordinary beauty into the humdrum.

In Sniffles' photos, Roberta Dee appeared fashionably attractive, the way half-a-hundred women on the street did; in the flesh, she was striking. Her face was older than Miss Corado's, and there was nothing virginal or innocent about it. But her slate-blue eyes were bright, clear, wide. She had soft waves running through her auburn hair which, though perhaps tinted or dyed, was thick and lustrous. Hers was a hard beauty, polished, like marble or jade.

She handed him the glass with Scotch in it. He took a sip and stepped over to the window. A perfect view of Grand Army Plaza. The arch. The new library. The park. A perfect view also of the bench from which he'd watched Babcock's comings and goings.

"Have a seat." She gestured to a large plush chair. The cushion was so soft and yielding Dunne felt for a moment as if his bottom might hit the floor. He planted his elbows on the armrests and jacked himself up. She sat on the couch across from him.

"You're lucky you're alive, Miss Dee."

"Aren't we all?" She folded her shapely legs and stretched her arms across the back of the couch, glass in her right hand, bodice of her knit dress tight against the firm curve of her breasts.

"Suppose you heard?"

"Who hasn't?"

"Didn't think you'd be this broken up."

She sipped the soda. "If you want to watch a woman have a good cry, try Garbo in *Camille*. It's still playing at the Kings Theater in Flatbush."

"Don't suppose the police have been here."

"I don't suppose you'll send them."

"I wasn't the only one saw Babcock come in and out."

"You, Morello the doorman, and Jimmy the elevator boy were the only ones who noticed. They're taken care of. Besides, last thing they want is to lose a couple of days work sitting around waiting to testify about a dead man's doings."

"Mrs. Babcock followed him *here*, you might be singing a different song."

"I always sang the same song with Clem. I made him take the train to Court Street and take a cab from there."

"Doesn't mean he couldn't be followed."

"By you? Yes. By his wife? She's not the type to travel all the way to Brooklyn. Look, in case you haven't figured it out, Clem and I had a business deal, pure and simple. I took care of certain of his needs. He did the same for me."

"Tell you he was off to The Commodore Hotel?"

"What he did when he wasn't with me was his own affair, and vice versa. I'm sorry about what happened to him and wish he'd been more sensible, which is probably the way you feel about Mrs. Babcock. Always hate to lose a customer."

Above her head, an elaborately framed painting of a beach at night, silver moon penetrating the clouds, shining across sand and angry sea, a pathway of light, looked like a candidate for the wall of some museum or movie lobby, except there was something foreboding about it, threatening, as though a body were about to bob to the surface. He'd seen it before. But where?

"Another?" Without waiting for an answer, she got up, took his glass and went over to the bar. She put more Scotch in the glass; quick spray of soda. She handed him the drink. "What say we get to what really brings you here?"

"Which is?"

"Elba Corado. I told her to look you up. Said you were an ex-cop who wasn't also a crook or an Irish son-of-a-bitch. Best of all, you know the homicide routine. She told me she'd used my name. I figured you'd be here before long."

"You seem to know a lot about me."

She went to the window, leaned back against the radiator cover and motioned with her head toward the street. "First time I looked out and saw you sitting there, I knew you were a tail. I watched you scribbling away in your notebook as Clem arrived and left. It wasn't hard to figure. Jimmy confirmed it for me."

"Jimmy?"

"The elevator boy."

"Likes to play both sides."

"He's got six kids. Plays any side that pays. Do you blame him?"

"You didn't let Babcock know?"

"Clem didn't hire me to be a private eye."

"Don't tell me Jimmy recommended me for the Corado case."

"No, Lenny Moss did."

He had to give it to her: She knew how to keep a conversation going. "I don't know any Lenny Moss."

"You did."

"That Lenny Moss got dead a while ago. If you were one of his girls, sorry to say I got no recollection."

"Sorry for who?"

"Whoever."

"I wasn't Lenny's girl. We grew up together in Brownsville and hung out in the same crowd on Rockaway Avenue. My mother worked with his in the needle trade. He was Lenny Moskowitz back then. Tall, handsome, and wild. We did a lot of partying together, then Lenny went away to jail. After he got out, I didn't see him again for awhile, not until he was arrested again and put on trial."

"Which trial?"

"The last."

"I testified at it."

"I know. His mother had nobody to go to the trial with her. She asked me."

"Lenny was a second-rate *shtarke* and a first-rate *stupe*. Let himself go to the chair for a crime he didn't commit." He could have added "third-rate pimp," but didn't. He searched his memory for some image of Roberta Dee. Not a trace of her but the trial was still there, fresh and vivid.

"Lenny knew he was a dead man," she said. "So he made a deal. If his mother were taken care of, he'd take the fall. He did, she was."

"Ask me, it was a lousy reason to let himself be electrocuted."

Brannigan had been put on the case on orders from the department's higher-ups. A deal had already been cut. In the wake of the general strike by the garment workers in '26, "Little Augie" Orgen had battled Legs Diamond for control of the industry's protection racket. Arnold Rothstein tried to broker a peace but just when it seemed ready to take, Orgen had two of Legs's men machine gunned on 14th Street. A professional tommy-gun job, combination of blunderbuss and Waring blender, ten rounds of .45 caliber bullets at a velocity capable of penetrating a quarter-inch of steel that blew Legs's men through the plate-glass window of Brookstein's Shoe Emporium and covered the display of suede and patent-leather footwear with a shower of blood.

The city's editorial writers hollered for investigations of the gangs, the police, the city administration. Mayor Jimmy Walker sat down with Rothstein. Tammany and the mob both wanted the heat off. Rothstein promised to deliver the culprit, or a reasonable facsimile thereof. Orgen offered up Lenny Moss as a sacrificial lamb. Brannigan pretended to investigate.

Dunne knew it was a set-up, but refused to go along. He didn't back up Brannigan's canned testimony when he was called to the stand. They got Moss anyway. On the way out of the courtroom, Brannigan pulled him aside.

*You're finished in the department, Dunne.*

*If it means never working with you again, Brannigan, score this my lucky day.*

After the Moss case, Inspector William Hanlon, a taciturn, honest cop, was pushed aside. Brannigan was promoted to Borough Inspector and made head of the Homicide Squad. He saw to it that any time an old man was found hanging from a light fixture, his last act before reaching the Happy Hunting Ground to shit his pajamas, Dunne was sure to get the case. Corpse in there three days with the windows closed before the neighbors call the cops. When some mop jockey gave his wife a hundred whacks with a rusty shovel and splashed her brains across the basement floor, everybody knew who'd get the call. Hubby doesn't try to run or get away. Cradles the corpse in his arms. Not exactly a case for Charlie Chan. The nights there were no bughouse homicides were spent at the morgue waiting for the results of one of Doc Cropsey's autopsies, listening to him gripe and guzzle cheap bootlegged whiskey.

That last night, in the spring of '29, there was a call from a warehouse on 12th Avenue. A clerk opened a locker that a renter defaulted on, pulled down a trunk that crashed to the floor, and spilled out the skeletal remains of three babies. Address of the renter turned out to be an empty lot in the Bronx. Doc Cropsey said the skeletons were full-term triplets. Suffocated at birth, probably. The most unglamorous, underreported crime of all: babies in varying states of decay in trash cans, basement corners, railroad restrooms, underpasses, wherever. He estimated they'd been dead several years.

It was a beautiful spring morning when the shift was over and it was time to get back to headquarters. The sky was streaked with hues of red and blue, dawn's early light. Dunne threw the badge on the desk. *You win, Brannigan.* The Hackett Building felt like heaven those first few months. He'd hardly given the homicide business another thought, until now.

Roberta returned to the couch and stretched out in the same position as before. "That day you testified, I was in the back, in a cloche hat, next to Lenny's mother."

"Didn't notice. I had other things on my mind."

"Lenny said you were the only cop who didn't lie."

"Got juiced all the same."

"I saw him in Sing Sing. He said he never met a cop but you who didn't lie when it was convenient or he was told to. He couldn't seem to get over it."

Dunne drained his drink. "So you wait ten years to look me up and let me know Lenny Moss thought I was okay? Wish I could say I was grateful, only I'd be lying."

"It was you looked me up."

She had a point.

"And after a view of me once ten years ago in a crowded court-room, you look out the window and recognize me from four stories up? Quite a feat."

"I didn't know it was you, not from here. I thought it might be. It wasn't till I tailed you back to your office I was sure."

"No man ever followed me I didn't know it."

"Last time I looked I wasn't a man."

The moon in the painting above her head contained the vague suggestion of a face, craters for eyes, a nose. Mister Moon seemed to be winking.

"All this to help the brother—excuse me, half brother—of your dressmaker? Sorry, Miss Dee, but I can't figure why you got involved in this, or better yet, why I should."

"Because Elba Corado is different."

"From what?"

"You and me. Elba thinks this is a world where the good, the true, and the beautiful should come out on top. You and me, we know that the beautiful does okay, long as it lasts, but where'd goodness and truth ever get anyone? Wouldn't it be nice, this once, to see the good and the true at least finish in the money? That's why I sent Elba to you. She loves her brother, and love can take us to the strangest places. It's made her so passionate about his innocence that it's like a religion with her. I figured any dick in this town gives her an honest shake, it'd be you."

"I already got a religion." He pushed himself out of the chair, feeling woozy as he did. He knew what he should do: go home, piss out the Scotch, have a nap, visit Brannigan, and start looking for another divorce case. "Besides, I don't come cheap."

"She has her own business. I'm sure she'll meet your terms, but she'll want her money's worth. What she doesn't want is some worm working from the cockeyed notion of turning this into a romance."

"Do I look like some dime-store gigolo?"

"You look like a man, which means it's better to be up front at the starting gate and let you know this is a race for geldings."

She led him to the door.

From where he stood, the picture on the far wall seemed to have darkened. Mister Moon was missing his smile. He remembered what it reminded him of: the cover of *Real Detective*, only the couple and the approaching thugs were missing.

"I'll let Elba know you've agreed. She'll be thrilled." She pecked him lightly on the cheek. The passing touch of her lips: a kiss, almost. Her breasts pressed for an instant against his arm, a professional goodbye. "You're a *mensch*."

The day had turned cloudy and rain seemed imminent. Grand Army Plaza was almost empty. The strollers were gone, and the WPA crew. No one around to defend or watch over, the figures on the monument seemed forlorn. Roberta Dee was up to something besides the pursuit of the good and the true. He'd had the same uneasy feeling with Mrs. Babcock. A feeling you couldn't acquire by reading *Real Detective*. It came the hard way.

Some day he might be smart enough to pay attention to it.

He lifted the notebook from his pocket and, starting to write a list of the people he'd want to talk to about Walter Grillo, realized he didn't even know the name of the nurse Grillo had been convicted of killing or the date set for his execution. A lot he didn't know. But the minute he put the notebook away and walked toward the subway, he knew he was being tailed.

# 2

Since taking power, Adolf Hitler has silenced or sent into exile most of his opponents. He has also won the loyalty of large numbers of Germans, many of whom were skeptical at best and hostile at worst. Georg D., a foreman in a shoe factory in the northeast part of Berlin that has lately been given over to producing boots for the army, is a case in point. He walks with a slight limp, the result of being shot in the hip by a British sniper during the war. "I work all the time now, but I'm not complaining," he says. "Better to be exhausted than unemployed. Three years I was out of work. We barely had enough to eat. My boy got crooked legs from the rickets." Each evening, after leaving the factory, Georg D. and his comrades stop in a nearby tavern to talk and drink beer. Most of the conversation is about sports, not politics. Georg D. observes that "Men talk only politics when they're frightened or unhappy. That is not the situation now."

Outside, away from the others, he sits on a bench to enjoy his pipe and muses about the changes that have occurred since the National Socialists came to power. "When times were bad and there was no work to be found, I thought about joining the Communists. But today I'm satisfied with matters as they are." He is happy also to see Germany's rightful return to its status as a great nation. From inside the tavern comes the sound of an accordion. Voices sing the anthem written by Horst Wessel, hero and martyr of the movement's street-fighting days (thug and pimp in the eyes of the opposition):

*Millions, full of hope, look up at the swastika;*
*The day breaks for freedom and for bread.*

"Our pride and prosperity have been restored, and all without a single shot being fired!" he says and taps his foot in time with the music.

—IAN ANDERSON, *Travels in the New Germany*

51

ABWEHR HEADQUARTERS,
72-76 TIRPITZ-UFER, BERLIN

*A*dmiral, *wake up. It's time for your lunch.*

A distant voice, a gentle nudge.

He listened first: drone of traffic, faint but reassuring sound of Berlin going about its business, then opened his eyes. The ceiling came into focus, followed by the broad, empty expanse of Corporal Gresser's East Prussian face, his hair as pale as Vistula sand. Behind him was the mantelpiece with clock and ship's model of the *Dresden*. The solid, reliable world.

"Gresser, I was dreaming, wasn't I?"

"Herr Admiral, you are the judge of that."

"Did I say anything?"

"You muttered, Herr Admiral, the way sleeping men do." Gresser moved to the window and pulled open the curtain. In the bathroom next to his office, Admiral Canaris ran cold water and splashed his face. He tried to recall his dream but couldn't. In the mirror, Gresser stood slightly to the rear, towel on his arm.

"I'll have a fresh shirt for you after lunch, Herr Admiral."

Canaris felt beneath his arms. Perspiration had soaked through. "I'll need a fresh undergarment as well." He took the towel from Gresser's arms and dried his hands and face. On his desk was a tray with a silver coffeepot, a plate laden with smoked herring, boiled beets, butter-slathered slice of bread.

Gresser poured the cup full, then retreated toward the door.

"Leave the pot," Canaris said.

"I've typed out your schedule, Herr Admiral. It's beside the phone."

Lifting the cup with one hand, Canaris slipped on his glasses with the other. *Conference at 3 on the situation in Spain. Meeting with the new British naval attaché at 4. Dr. Arnheim at 5:30.*

"Gresser, I didn't ask for an appointment with Arnheim, did I?"

"He requested it with you, Herr Admiral."

"Didn't you think to check with me first?"

"He was here in person during your nap, Herr Admiral. Said it was urgent that he have a few minutes with you. I checked your schedule. The time is available."

"Well, call him back. Tell him you were mistaken. Tell him I'm otherwise engaged or been called away on an emergency. Anything."

A once-a-year obligatory physical was more than enough of Arnheim's ashen face, sharp snout, and sour mouth better suited to an undertaker than a doctor. A high-ranking officer in the National Socialist Physicians League, an old Party man, noted expert in the field of racial hygiene and friend of Dr. Karl Brandt, the Führer's personal physician, Arnheim had lost no time in assuming the practices of first one, then several Jewish doctors who'd been forced to leave the country by the anti-Semitic provisions of the Reich Physicians Ordinance and the Nuremberg Race Laws. He liked to talk. A vexing habit in many doctors, chattering away when they should be quietly focused on their duties. Worse, he gave the same speech at the end of every annual examination.

*Good health is part of our duty to the nation and the race. That's why over half the doctors in this country have joined the party! No other profession can make such a boast! Not even lawyers! The Führer is a model for us all. Never smokes. A vegetarian. Refrains from coffee and tea. A living testament to the venerable truth of* mens sana in corpore sano. *A sound mind in a sound body.*

The metal dish of Arnheim's stethoscope slid across Canaris's hairless chest, a cold sensation that made him shiver. *You need more exercise, Herr Admiral, and stop drinking so much coffee. Caffeine is ruinous to the stomach. If your bowels bother you, here's the culprit: coffee! The German people look to its leadership for example, Herr Admiral. The Führer's put us in the vanguard of racial health and eugenical progress. We've overtaken the United States in these areas. We must not falter!*

Canaris blew on the coffee and took a gulp. Liquid in, liquid out. Chronic diarrhea. He snapped open the gold lighter on his desk and puffed alive the cigarette. *We who are about to shit, salute you!*

He walked quickly to the bathroom. The third time today. As soon as he sat, there was a hesitant knock.

"What is it, Gresser?"

"Herr Admiral, while you were asleep, you had a call you may wish to return before too long." The thick mahogany door made Gresser's voice sound distant and insignificant.

"Speak up, Gresser. Who called?"

"General Heydrich."

"Did he say what he wanted?" The knot in his stomach seemed to momentarily tighten.

"His secretary said that the General was sorry you couldn't join him for a morning ride. The General is concerned for your health. He wishes you to call."

"Assuredly, Gresser." There was little Heydrich needed to be told. He probably read Arnheim's reports before they were typed. Knew better than the patients themselves the condition of heart, brain, liver. Search for some lever. Syphilis. Epilepsy. Alcoholism. Peer at blood specimens through the lens of a microscope to spot any tiny, telltale swarms of Mogen Davids.

Again the knock, the muffled voice.

"What is it now?"

"Your wife, Herr Admiral. She also telephoned. You're meeting her at six-thirty at the Capitol Cinema. She was quite firm. You're not to be late!"

Erika had the Berliner's passion for moviegoing. He rarely went except on occasions like tonight, her birthday, or when she grew sullen and withdrawn, feeling he was neglecting her. Most times they went to American films, especially the romantic comedies, which were her favorite. He found them predictable and boring. He stopped paying attention after a few minutes. He liked the American cartoons, which sometimes preceded the movie, anthropomorphic ducks and rodents in their inevitable melee, a Walpurgisnacht of frenetic *thwacks* and *bonks* from which everyone emerged unscathed.

Once, before the newsreels had acquired their present level of hysteria and bombast, he had seen himself in one. Erika jabbed her elbow into his ribs, "Willi, that's you on the screen!" He was among the dignitaries and officials bidding *bon voyage* to the airship *Graf Zeppelin* as it left from Tempelhof Airport on a mission of polar exploration. Aboard was a company of distinguished scientists and a small group of naval intelligence officers who were undertaking a journey of 8,000 miles that was to be covered in just nine days. The excitement was manifest, the spectators scooting this way and that, waving, saluting. He was on and off the screen in an instant. A casual observer might not have noticed his awkward discomfort at being caught by the camera, but he did, every bit of it, clumsy gestures, half salute, his inane, unnatural smile.

"You're a movie star!" Erika said as they exited the theater.

He dropped the cigarette butt in the toilet and flushed. It spun around like a ship caught in a maelstrom and vanished down the pipe. He washed his hands. The face in the mirror had black circles beneath the eyes; yellow nicotine stains on the upper and lower teeth. He pushed the hair back from his forehead. A line in a slow retreat. Premature gray giving way to white. Some movie star.

Arnheim was right. He needed more exercise. Once he had been rigorous in his devotion to physical fitness. It was particularly important for sailors who spent months at sea. He'd seen enough officers trussed up in corsets so they'd look suitably trim in their dress uniforms to know the dangers of idleness. He'd walked the decks and went up and down ladders till his legs hurt. On land, he'd been a faithful visitor to the officer's gymnasium. Now, given the demands on his time, the best he managed was horseback riding or the strolls with Lieutenant Colonel Hans Oster, his deputy at the Office of Military Intelligence. But it would be untrue, he knew, to ascribe the strolls to a desire to stay fit. It was Oster's outspokenness—more and more venturing beyond frankness to recklessness—which drove him outdoors, away from the casual eavesdropping of co-workers or subordinates or passersby.

Canaris was barely back at his desk when Oster entered in his usual manner, sauntering past Gresser and not bothering to knock. He'd ignored complaints about his unannounced entries for so long that Canaris stopped making them. Oster fell onto the couch, sprawling rather than sitting.

Although only a year older, Canaris felt far senior, like a professor indulging a bright but undisciplined undergraduate. He recognized in Oster one of a type: the veterans forever changed by the *fronterlebnis*, the shared experience of the Western Front. They were marked by the same insouciance and cynicism; the same adolescent impatience with rank and routine; the same spirit that helped drive the Freikorps, the soldiers and sailors who'd joined together at the war's end to put down the Reds. It had also been on display in the Brown Shirts, or SA, the Storm Troopers who'd spearheaded the rise of the National Socialists. Like the vast majority of the officer corps, Oster had been in sympathy with them at the start. But, unlike most, he'd soured rapidly on what he saw as a regime incurably poisoned by thuggery, corruption, and overreaching ambition. To one degree or another, there were other officers with similar opinions, a relatively small percentage to be sure, but few as poor at masking their contempt as Oster.

"Have you seen Piekenbrock's report?" Oster said.

"You know my feelings on the matter." Canaris initialed a stack of requisition forms. He would not be drawn in. He had stated his views on the subject emphatically, so no one could infer a different interpretation, or leap from a criticism of particular acts to an attack on the regime.

"You've read it?"

"Of course." The actions that had followed the annexation of Austria in March, the orgy of SS confiscation and violence directed primarily at the Jews, had become a constant theme of Oster's visits. He had underscored parts of Colonel Hans Piekenbrock's confidential summary so Canaris couldn't miss them. *SS Officers Kaltenbrunner, Globocnik, and Eichmann were particularly odious and brutal in their behavior. The regular army made no attempt to stop or mitigate their conduct, and in many ways abetted it. The SS and Gestapo proceeded with impunity.*

"A vile bunch."

"I have said all I'm going to say on the matter." Canaris said it publicly, glass in hand, at the Naval Ball held a few days after the annexation, into a microphone: *All of us are still dazzled by the experience of the great German consolidation. It exalts every heart!*

The audience answered in a single unanimous shout: *Heil Hitler!*

From his first days with Military Intelligence, Oster had made it clear that he would say what was on his mind and if Canaris didn't like it, he was welcome to dismiss or arrest him, whatever he pleased. Occasionally, he warned Oster about the tone of his remarks and the ease with which they could be misconstrued as treasonous, especially his acerbic asides on the regime's leading personalities. It did little good. Several weeks before, he'd taken Oster with him to attend a reception for a visiting delegation of Japanese military officers in the new Reichschancellery, on the Wilhelmstrasse. It was Oster's first visit inside the still-unfinished building, and he seemed on his best behavior, as reserved and stiffly formal as the other members of the officer corps present.

On the way out, they walked beside the building's architect, Albert Speer, who didn't lose a moment in underlining how close he was to the Führer and how the Reichschancellery was just a small foretaste of their plans for rebuilding Berlin on a truly heroic scale. Oster stopped to gaze at Arno Breker's towering bronze nudes, *The Party* and *The Army*. He pointed at their genitals. "Here we have a perfect recapitulation of your architecture, Herr Speer. Oversized but flaccid." Oster strolled ahead and left Canaris standing with the flustered architect.

Oster rose from the couch and prowled the room. "Sooner or later, our Austrian corporal will push too far," Oster said. "There are no restraints. We'll be plunged into a war we cannot win. It's only a matter of time. Mark my words."

Outside, Gresser was at his desk. Figures moved past in the corridor: secretaries, orderlies, officers. Was it only a matter of time before someone overheard and repeated it to those whose business it was to nose out such sentiments? "Come," said Canaris. "Let's go for a stroll on the Embankment. My doctor advises I need more fresh air and exercise." They walked to the main entrance of the War Ministry, past the busts of Moltke and Blücher, Prussia's two great vanquishers of the French, out along the Tirpitz Embankment, beside the canal. Across the hall, stuck in a corner, was a small bust of Baron von der Goltz, Prussia's original spymaster. He had formed what was among Europe's first professional intelligence services at the behest of Frederick the Great, the king who'd abolished torture as an instrument of state.

Unburdened of frigid, insistent darkness, Berlin was any city of the north awash in the high tide of spring. Oster lit a cigarette by the Embankment wall. He cupped his hands to shield the match from the breeze. Two nursemaids halted their perambulators several yards behind, leaned over to adjust the blankets covering the infants within, chatting as they did.

"Do you know the story of the cat and the rat?" Oster said.

"I suspect that I've heard every cat and rat story," Canaris said. "Don't tell me you have a new one."

"An old Swabian tale, but perhaps it will be new to you. In it, the rat succeeds in convincing the cat that he isn't a cat at all but a rat."

"Stupid cat." Canaris casually surveyed the parade of pedestrians on the Embankment. The nursemaids trailed behind.

"Clever rat. Eloquent and impassioned, he gradually gets the cat acting like a rat. The cat starts to scurry around on its belly, lives in sewers, doesn't clean itself, feasts on garbage, becomes one of the pack. Most wonderful of all, the cat soon realizes he doesn't miss being a cat one bit. He feels quite free now that the burdens of independence, cleanliness, and self-respect have been lifted. He is filled with gratitude toward the rat."

Canaris resisted the impulse to turn and see if the nursemaids were still following. "But how do the rats feel about having a cat in their midst?"

"Oh, after a while the cat so much enjoys the role of rat that the hair falls off his tail. His round puss narrows into a rodent's malevolent snout. Legs shrink into rat's stubs. He is at home with the rats and they with him. Other cats see how happy he is, how prosperous and carefree, and they join the rats."

"This sounds very *unlike* a Swabian folk tale."

"Truth is, an Englishman, a writer, told it to me."

"Since when do you associate with Englishmen or writers?"

"A mutual acquaintance prevailed on me to see him. He needed help facilitating the departure of a Jewish doctor whose exit was complicated by her former Communist ties."

"You keep strange company."

"These are strange times. Let me finish my story. One day, the clever rat gathers together his brother rats, and the rats who once were cats, and the cats in the process of becoming rats, and tells them they can fly."

"They believe him?"

"Not at first. But he reminds the rats how he's transformed the cats and conjured away their enemy. He points out to the cats how free he's made them. Given such success, why shouldn't he be able to make them fly? There are still doubters, but they stay quiet and are swept along with the rest as the clever rat leads them to the highest cliff he can find. 'Forward, my brothers!' he cries. 'Over the edge! Fly!'"

"*Finis*, I suppose?"

"The storyteller posited two possible endings. First, the cats and rats follow their leader over the cliff to destruction. Second, they hesitate at the edge, doubtful at last of their leader, and at that moment a conspiracy of cats still in possession of their souls deposes the clever rat."

"There's a third possibility, Hans, for your storyteller to consider."

"What's that?"

"Perhaps he can fly." Canaris had watched in person as a quarter of a million people filled the Heldenplatz, in Vienna, trampling each other to get closer to the gleaming Mercedes, a chariot from heaven, the god within once more defying the timid counsel of generals and diplomats, jumping from the cliff and landing on his feet.

"He's been lucky, that's all. The next jump will very likely be from a deadly height." Oster tossed his cigarette into the canal.

They turned back toward the Ministry. The nursemaids went by, still in conversation. The two officers touched their caps and bid the women good morning. Each carriage contained a fat, pink-cheeked infant, small hands clutching at the air. The women nodded and pushed the carriages along the Embankment.

"I've no more time to waste." Canaris walked at a brisk pace. Oster stayed beside him but said nothing. Canaris welcomed the silence. He knew Oster would return to the discussion he was having with other officers, about what to do if the order was given to move against the Czechs. General Ludwig Beck, Chief of the General Staff, was involved. A growing conversation. That ugly, unsoldierly word: *Mutiny.*

"The Czechs will fight," Oster said. They stopped beneath the portico of the Ministry. "The British and French will stand by them. They've already made that clear. When the people know the days of easy conquests are over and face a war more punishing and destructive than the last, their mood will change. The cats' hour will have come. It will be our final chance."

"The desire to take wishes for facts is the deadliest of all temptations for an intelligence officer," Canaris said. He knew as well as Oster the feelers that had been put out to the French and British. Gördeler had carried the message to the Foreign Office in London: *The only way for war to be avoided is to reject the demands being made on the Czechs. Prepare to resist. There are elements in and out of the German armed forces that are ready to seize the opportunity to put an end to the regime.* A response somewhere between bewilderment and disdain. A palpable awe of the new Germany and its leader. If there were any wish to challenge him, the French and British were doing a skillful job of disguising it.

"Sooner or later," Oster said, "either we Germans will have the courage to turn wishes into facts or be damned by our own cowardice."

The nursemaids doubled back and came past the portico. The day before, during the morning ride in the Tiergarten, General Heydrich stopped his horse. Canaris stopped, too, thinking perhaps Heydrich wished to dismount and give the horses a rest. Instead, Heydrich leaned out of his saddle and said in a quiet, solemn voice, "Wilhelm, there are rumors that, if true, could implicate certain members of the officer corps in treasonous conversations. We must work together to search out and destroy such a conspiracy, if it exists. We will show no mercy to such scum, even though they wear a German uniform." He patted Canaris's shoulder. "We, the loyal servants of the Reich!"

Oster lingered with another cigarette beneath the portico. Alone, Canaris mounted the stairs to his office. At the second landing, he caught a glimpse through the two-storied Palladian window of the nursemaids as they crossed the street. If surveillance had been ordered, it would probably be less clumsy and obvious. Or perhaps not. As fast as the Abwehr has grown, Himmler's SS empire had grown far faster. At last count, Pieckenbrock's Section I of Military Intelligence estimated that Reichsführer-SS Himmler and his deputy, Reinhard Heydrich, the head of the SS Security Service, or SD, employed 40,000 Gestapo men, 60,000 agents and 100,000 official informers. Along with the main concentration camps at Dachau, Sachsenhausen-Oranienburg, Buchenwald, Flossenburg and Ravensbrück, they had camps under construction at Mauthausen, in newly annexed Austria.

The night he and Erika watched the newsreel of the Führer's entry into Vienna, they dined in a restaurant right off Potsdamer Platz. Berlin wallowed in its new prosperity. Construction scaffolds were everywhere, new automobiles, crowded stores, high-toned cafés. The restaurant was filled with handsome young officers in uniform, women in well-cut clothes, plump businessmen with UFA starlets on their arms.

There seemed no hint of the other Berlin, the underworld of wiretaps, informers, arrests, interrogations, and internment on suspicion of disloyalty. The masses of obedient and loyal citizens had nothing to fear. But along with the carrot of Germany's renewed strength and power was the insinuation of the stick, a self-correcting mechanism for the few who might prove too overt in their dissent, an underlying dread threaded into the neon and newly poured concrete and traffic-choked streets, medieval torture chambers housed next to movie theaters, the soundtracks loud enough to obliterate any noise that might miraculously escape the impervious prison walls.

At first Canaris had been incredulous at the reports that Colonel Piekenbrock sent him on the self-contained network of concentration camps the SS had set up. The Stormtroopers' assault on Reds, socialists, and radicals, the first violent outburst after the National Socialists had taken power, had been transmogrified into a permanent terror. The reports of floggings, beatings, clubbings, prisoners drowned in latrines, whipped with barbed wire, strung up on racks, their genitals crushed, seemed a preposterous rehash of the prurient novels on the Inquisitions, with their cheap, lurid paper covers, that salesmen and students bought for a few pfennigs at railway news-stands. But the consistency of the reports gradually erased any doubts about their authenticity. Theodor Eicke, once an inmate of a psychiatric clinic in which he'd been consigned to a straightjack-et, was now in charge of more than 10,000 well-trained and armed SS Death's Heads Units responsible for policing the camps. In Columbia House, the SS center on Potsdamer Platz, one of the interrogators kept a drawer full of the teeth he knocked out of detainees' mouths.

The nursemaids sat on a bench. They rocked their carriages back and forth. Perhaps they were intended to be noticed. A casu-al but deliberate warning: *Admiral, no one is above suspicion.* Gresser jumped to attention when Canaris re-entered his office, shoulders back, chin up, eyes ahead, the pose of a loyal and obedi-ent subordinate.

What were the chances, Canaris wondered, that he answered to other masters as well?

Canaris put on the fresh shirt and undergarments that Gresser had laid out. He attended the conference on the situation in Spain, a topic that usually absorbed him, especially since the progress there was so notable, Franco's Falangists growing stronger each day. He doodled on a pad during the presentation by the Luftwaffe officer who reported on the performance of various aircraft. He found it impossible to focus his attention on what was being said, a condition he had endured for a prolonged period over a decade ago, in the time of the Weimar Republic, when his career seemed stalled and he began an affair with a woman he'd first met as a naval cadet.

He was certain his wife had no idea. Yet after weeks of reveling in the physical intensity of his illicit relationship, he fell in a funk that left him unable to concentrate and finally brought him to the point where he felt a vacuum had formed inside his head, a void that made thinking itself seem absurd. He went through the motions of work until thoughts of suicide drove him to see a doctor who referred him to a respected neuropathologist and psychotherapist, Doctor Manfred Stern, a half Jew married to the daughter of a minor Bavarian nobleman.

Careful to make sure his visit took place at the doctor's private office in the early morning hours, Canaris arrived by taxi, in civilian clothes. Doctor Stern was solicitous. He encouraged Canaris not only to describe his mental anguish but also to speak freely about his life. Canaris did so hesitantly at first, then surprised himself by going on for longer than he intended, though he left out any mention of his affair. Doctor Stern asked no questions until Canaris fell silent. "What about your wife?" he said.

"What about her?"

"You've never mentioned her."

"I'm here to get medicine for my nerves, not to discuss my marriage."

"Do you know that line from *Hamlet*: 'We know what we are, but not what we may be'? Sometimes, the opposite can happen. A man loses a true sense of who he is yet feels he's changing into something he loathes and there's nothing he can do to stop it. It's characteristic of over-supple minds and can induce a kind of psychic paralysis." The doctor recommended valerian drops as a mild sedative. "This may help relieve the symptoms. If you wish to treat the cause, I'd be glad to take you on as a patient."

Canaris never went back. He ended the affair and threw himself into his work. The sensation of numbing distraction came back only very sporadically, as it had this afternoon. Returning to his desk, he tackled the backlog of reports and letters stacked on his writing stand where he'd left off before his nap. The clock on the mantle chimed four. Gresser reappeared to announce the arrival of the new British naval attaché. The British had their faults. Tardiness wasn't among them. Germany's friends in Spain and Italy could learn a lesson from them.

The attaché had none of the silly hauteur of his predecessor. Formal but pleasant, he surveyed the office with the studied sweep of a deck officer on watch and pointed at the model of the *Dresden* on the mantle. "Von Spee gave us a quite a scare. I lost two close friends in 1914, at Coronel."

"I was the *Dresden*'s First Lieutenant," Canaris said. "We were all proud to serve with Admiral von Spee." Days so different from now, the endless Pacific sky; at night the spectacle of the Southern Cross, the pyrotechnics of shooting stars. The war was still exciting; victory still a possibility. The *Dresden* put into San Miguel on Michaelmas, a propitious coincidence, everyone agreed. Canaris spent several nights with the same whore, a half-Indian, half-German girl, a face so lovely he'd never seen its equal. Soon after, the *Dresden* rendezvoused with von Spee's squadron and formed a small flotilla that posed a potent threat to British shipping.

The Royal Navy wasn't long in coming, steaming ahead with all the cocksure arrogance for which it was famous. Von Spee waited outside the port of Coronel, in Chile, and let them run into his guns. *Monmouth* and *Good Hope* each took direct hits, erupting into the twilight with the force of volcanoes, and sank with all 1,600 sailors aboard. Von Spee directed there be no cheering. An unnecessary order. The men knew that the Royal Navy would do everything in its power to undo such an atrocious defeat, the worst in more than a century, and that the charred and broken corpses floating in the water might soon be their own.

"The *Invincible* and *Inflexible* put an end to the Admiral's success," the attaché said.

"Yes, but the *Dresden* got away."

"Quite right. It was the *Glasgow* that finally caught up with you and sent the *Dresden* to the bottom, was it not?"

"We were hit by *Glasgow*, but we scuttled it ourselves and fled ashore. The crew was interned, but I was too young to waste away in such a place, with nothing more exciting to look forward to than a daily siesta. I escaped across the Andes, reached Buenos Aires, and sailed with a Chilean passport through Plymouth to Rotterdam."

"The one that got away!"

"That time at least."

They'd watched from a nearby hill as the *Dresden* reared up out of the water, heaved its stern in the air and keeled over to expose the gaping, smoking, fatal wound in its starboard side. The sturdy, reliable, hardworking *Dresden* slipped rapidly into the green sea. An oil slick spread over the surface of the water like a blood stain. It felt as though they witnessed the death of an old and trusted mate.

Three of the crew died from cholera while interned on the bleak island of Quiriquina. Another went mad. One slit his wrists. He was surrounded by death, certain it would come for him if he stayed, so he fled, across the Andes, death a pace or two behind. The commendation that accompanied his Iron Cross saluted his "heroic determination to rejoin the struggle for the Fatherland and fight unto the death." But it was fear—the fear of death—that drove him to escape, not heroism.

Gresser served tea. The attaché spoke of his hope their countries wouldn't be adversaries again. He recognized Germany's claim on territorial adjustments to the Versailles Treaty. "But all this saber rattling is putting everyone on edge."

"Wanton aggression must be strongly opposed," Canaris said. "The security of Europe depends on it. Your government must face up to that."

"Come, Admiral, I'd hardly call the Czechs 'wanton aggressors.'"

"Neither would I."

The attaché stared at the tea leaves in the bottom of his cup, as if the meaning of Canaris's implicit criticism of his own government might be found there. After an unnatural pause, he described a motor trip he'd taken on the new autobahn, the wonders of its broad lanes, no lights or crossways or local traffic. He had an Englishman's love of monologue as well as a talent for it. Canaris was delighted to be relieved of the burden of conversation. They parted with an amicable handshake.

Canaris finished up his work and prepared to leave. The nap hadn't done much to relieve his sluggishness, and the reminiscences of the *Dresden*, of what seemed a lost, irretrievable innocence, left him nostalgic. He'd served on the *Dresden* in a different time, a different world, when the sea and its endless horizons encouraged dreams and illusions that duty and the war obliterated.

He remembered one time in particular, during the last full summer of peace, in 1913. The *Dresden* had been temporarily relieved from South American patrol and sent on a goodwill call to the city of Baltimore, for the occasion of the American Independence Day. Passing up an invitation to visit Washington, D.C., Canaris and another officer took a train to New York on a three-day leave. After some stretches of open country, the rail corridor they rode through became thick with an impressive array of bustling warehouses and smoke-belching factories. They were quite prepared to dislike New York, a town of legendary political corruption, filled with lumpen Irish and the dregs of Naples and the Polish shtetls. But as the train sped across a great marsh, and the tops of the city's tallest buildings could be seen twinkling magically, like the evening star, in the purple gloaming, Canaris felt a sense of excited anticipation.

The train plunged into a tunnel and emerged a short while later in the great steel and glass-covered cavern of Pennsylvania Station. The German deputy vice-consul of New York was there to meet them. He led them to a broad traffic-choked avenue ablaze with electric lights and into a waiting automobile. After they checked into their hotel in an area every bit as bustling as that around the station, the deputy vice-consul escorted them to an outdoor Italian restaurant where a tan-skinned cantatrice sang about love and broken hearts. In the morning they visited the zoo in the Bronx, the thinly populated northern part of the city. Later, they toured the metropolitan art museum and went to the top of the newly opened Woolworth Building, traveling everywhere on the city's efficient train and tram system. The deputy vice-consul was a man in his mid-thirties, a florid and rotund Bavarian, who seemed as inured to New York as any native. That night, in the intermission of the play he took them to—a comedy they barely understood but that drew incessant laughter from the audience—he flirted with several women. He consorted with every cab driver and doorman as though they were mates of long acquaintance.

The manager of the hotel was waiting for them when they came back. He was the grandson of a Berlin composer, a Jew, and welcomed them warmly. He opened a bottle of fine Riesling, and when that was gone, brought out a bottle of American whiskey, which had a coarse, smoky taste. Canaris's companion excused himself, explaining that they had to catch a train early the next morning back to Baltimore. Canaris followed him out but didn't return to their room. He needed some fresh air. He rode the elevator to the hotel's roof garden, where he drank wine at the bar and stared at a lovely girl in a violet hat and dress who sat between her parents beneath a lattice entwined with paper flowers. The parents didn't seem to notice him, but the girl did. She smiled at him.

The warm night air and the flow of the wine fermented silly, evanescent thoughts. He would propose to the girl. Their wedding night would be in this very hotel, her in the bed in frilly white undergarments, waiting for him as he packed away his uniform in the bottom of their traveling trunk, where it wouldn't be discovered until decades later when a grandchild went rummaging about in the attic of their house. He would seek employment in the tumultuous commerce that drove the city, import-export perhaps, and assume the same style as the deputy vice-consul, the unguarded bonhomie. The girl and her parents left. She looked over her shoulder at him as she went out. A look of desire. In the distance, beyond the roof garden, the broad, well-lit, heavily trafficked avenues stretched north, toward the great open space of America.

He drank more wine. How easy this city had it. Berlin had been raised to greatness not by the River Spree or the luck of geography, but by struggle, battle, the concentrated willpower and firepower of a state with enemies on every side. New York was handed greatness, wide river, deep, capacious harbor, the ocean at its door. Soldiers were nowhere to be seen. There was no rival military power for a radius of three thousand miles. Even the police lacked any sense of military bearing—fat, slovenly Irish peasants who strutted about with the gait of a farmer taking a cow to market.

The sharp, unceasing pain in his head the next morning was made all the worse by the unrelenting cacophony of the New York streets. He couldn't remember the face of the girl at whom he had stared so intently. He boarded the train to Baltimore. The *Dresden* sailed that evening. When the war came, and she went to the bottom, he made his epic, dangerous journey back to the Fatherland, took the assignments that were given to him without protest or complaint, even desk work in Berlin, sitting bolt upright, mind harnessed to the iron coulter of military paperwork.

Occasionally, as he did now, he recalled his visit to New York. The roof garden. That girl. Her look. Violet. Memories that grew fainter. Besides, the city he visited had long since disappeared. Like the rest of America, New York had fallen on hard times. Unemployment rampant. The busy gaiety of the city gone. Streets overrun by competing mobs of gangsters who fought gun battles for control. The chaos that democracy inevitably brought. But there'd been a moment when it enticed him, possibilities never pursued that now seemed only wild fantasies.

WALL STREET, NEW YORK

The sustained buzz of the intercom drew Donovan's attention from the nagging pain behind his knee. His secretary had probably been pushing the button for some time. He put the switch in the "on" position and bent close. "Yes."

"Colonel Donovan, sorry to interrupt, but I have John Foster Dulles's secretary on the line, and she wants to change your luncheon appointment from the River Club to the dining room at the law offices of Sullivan & Cromwell. Mr. Dulles's back is bothering him and he'd appreciate not having to travel uptown."

"Fine."

"And she wants to know if you mind that District Attorney Dewey will be joining you."

The constriction behind his knee became almost unbearable. "Oh, Christ."

"Does that mean you don't wish Mr. Dewey included?"

"No, no, I'm sorry, my leg is acting up, that's all. Include Mr. Dewey by all means."

"Shall I bring you some aspirin?"

"That's not necessary. It'll pass. It always does."

Then again, Donovan thought, aspirin might lessen the headache that sometimes followed John Foster Dulles's ponderous monologues. Dulles had brought Tom Dewey with him before, obviously convinced that the Racket Buster was his great white hope for putting a Republican in the White House and elevating himself to Secretary of State, a position held by his grandfather and uncle. Dewey and Dulles together would make for a grimly serious lunchtime. "On second thought," he said, "yes, please bring the aspirin."

The ache settled into a concentrated throb. Standing usually helped. This time it only made it worse. "A phantom pain," the doctor said. "The bullet shattered all the nerves and blood vessels. You couldn't have any sensation there."

Couldn't, but did.

Donovan sat down again and drove his knuckles into where the throbbing had intensified. Years ago, he'd rubbed a spot nearby and felt something sharp. It turned out to be a sliver of shrapnel that had worked its way to the surface a full decade after it had entered. The common phenomenon of wounds working beneath the skin, invisible, but still there, still capable of making their presence felt. He could never remember when exactly he'd been hit by shrapnel, but it had to have been soon after he crouched on the lip of the shallow trench the men had dug, stood, and blew his whistle.

*Ahead, behind a shroud of fog, the furious syncopation of the German machine guns seems to come from all sides. As he turns to look behind, the impact of a bullet knocks him flat. Stunned for a moment, he struggles to his feet. Sergeant Kane is struck by a burst of machine gun fire that shreds the lower part of his face. Tumbling backwards, Kane drags them both into the trench they'd just left.*

*The heaving of the ground brings him to his senses. The high, thin, hysterical shriek of the German 210 millimeter shells inches closer, finding the right range. At the far end of the trench, three soldiers huddle close to the earth. They're too scared to be embarrassed at having failed to follow the others out of the trench. The dirt streaked across their faces can't disguise or diminish their terror. They're the three youngest men in the unit, boys really. "Are you all right, Major Donovan?" one of them calls. His hands are cupped together like a football coach calling across the field to one of his players.*

*Another shell hits, closer than before. Amid a gray, grizzled crimson-flecked shower of dirt and pulverized flesh, a perfectly butchered human leg, puttee and laces still in place, bone as white as soap, lands next to him. He's sure that the severed limb belongs to the boy who'd yelled over a moment before. He looks at where they'd been. Two were gone. Obliterated. The third, the youngest, is missing his legs but still alive. He's shouting, "O shit! O shit!" A soldier reappears through the mist. He thinks at first it's a German stormtrooper come to finish the job. He gropes for his revolver, barely getting it out of its holster when he realizes the soldier is one of his own boys, returned to carry him to safety. They just make it out before the next shell hits. He stays where he is for the next five hours, in shivering agony, refusing to be evacuated or to order a retreat. The Germans are waiting for that. The instant a withdrawal begins they'll throw in their reserves and turn it into a rout.*

*When a stretcher finally arrives, one of the bearers is Tommy Scanlon, who'd been with the 1st Battalion of the 69th since those early days at Camp Mills. He's been among the hardest to win over, a Hell's Kitchen brat resentful of the commanding officer with an Irish name but Brooks Brothers breeches and Ivy League manners. Scanlon hadn't changed his attitude until the Ourcq. The battalion had been cut to pieces and he went wild, shooting three German prisoners. After he took away Scanlon's pistol but didn't report him, Scanlon conferred on him the nickname "Wild Bill" Donovan, a misnomer if there'd ever been one, since he'd been in charge of calming the men after they'd lost 66 officers and 1,750 soldiers in the fighting at the Ourcq, almost two thirds of the regiment's original 3,000 men.*

*"Well, Major, guess the krauts won't be satisfied till they done us all in."*

*Scanlon holds a corner of the blanket that they're using as a makeshift stretcher. His face is directly above. He's always thought of Scanlon as a grown man. Suddenly it's obvious: He's just a kid. A kid in the wrong place. There isn't time to reply before a bullet strikes Scanlon just beneath the rim of his helmet, one neat hole in the head, dead. The others drop the blanket. His bullet-broken knee takes the brunt of the fall. His howl is swallowed by another round of mortar shells. Scanlon is crumpled next to him, eyes bulging with fatal surprise. The day he accepts the Congressional Medal of Honor, he thinks of Scanlon's expression. He deposits it at the 69th Armory as a memorial to Scanlon and "our brave and unforgotten dead."*

*Unforgotten by whom? Who remembered Scanlon? When it's over, people can't forget the war fast enough.*

His secretary entered with a bottle of aspirin and a glass of water on a teak tray. She rested the tray on his desk along with a folder containing the morning mail. "They want to make you a star."

"Who wants to make me a star?'

"Warner Brothers. It's the first letter."

He took the folder to the window and stood while he read. The pain ebbed slightly. Addressed to "Colonel William J. Donovan," the letter was a follow-up to a phone call from a studio executive informing him that Warner Bros. was considering a film about the wartime exploits of the 69th Regiment: "As the distinguished commander of that outfit, as well as the most highly decorated American officer in the Great War and winner of the Medal of Honor, you, Colonel Donovan, would be prominently featured." The letter asked his technical assistance in developing the idea. "While we are only in the initial stages, we are hopeful this project will be brought to completion."

Till now, films about the war had been scant. America had its fill of *Over There*. The Depression concentrated attention *Over Here, Over Here*. The second page contained some preliminary information intended, the executive wrote, "to convey the seriousness with which we approach the project." Academy Award-winning screenwriter Norman Reilly Raine and director William

Keighley, the team responsible for the current Warner Bros. hit *The Adventures of Robin Hood,* were being considered for the film.

There was no mention of who'd be cast in the movie, and Donovan knew there was no telling. With God, said Saint Augustine, all things were possible. How much more so with Hollywood, where no truth, physical, spiritual, or historical, would be allowed to stand in the way of box-office success? Who'd be cast as Father Duffy, the regimental chaplain, a restless intellectual dismissed from his post at the archdiocesan seminary for his theological explorations, and a priest utterly unjudgmental of the moral failings of the troops he ministered to? Probably be reduced to a pious silhouette. Pat O'Brien, perhaps? *All Quiet on the Western Front* meets *Boys Town,* another Warner Bros. hit. James Cagney as William Donovan? Or Errol Flynn? Or borrow Mickey Rooney and Spencer Tracy from MGM?

"How about your autograph?" His secretary returned with another folder that contained the letters he'd dictated to her first thing that morning.

"You mean my signature." Sitting behind his desk, he scribbled his name at the bottom of each.

"No, your *autograph.* Looks like you're on your way to stardom." She had come to work for him after his defeat in the 1932 New York gubernatorial election with the caveat that her true profession was acting. As soon as she landed a role, she'd be gone. That was six years ago. She took the folder back to her desk, closing the door harder than usual.

He switched on the intercom. "Anything comes of this movie business, I'll see to it that the Warner Brothers are alerted to your theatrical aspirations."

"*Abilities.*"

"You know what I mean."

"My *aspirations* are to the legitimate stage, not an assembly line in some Hollywood movie factory in hopes of becoming 'The loftiest star of unascended heaven; pinnacled dim in the intense inane.'"

"Shakespeare?"

"Shelley." A sharp crack signaled she'd switched off the intercom.

If truly disinterested, she was in a small, ever-dwindling minority. Donovan saw it on his travels. The lure was everywhere: the spectacle and stars of filmdom, an outsized, nonstop rebuttal of all the quotidian misery and ordinary squalor that had overwhelmed the country. A few nights earlier, the day after his wife left on a trip to California, he went for a walk and was halfway across town when it began to rain, a convenient excuse to duck into a movie theater. He hardly cared what was playing as long as it offered some diversion from worrying about his wife's long spells of paralyzing sadness. He caught the second feature, *Racket Busters,* a low-budget Warner Bros. picture with Humphrey Bogart in his usual role as a villain and George Brent as an honest trucker trying to resist the grip of the mob.

It proved diverting enough, though the suave George Brent seemed particularly unconvincing as a truck driver. The chief racket buster, played by Walter Abel, embodied yet another tribute to the growing fame of the real-life nemesis of the mob, Tom Dewey, the man who'd nailed Lucky Luciano, broken up a string of rackets, and was hot on the tail of the Tammany Tiger and its corrupt politicians.

Donovan was struck by how the audience clapped at the end, applause directed not to the actors on the screen but to the boy wonder from Owosso, Michigan, the crusader who'd inspired anti-corruption drives across America. The year before, it seemed as if Dewey were ready to lay down the mantle of special prosecutor in charge of breaking the hold of the rackets on businesses and entire industries for a lucrative position in private practice. Foster Dulles crowed loudly about how he'd hooked Dewey for Sullivan & Cromwell with an offer of $150,000 a year. But Dewey changed his mind and announced he was running for D.A. His work wasn't done. Crooks, grafters, and murderers still abounded. The decisive victory had yet to be won. His picture seemed to be everywhere, his voice, too, in thundering radio addresses. It was said you could tell where he was from several blocks away by the intensity of the flash bulbs.

Dewey was easier to admire, Donovan came to realize, than to be around. Cocky and aloof, he wore a dismissive smirk that followed the thin horizontal line of his mustache. "Bill," Dewey said when Dulles introduced him to Donovan, "if I ever run for governor of New York, I don't intend to get trounced the way you were." Now it seemed likely he'd not only have his shot at governor but even higher.

"Tom is an authentic American hero," Dulles said at that first meeting. "If anyone can end the long reign of Democratic misrule, it's he. *Vir horae.* The man of the hour!" He lifted his glass in a toast. Dewey held up his glass as well. A toast to himself. A full smile exposed the space between his front teeth and made his young face seem almost adolescent. His eyes glowed. With what? Ambition? Scotch? Amid the crowded, stuffy ballroom of the Roosevelt Hotel, he remained cool and self-assured, off by himself, pinnacled on some dim and distant peak.

Donovan's secretary was in front of his desk. He hadn't heard her return. She placed a letter on his desk. It was postmarked London. "A Mr. Anderson is requesting a meeting with you. He claims you know him." She left without another word, her pique unspoken but palpable.

He recognized the name immediately, though Anderson thought he wouldn't: *"Perhaps you don't remember me, but . . ."* It was either a typical example of British self-deprecation or more likely the reflexive cover of a professional intelligence officer, in which capacity he was serving when Donovan first met him, near the end of the war. The two weeks of instruction had come as a much-welcomed respite from the trenches. Though it was the early autumn of 1918 and the war's end was less than two months away, the Allies seemed a long way from decisive victory, with the Germans, sensing their backs were to the wall, still fighting like demons. The American officers were told they'd been selected for special training in "advanced field tactics."

When they arrived at the chateau where they were quartered, it was revealed they'd been chosen for schooling by the intelligence service of the British Army. "The British are the best in the world at such things," said the divisional commander, Douglas MacArthur, who made a brief appearance. "Consider yourselves honored."

Major Ian Anderson was in charge. He instructed them not only in debriefing German prisoners, extracting valuable bits of truth from the deliberate lies and confused misreporting, but also in searching out the disgruntled prisoners who, with proper encouragement, would tell everything they knew and might even inform on their fellow prisoners and provide added information. "The whole genius of any proper intelligence operation," he said, "is in spinning a web of relationships that gives you entry to the minds and souls of your opponents." He made a point of eating each night with Donovan and bringing along a bottle of port, which his American companion never touched.

On their last evening together, Anderson was blunt. "The Hindenburg Line is guarded on its flanks by the Michael, Wotan, Hermann and Kriemhilde lines, all of them baptized with good Wagnerian names and properly symbolic of the bloodbath that will occur when we storm them." Anderson was sure the Allies would eventually triumph but less sure of what would follow. "Once upon a time, Donovan, I was a history professor by trade, and there's no greater barrier to ordinary human happiness than exposure to too much history. That's why you Americans are so optimistic. Europe has so much history crammed into so small a space, and you have so little in so large."

Anderson finished the bottle of port that last evening. He recounted his experience at the Somme two years before, when he'd been shot and gassed. "It was done like an assembly line," he said. "Row after row cut to pieces. Two hundred battalions, 100,000 men thrown against the German position. We weren't so much soldiers as part of a new manufacturing process, industrialized murder. 20,000 killed and 40,000 wounded that first day, ground up with machine guns and high explosives, hung up on barbed wire, smothered with gas."

"Perhaps we've made war too terrible to fight."

"History says otherwise." Anderson slurred his words. "We've turned science to the service of mass murder. We've yet to see what final place it will lead us."

In his letter, Anderson rambled on for several paragraphs about his present travels in Europe as a freelance journalist. Again, Donovan thought he was either being typically British, expressing the national passion for commenting on the manners and customs of the world, or reinforcing his false credentials. At last Anderson got to the point, or what he pretended was the point: "I would be grateful for the opportunity to interview you for an article I'm writing on the exploits of the American Expeditionary Force in the Great War."

There'd always been something odd about Anderson, not merely eccentric, but an air of the mystical and exotic. Perhaps he'd been raised in India or some other part of the empire where he'd been touched by the beliefs of the East. It was known to happen among Brits far from home. Whatever Anderson's reason for coming, Donovan looked forward to seeing him again. They had the bond of having served together in the war, a tie that neither distance nor time could erase. He scribbled a note instructing his secretary to schedule a meeting the next month, when he returned from one of his periodic visits with the firm's banking and industrial clients in Chicago and Detroit, a solid corps of orthodox Republicans more eager to discuss politics than business, and how best to drive "that man"—some were so filled with loathing for Franklin Roosevelt they carefully avoided using his name—from the White House before he involved the country in another war; or used such a crisis to do the unthinkable, an act without precedent in the history of the Republic, and seek a third term.

# 3

Doctor I. is among the minority excluded from participation in the new Germany. A woman of delicate beauty, an accomplished medical specialist, former resident of a prestigious research institution as well as wife of a physician who is a decorated war veteran, Doctor I. is a Jew. Though living close to the bustle and excitement of Berlin, she rarely pays a visit to town. Instead, she spends most of her days in a villa, in the bosky suburb of Wannsee, where she and her husband reside. Even in private, she hesitates to criticize the actions of the National Socialist regime. "Germany is entitled to whatever form of government it wishes," she says. Her only desire is to leave, which, she explains, has been temporarily complicated by her former political associations with the now-banned Communist Party. Strolling in her garden, amid the chill of an autumn-laden evening mist, she pulls her sweater close around her thin frame. "Ideally," she says, "if things had turned out differently, I couldn't imagine leaving Berlin. But all I wish today is to go to a city such as New York and resume my research undisturbed." Doctor I. shivers slightly and continues her walk, into the night, into the fog.

—Ian Anderson, *Travels in the New Germany*

## Abwehr Headquarters, Berlin

Faced with the drudgery of reports and requisitions, Canaris grew drowsy. Lately, he'd found it easier to sleep in the day. The night before, Erika awoke and saw him sitting in the chair, staring at her. She sputtered a reproach. *Willi, come to bed. It's already so late.* He lay down beside her for what seemed an interminable time before he felt himself drifting off. He hoped he wouldn't have one of his nightmares and disturb her with his fitful muttering and crying.

He told Gresser to hold his calls. He pulled the curtains shut, the new ones issued in case of air raids, and lay on the couch. The breeze he'd felt during his walk on the Embankment pushed the curtains and momentarily held them apart. A shaft of light fell across his desk and touched the gold cigarette lighter Erika gave him for their first anniversary. Engraved beneath the date of their wedding was *Wie geht's?* A private joke. *How's it going?* That first night of their honeymoon, almost twenty years ago, in the old inn on the Baltic, they barely slept, talking and making love till dawn, and didn't leave their room until lunch the next day. The old waiter winked at them, said with a knowing grin, *Wie geht's?* They all laughed, even Erika, her face red with embarrassment.

The lighter glistened in the light, until the curtain fluttered back in place. The room was dark again. In the quiet after their very first lovemaking, Erika whispered, "Will, we are each other's destiny. It's written in the stars." He refrained from saying what he thought. *The stars have no power over us. Distant suns, useful for navigation. That's all. The rest is romantic claptrap. Superstition.* The curtains parted once again and a beam struck the lighter as before, making it shine. Like a star. The previous March, on the day of the national celebration of the annexation of Austria, at the reception in the Chancellery, the room exploded in cheers when the Führer entered. He surveyed the crowd coldly and moved deliberately toward the corner where Canaris stood. He extended his hand. "Admiral," he said, "I have learned the greatest truth the gods can teach. My destiny is out of human hands. It is written in the stars!"

How dim and distant that constellation had once appeared, and how suddenly it flared across the heavens. Several months before Hindenburg, war hero turned dottering octogenarian, made Hitler chancellor, the commander in chief of the navy gathered his aides and reported on the meeting that the leadership of the armed forces had with President Hindenburg. "The President assured us that he would never make that rabble-rousing outlander a cabinet minister, never mind chancellor," the commander said. "And let me tell you, gentlemen, the thudding of hands on that conference table left no doubt of where the military stands."

On January 30, 1933, the morning of the day Hindenburg did what he said he would never do and asked Hitler to form a coalition government, Canaris surreptitiously disembarked from his post aboard the battleship *Schlesien*, which was carrying out gunnery exercises in Kiel Bay, and traveled in mufti to rendezvous at the Hotel Adlon, in Berlin, with a friend in the naval ministry who was highly sympathetic to Hitler's ambitions. "The oldtimers are hopeless," the friend scoffed when Canaris repeated what the commander said. "They're still waiting for the Kaiser to return. The rest of us are more than willing to give Hitler a chance. God knows, he can't be worse than what we've had." He took a cube of sugar and placed it in the middle of the table. He banged it with his spoon. "Hitler is the anvil on which the Reds will be pounded into powder." He scooped up the pieces with the spoon and dropped them in his coffee. "And as long as he respects and serves the wishes of the armed forces, we should have no problems." He stirred his coffee and sipped. "Just right," he said.

In the flyleaf of the Bible his parents had given him the morning he left for the naval academy, Canaris had scribbled a note to himself. *What men wish to believe, no matter how absurd, they will allow nothing to stand in the way of their belief.* It was a student's declaration of independence, made in the heat of having read *Zarathustra,* a sneer at absurdities enshrined at the heart of all formal religions. Over time, he'd lost his taste for Nietzsche and come to value the worth of Christianity as a bulwark against anarchy and communism. Erika was a sincere believer. After their marriage, he occasionally accompanied her to church. She sang the hymns with great skill and feeling. Once at the Easter service that took place after Erika's first miscarriage, during the choral celebration, her belief in the myth of a crucified and resurrected god carried her away. Her beaming, raptured face was streaked with tears. "Heal me, My Savior," she whispered, "heal me."

Erika never shared his growing faith that the National Socialists represented the best hope for restoring Germany's military strength and national greatness. She had a special disdain for the rowdy street fighting spearheaded by the SA and the loose talk among the radicals about forcing a "showdown" with the Christian churches. But that night, five years before, when Hitler was sworn in as chancellor, as they stood together in the Pariser Platz and watched the immense parade of torch-bearing Brown Shirts on their way to hail Germany's new leader, her face had the same look as in church, an overpowering joy and hopefulness. For the first time, he too knew how it was possible to be so elated, so filled with hope, tears became unstoppable.

For weeks following, magazines and rotogravures were filled with photographs of the procession. Göbbels, the new Reich Minister of Propaganda, even restaged the event so it could be properly lit for filming. But neither photographs nor newsreels nor reenactments could touch the emotions in those streets, the spontaneous singing, a three-dimensional formation of light flowing like an incandescent river, the decade-and-a-half nightmare of humiliation being washed away, shock of defeat, harsh peace, reparations, coups and uprisings, devastating inflation, the decadent republic, a rage for novelties and self-indulgence followed by the cold bath of the Depression, idle men and hollow-eyed children lined up for soup, paralyzed, ineffectual politicians mouthing endless platitudes, arrogant seditious Reds promising revolution, blood running in the streets—over, at last! *Heal us, our Savior, heal us.*

On a wet, late-February afternoon, his car stopped by a large crowd, Canaris watched through his windshield as throngs of wind-whipped Social Democrats left an anti-Hitler rally in the Lustgarten. A solitary policeman halted them to let the traffic pass. Canaris glimpsed them in his rear-view mirror as he pulled away. Sodden and dispirited, beaten by more than weather, beaten by history, they slouched into the winter dusk. Good riddance, he thought, to the mob that had deserted Germany and its Kaiser in their hour of greatest need, to the rabble that made a mockery of military discipline and overthrew centuries of tradition, to the democratic dreamers who cooked up the Weimar Republic and tried to win the respect of the Great Powers by playing the role of model pupil, thus ensuring their contempt.

Erika came home one afternoon shaken and pale. She and a

friend had been lunching at a restaurant in the Alexanderplatz when the Brown Shirts had pulled a workingman off a tram, hand-cuffed him, and kicked him to death in full view of everyone. "We watched through the window. I pleaded with the maître'd to call the police. 'Madame,' he said, 'the Brown Shirts *are* the police.'" The incident in the Alexanderplatz was no aberration. The Brown Shirts broke into homes, flats, cafés, pulled people out of schools, the-aters, factories, pushed, punched, whipped them, dragged them off to impromptu detention centers throughout the city. At the Naval Club, Canaris joined several other officers for a drink. Among them was a rigid, old Prussian who complained about the public disorder and the flouting of legal regulations by the supporters of the new government. "Well, I suppose you can't clean out a sewer without causing a stink," Canaris said. The table of officers laughed and even the Prussian nodded in agreement.

Canaris accepted an invitation from his friend in the naval min-istry to accompany him to the ceremony scheduled for the Garrison Church in Potsdam the next day. Among the last to squeeze their way in, they stood in the back, by the door that led to the choir loft. President Hindenburg and Chancellor Hitler entered together. Bedecked in full military regalia, the old Field Marshal walked with the stiff, jerky gait of a marionette. Hitler seemed visibly uncom-fortable in striped pants and formal coat. They processed up the aisle, beneath the battle flags dating back to Frederick the Great's Silesian campaign, the groom of the old Germany and the bride of the new. They bowed before the altarpiece, with its martial and tri-umphant Christ. The audience rose in unison, unprompted, to sing the national anthem. Hitler spoke of national unity. There were no gutter theatrics. When the ceremony was almost over, the com-mandant left to join the naval guard of honor outside the Church. He winked at Canaris and banged his right fist into his left palm, like a hammer on an anvil. "Mark my words," he mouthed.

In the days that followed, the commandant's prediction was not only fulfilled but exceeded. The National Socialists became both hammer and anvil. A spontaneous adventure in rampant revenge and score-settling was quickly transformed into an effi-cient apparatus of state power. The burning of the Reichstag, an alleged act of Communist arson, resulted in the passage of the Enabling Act. The Chancellor was granted extra-legal powers. Two days after the ceremony in the Garrison Church, the members of the Reichstag convened in the Kroll Opera House, the wet, charred odor of their former home hanging in the air, and in effect voted themselves out of existence. On Prinz-Albrecht-Strasse, not far from the Reichschancellery, Hermann Göring took over the premises of the School of Applied Arts and installed the offices of the Secret State Police, the Gestapo. In Bavaria, Heinrich Himmler was made police chief. An unused munitions factory at Dachau, on the outskirts of Munich, opened as a temporary detention center and then became a permanent concentration camp under the supervision of Himmler's SS, a prototype for the other camps that were being opened. No sooner had the Reds been squelched than Hitler turned on the SA, his own Brown Shirts, cracking down on the wild men who threatened to take over the army, attack the church, and pillage the wealthy. Pretending to have only recently been made aware of SA leader Ernst Röhm's flagrant homosexuality, Hitler used it as a pretext to have Röhm summarily executed and his circle of SA comrades purged.

The reports of the successful moves against the SA gave special attention to Reinhard Heydrich, Himmler's deputy. Erika cut out a glowing profile of him from a newspaper and left it on Canaris's desk. The face in the picture was the same smooth, creaseless one he remembered from the training cruiser *Berlin*, the sharp-featured cadet with the half-hooded, almost Asiatic eyes and slender hands, who made few friends and spent most of his time practicing his fencing. Canaris rarely spoke with the cadets. But once or twice, while standing on the bridge, he had noticed Cadet Heydrich staring at him with that same watchful, haughty gaze he trained on his fencing opponents as he donned his mask and prepared to humiliate them, as he invariably did.

It wasn't until they had finished a three-month training cruise and were back on land that he got to know Heydrich better. Cadet Heydrich showed up on a Sunday morning. Canaris was in his robe and slippers. Erika was getting ready to go to church. He was taken aback by this uninvited visit at his home by so junior a subordinate.

Heydrich spoke some inane pleasantries, then said, "I'm told your wife is an accomplished musician." Canaris's surprise gave way to indignation. When had a cadet ever gone so far as to make an inquiry about an officer's wife? He was about to give this upstart a suitable tongue-lashing when he heard Erika behind him. She was dressed for church. "Wilhelm," she said, "don't be so rude. Please, invite our young guest in!"

Heydrich stepped into the vestibule. He spoke of how he missed playing the violin and the effect music had on his soul, the peace and comfort it brought. Erika mentioned the musical ensemble to which she belonged. They played every Sunday afternoon here, in their house. "Would you be interested?" she asked. He bowed to her. "Imagine, I came to pay my respects to an officer whom I admire and whose passions for the navy I share and find that my passion for music is shared as well!"

He surprised everyone with his musical skill. His long slender fingers moved the bow with authority and virtuosity. Although it was obviously untrue, he insisted Erika was the better musician. He lauded Canaris's abilities as an officer and offered heated support to the role he'd played in crushing the Red uprising at the end of the war. Gradually, his unctuous style began to grate on Canaris.

It was Erika who called a halt to his visits. There was no formal break. When they returned from the next cruise, the Sunday performances weren't resumed. Heydrich remained cordial and solicitous. Not long after he was commissioned, Heydrich became involved in an affair of honor and was dismissed from the navy for behaving in "a reprehensible manner."

Canaris lost touch with Heydrich until he re-emerged as a rising star in the new leadership. Captain Patzig invoked his name during this conference at the War Ministry, when he formally turned over the job of military intelligence chief to Canaris. "I have no skill for diplomacy," Patzig said. "It's hard enough keeping track of military developments in France or Russia without being tripped up by the clumsy zealotry of these Party types."

"Military intelligence is a difficult job under the best of circumstances," Canaris said.

"Thanks to God and the General Staff, it's yours now." Patzig smacked his lips as he drew on an empty pipe. "The higher-ups were mighty impressed to hear that Heydrich is an admirer of yours. What is it he sees in you?"

Annoyed by Patzig's cynical demeanor, mechanical smile, long silences interspersed with the draining noise of his vacant pipe, Canaris ignored the question.

Patzig burped and tapped his chest with his fist. "Pardon me," he said, "I should never have cabbage for lunch."

Canaris stood. "On taking over, I feel well disposed toward these youngsters. The more familiar we become with National Socialist ideas, the more, I'm convinced, we'll discover they are truly soldierly ideas."

"I suppose." Patzig shifted in his chair, leaned to the side, lifted his rear, and broke wind. "Pardon me again," he said.

A short while after, a lieutenant from the cryptography section, a highly competent naval officer, thin and very blonde, handsome in an adolescent, almost androgynous way, reported that he'd been visited at home by the Gestapo. He requested to see Canaris.

"They asked if I knew someone named Otto Kerstein." The lieutenant fidgeted in the chair, seemingly unable to find a comfortable position.

Canaris offered him a cigarette, which he declined. "Kerstein's a mate of yours?"

"No. He was the director of a theater company I belonged to as a student. It was only for a single summer. Some time afterwards, he became a leader in the Workers' Theater League. I'd lost touch with him by then. The agents informed me he'd been arrested and sent to Dachau."

"How'd they know of your association?"

"They said they'd found some old letters among his papers."

"Did they make any accusations against you?"

"They said Kerstein was a communist. I told them the truth. We'd never talked politics, only the theater. I didn't know what he was. 'Were you also unaware,' they asked, 'that he's a yid and a fag?'" The lieutenant sat still and looked down at his hands.

"Were you threatened with arrest?"

"They said I would be summoned for a formal interrogation. Either that or perhaps we could have an 'understanding' and the matter be dropped."

"They wanted you to spy?"

"Yes, Herr Admiral."

"On me?"

"On the whole operations."

Canaris took out a sheet of official stationary, scratched down a paragraph and handed it to the Lieutenant. "You've done admirable work, and I commend you for your loyalty. An officer of such caliber should be at sea, not behind a desk. I'm reassigning you to the North Sea Squadron. Your transfer is immediate."

In the wake of Hitler's decision to put Himmler in charge of the Reich's internal security forces, Himmler elevated Reinhard Heydrich to head of the SS Security Service and Gestapo. Following a brief chance meeting with Heydrich while strolling on the Dölle-Strasse, an invitation came from him to visit his new Berlin headquarters, in the Prinz Albert Palace, around the corner from Gestapo headquarters. Canaris followed a burly SS trooper through the freshly painted barrel-vaulted halls into a large, elegant, ballroom-sized space. At one end was an immense altarlike desk; at the other, a towering gilt-edged painting of Adolf Hitler. Heydrich appeared through a door behind the desk, his boots striking the uncarpeted floor with a hard, martial click as he approached.

"Wilhelm, welcome!" Heydrich extended his hand. His broad smile exposed his large, bone-white teeth. "Tell me, how is your dear wife?"

"Erika is well."

"Tell her SS General—no, *Cadet*—Heydrich sends his compliments to the handsomest wife of the finest officer in the German navy!"

"Your exaggerations are excessively generous, at least in my case."

Heydrich watched amusedly as Canaris gazed about. "You

must think I've let my position go to my head. But don't worry, this is only for ceremony. Come, see where my real work is done."

Canaris remembered the plan of this security complex secretly obtained by Colonel Piekenbrock indicated a honeycomb of basement cells designed so no prisoner's screams could escape. Heydrich led the way, back through the door from which he emerged.

The room was far smaller than the one they'd just left. The bookshelves that lined the walls were filled with handsome leather-bound volumes. Heydrich ran his fingers over the spines. "I think it's fair to say that what you find here is a representative selection of the top scientific and legal texts on racial hygiene to be found in Germany." He picked out a book and held it so Canaris could see the title. "Here we have Alfred Rosenberg's *Myth of the Twentieth Century*. Though turgid and dull in places—and the same, I suppose could be said of its author—it is overall a useful text." He gave the cover a hard pat, which Canaris interpreted as a small symbolic blow against one of the many Nazi higher-ups contesting for the Führer's favor, and replaced the book.

Heydrich perched on the edge of an elegant oak writing table and gestured to a shelf almost directly at Canaris's eye level. "There, in front of you, are translations of American classics, such as Madison Grant's *Passing of the Great Race* and Stoddard's *Revolt Against Civilization*. Next to them are specially bound volumes of *Volk und Rasse,* and Dr. Shulz's treatise on the unique disease-bearing capacities of the Jew. Beneath are the official commentaries on the Sterilization Laws and farther down the original drafts of the Nuremberg Laws, along with a book of essays describing the ways in which this prophylactic legislation has halted the spread of the Jewish viremia."

Heydrich handed a slim volume to Canaris. The title was tooled in gold letters on the leather cover: *Biology and the Survival of the Volk*, by Professor Hans Luxemburger. "Look at the pictures on the back," Heydrich said. Canaris flipped through pages of infants with swollen heads, Mongoloid children, old drooling men in smocks, mouths agape, women with shaved heads and blank, expressionless eyes.

"There's the future, Wilhelm," Heydrich said. "Unless we have the intelligence and will to do something about it. The Führer has stated that if Germany were to have a million children a year and do away with the weakest 700,000, we would finally be assured of permanent racial superiority. Perhaps that sounds harsh. But does one show pity to the smallpox bacillus? Believe me, the day will come when we must face our moral duty to exterminate whatever threatens the future of our people."

He put the book back on the shelf, took another from his desk and stuck it beneath his arm. "I've ordered tea served in the garden. It's too lovely a day to stay cooped up inside." They crossed the ceremonial office and went out into the Palace gardens, an exquisitely tended courtyard filled with flowers and shrubs. A table was set with tea and cakes. Heydrich sat beside a bush of dark-red roses. An SS orderly brought a chair for Canaris, placing it directly in the sun.

The orderly poured their tea. Heydrich put the book on the table, patted Canaris's knee, and leaned back. "I so much look forward to our working closely."

Canaris took a gulp of tea. "We are in charge of different jurisdictions. Mine is foreign intelligence, yours domestic security."

"Of course. But we've common concerns."

"Some of your underlings seem to have trouble grasping that fact. They've attempted to spy on my operations, as though we were the enemy."

"The young man in the cryptography section wasn't exactly a wise choice for such a sensitive position. I think you'd be shocked if I showed you the file we have on him."

"His position and fate are a matter of concern for my office, not yours."

"I suppose you're aware, then, that he's resigned his commission and gone ashore in Copenhagen?" Heydrich bit into a cake.

"I'm sure the news will reach me through the proper channels." The sun beat down hard. Canaris raised a hand to shield his eyes.

Heydrich finished his cake. Right leg crossed on the fulcrum of the other knee, he sat back and rocked a perfectly polished boot back and forth. "You know the admiration I've always had for you. That's why I invited you here. Two old shipmates like ourselves should be able to act together in the best interests of the Führer and the Reich." The boot slowed into a steady to-and-fro, as if to the beat of a march.

"The interests of the nation must come first, of course." The sunlight was so intense Canaris found it hard to make out Heydrich's face. "Would you mind if I moved my chair?" he asked.

Heydrich indicated to the orderly to place the chair next to his, out of the sun. He unfolded his legs and leaned toward Canaris. "We're in the twilight struggle for the survival of our race. What we require are those willing to rid Germany of everything that threatens its future. We must not only march in the same step, but our hearts must beat to the same rhythm. Do you agree?"

The intensity of the inquisitor's stare made Canaris uneasy. Heydrich was searching his eyes. *For what?* Heydrich took the book from the table beside him and put it in his lap. "When you arrived earlier I was reading *Die Rassenhygiene*. It is a classic in the field of eugenics, summarizing the work of giants like Ernst Haeckel, Eugene Fischer, August Weismann, Alfred Plötz, and Karl Binding. It was written in 1921 by Josef von Funke, a young doctor who marched with the Führer in Munich in '23, and is more relevant now than when written. It has proved to be a work of prophecy. Here, listen to one small passage and see if you don't infer the same urgency and realism as in *Mein Kampf*."

He opened the book and held it at arms length, adjusting the distance until he could read it without the glasses he so obviously needed: "'Unless we are willing to cleanse ourselves of everything weak, crippled, infected, and alien, that is, to remove the crushing burdens of hereditary and racial degeneracy which threaten to overwhelm us, the destruction of our race is assured. What we must enter upon is a struggle more medical than political, directed not just at a change in government but at a transformation of sentiment. This is not work for the faint of heart or the weak of will. As always in nature, strength is the highest wisdom. Kindness to the weak is subversion of the fit. Compassion toward the unfit is treason to the race. Victory belongs to the merciless.'"

Snapping the book shut, Heydrich put it back on the table. His fingers played on the cover. The fingers of a virtuoso. "The words of a medical doctor, but a doctor with the heart of a German poet."

"Medicine has never held much interest for me."

"Come, my friend, why do you think our Führer ended the thuggery of the Brown Shirts, if not so that the principles of racial therapy could be carried out in an orderly fashion? Today, we have a eugenic dossier on every single member of the SS tracing his ancestry back to 1800, 1750 in the case of officers. We are the first organization in Germany to achieve racial purity, to be utterly and demonstrably Jew free. This is the reason we've gone from a band of bodyguards into the vanguard of the nation's destiny!

"You must know how important this is to the Führer and to SS Reichsführer Himmler!"

"I suppose I must." A file locked away in Canaris's desk contained confidential reports on Himmler's strange ceremonies at Wewelsburg Castle, he and his SS acolytes walking around with wreaths of oak leaves around their heads, muttering mystic incantations to ancient Nordic gods. Oster had glanced through the file. "They have created something entirely new," he laughed, "Teutonic voodoo!" He threw it aside. Of more interest to him were the other, thicker files containing the data on the steady increase in armaments and combat training for the SS, a multiplication of resources that was turning Hitler's bodyguard into the nucleus of a new army.

"Wilhelm, we must put aside old rules, old notions of hierarchy and divisional jurisdictions, old moralities, in the service of our new Germany. Sometimes, as you know, our old navy comrades can be particularly stubborn. I'm sure I can count on you to intervene where necessary?"

"That depends."

"*Depends?*" Heydrich's question was laced with a harsh, skeptical tone. "On what?"

"On the specifics of each case. Admiral Dönitz, for example, has been adamant about not using his U-boats for anything but purely military purposes, especially since we are at peace and could risk embarrassment as well as the loss of advanced equipment. He makes a convincing argument."

"Specifics!" Heydrich rose from his chair. The orderly came to his side. He handed him the book. "As long as we agree on the destiny of the *Reich* and the German *Volk*, the specifics, as you call them, will take care of themselves." He bowed slightly and offered Canaris his hand. "Meanwhile, we mustn't spend all afternoon chatting and eating cake. There's much work to be done."

Tired but unable to sleep, Canaris went to the window and pushed back the curtains. Oster was already acting as if a conspiracy were in motion. But getting members of the officer corps to move from murmured disgruntlement to outright treason went against its tradition, training, and history.

He wasn't long at skimming through the weekly naval surveillance survey of the British fleet when Oster returned, a folder beneath his arm which he plopped on Canaris's desk. "For your reading pleasure, the latest outrage by the SS."

"I'll read it later. Right now, I'm busy." Canaris placed the folder on top of a pile of intelligence reports and went back to reading the survey.

"They've sent their own agent to the United States." He lit a cigarette with Canaris's lighter. "They have no business meddling in foreign intelligence. It's an affront to your authority and the role of the Abwehr."

Canaris slowly turned a page of the survey, as though absorbed in what he was reading. "Perhaps it's an internal matter that pertains only to the SS."

"Perhaps the Atlantic Ocean is really beer." Oster leaned his tensile, elegant form across the desk, retrieved the folder and placed it open in front of Canaris.

"How was he sent?"

"He traveled by commercial liner to Mexico, then headed to New York."

"As soon as I finish my present business, I'll give it a look." Canaris kept his head buried in the survey.

"His name is Gregor Hausser, a graduate of the SS Officers Academy at Bad Tolz. He served in the Death's Head battalion at Dachau. An odd choice, wouldn't you say, for a secret agent?"

Aware he'd get no peace until he paid attention to the folder Oster put before him, Canaris laid aside the survey and picked it up. The single sheet inside contained little more than the information Oster had already recounted. "There's not much here."

"Perhaps the SS is interested in using the German-American Bund. There seems to be quite a few National Socialist sympathizers in America, both in the immigrant community and outside it."

"Germany seemed to have a lot of sympathizers in America before the war, but once the U.S. entered on the side of the British, they disappeared. As for the Bund, I wouldn't expect much from that collection of clowns, at least if they're at all like their Bundesführer."

"Fritz Klein?"

"Fritz *Kuhn*. A sorrier specimen of the *Volk* would be hard to imagine."

Canaris had shaken Kuhn's hand during a visit by officials of the *Amerikadeutscher Volksbund* to the Berlin Olympics. A chemical engineer and veteran, Kuhn had left Germany after stealing 2,000 marks from a Jewish acquaintance and eventually landed a job at the Ford Motor Company, in Detroit, an employer he admired on account of its founder's outspoken anti-Semitism.

Walther Darré, the regime's expert on the mystic ties of "Blood and Soil" among Germans at home and abroad, prevailed on the Führer to accept an impromptu drop-in by the Bundesführer, an interview made more awkward when Kuhn, already utterly flustered and almost unable to speak, handed Hitler a check for 3,000 dollars, which was intended for the Nazi relief fund but whose purpose Kuhn forgot to explain. Canaris conjectured that the Bundesführer's perplexity was a joint result of nervousness and the distraction of trying to keep his bulging gut sucked in while in the Führer's presence. Kuhn's room at the Hotel Hollstein was bugged by the Gestapo, who found the recordings of Kuhn's nightly sexual antics with two prostitutes, and particularly his pornographic exclamations, so amusing they circulated copies.

Oster took a long drag on his cigarette and exhaled through his nose. "We need to find out what Hausser's mission is. The regime's official policy is to do all that's possible to placate American sentiments and encourage their people's desire for neutrality. Here's a chance to expose and embarrass the SS."

"I have other priorities at the moment. We have no idea what's involved here. It could be something trivial. One agent isn't exactly an invasion force. I'll assign Piekenbrock to look into this."

The intercom signaled that he had a phone call. "Line one, Herr Admiral," Corporal Gresser said. "General Heydrich's office wishes to know if you'll be joining him tomorrow on his morning ride in the Tiergarten."

"Tell him yes," Canaris said.

"You could always ask Heydrich directly about this agent in New York," Oster said. "Get an answer straight from the horse's mouth, so to speak. It will undoubtedly be a lie, but a clever one."

"And I'd be alerting him to our distrust."

"Ha! As if he's not already alert to that." Oster put the lighter back on its stand, the inscription facing Canaris: *Wie geht's?*

NEW YORK

Whoever tried to follow him from Roberta Dee's place, Dunne decided, was either an amateur or an out-of-towner. Probably both. He lost him easily switching trains at Atlantic Avenue. Arriving on his block, he scanned his apartment building. There was no sign of surveillance but, taking no chances, he went in through the basement, up the stairs to the roof, climbed down the fire escape, and jimmied the kitchen window open. He added what was on the bed to the pile on a nearby chair, stripped to his underwear, and lay down.

In the morning, he went to the Records Office of the New York State Supreme Court, on Foley Square, to read the transcript of Grillo's trial. Sollie Feldman, the chief clerk and a former cop, made sure he had everything he wanted. "Better read quick," Feldman said. "Grillo made the mistake of being one of the first homicides tried under Tom Dewey. A new district attorney is always a man in a hurry, especially the reformers. Dewey made a show of being in

the courtroom to congratulate the assistant D.A. who got the conviction. No secret Dewey's got his sights set on the governor's chair.
Governor Lehman's already running scared remembering how
Charlie Whitman parlayed the Manhattan D.A.'s job into the gov-
ernorship. Not a chance in hell Lehman's gonna stop Grillo from
getting juiced." Dunne spent an hour paging through the transcript.
The prosecutor, Assistant D.A. Tom Regan, came across as well
organized, efficient, and tough. He rolled over the defense. Walter
Grillo hadn't made it hard.

Chief Robert I. Brannigan testified that he led the first party of
detectives to the crime scene, the apartment of Miss Mary
Catherine Lynch, unmarried white female, age fifty-six. A neighbor
had seen her door ajar. Knocking and getting no response, she summoned Patrolman Michael J. Rath, who discovered the victim's
body. Brannigan had the apartment sealed, the building searched,
and immediately sought out the building's superintendent, who was
nowhere to be found.

A top-to-bottom search of the building by Brannigan and
Detective Matt Terry discovered a pair of shoes beside the boiler.
Turned out they belonged to the superintendent, Walter Grillo, who
was still in them. Grillo lay in a drunken stupor on the floor. A few
feet away, wrapped in a bloody towel that had been taken from
Miss Lynch's bathroom, was the carving knife that was later identified as the murder weapon. Grillo denied the knife was his. The
prosecutor established Grillo's prints were on the handle, although
no others showed up in the victim's apartment.

Several residents in the building testified that Grillo was often
drunk and had a violent temper. The defense brought out that
Grillo's behavior had never gone beyond an occasional verbal outburst, usually in reaction to the non-stop complaints of the building's congenital gripers. Most of the time, he had done his job to the
satisfaction of landlord and tenants alike. There was no evidence
that he had ever had any disagreement with Miss Lynch or har-
bored any sexual interest in her. On the contrary, a neighbor testified that Miss Lynch was one of the few residents in the building for
whom Grillo always showed "a gentlemanly regard."

Dr. Joseph Sparks testified that Miss Lynch worked for him as a nurse during the month before her death. Although in only a temporary position, Sparks said, Miss Lynch impressed him with her professionalism. The day before her murder, she came to his office to pick up her paycheck. They exchanged a few pleasantries. She expressed her appreciation for the chance to work with him and left, he said, "in good spirits." His chauffeur drove him soon afterwards to a medical appointment. He returned home late and didn't learn of the murder until the next day. Grillo's lawyer had no questions.

Dunne skipped to Grillo's testimony. His lawyer established that Grillo wasn't the ordinary kind of super who'd been knocking around the janitor trade since dropping out of grade school. Elba Corado had told the truth about her brother, at least about his professional credentials. He'd been a lawyer and a professor at the University of Havana Law School who fled in 1931 due to an argument with the government. After arriving in New York, Grillo had difficulty finding work. Living in a building that the superintendent left dirty and ill cared for, he took to sweeping the lobby and cleaning up the trash. Finally, the landlord fired the super and offered Grillo the job. Didn't pay much but the rent was free. Grillo took it.

Assistant D.A. Regan took Grillo apart on the witness stand. Grillo claimed he was in Riverside Park between 5:00 and 8:30 P.M., the time established for the murder.

Q. Where exactly did you walk?

A. Around, in many parts.

Q. Did you see anyone you knew during that time?

A. Not that I can bring to my memory.

Regan asked Grillo if he had ever used the services of a prostitute. The defense objected. The judge directed Grillo to answer. No. Was Grillo ever driven by "uncontrollable sexual urges"? The defense objected again. Sustained. But the point was made. Regan asked about Grillo's drinking habits.

Q. You were frequently drunk on the job, isn't that true?

A. Sometimes, yes. Mostly, no.

Q. Were you drunk on the night of Miss Lynch's murder? Yes or no?

A. I had drinks that night. How many I don't know.

*Q. Big drinks or little drinks?*

*A. Drinks.*

*Q. Big enough to render you into the unconscious position in which the police found you?*

*A. My memory is not clear.*

*Q. The memory of how you overcame whatever vestiges of decency that might have held you back from using your key to enter Miss Lynch's apartment?*

*Objection.* Dunne read on to the end of the transcript. Regan delivered a blistering summation. He asked the jury to send a message to all the murderers, rapists, and hoodlums who'd become accustomed to having their way in New York: *Tell them loud and clear that their day is over. Show them that Lady Justice has picked up her sword once again and will wield it with a sure and terrible swiftness. Convince them that the decent, law-abiding citizenry of New York will no longer tolerate the depraved assaults of conscienceless criminals.* Grillo should have listened to his lawyer. Maybe he could have wrangled a life sentence by pleading guilty. The jury telegraphed its verdict with a speed that would make Western Union proud. *Adios, Wilfredo.*

Feldman wasn't in his office when Dunne left. He bought a pack of cigarettes at the newsstand in the basement of the court building and got change for the phone. He waited a few minutes before a booth was available. Most murders, no matter how seemingly cut-and-dried, had their peculiarities. Put the puzzle together, and though the picture was clear, there'd be one or two pieces missing or out of place. The defense made a living getting juries to ignore the doughnut and focus on the hole. Most probably there'd be an odd or absent piece in the Grillo case. Wouldn't know whether it was enough to reopen the case or sustain a reasonable doubt until you found it.

He entered the booth. A thin-faced man in a sweat-stained pearl-gray fedora immediately knocked on the glass. It was impossible to tell if he was a lawyer or defendant. Dunne ignored him and dialed the Shack. No use trying to get anything new out of the cops. They'd all be in lockstep. But if the Professor had been on the scene, which seemed likely, he might provide a place to start. No answer.

Dunne hung up and dialed again. There was another round of hard rapping on the glass.

Corrigan finally answered the phone. *No, he didn't know the Professor's whereabouts but the possibilities were limited, weren't they? Either the usual gin mills or the disrobing palaces on the Deuce where he was sure to turn up later in the day.* Dunne cut the conversation short when Corrigan started to ask about the Babcock case. He grabbed the phone book, suspended in a black metal jacket at the end of a short chain, flopped it open and looked up Doctor Joseph Sparks. There was only one, at an East Side address. A feminine voice, cozy as terry cloth, answered. "Good morning," the voice cooed, "This is Dr. Sparks's office. How may I help you?"

"I need an appointment."

"You're a patient?"

"No. This is business."

"Please leave your name and number. The Doctor will get back to you."

"How about a quick in-and-out? Be up in half an hour."

The tone turned abrupt. "Who is this?"

"I'm on an insurance claim. All I need is a few minutes."

"The Doctor is never here on Wednesday afternoons. He leaves at noon." The warmth came back into her voice. "If you leave a message, I'll be sure he gets it."

"I'll try some other time."

"Thank you for your call." The receiver slammed into its cradle, the hammer inside the terry cloth.

The nervous Nelson in the pearl-gray fedora was gone when Dunne hung up, but a globule of spit trailed down the glass. A lawyer, definitely.


Dr. Sparks's office was on a quiet, elegant, tree-lined street, just off Park Avenue. Around the corner was one of those silk-stocking clubs where the *Social Register* types had lunch. Their limousines were lining up along the street like a row of battleships. The chauffeurs leaned against them, smoking and schmoozing. Sparks's office, on the ground floor of a stately building, had its own entrance, a black door with a well-shined knocker and a brass plaque set into the wall. No one answered when Dunne knocked. The doorman at the building's main entrance gave him the once-over that every doorknob polisher in the swank districts kept on ice for strangers, a look more of snobbery than suspicion, as if serving the rich made him one of them.

"I'm suppose to see Doctor Sparks," Dunne said. "But the office is closed."

"Always is, Wednesday afternoons. Musta' got your days mixed up." The doorman turned to help a well-to-do-looking woman with fat ankles exit a taxi. She entered the building without bothering even to glance at him. Dunne slipped him a dollar. Frost gave way to spring. "The Doc lives upstairs," the doorman said. "Plays tennis every Wednesday on Long Island. His car will be here in a few minutes. But do me a favor."

"Name it."

"Wait across the street so he don't think I'm playin' tipster on him."

After only a minute or two, a racket-carrying man in tennis whites, with a sweater draped over his shoulders, its V-neck outlined in red and blue stripes, exited the building. The doorman nodded casually in his direction.

Dunne intercepted him at the curb. "Doctor Sparks?"

He took the racket from beneath his arm, swung it to his shoulder, and smiled at Dunne. He had an open, friendly face, smooth skin, smile right out of a toothpaste advertisement. "Yes," he said, "how can I help you?"

Sparks's tennis whites were crisp and spotless. Trim and fit, brown hair flecked here and there with gray, he looked younger than the forty he probably was, an impression his shortness helped reinforce. He removed the racket from his shoulder and toyed with the iron butterfly nuts on the brace. He seemed ready to start playing, substituting the sidewalk for the courts at Piping Rock or the Creek Club. He went up on the balls of his feet, and Dunne noticed the tennis shoes were thickly padded, a way of adding spring to his game along with a few inches to his height.

"I need just a minute," Dunne said.

Sparks squinted. Webs of small wrinkles radiated next to his blue eyes. "My patient list is full, I'm afraid. Speak with my secretary, she'll provide you with a referral." He looked down the street. "Damn," he said, "I'm going to be late."

"It's about the murder of Miss Lynch."

"You're a reporter, aren't you? I should have realized such a visit was inevitable given the pending execution of Mr. Gonzalez." Sparks let the racket drop to his side. "I'm a doctor, not a ghoulish commentator on other men's crimes, so you'll forgive me, I trust, if I make no comment whatsoever." He wasn't the professional physician type that the guard dog of a secretary led Dunne to expect, eyes encircled by steel frames and thick lenses, as though he were examining you through the lens of a microscope, same bland expression they hand out in medical school for telling you your mother just died or to see the nurse about the bill.

"Grillo. Walter Grillo, that's the name of the guy they convicted, and I'm not a reporter. I'm a private investigator."

"Whoever you are, you've heard all I have to say on the matter." He turned to the doorman. "Johnny, do you know what's keeping Bill?" The words were barely out of his mouth when a big handsome Buick pulled around the corner. "At last," he said.

"I just want to go over Miss Lynch's movements the day of the murder."

"I barely knew her. She worked for me for a few weeks while my regular nurse was away. What happened to her was despicable. But I told everything I know to the police and repeated it at the trial." The racket moved back and forth, rhythmically. "There's nothing to add."

"I'm checking facts for the insurance company that has to pay on Miss Lynch's policy. Routine stuff." He handed his card to Sparks, who studied it intently.

"This says 'Matrimonial and Divorce,' Mr. Dunne. You seem somewhat afield."

"These days I grab whatever it takes to stay afloat."

The Buick pulled up in front of Sparks. "I wish you luck." His handshake was prep-school firm; his smile, softer. Maybe close to snide.

Broad-shouldered with an outsized jaw, the chauffeur came

around the front of the car, opened the rear door with one hand, put the other on Dunne's chest, and gave a sudden shove. "Beat it," he said.

Caught off balance, Dunne stumbled backwards. He grabbed one of the metal poles that supported the canopy and steadied himself.

Bill closed the car door behind Sparks and walked back to the driver's side. The spread of his shoulders was accented by the double rows of buttons on his black tunic. Unfastening the top buttons, he stood with his hands on hips.

Sparks leaned through the window. "I apologize, Mr. Dunne. Bill's a bit over protective. Happy hunting." He rolled the window up. Bill climbed into the driver's seat. Dunne came around and stood next to him. "Sorry, I didn't realize you knew the Doctor," Bill said. "I thought you were a pan handler or an organ grinder."

"If I was an organ grinder," Dunne said, "I'd use you for the monkey."

"Stand back, unless you want to start a pushing contest with this car." Bill leaned forward and shifted into first. The flap of his tunic fell open. The butt of a pistol, cradled beneath his armpit, poked through.

"I should've warned you," the doorman said. "Bill's got a tiny fuse."

"And a brain to match. I'm half-tempted to stick around and continue our conversation when he gets back."

"Please, buddy, have it somewhere other than here. Any trouble like that and I'll be lookin' for another job."

"Better tell Bill that."

"I already did."


At the head of the car, the conductor yelled, "Next stop, Sing Sing!" The train arrived on time. The spring morning, ripe with summer, had spoiled into a humid, sunless afternoon. The walls of the prison blended into a sky the color of wet concrete. The machine guns in the turrets pointed east and west, as though to stop civilians from breaking in as well as convicts from breaking out. A guard led Dunne through a series of bare rooms, each with a metal gate. They stopped in a closet-sized cubicle, where Dunne was frisked and the contents of his pockets examined. A small black truck took them a short distance to a squat unmarked building. The acrid smell of burnt rubber hung in the air. Maybe it was from the truck's brakes; or maybe it was a permanent part of the place.

Although Dunne had expected it might take a while before he was allowed to see Walter Grillo, the prison official on the phone said he could come up that afternoon. As long as his name was on the appointment list and Grillo didn't object, he'd be admitted. Padding ahead on felt-soled shoes, the guard led the way through another series of hallways, checkpoints, and steel doors, until they reached a door marked VISITOR CENTER. There was a set of rules posted on the door, but the guard opened it before Dunne could read them. He directed Dunne to sit at a large oak table on the side opposite the door. A single light hung over it. The room was cool and quiet as a morgue. "Be a few minutes," the guard said.

Two guards escorted Walter Grillo. Taller than Dunne imagined, older too, with hair that shaded from ash gray to white, he wore a capacious white shirt, with embroidery on the front, that obviously wasn't standard prison garb. It hung off him like a shroud. The guards bookended Grillo as he sat in a chair across from Dunne. "Got fifteen minutes," one of them said. Grillo nodded. The concave creases in his cheeks made his nose as prominent as a beak. "You know me, Joe, I never go over."

The guards retreated just outside the open door. Grillo slumped in the chair, head down, hands in his lap. Dunne sensed the relaxed attitude of the guards had less to do with pity for a condemned man than with Grillo's obvious passivity.

"I'm Fintan Dunne, a private investigator."

"I know. Elba called. She thinks you're Jesus Christ come to save me." Grillo removed a pack of cigarettes from his shirt pocket, lit one, and tossed the pack on the table. "Funny, you don't look like Jesus Christ."

"I don't walk on water. But maybe I can save your life."

"Forget about this. That way you'll save your time and Elba's money." Grillo blew a stream of smoke toward the light over the table. "The State of New York has promised to put me to death. A great state like this won't go back on its word."

"We produce the right evidence it will."

"This isn't about evidence. It's about politics. There's an election for governor in the first week of November. I'm scheduled to die on September twenty-first. Both the governor and his challenger will want to make sure I keep my date with the executioner."

"Your sister is convinced you're innocent. Let's say you play along, tell me what you know, and I'll find out whatever I can. What's the harm?"

Grillo stared up at the light and the trail of smoke that crossed it. "I have accomplished two things in prison, Mr. Dunne. When I came here my English was inferior. I knew enough to get by, but it always struck me as a crude, clumsy tongue. I didn't bother mastering it. Now I've come to enjoy and savor it. Also, I've made my peace with God. I never was a religious man. I'm still not what you'd call devout, but today I know that I'm a believer, which I'd never given much thought to before. I'm at peace. I've confessed my sins to a priest."

"In English or Spanish?"

"Pardon?"

"Did you confess in English or Spanish?"

"Does it matter?"

"I guess not. Rape and murder are rape and murder in any language."

Grillo sat up. He had the same brown eyes as Elba, alight with the same indignation. "I confessed my sins, not the lies told by the police and repeated by the prosecutor."

"Which lies?"

"All of them."

"Name one."

"Ah, bravo, Mr. Dunne. You know how to prod a witness." Grillo sank back in the chair. "You would make a good lawyer."

"Where were you the night of the murder?"

"In the park, walking."

"I don't believe you."

"Neither did the jury."

"There's nothing you can tell me about what happened that night? Give me something to go on, I promise I'll do what I can to get you out of here."

"What it takes to get me out of here is down the hall, in the chamber that holds the electric chair. That's how I'm destined to leave. It's the wish of New York State. And God's will." Grillo stood. "Joe," he called out. "I'm ready."

The guards re-entered. They flanked Grillo in an informal, familiar way.

"And Roberta Dee, what can you tell me about her?"

If the name meant anything to Grillo, he gave no sign. He shrugged and picked up his cigarettes. "Goodbye, Mr. Dunne. Give my love to Elba." The guards walked out behind him. A gate shut with the uncompromising finality of steel against steel.

WALL STREET, NEW YORK

Donovan was late for lunch. The receptionist advised that Mr. Dulles was also running late but Mr. Dewey was already in the dining room. She buzzed and a formally attired attendant came to the front desk. He led Donovan down the heavily carpeted hallways. Except for occasional echoes of smothered shouting from behind heavy oak doors, a churchlike quiet prevailed. The pain had returned to his knee during his walk up Wall Street and was throbbing once more. He limped slightly entering the dining room.

District Attorney Dewey studied the smoldering tip of his cigarette. He stood when Donovan came in. "Bill," he said. "Glad you could make it." Neither his enthusiastic handshake nor smile disguised the slow burn he'd been doing at being kept waiting. Two colored waiters in starched and spotless white jackets appeared and served them each a chilled glass of tomato juice. The chief attendant stayed in the corner until they'd been served. "Mr. Dulles apolo-

gizes for the delay," he said. "He's on an international call and will
be with you shortly."

"He was on the same call ten minutes ago." Dewey rubbed out
his cigarette in the saucer beneath the tomato juice. "I wish I'd been
told ahead of time. I rushed through a review of one of our capital
cases to get here. Thank God it was an open-and-shut case, the perpetrator caught red-handed. He's set to be executed the twenty-first
of September."

The phone on the sideboard rang softly. The attendant picked
it up on the first ring, hung up without saying a word, and hurried
to the door. John Foster Dulles entered a moment later, moving
deliberately, like a prelate in a liturgical procession. He nodded
toward Dewey and Donovan. He laid his hand on Dewey's shoulder as he walked past to the far end of the table.

"Gentlemen," he said as he passed, "please accept my apologies
for the delay. It was unavoidable." The attendant stood ready to
pull out Dulles's chair but was waved away. Dulles stayed erect,
holding the knobbed spires on the back of the chair, arms stiff, neck
arched, face upturned.

"Are you in pain, Foster?" Dewey asked.

"My back. It will pass. These things always do." Dulles reached
behind and stuck his thumbs into the base of his spine. "I'm particularly grateful to you, Bill, for accepting this change in venue and
making the necessary alterations in your schedule."

"I should thank you. You saved me a cab ride uptown."

Dulles bowed his head, as if about to pronounce a blessing on
their meal. "I didn't want to postpone this meeting because I believe
there's a growing urgency to events." While he spoke, the waiters
glided noiselessly around the room and served a lunch of chicken in
cream sauce, salad, and ice tea.

"Please, gentlemen, go on with your meal." Dulles could have
been addressing an audience or congregation of two hundred
instead of two. "The bankruptcy of the current administration in
Washington is self-evident. Having failed to return prosperity to
the United States, with nine million people still out of work, it
hopes to turn to foreign adventures to cover its domestic sins. It's
among the oldest ploys of demagogues, and few demagogues in

history have been as utterly unscrupulous as the present occupant of the White House."

"Or as tolerant of corruption," Dewey interjected.

"Exactly, Tom. The New Deal has brought a new stench to the open sewers of corruption that disgrace so many of our cities."

"But we're closing those sewers down here in New York, cleaning them up, showing the whole damn country how." Dewey thumped the table for emphasis.

Dulles's contented smile was the kind a preacher might bestow on his brightest Sunday school pupil. "It is precisely such vigorous prosecution of wrongdoing that has led to Tom Dewey being the choice of an ever-growing number of Republicans for the upcoming presidential nomination."

"Have you seen the movie *Racket Buster*?" Dewey said. "I'm told it's a hit."

"I thought George Brent was miscast," Donovan said.

"Yes, yes, all well and good." Dulles was visibly displeased with the turn of the conversation. "But not really relevant to our discussion. As my grandfather John Foster was fond of saying, 'Fame is ephemeral. It's a man's character that endures.' Though grandfather never sought the presidency himself, his service as Secretary of State left him well-schooled in the requirements of national leadership."

"We're getting ahead of ourselves, don't you think," Donovan said.

"You're absolutely right, Bill." Dulles put his hands together, in a small, silent mimic of applause. "That's why I felt this meeting was so urgent. While Tom's success as a prosecutor has brought him national attention, he needs a higher platform from which to seek the presidency, an executive position, such as governor, in which his sterling leadership qualities will be fully displayed. But he'll need a good deal of guidance in putting together a proper campaign that can unseat the incumbent."

"I lost for governor by more votes than any candidate in history," Donovan said, "and against the current occupant."

"Nineteen thirty-two was an *annus horribilis* for Republicans. Besides, before running your own campaign for governor in '32, you helped manage a presidential campaign in '28, and *won*."

"Hoover won. I was a mere accessory."

"You're too modest," Dulles said.

"Too honest, that's all."

Donovan knew that he hadn't been an accessory during the election of '28. An upstate Irish Catholic, he helped manage the campaign of Herbert Hoover against Al Smith, another Catholic Irishman from New York. But he most certainly felt like one afterwards, when the electoral votes of five southern states, formerly firmly Democratic, went into the Republican column. The Rebels from the South joined with the Yankees from the North to ensure that the position of Attorney General didn't go to Donovan, the man whom Hoover had promised it, a "mackerel snapper" from New York, but to a true-blue one-hundred-percent-loyal American Protestant. "It's just politics, Bill," said an emissary from the president-elect. "Don't take it personally." *The problem is, if I take it professionally, it hurts even more.*

"The Republican Party is ready to stand behind me for governor. That's already clear. They're hungry for new blood, fresh ideas. Like every Democratic governor, Lehman is dependent on the big-city bosses, and the people are fed up, ready to throw them out, not just in New York but across the nation!" Dewey was red-faced when he finished.

"There, there, Tom. 'Elections are like wars,' my uncle Robert Lansing used to say. 'They are won not by speeches but by clear purpose harnessed to sound strategy.'" Dulles launched into a discussion of his uncle's service during and after the war as Woodrow Wilson's Secretary of State, a monologue that continued as the waiters cleared the table, including the plate he'd never touched. Finally, he sat. He turned toward Donovan. "We need men of stature and experience in this campaign. Men with national connections who know the New York electorate and aren't afraid of a good fight."

"Fighting Irishmen like you, Bill." Dewey dug into the vanilla ice cream the waiters had just delivered for dessert.

Dulles winced, perhaps because of his back, more likely from the mention of the sort of ethnic appeals he despised, the age-old specialty of those who subverted the rule of men of true standing, those predestined by pedigree and education to stand above the passions of the mob and direct affairs of state. He resumed his monologue, steering it into a discussion of foreign policy, speaking with the tone of high certainty that Donovan imagined Dulles's minister father must have used to lay down the Calvinist doctrine of justification to his congregation. The events in Europe were none of America's business, Dulles said. They involved the eternal struggle between dynamic and static forces to find a proper balance, a *natural* balance, which could only be achieved if the U.S. kept its thumb off the scale. The *right* Republican in the White House, surrounded by *responsible* advisers, were the best guarantee of such an outcome.

"What about those who argue that National Socialism is incapable of accommodation, that its motives and purpose must inevitably be directed toward conquest?" Donovan knew Dulles's deep dislike for having his opinions questioned in any way. He hoped it might agitate him sufficiently to get to the point.

"That's the kind of alarmist poppycock the Democrats will use to retain the White House. It's why they must be stopped and why we need men like you to help see to it."

"Yes, I'd welcome your advice." Dewey extended his hand. "Too bad there's not a photographer to get a shot of this," Dewey said when Donovan shook it.

Dulles stood, a signal the lunch was over. He put his palms on his lower back. "Are you all right, sir?" the attendant asked from behind the chair.

"A cross to bear. We're all given them." He spoke directly to Donovan, as though he'd asked the question. "The country cries out for men willing to take up their crosses. I hope we can count on you, Bill." Dulles's shoes shuffled across the carpet in a short, slow *Via Dolorosa*.

"I'm looking forward to the campaign," Dewey said.

"Then work on our friend here, Tom," Dulles said as he left the room. "You're the master of swaying the wavering juror." He raised his hand in farewell, or benediction. *Take up your cross and follow me.*

Donovan watched Dulles's stooped figure move slowly down the hallway. When he'd turned down the ambassadorship offered by president-elect Hoover as a sop for not being named attorney general, he was told that Dulles had described his behavior as "childish petulance." Donovan's informant said that Dulles had declared, "The interests of our country must always come before pride or profit or *any* personal consideration."

Here, of course, Donovan came to realize, was Foster's genius. He did his business atop Mount Sinai, untainted by base desires, successfully erasing in his own mind any difference between his best interests and those not only of the nation and the world but also of the Godhead. He spoke from the heights, seemingly apart from the travails and concerns of those enmeshed in the fleshpots of Egypt. The connections of his firm, Sullivan & Cromwell, extended past Wall Street to the entire international business community. The firm had overseen the investment of $10 billion in foreign securities that had been battered by almost ten years of Depression and defaults, and it fell on Foster Dulles's shoulders to act as a human flying buttress, doing his best to prop up the cracked and weakened structure of global finance. So many burdens at one time: ensuring that the beleaguered republican government of Spain couldn't raid that nation's banks and sell the assets abroad to finance its war against the surging forces of General Franco; protecting General Aniline & Film Corporation, the largest North American subsidiary of I.G. Farben, the German chemical cartel, so that if the unthinkable happened, if America was dragged into war, its operations would be safe from confiscation; running the board of the International Nickel Company, Inco, in a reasoned, calm way that didn't take the bait of the scaremongers who railed against its extensive contracts with the German arms industry. Business was business, yet with Foster Dulles the motive was never for personal profit or gain, though such rewards might result. Dulles's motives were higher, purer—world order, peace, the inexorable unfolding of God's designs as carried out by His predestined designees.

On the way down in the elevator, Dewey told Donovan that while he was sure he could win the gubernatorial nomination at the Republican state convention in September, in Saratoga, it would be hard to defeat Lehman in November. "In a close election, the Democrats are still in control of the political machines. In places like Albany and the Bronx, the bosses will steal whatever votes they need to win."

"If you make it close enough, it'll be the same as a victory, at least on the national level." Donovan stopped short of making the commitment that Dewey and Dulles both sought. He'd become an observer of politics rather than a player. Disappointment was part of it, but there was something else as well.

At the last meeting he'd ever had with Herbert Hoover, the president-elect squeezed his arm, an imitation hug accompanied by a frozen smile. "Bill," he said, "you know from your football days that not everyone who tries out for the team gets to play." The round, blank face above the stiff collar had the appearance of a boiled egg in its cup. Try as he did, Hoover couldn't forge the unspoken bond of human empathy that gave the impression he knew what others felt and felt it himself. The ability to forge that bond—or at least to give the appearance of doing so—was a gift, like grace, randomly bestowed. Men like Dulles rejected it. Others, like Dewey, craved it but were passed over.

Despite the close ties he could make with individuals, even with groups as large as the regiment he'd taken to France, Donovan knew it was a skill that failed him in the open arena of politics. He knew it for certain at the end of his campaign for governor, when it was clear not only that Lehman would swamp him but that then-Governor Franklin Roosevelt would evict Hoover from the White House. In the last week before the '32 election, Roosevelt serendipitously appeared in the lobby of the Ten Eyck Hotel in Albany. He leaned on his son's arm waiting for his official limousine, a cane in the other hand. Seeing the Republican candidate for governor coming toward him, Roosevelt beamed a broad smile and, unsatisfied with a handshake, gracefully hung the cane on his son's wrist and put his hand on Donovan's shoulder.

"Now, Jim," Roosevelt said to his son, "I want you to shake hands with one of nature's rarest creatures, Bill Donovan, an Irish Catholic *Republican*." Roosevelt gleefully observed his son's discomfort at this chance encounter with the opponent of his father's handpicked successor. Throwing his head back, Roosevelt laughed loudly. "It's okay, Jim, back in our school days, before his apostasy from the Democratic Party, Bill and I forged a lasting friendship based on our mutual love of football."

It was an utter fabrication. Roosevelt had been an undergraduate at Harvard and a pampered student at Columbia Law School, treated with deference by professors in awe of his name and social standing. He'd never appeared anywhere near a football field. He and Donovan were never more than passing acquaintances. But Roosevelt told the story with such good-natured certainty that Donovan found himself nodding in agreement and joining in the laughter, unbothered by the lie or the patrician accent that, in another man's voice, might have had an edge of condescension.

"The reign of Roosevelt is at an end," Dewey said. "A Republican victory here in New York, in his own home state, will be a clear signal that the time is nigh."

"And if it isn't, we can always start our own law firm, Dulles, Donovan, and Dewey," Donovan said. "It's got a ring to it."

Dewey shook his head. He seemed to take Donovan's joke seriously. "Foster will never surrender his interest in Sullivan & Cromwell. He regards his firm the way a minister does his church. For my part, my interest is in public service, in cleaning out the crooks and corrupters and returning American government to the hands of honest, capable men."

Dewey seemed ready to slip into a campaign speech. Donovan declined the offer of a ride before it was even made. He promised to call Dewey as soon as he returned from a meeting with clients in the Midwest. They said goodbye in front of the building. Flanked by bodyguards, Dewey looked around, waiting to be noticed by the lunchtime crush of brokers, clerks, and secretaries. After a minute of watching the crowd and sensing their lack of interest in anything save stocks and bonds and ogling each other, he ducked into the car and was gone.

*   *   *

109

## 42ND STREET, NEW YORK

Dunne arrived back at Grand Central around seven. The stars painted on the ceiling above the station floor served as a substitute for those the city's incandescence made invisible. There was no need for the occasional passengers who bothered to gaze up to trace the outlines of sky creatures the ancients claimed to see— bear, lion, lamb. The New York Central Railroad had done it for them. He exited on Forty-second Street and walked west along the Deuce, past the north side of Bryant Park. Beyond the flashing lights of the movie marquees, the horizon was streaked with the fading purplish-red remains of a sun that had just sunk behind the Palisades.

At the corner of Broadway, a shill in a white hat tried to sell him a ticket for a bus tour of Manhattan. He waved him off. At the light, a voice behind him said, "Hey, mister, postcards from Paris. Interested?" He crossed the street without looking back. The usual crowd of pasty-faced ghouls loitered in front of the Rialto, eyeing the posters for the double bill of zombie-voodoo films. Male gawkers were everywhere, walking with the feral, furtive look of men hunting for forbidden thrills. Some stopped in front of the grindhouses and stuck their noses close to the glass-encased stills touting cut-rate reels, NEVER BEFORE SEEN ON SCREEN! SHOCKING! UNCENSORED! *Slaves in Bondage, Girls of the Street, Forbidden Desires, Jungle Virgins*. Two sailors studied the window of a dime museum and novelty shop. The banner above advertised "The Hidden Secrets of Sex as Approved by the French Academy of Medicine, Paris." They paid their dimes and went in to be educated.

Across the street, the belt of bulbs zipped around the Times Tower spelling out electronic headlines that almost everyone below ignored. One day Walter Grillo's name would be up there, sharing the Square with the movie stars, headliners, and top billers. In Grillo's case it'd be a once-only appearance. A tourist couple planted themselves in front of Dunne. The man posed the woman for a picture, her back to the huge sign across the Square advertising Wrigley's

Spearmint gum, the same spot Dunne stopped with Danny Cassidy when they returned to New York from France.

The sign, a towering wall of light flashing its electric hymn to Mr. Wrigley's sweetened chicle, hadn't been there when they'd left. But it greeted their return. They'd come to Times Square directly from the regiment's last march. They'd assembled by companies at 110th Street. Unlike most regimental commanders, Colonel Donovan didn't ride a horse but walked with them down Fifth, then over to Lexington, for their formal dismissal at the 26th Street Armory. They stood around, awkwardly, congratulating one another on still being alive, leaving unmentioned their haunted, guilty recollections of the dead. Donovan walked the ranks. He stopped in front of Dunne and extended his hand. Neither of them had the words to express what had taken place between them.

Nor the inclination.

Dunne and Cassidy strolled up Park Avenue. "Let's go to Gyp O'Connor's and get drunk," Cassidy said when they reached Grand Central.

They drank beer in Gyp O'Connor's saloon all afternoon. On the house. "You boys done your duty," O'Connor said. "More than can be said for them bluenose sons of bitches in Washington who've enacted Prohibition and kilt the liquor trade! Drink up, boys, while you've the chance. Soon New York will be dry as the Sahara! Times Square will be as quiet as a Quaker meeting house. Mark my words, boys. Mark my words." In the evening, O'Connor's patrons took their beer mugs and went outside and bathed in the glow of Wrigley's advertisement. One by one, they went back, got their coats, and joined the parade of strollers and theatergoers moving through the Square, people and traffic sharing Broadway's biggest, grandest stage.

The Square had a different feel now, but not that of a Quaker meeting house, unless the Quakers had converted to honky-tonk. The movies strangled vaudeville, Prohibition took care of the fancy restaurants, and the Depression made straight the way for Minsky and burlesquedom, the disrobing beauties who filled the seats the producers and playwrights couldn't. *Take it off, girls!* Dunne shadowed his share of wayward husbands to the stage doors. The burlesque business prospered as steel and autos and the rest of the economy went south. The reformers squawked and complained without much effect until the Mayor and the holy company of gangbusters decided such displays of female flesh were a threat to public health and morals and set out to take away their licenses. Couldn't even use the word burlesque for fear of the civic impurities it might instigate. But the crusaders had a ways to go from the look of the Deuce.

A fat man in a gold velvet vest and a straw hat yellow with age barked outside a nearby theater, "The show is about to start! Hurree, hurree, see the most beautiful girls in New York! Yes, siree, tonight, straight from her special performance before the Sultan of Madagascar, the Magnificent Monique! Lookee see, my friends!" He rested his hand on a cardboard simulacrum of a turbaned woman, with a half-veiled face, wearing harem pants and a sequined vest. A crowd gathered.

Dunne shouted over their heads, "Hey, Morrie, is the Professor in there?"

"As usual, backstage." Morrie went back to his pitch. When no one stepped forward to buy a ticket, he snared an elderly gent by the elbow and half led, half coerced him to the box office. "Money-back guarantee," he said. "Monique don't get your ticker beatin' faster, show's on me." A line formed to buy tickets.

Morrie joined Dunne at the curb. "Go ahead to the back, Fin. Max is at the door. Tell him I said it's okay." He took off his hat and mopped his bald head with his palm. "You followin' someone?"

"No, I just need to talk to the Professor."

"Gotta get back to work." He put his hat back on. "Christ, who'd ever think it'd be so much work to get men to stare at naked women? Ask me, it's gonna take another war to restore the red-blooded vitality of the American male."

"No thanks, Morrie," Dunne said, "I already had my war."

At the rear of the theater, on Forty-third Street, Max, the stooped, ancient doorkeeper, mumbled hello and led him to a small, windowless dressing room. The walls were the same lifeless, defeated beige as the visitor's room at Sing Sing. The Professor sat in a decrepit lounge chair, reading a book. Next to him was a tall multipaneled screen, various articles of women's undergarments draped over it. The Professor glanced up, eyes fiery red, an expression of serenity across his face. "Dunne, my good man, what brings you to this seraglio of galluptious femininity?"

"Corrigan thought it was a good bet I'd find you here."

"A pity my peregrinations have become so predictable." The Professor reached beneath a skirt covering the dressing table, lifted out a bottle of Four Roses and two glasses. "The management discourages the consumption of spiritous liquors upon the premises for fear it might impair the concentration of the performers." He poured a finger of whiskey into each glass and handed one to Dunne. "But since neither you nor I fit into that category, I see no harm."

"Who you talkin' to, Jack?" The question came from behind the screen.

"A gumshoe extraordinaire and former member of the metropolitan gendarmerie."

"You in trouble?" A face peeked around the side of the screen, pretty beneath a heavy veneer of makeup.

"No, Mr. Fintan Dunne and I are comrades."

"Hi, I'm Monique." She flashed a smile at Dunne. "Jack, pass me them pants, will you?"

The Professor handed her a pair of diaphanous silk harem pants from a rack beside his chair. Her head disappeared once more behind the screen.

"I've yet to scare up any business for you, Fin," the Professor said, "if that's what brings you here." He gently tapped his glass to Dunne's. "But I haven't forgot."

"I'm on a temporary assignment. Been hired to look into the Walter Grillo case."

"Grillo?"

"Short-term tenant of the death house. Convicted in the murder of a nurse, Miss Mary Catherine Lynch."

"Ah, of course, 'the West Side Ripper' as dubbed by my colleague, Mr. Corrigan. Bit of an exaggeration since Grillo only struck once and was too inebriated to make his escape. Yet the Cubaño did manage to savage a sixty-year-old virgin, deflower her, and rip her apart with a stiletto. One needn't be inspired by Melpomene to lament the nature of that poor woman's demise."

Monique's head appeared again. She'd put on a turban. "Mel Pomeno?" she said. "I knew his sister, Gina Pomeno. If I remember correctly, she works in Billy Field's Follies." She withdrew behind the screen.

"Melpomene is the Muse of Tragedy. She has eight sisters, but as far as I know none has a position with the Follies." The Professor refilled his glass.

"You covered the murder for the *Standard*?" Dunne asked.

"Who else? But why pursue such a piece of soon-to-be-forgotten history?"

"Business, that's all."

"Not much to tell."

"You were in her apartment?"

"First of the crime scribes on the scene, as usual."

"Anything catch your eye?"

"Something always does at a murder scene, usually the corpse."

"Other than the corpse?"

"You're fishing, Fin."

"Give me a nibble, I'll go away."

"Have you talked to Brannigan about the Babcock case?"

"Soon."

"Don't goad the Minotaur, my boy. He'll prowl the labyrinth until he finds you and take you apart when he does."

"A nibble, Professor, that's all."

"Oh, well, it was a nicely done-up little *appartement*, with an elegant highboy, or chest of drawers, that showed, however small her means, Mary Catherine Lynch was a woman of good taste. And there was the jewelry box."

Monique came out from behind the screen, in a pink satin robe, tied at the waist, which reached down to her ankles. "Well, it's time." She bent over and kissed the Professor on his head. "We'll get down to business soon as I get back," she said. "No more dilly dallying. I promise."

"A promise to which I shall hold you." He kissed her hand.

"What about it?" Dunne asked.

"What about what?" the Professor studied Monique as she went into the hall.

"The jewelry box."

"It was odd the way the pieces were arranged atop the bureau, as though Grillo had been sifting for something in particular. Unusual for a drunken maniac in the grip of a sexual delirium to take such care. That's all the nibble I can give. Now go offer some propitiation to Brannigan."

"Doc Cropsey do the autopsy?"

"I suppose."

"Wasn't sure he was still in the business."

"He switched from drinking whiskey to formaldehyde. It keeps him most wonderfully preserved."

The thump of a drum and a wave of raucous shouts reverberated from the hall. "There she goes," he said. "The Magnificent Monique nightly fulfilling the prophecy of Job, 'Naked came I out of my mother's womb, and naked shall I return thither.'"

Dunne put down his glass, the finger of whiskey untouched. "Better be off."

"I take it's money alone draws you to this case."

"Pure and simple."

"Nothing else?"

"Now it's you who's fishing. For what?"

"The Ripper's sister. I was tipped off about her. I could've dragged her into the story. But didn't. I hope she hasn't lured you into this folly."

"His sister? Too young for me. Believe it or not, I think Grillo may be innocent."

"Never be afraid of youth, especially in a woman. Take Monique, for instance. A girl from the Jersey City proletariat, née Monica Mauro, without benefit of a high school diploma but gifted with an incisive intellect and a true enthusiasm for the classics." The Professor opened the book he'd been reading. "Listen to these lines: '*Odi et amo. Quare id faciam, fortasse requiris? Nescio, sed fiere sentio et excrucior.*' Has the torment of the lover's mixed emotions ever been better expressed?"

"Beats me."

"I think not, and as we read these lines earlier this evening, it was Monique who pointed out the poet's genius in linking '*odi et amo,*' love and hate. 'They aren't opposites,' Monique said. 'The *et* makes that clear. They're Siamese twins. They share one heart, one spleen.' A profound insight, beyond what any student of mine at Princeton ever managed, and one that belongs to youth, to those still in the grip of their passions."

The sound of the drumbeat grew louder, as well as the cheering and whistling. The Professor poured himself another whiskey. He handed Dunne his untouched glass. "Spare me the indignity of being forced to drink alone."

Dunne held the glass to his unparted lips.

"Thirty-six years ago, yet the wound is still fresh. A quick end to my employment at Princeton and what seemed destined to be a brilliant career teaching the classics. A colleague's wife and I were indulging our shared literary passion for Catullus. *Cras amet qui numquam amavit; Quique amavit, cras amet.* The intoxication of words! The seductive power of poetry! 'Let those love now who never loved before; Let those who always loved now love the more.' The irresistibility of those sentiments drove us to an act of spontaneous coition on my desk, alas, at the very moment the department head chose to speak with me on some trivial matter."

"Bad timing," Dunne said. "We both seem to suffer from it." He'd heard it all before, and seeing the condition the Professor was in, knew he'd hear it all again.

"Not timing alone. Given my academic achievements and unblemished record, it might have been settled with a mild reprimand. Even the husband, a notorious wittol, agreed. The university's president, however, that loathsome Presbyterian hypocrite, Mr. Woodrow Wilson, would hear none of it. He demanded my scalp, which he promptly got. Of course, *his* first wife was buried but an hour before he was off romancing another. I trembled for my country when that moralizer was elected president. Never doubted that once those guileful Europeans got their hands on him at Versailles, they'd pluck and dress him like a freshly killed turkey."

The Professor stared into his drink. The mix of drums and shouts from outside neared a crescendo. "I'm not a satyr, Fin."

"A what?"

"'Professor Lockwood is a sensualist and materialist, more satyr than man.' That's what Wilson said of me. I love beauty, in nature, in poetry, in the human body. I share that love with Monique. Unschooled as she is, she has a deeper, more genuine desire to know the beautiful than any academic I ever encountered."

Dunne stood by the door. He knew a longer lecture would follow. "Anything else comes to mind about the Grillo case, call me."

"Do me a favor, Fin."

"What's that?"

"Don't turn into one of our modern-day crusaders whose invincible sense of right confers on him the conviction he must undo all that is wrong with the world."

"Just out to make a buck."

"Stay that way. There are enough crusaders as it is. Gotham is being scrubbed clean by Mayor Savonarola and District Attorney Oliver Cromwell. Slot machines and soubrettes alike are banished to ultima Thule. An artist like Monique faces imminent exile to Hoboken. The Guardians of Purity and Public Morality are winning the field. Still, if I were a wagering man, a vice I've had difficulty in indulging since my local bookie was dispatched to the new penal institution on Riker's Island, I'd bet on sin. In the end, sin will be the winning horse, no matter what handicaps are laid upon it."

"Cross my heart, Professor, I'll stick with sin."

The music was swallowed by a frenzy of shouting and whistling. The Professor joined Dunne at the dressing room door, stumbling as he approached. He steadied himself on the door. Monique sashayed down the hallway from the stage, naked except for a turban, high heels, and a wedge of spangled satin in the V between her legs. Her ample breasts bounced jauntily against her chest, up and down, like wave-riding buoys. She waved and smiled broadly. "Okay, Jack," she said, "time to get back to our poetry."

"Ah, yes, our poetry," the Professor said.


The front door of the Hackett Building was bolted from inside. Dunne banged on it until Hubert, the Negro porter, came by steering a wheeled pail with the handle of a mop. Hubert peered though the glass. The minute he saw who it was, he pulled on the chain attached to his belt and fished a thick knot of keys from his pocket.

"People askin' where you are," he said.

"Nice to know I'm missed."

"Wouldn't go that far." White-haired and dignified, Hubert grew old trying to keep the building clean and shiny as it slid toward decrepitude. At night, the sound of his saxophone drifted up from the basement through the building, sometimes happy notes, an April day filled with the hope spring would stay forever; other times, it was solitary and haunting, memory of a voice, a face, a rainy winter morning. Nobody complained.

"Looks like they're sprucing up the place," Dunne said. The hallway was half-covered with scaffolding. The receptionist's station had been demolished.

"Today was Miss Marlene's last day. Landlord says the tenants can answer their own phones. Put her out to pasture, if that's where they put she-cats the likes of her."

"Place will never be the same."

"That's what the landlord hopin'. He thinks he can get a better class of tenants. Least he's sure he can't do worse." Hubert rode the elevator with Dunne. "You know, the cops been here lookin' for you. Wanted me to let 'em in your office but told 'em you changed your lock and never give me a duplicate. Mind yourself. What I seen of 'em, they'll kick your ass good, they get the chance."

"Trick is, don't give 'em the chance."

"A trick for the white man, a miracle for the colored one."

The mail that Dunne found stuck beneath his door included several bills and a notice from the landlord announcing the receptionist's termination, the start of the Hackett Building's refurbishment, and an upcoming rent increase. There were also three phone messages, two from Elba Corado, one from Roberta Dee. He took off his suit, hung it in the closet, and lay down on the couch beneath the thin blanket he stored for nights like this. He was almost asleep when he heard the faint but distinct music of Hubert's sax waft up the elevator shaft. A reminder of lyrics he'd rather not recall:

*Yes, you're lovely*
*With your smile so warm*
*And your cheek so soft*
*There is nothing for me but to love you*
*Just the way you look tonight.*

He rolled over on the couch, face against the cool, worn leather, and pulled up the blanket till it almost covered his head. Two years ago, the last night he spent in Lily's apartment, the singer next door practiced those lyrics over and over, her voice mingling with other sounds, traffic, sirens, the rattle of the El, all one melody. Lily undressed in the bathroom, as she always did, and got into bed naked, her handsome body exposed, that scent of hers all around. Sweet. The singing next door continued. *There is nothing for me but to love you.* When they were finished, he draped his arm over her.

"It's about time, Fin, isn't it?" she said.

He looked over at the alarm clock. It was nearly midnight. "Time for what?"

"We're running out of it."

"I guess." He took away his arm and went to sleep.

On a sleeting December day, she left on a week's vacation from her job as the choreographer at the Diamond Horseshoe and went home to Perry, Iowa, a town he'd promised to visit with her but never found time. He escorted her to Penn Station. Kissed her goodbye in front of a poster touting a vacation in Nevada. In it, a cowboy stood beside a cactus, open space all around, the sky innocent of clouds. She laughed and went on about how they could start over in a place like Nevada. Life would be easier than in New York. Open roads, no crowds, no snow.

"Give me a home where the taxi cabs roam," he said.

"It's a big country, Fin."

"I got small ambitions."

"Add mine to yours, they'll be big enough."

"Subtract mine from yours, they'll be small enough."

Just before the train left, Lily dashed upstairs to get a magazine. He followed the obtuse angle of her thigh and calf, leg against impressionable silk, faint outline of her undergarments. His unspoken thought: *I'm no good at holding on to things. Never have been. But we'll talk about it as soon as you get back. Promise.*

She kissed him hard, pressing her lips onto his. The taste stayed a long time. A week turned into a month. A postcard arrived from Quebec. She was on her honeymoon. The taste of goodbye. *P.S. Sorry, Fin, I grabbed it before it passed by. Afraid it was my last chance. Au revoir, Lily.*

*Au revoir.* French for what? *Time, Fin: we're out of it.*

He missed her most in this moment, on the edge of sleep, and in the one that followed, waking up and realizing she wasn't next to him. What he remembered: angle of her leg, her kiss, laughter, that sweet smell, same as her name. Fleur-de-lis. The Signature Perfume of the House of L'Espere. In the Catholic Protectory, Brother Flavian lavished attention on his African lilies, dug them up each fall, and stored them in sand, in a corner of the dining hall he turned into a makeshift hothouse. "Lilies are the only flower Our Lord ever spoke of," he said. "'Behold the lilies of the field.' Theirs is a holy scent." Hers: the sweetness of succulent fruit, luscious. No hint of holiness.

Just after dawn, he got up, shaved, and washed in the bathroom down the hall. He put on the clean shirt and tie he kept in the bottom drawer on his desk. He took the elevator to the basement, where Hubert maintained a small, meticulously neat living area. Up to now, given the landlord's neglect of the Hackett Building, Hubert had been allowed to reside where he worked. Pretty soon, Hubert's quarters would probably follow the receptionist's stand into oblivion.

Hubert sat on the edge of a neatly made cot, reading last night's *Standard*.

"There a phone I can use?"

"What's wrong with the one you got?" Hubert didn't look up from the paper.

"Only good for wrong numbers."

"Afraid it's tapped?"

"Crossed my mind."

"There's a phone by the delivery entrance. Need a nickel, use this." Hubert put down the paper, took several slugs out of his pocket, and handed them to Dunne.

"Slugs are illegal."

"You complainin'?"

"Not if you cut me in next time you get some."

"Not likely."

The phone down the hallway was on a wall covered with phone numbers and the odds on races at different tracks. A bookie's station. Mingled in was the name Linda. It was repeated several times, always with a different phone number. Good bet that whatever Linda was riding it wasn't horses. Dunne was about to hang up when Elba answered. She went on for a minute about how upset her brother had been by his visit to the death house. He cut her short.

"You drive?"

"Why, yes."

"Own a car?"

When she answered yes, he gave a corner and time to meet. If he wasn't there, he said, keep driving. He'd call that evening. He went out the delivery entrance, rode the subway to Rostoff's, and arrived at the tail end of the morning rush. A short time earlier, it would have been packed, Rostoff urging the tray boys to grab every empty dish and banging a rolled-up newspaper on the table to remind the lingerers that if they wanted to sit and read, the city had gone to great expense furnishing its parks with benches.

For now, the cafeteria had the quiet repose of a library. Dunne spread the newspaper in the space that the tray boy had cleared. The Babcocks were already off the front page, replaced by Sudeten-German civilians battling Czech police. On the Society Page were the usual pictures of the usual crowd in the usual poses in the usual clubs. Gent in a satin-collared tux, cigarette in one hand, the other on the shoulder of some smart-gowned debutante, or some American rich girl hanging on the arm of a defunct aristocrat, or vice versa. Stalwarts of the café set, the Babcocks were gone from these pages too. Those left behind were doing their best to carry on. From the looks of it, they were doing just fine.

The tray boy came back down toward the kitchen, cart piled

high with dishes. He drummed a spoon on a steel handle, the short percussions accompanied by his falsetto:

*The man who only lives for making money*
*lives a life that ain't necessarily sunny,*
*like the man who works for fame.*

Jules Rostoff looked up from the newspaper atop his idle cash register, took the cigar out of his mouth and yelled, "Rudy, shut the mouth, please." The tray boy cleared a nearby table of cups and yolk-streaked plates, cigarette butts crushed into the hardened yellow goo. He hummed loudly, then resumed singing:

*Fact is, the only work that really brings enjoyment*
*is the kind that's for girl and boy meant,*
*that's the best work if you can get it,*
*and if you can get it, won't you tell me how.*

A loud repeat of the tattoo seemed a prelude to more singing. Rostoff came out from behind the cash register, into the aisle. "For the last time, Rudy, shut up!"

The tray boy shrugged. "Durante started this way."

"Durante got talent!"

The mild, windless morning convinced Dunne to walk to the building where Mary Catherine Lynch had lived. A kid of about twelve in a felt cap, its brim turned up and serrated like a crown, sat on the front steps. He bent over so he could tighten his skates with the key hung around his neck.

"Hey, champ," Dunne said, "where can I find the super?"

The kid stopped tightening his skates and glanced up. "Maybe across the street in Murtagh's Bar or maybe sleepin' it off on the roof. Then again, could be in the basement playin' ring-a-lievo with the cockroaches."

"What's your best guess?"

"What's it worth?" He held out his hand, gimme-style, palm up.

Dunne pulled him to his feet. "There, I helped you up. We'll call it even."

"Nothin' more than a bum's handshake?"

"You're below the minimum age for shakedown artists."

"Try the basement."

"What's his name?"

"Henry Draub. We call him 'Heinrich the Slob.' Last super was a spic, but clean. Go figure." He crouched and began to skate with short, hard motions. In an instant, he disappeared around the corner. Dunne followed him as far as the alley, passed a row of badly dented garbage cans, and ducked into an open entranceway. Down the hall was a battered metal door, SUPERINTENDENT stenciled on it in cracked white letters. A balding man answered. Slob was a good description. Or schlub. He looked as though he'd just got out of bed. He didn't talk. His scowl did it for him.

"The Lynch apartment been rented?" Dunne asked.

"You ain't no cop."

"Who said I was?"

"Who are you?"

Dunne tucked a folded bill into the super's shirt pocket. "Dick Tracy."

"Ain't rented but ain't ready to be shown."

"Need a look, that's all."

"How bad?"

"Look in your pocket."

The super kept his eyes on Dunne. "Ain't enough."

"Add this to what's already in your pocket." Dunne waved a bill in front of the super's face. "That's all you're gonna get."

The super lifted the bill from his shirt pocket, then shoved it back in and snatched the other out of Dunne's hand. "I'll get the key." He tried to close the door.

Dunne held the door open with his foot. "I'll make sure you don't forget to come back." He followed the super into a square room that contained an armchair and a sofa, both in the process of disgorging whatever, long ago, they'd been stuffed with. The only light struggled through a dirt-streaked basement window set high in the far wall. Beneath, looking forlorn and out of place, a tall, regal-looking chest of drawers stood on skinny, delicate legs. It was topped by a curbed, graceful pediment.

The super turned left, down a dark, narrow hallway. He switched on the light in a small kitchen. Half a dozen cockroaches zigzagged into the stove. He fumbled at a rack covered with keys draped on hooks, removed one, and held it up to a light fixture from which dangled a coil of yellow fly-studded adhesive. He examined the soiled, wilted cardboard circle attached to the key, which had the apartment number inscribed on it. "I'll tell you right now, place was cleaned out a long time ago."

Dunne ducked to avoid the coil of dead flies. "Just need a look, that's all."

"Let's go." The super stuck the key in his pocket and brushed past.

Dunne took another look around. Lawyer and professor, raised in sun-drunk Havana, Walter Grillo ended up here, endlessly pestered with complaints, not enough heat, too much heat, the water's too cold, too hot, perpetual whiners yapping in a language he only half understood. Drive anybody to the edge. Maybe over.

"Come on, will you," the super said. "You're payin' to see Miss Lynch's apartment, not live in mine."

"Wouldn't worry about that I was you." Dunne followed the super up three flights of stairs. They stopped in front of a door at the far end of a badly lit hallway. The super opened the door and stood back. "Don't stay all day," he said.

"In like Flynn," Dunne said. "Out just as quick."

The layout of the place was different from the super's: bedroom straight ahead, bathroom right beside it; to the right, a tiny kitchen; to the left, two windows facing the street. It was no surprise the furniture was gone. Dunne's footsteps echoed on the bare floors as he crossed the living room to the bedroom. Except for a few dust balls, the closets were empty. Same with the kitchen and bathroom cabinets. Mother Hubbard's cupboard all over again.

From outside came the muffled commotion of traffic, clash of roller skates on concrete, kids shouting, laughing, sounds that might have been among the last Miss Lynch heard. According to the trial record, it had been sometime after 8:30 P.M. that a neighbor noticed her door ajar. The neighbor knocked and called her name. Fearful and suspicious when she got no answer, she went to find the super. No answer there either, she left the building and corralled Patrolman Michael Rath. He entered the apartment and found

Miss Lynch sprawled amid the caked, clotted gore on her bed-clothes and summoned the homicide squad.

Though it was possible Officer Rath had guarded the apartment until the other cops arrived, touching nothing and making sure no one else did until the place got an official going-over, Dunne knew from experience that it was more likely Rath had made a quick search through dressers, trunks, closets, under the mattress, for "spinster's gold," the fabled horde accumulated by those thrifty souls who stowed away cash and jewelry against the possibility of an old age spent in poverty. Several years before, two sisters had been discovered in a room they hadn't left in a quarter century with nearly a million dollars in cash and negotiable bonds. The Surrogate's Court glommed the goods that time, but with each homicide or suicide or unexplained death, the treasure hunt went on more fervidly than ever, cops, ambulance men, whoever was in first on a mad dash to find the trove before the next wave of detectives, fingerprint boys, and photographers arrived.

He lit a cigarette in the bathroom and tossed the match in the john. Wisps of smoke hung in the dead air. After a while, the place would have been thick with cops, some working, most standing around and kibitzing. Maybe somebody noticed a crucifix on the wall and called a priest. Anybody's guess how much evidence was lost and how much gathered before the morgue crew stuck the corpse in a heavy canvas bag and hauled it away. *Requiescat in pace.* The person who searched Miss Lynch's jewelry box did so carefully, the Professor said, piece-by-piece, as though searching for something in particular. Didn't seem likely he'd been part of this crowd.

The super was in the hall, leaning on a mop. There was no pail. "Satisfied?"

"How about a word in private?"

"This is private."

A wide, frightened eye stared at Dunne through the peephole in the door behind the super. The fate of Miss Lynch helped confirm the impression of a horde of homicidal lunatics continually on the prowl, which the Professor and his fellow tradesmen earned their daily bread reinforcing. The fact that there were a few hundred murders a year in a population of eight million, most involving people who knew one another, didn't exactly match the tabloids' version of nonstop mayhem. But good luck trying to convince the one-eyed peepers that they have about as much chance of being hit by lightning as getting chopped in pieces by a new, improved version of Jack the Ripper.

"More private," Dunne said. "Your place."

"No way."

Dunne drew close and nudged him with his shoulder, a wordless invitation: *push back or start moving.*

"Don't try that tough guy stuff with me." The super banged the handle end of the mop on the floor for emphasis.

Dunne nudged him again. *"Move."*

The super hesitated, then turned and walked ahead of Dunne. He halted a few feet inside his apartment, the mop at his side like a spear. "Okay, Aladdin, this is your last wish. Make it quick."

"Tell me, genie, where's the highboy from?"

"Who?"

Dunne nodded toward the piece of furniture at the far end of the room. "The chest of drawers."

"That? It was in the storage room when I moved in. Nobody knew who it belonged to, so I took it."

"No chance it belonged to Miss Lynch?" A hunch dressed up as a question: the out-of-placeness of the piece plus a recollection of the Professor's mention of the elegant furniture in her apartment.

"Suppose it did? Finders keepers."

"Furniture at a murder scene should have been impounded by the Sheriff's Office." Dunne's memory of the evidentiary rules for homicides was rusty, but it sounded right, and the super seemed disinclined to argue about it. "This amounts to suppression of evidence. A crime. Losers weepers, if the D.A. hears about it."

"Ain't givin' it back, if that's what you're anglin' for."

"Can't imagine you would. Goes so nice with everything else."

The super stood aside. "Have a look. Nothin' in it anyways. Then scat. Your welcome's run out."

The top drawer glided out smoothly and noiselessly. Dunne repeated the process with the drawers beneath. They were as empty as the super promised. Dunne felt their undersides. No fake bottoms. The trial record indicated that though Grillo's prints had been found on the murder weapon, he'd managed to turn the place upside down and meticulously search the jewelry box without leaving a print anywhere else. Odd.

"Time's up." The super was at the door, cradling the mop in both hands, more like a rifle than a spear.

"Another second." Dunne knelt and put his hand beneath the highboy. He ran his index finger along the inner rim, from corner to corner, and touched something that had the feel of an old wad of gum stuck underneath a movie seat. He pried it loose with two fingers. It fell into his hand. As he stood, he brushed his pants with his hands and  dropped the wad into his pocket. "Nothing," he said.

The super smiled for the first time. "I told you."

"Next time I'll listen."

"Next time?" The smile vanished. "There ain't gonna be no next time." He pulled the door open and stood next to it, mop by his side. "Now get out!"

Dunne stepped into the hallway. He pointed at the mop. "Try it with soap and water. It works better."

"Kiss my ass, Dick Tracy." The super flung the door shut.

Skates slung over his shoulder, the kid in the felt cap was on the corner when Dunne came out of the alley. "Find him?"

"Bigger charmer than you let on." Dunne tossed him a quarter.

"Hey, thanks. Figured you for a cop when you wouldn't let go a nickel. Them guys is so tight, they squeak a block away. Crawled all over the neighborhood after old lady Lynch was kilt and didn't spring for a glass of seltzer." The boy put the quarter in the pocket of his knickers. "Guess I was wrong about you."

"Cops question you?"

"Questioned everybody."

"What'd you tell 'em?"

"Gettin' the feelin' it's time for another quarter."

"Tell me what you told the cops, I'll tell you what it's worth."

"Ain't worth much, least the fat cop in charge didn't think so, but Miss Lynch had a brother, a wino bum. Came by every once in a while. Got the neighbors upset, a hobo hangin' around, but she'd smooth it over, give him a meal and some money, I guess, and send him away before people got too angry. Anyways, I thought I seen him here the day she was kilt, late afternoon like, little after she come home."

"You weren't sure?"

"Maybe yes, maybe no. Didn't matter much till Miss Lynch was dead, if it was him or not."

"That the last time he came around?"

"Was the last time I seen him. Or maybe it wasn't. Me and my friends, sometimes we go to the river to fish, down by the Hoover Flats, and the bums is lyin' on the pier sunnin' themselves. This one time, I thought I seen him there but, hey, like the fat cop said when I told him about thinkin' I spotted Miss Lynch's brother, 'Seen one wino bum, seen 'em all.'"

"Here, buy you and your friends some sodas." Dunne handed the kid a dollar.

"Man, now I know for sure you ain't a cop!"

Arriving early at the corner where he'd arranged to meet Elba Corado, Dunne went into the 5 & 10 and ordered a cup of coffee at the luncheon counter. He took the wad from his pocket, laid it on the paper napkin, and pressed it with his finger. There was something hard at its center. He scraped away the gummy covering with his penknife and exposed a key, an embossed circle at one end, two teeth at the other. Its small size seemed fit for a dresser or cabinet drawer. The highboy didn't have any locks. That narrowed the search down to the several million drawers and cabinets throughout the five boroughs. But somebody had gone to the trouble of hiding it. Perhaps it was what the killer had searched for in Miss Lynch's jewelry box. At the post office next door, he bought a stamped envelope and mailed the key to himself in the Hackett Building.

Elba Corado arrived in a two-door Ford coupe, a sporty maroon model that looked faster than it probably was. He was barely in the passenger seat when she stepped on the gas. Dunne braced himself against the dashboard.

"I can't tell you how excited I am that you've taken Wilfredo's case," Elba said. "It's the first ray of hope in such a long time."

She braked at the last moment for a red light. A cab almost slammed into their rear. The driver honked and screamed. She paid no notice. "I have such faith in you, Mr. Dunne. I knew from the minute I saw you, you were the one to help Wilfredo." She raced ahead, coming to another abrupt stop at the next light.

"Just buy the car?" Dunne asked.

"You can tell?"

"Dress business must be good."

"Thank God, Mr. Dunne, it's something I can rely on." The car moved away from the light at a slower, more deliberate speed. "Where are we going?"

"Where we can talk. Go straight for now." He lit two cigarettes and handed her one. "What's Wilfredo's secret?"

She drove with one hand; held the cigarette to her lips with the other. "Secret?"

"He'd rather go to the chair than reveal it, whatever it is."

"He told you that?"

"Didn't have to. It was obvious."

"So you think he killed Miss Lynch?"

"Whatever his secret, it's not *that* obvious."

She pulled over to the curb, drew deeply on the cigarette. "This is very emotional for me. Would you mind driving?"

"Sure." He came around and opened the driver's door. She slid across the seat.

"You have a license, don't you?"

"Been a while since I've been behind the wheel, but I'll be fine." He re-entered the stream of traffic and glanced in the rearview mirror. A beer truck was right on their tail. The driver honked twice.

"He wants you to go faster."

"Faster it is." Though he'd never bothered with the formality of a driver's license, it came back to him quickly, the feel of shifting the clutch, up and down, in and out. The engine responded smoothly.

"You drive well," Elba said.

"Thank Uncle Sam for that. I learned in the army."

His first time behind the wheel was in France. They'd marched through a blizzard in the same uniforms issued the previous summer. Next morning, the sun came out and turned the roads to pudding-like slime. In the early afternoon, weary from trudging though miles of muck, they sat on the side of the road as a motorcade went past, a roaring, sputtering caravan of British and French touring cars, Rolls-Royces, Emersons, Grand Days, Courbots, and Renaults, each with one or two army brass, dry and warm inside and oblivious to the exhausted, sodden, mud-splattered soldiers on the roadside.

The troops grumbled and complained, then resumed their march. Dunne remembered what Vincent Coll said in the Protectory when they'd managed to get out of slaving in the laundry and were assigned to Brother Flavin's garden detail. *Gettin' what you want, that's the game, Fin, not grousin' about not havin' it.* Soon as they were quartered in a local village, Dunne went to the garage next to the church and drafted the rotund, gray-haired proprietor into teaching him to drive. The Frenchman knew only one abbreviated English phrase: "Eyes on zee road!" But thanks to his impassioned pantomime, Dunne got the hang.

By evening, they were ripping across moonlit roads and lanes, the Frenchman yelling what Dunne chose to interpret as encouragement. For the next month or two, Dunne chauffeured regimental officers to historic churches and handsome bordellos, until the fighting started and every available man went into the trenches.


Dunne turned onto Riverside Drive. "Where you taking me?" Elba asked. "Canada?"

"Farther. The North Pole." He glanced at her.

A rush of air shook the frilly collar on her dress, tugged at her hat, and rippled across the soft waves of black hair beneath it.

Tempted to leave his gaze fixed on her, Dunne remembered: *Keep your eyes on the road.* He looked ahead.

Without any prompting, she began talking about her brother and herself. She was nearly twenty years younger than Wilfredo. They had the same father, but Wilfredo's mother died when he was a boy; Elba's died giving birth to her. Their father died in a boating accident soon afterwards. She was raised by her maiden aunt and, in a way, by Wilfredo, who had always seemed more an uncle than a brother. The family was well supported by a sugar business they'd owned for more than a century. Wilfredo trained to be a lawyer, and had even come briefly to New York to attend Columbia University School of Law. Eventually, instead of joining the family business, he became a professor of law at the University of Havana and advisor to the Student Federation.

"Do you know anything about Cuba?" she said.

"Rum, cigars, best nightclubs in the world." He drove across the 207th Street Bridge into the Bronx, turned right onto Kingsbridge Road, and went up Marble Hill.

"Have you ever heard of Machado?"

"A brand of cigars?"

"Oh God, you're such a typical *yanqui!* Machado was the president of Cuba. He turned himself into a dictator and ruled with the support of the army and the rich. Wilfredo helped lead the movement to reform the university and open its doors to the children of the poor. Before long, Wilfredo sought to consolidate an even wider coalition to seek real democracy and true independence."

Dunne braked at the light where Kingsbridge Road passed beneath the Jerome Avenue El, in a patch of track-striped Bronx sunshine. "Would you light me another cigarette, please?" she asked. He lit two simultaneously and handed her one.

She took a quick, deep drag. "You Americans are so ignorant of what goes on in Cuba, or what your government supports," she said. "For you Cuba is a playground. 'Cigars and nightclubs' as you put it, along with casinos and brothels. You behave there the way you can't here. For us, it's a struggle for self-rule and democracy. It's impossible to understand who Wilfredo is, how incapable he is of the crime he's been convicted of, without knowing the role he played in our homeland."

Dunne blew a trio of smoke rings out the window toward the looming bulk of the Kingsbridge Armory. A nice notion: hometown hero can't turn out to be a criminal. The history of crime said otherwise. So did the jury that condemned Wilfredo. He kept the thought to himself and drove straight ahead when the light changed.

She reached in the glove compartment and took out a photograph. At the next light she handed it to him. "This was taken of Wilfredo in Havana, when he was a professor. No matter the changes, this is how I'll always picture him."

A tall, thin gentleman in an elegant white suit posed on a battlement beside a cannon. The sea was behind him. He had his hat in one hand and leaned on a cane in a lighthearted way that made clear it was there for fashion, not support. A broad smile pushed his mustache out toward his ears. It was a handsome, enthusiastic face, devoid of the resignation that had stared across the table at Dunne in Sing Sing. He had the same wide, intelligent eyes as his little sister, and in Wilfredo's youthful face, the resemblance between the two was particularly striking.

The car behind honked. The light had changed. Dunne saw in the rearview that the impatient horn belonged to a patrol car. He handed the photo back to Elba and drove at what he hoped was an unsuspicious speed, not too fast, not too slow.

"This was taken in the last of the happy times," Elba said. "Soon after, President Machado canceled the election, closed the opposition's newspapers, arrested the union leaders and shut the university. Wilfredo was among those who organized a protest. The authorities broke it up. There was violence and shooting. Wilfredo was indicted for treason and went into hiding. They searched our house, smashed the furniture, ripped apart books and bedding. My aunt was so frightened her heart gave out and she had to be taken to the hospital. Our whole world was collapsing."

The thin whine of a siren rose into a wail. The traffic on Fordham Road made it impossible to think about escape. He slowed down. The patrol car swerved past and zoomed left on to Third Avenue, the siren trailing away in the distance.

"I thought for a moment they were after us," Elba said. "But we've done nothing wrong, have we?"

"Not today."

She propped the photo of Wilfredo on the dashboard. "And he's done nothing wrong either. It's important to remember that."

Dunne threaded his way through the congestion. Wilfredo's photo sat on the dashboard like one of those holy cards people kept to ward off accidents and flats. Dunne couldn't remember the photo the newspapers used of Walter Grillo when he was arrested, but it was a safe bet it didn't bear any resemblance to a holy card. More likely it wasn't any different from the unholy pose beloved of Brannigan and company, handcuffed defendant, head bowed, cop on either side, each holding an arm, the accused convincingly transformed into guilty-as-sin perpetrator. Pop goes the flashbulb: *Hey, Grillo, say cheese, say whiskey, say guilty until proven innocent.*

"At the trial," Elba said, "there was barely a mention of his stature in Cuba."

"I know. I read the transcript."

"Roberta Dee convinced me not to attend. She said the press would hound me and that would only make things worse for Wilfredo."

"She was right."

"Still, I felt guilty that I wasn't there."

"You do whatever Roberta Dee tells you?"

"She's been very kind to me."

"How'd you meet?"

"She came into my shop soon after it opened."

"Out of the blue?"

"She was in the neighborhood, shopping. She's a very stylish woman. She became a steady customer. Now she's a good friend."

"How's she support herself?"

"She's a widow. Her husband was in the garment business. He left her comfortably provided for."

"She tell you that?"

"Yes, she told me." The tone of annoyed frustration Elba had used in their first meeting, at Dunne's office, returned. "Why must you always sound so doubtful, Mr. Dunne? I'm trying to save my brother's life. Why would I lie?"

"It's my job to be skeptical. Don't take it personally. And by the way, there's no need for 'Mr. Dunne.' Fin, that's what everybody calls me." He'd wanted to tell her that since he got in the car.

"All right then, 'Fin' it is." She smiled.

Wide and green, Pelham Parkway had far less traffic than Fordham Road. He stepped on the gas. The picture of Grillo fell from the dashboard and fluttered to the floor. She picked it up. "This photograph was the only reminder I had of Wilfredo when he left Cuba. He escaped on a cruise ship to New York. He wrote us and promised that as soon as Machado was overthrown, he'd return. But when Machado was kicked out, it was by Fulgencio Batista and his army buddies who, with the blessing of the American government, installed a puppet of their own. One gang of thugs replaced another. Wilfredo stayed where he was."

"And you came here to be with him?"

"I stayed in Cuba another year, then my aunt died and I had no one. Wilfredo was afraid for me. He wired the money for me to come to New York. I was shocked when I saw him. His face was puffy and sickly. He was drinking heavily. He'd cut himself off from the other Cuban exiles in New York. He was bitter and alone. He was also afraid, I think, that Batista might use his friends in the Mafia to eliminate him."

"You lived with him?" Dunne couldn't picture Elba in the dungeon that Henry Draub now occupied. An orchid in a coal bin.

"Wilfredo was deeply embarrassed by where he lived and his job as a janitor. He'd arranged for me to reside as a student at Mount Saint Vincent College. I don't know where he found the money, but he did. The nuns were strict. I hardly left the campus. When summer came, I got a job in a dress shop in Manhattan and shared an apartment with two other girls from the college. In the autumn, I refused to go back. Wilfredo was very angry, but we have the same blood in our veins, and I can be as stubborn as he. I stayed at the dress shop. The owner made me assistant manager. I had a flair for the business. I began to save for the day I'd own my own shop. It was my dream, and I shared it with Wilfredo. One day he met me after work and handed me a check. He'd received a settlement of my aunt's estate in Cuba and he wanted me to have it all, his share as well as mine, so that I could open my shop. 'If your dream comes true,' he said, 'mine does too.' That's the kind of brother Wilfredo is."

Crossing the City Island causeway, Dunne shifted into second and slowed the car. The salty tang of low tide tainted the air. Using a handkerchief from her pocketbook, Elba wiped her eyes and softly blew her nose. "I'm sorry," she said. "But each time I think of what has happened to him, the wound becomes fresh."

In the distance, the towers of the Whitestone Bridge, bright and new as the chrome on Elba's car, poked above the foliage of Throg's Neck. "Where are we?" she asked.

"City Island."

"It's so quiet, so quaint. We could be in New England."

"Don't worry. You're safe. We're still in the Bronx." He drove slowly down the leafy, uncrowded street. A few women were out shopping. Workmen from the nearby shipyards lolled outside a tavern. She put away the handkerchief.

He'd seen her kind of wound before: beneath the outward sophistication, woman's shape, makeup so expertly applied, a young girl's hurt at discovering the world's indifference to her hopes and dreams. Sooner or later, to one degree or another, everybody got taught that lesson and was disabused of their belief in the inevitable triumph of the good and the true. Roberta Dee thought she could preserve Elba's innocence. But she couldn't. Nobody could.

They parked at the very end of the street, in front of a cinderblock snack bar with a veranda facing Eastchester Bay. At a white enameled table, beneath a frayed, sun-bleached umbrella, Dunne ordered a bucket of boiled shrimp and a pitcher of beer. Elba nibbled at a few shrimp and took a single sip of beer. She talked more about her girlhood in Cuba, itemizing her memories, the way people recalling an especially happy (or unhappy) time will do: doors and windows that open on the blue-white expanse of the Caribbean sky, sun-drenched balcony, wooden jalousies rattled rhythmically by a gentle, constant, flower-scented breeze.

"Oh, Fin, you can't imagine how beautiful Cuba is."

They walked past a row of sail shops and clam chowder joints. She went into a second-hand clothing store, and he followed. She wandered the aisles, fingering pea jackets and yellow rain gear. "With the right design," she said, "this could be an attractive line of women's wear." After the store, they proceeded slowly down the leafy street. He sensed her reluctance to return immediately to the city. He shared it. It was early evening by the time they were finally ready to leave. She asked him to drive again.

"Where to?" he said.

"I'm not ready to go home, not yet."

"Me neither." He took the first right over the causeway, pulled into a large, mostly vacant parking lot and stopped in front of a row of skinny saplings.

"Where are we now?"

"Orchard Beach. Come on, let's walk."

Ahead was the curved façade of a large bathing pavilion, a structure whose size and sweep belied its simple function as a place to change or go to the bathroom. They emerged through a tunnel that ran beneath the pavilion onto a crescent-shaped beach. A scattering of people sat on towels or stood at the water's edge. Elba put her hand on his shoulder, steadying herself as she unstrapped and removed her shoes. Dunne took off his suit jacket and laid it down. They sat on it, facing the water.

The early-evening sky was filtered at its edges with a pinkish blue light, land and water aglow in the sunset, nothing yet lost to the night. They sat and smoked. Elba let a handful of sand run through her fingers. "This is as white as the sand in Cuba, and as fine as the sand in an hourglass."

"Or in an ash tray." He buried his cigarette butt in the sand. "The WPA hauled it here from Long Island when they built the place."

"It seems like it's been here forever."

"Nothing in the Bronx has been here forever. Except maybe the rocks. The rest of it, sand, people, and the animals in the zoo, all arrived from somewhere else."

"Are you from the Bronx?"

"Spent time here."

"Your childhood?"

"Mine ended before I got here." Dunne stood and brushed off his trousers. "Let's go. Be dark in a minute."

*He slips into his mother's bed in the middle of the night. The room is freezing, but it's warm next to her, beneath the heavy quilt, snuggled into the flannel curve of her nightgown. She draws him close, strokes his head, and whispers, "Your father's at peace. He's happy with his parents in heaven. Pray for the repose of his soul." He watches the flicker of the votive candle in front of the small statue of St. Anthony on the bureau, a steady flame encased in red glass, part of the reassuring warmth that surrounds him. Her breathing purrs on his neck. He prays she won't die. His father had taken forever to die, relentlessly wasting from the strapping man called "Big Mike" by his friends into a wheezing relic propped on pillows by the fire escape.*

*Each night, his mother had waited for the darkness to carry a milk bottle filled with scab-colored sputum down four flights and pour it into the sewer. The shadow next to the window struggled for air, rib cage moving up and down like a pump. She shaved off his mustache. He smiled at the children as she wiped his face, and Maura burst into tears at the sight of the grinning death's head. Not long after, the visiting nurse removed him to the hospital, where he died.*

*During the funeral mass, he keeps looking at his mother. He watches the way she breathes, listens to her sigh. She holds his hand at the graveside.*

*"I'm cold," he says.*

*"Offer it up," she replies softly.*

*The priest reads Latin prayers from a book and sprinkles holy water on the coffin. You can tell that it's almost over the way the gravediggers fidget with their shovels. The priest finishes and closes his book. Dunne tugs at his mother's hand. He wants to go home. Suddenly, she lets go of his hand, raises both palms to her face, beneath the veil, and releases a sob from somewhere deep inside, from a hidden, private place. She convulses with sobbing. He begins to wail at the choking sound she makes, certain she will die as his father had, retching up her insides.*

Elba stared ahead silently, seemingly lost in a momentary reverie of her own. "It's so peaceful," she said. "Thank you for bringing me here."

An old-fashioned steam-powered tug chugged toward a small island dotted with a few one-story buildings and a water tower. The tug sounded three high-pitched blasts on its whistle as it approached a concrete pier.

"What's that place?" Elba asked.

"Hart's Island."

"Is it a school?"

"A prison for the cons who can't swing it in the pen. Cripples, crazies, geezers, the ones who'd get eaten alive in a regular lockup. The city has them repair furniture and care for the Potter's Field."

"There's a cemetery there too?"

"The twin populations of Hart's Island: cons and cadavers."

"You seem to know a lot about the place."

"Work the homicide detail long enough, you know about criminals and corpses, and where they get sent." He reached his hand down to her. "Come on, it's against the law to sleep on the beach."

She got to her feet without taking his hand. He picked up his jacket, shook it free of sand, and started toward the car.

"Wait, Fin." He held her shoes in his hand. "Just a moment longer."

The lights in the buildings gave the appearance of a ship anchored off shore, a ship with nowhere to go, and a cargo nobody wanted. His brother Jack was over there on the island. He had gone quickly, with no fuss. That's the kind of kid he was, a six-year-old with shriveled legs, a haunted look. Never caused a stir. There was no money for a grave. The priest who said the funeral mass promised to do what he could. Whether he tried or forgot, John Francis Dunne ended up on the tug to Hart's Island, to a pauper's grave, laid to rest in the children's section beneath a single granite cross and its one-size-fits-all inscription:

HE CALLETH HIS CHILDREN BY NAME

*Sleep tight, Jack.*

"I'll be in the car," he said.

She wasn't long in coming. Dunne was already in the passenger seat, so she drove. Once they were out of the Bronx, he nodded off. She poked him awake at 86th Street and Broadway. They were pulled over in front of a newsstand. "I don't know where you live," she said. For an instant, he weighed spending another night at Cassidy's, but decided against it. Too many nights on cots and couches, his back went flooey. He looked at his watch. There was time for one more stop. That way he'd get home late enough that any cop watching the place would probably have packed it in and gone back to the station.

"Go down Broadway."

"How far?"

"Till I tell you to stop."

Once they crossed Canal Street Elba said, "There's not much of Broadway left. Pretty soon we're going to be at the Battery." The streets were empty, the office buildings dark and locked. He told her to make a left on Worth and to stop in front of a squat building in which the lights were still on.

"Mind if I ask where you're going?"

"To see a doctor."

"Are you ill?"

"No, but I'll be a while."

She took an envelope from her pocketbook and handed it to him. "I know we haven't agreed on formal terms, but this is intended as a retainer and as partial remuneration for the time you've already spent."

He jammed the envelope in his pocket. A hefty feel. "I'll mail you a contract."

"I don't know if anything I told you is useful. I appreciate what you're doing." She leaned across the seat and gave him a quick, sisterly peck.

"Can't solve a puzzle without the pieces. The more pieces, the better the odds. Get home safe." He slammed the door and went into the building.

Doc Cropsey was in the same office as the last time Dunne had seen him, his final morning as a homicide detective, nine years earlier. Same green walls, battered desk. "So, the Prodigal Son returns." The Doc's frown hadn't changed, either. "I thought you died. Or got married and moved to New Jersey. Not that there's much difference."

"I went out on my own. Matrimonial stuff."

"I hope you didn't come looking for clients." He nodded at the opposite wall, at a clock and a calendar hung next to each other, at crooked angles. "I'm scheduled to be at the morgue in half an hour, so whatever brings you here, make it quick."

"Friend of mine asked me to look into the murder of Mary Catherine Lynch."

"Not much of a friend."

"The Professor told me you did the autopsy."

"That drunk is losing his grip. Understandable, I guess, after a career spent slinging slops in that trough called the *New York Standard*. Instead of waiting for cirrhosis to eat their livers away, he and his cronies should toss themselves in the river and get the job done quick. Drowning can be a fast way to die, long as you don't resist."

"Who examined her?"

"One of the so-called scientists now in charge of this place. Today it takes a week to do what once took a day. When I started, in '08, the coroner was elected, and we got paid ten dollars per inquest. Most of us were good Tammany men, and we all had practices on the side. Get the job done in a flash and be off to see your own patients. Then they installed all this civil service flummery, exams, reviews, keep you all day filling out forms. Isn't an autopsy any more, but a 'scientific inquisition of the dead body.' Lotta crap, you ask me." He pointed at the calendar. "Another ninety days or so, I'll have my thirty years. Anyone tries to stand in my way will have a heel print in the middle of his forehead. Miss Lynch was the last straw."

"Thought you said you didn't do her autopsy."

"It was complete by the time I came in. Botched it good." Cropsey came from behind the desk, removed his medical apron from the back of the door, and stuck it in his briefcase. "For chrissake, this boy genius missed she was strangled as well as stabbed. Even in my drinking days never made a boner that bad. Hyoid bone in the throat crushed, hemorrhaging between the broken fragments, and engorgement of the mucous membrane of the wind pipe, and he didn't see it."

"You add it to the report?"

"I wasn't about to reopen the inquest and start another round of paperwork."

"Was that all that was left out?"

"Wasn't that enough? Sorry, Fin, can't stay and chat. Got my job to do. I was you, I'd stick to the divorce business. The one they got for the Lynch murder will fry sure as sunshine follows rain."

"Always had an eye like no other."

"The eye isn't what it was. Saving what's left for the fish. I still got the shack in Southold. Once I leave here, that's where you'll find me, gutting porgies and blues."

"Seems like someone wanted to make sure Miss Lynch was dead, strangled *and* then stabbed her. One did the job, don't you think?"

"Think?" Cropsey walked to the wall and straightened the calendar. "Something like 75,000 people died in this city last year. Almost 15,000 got referred to the Medical Examiner's Office. That's forty-three cases a day, everything from infectious diseases to falls, car accidents, fires, suicides, homicides, you name it. After a while, it isn't much different from gutting fish. You don't *think* anything."

"Nothing else you noticed?"

"Depends on what you mean by 'noticed.'" He shoved his hands deep into the pockets of his jacket. "Seen a lot of stab wounds, especially before the war, when the fashion was more the stiletto than the gun. Whenever sex is involved, the savaging is more pronounced, which was evident in the Lynch case. But there was also what might be described as, well, an incision from the suprasternal notch to the symphysis pubis. I was a bit surprised this sex-crazed, liquored-up Latin could cut her up in such a careful, dispassionate way. But there's no explaining everything a killer does, is there, Fin?"

"That's what I need to figure out."

"When you get tired, come see me in Southold. Be glad for the company."

\* \* \*

The lone taxi careening across Worth Street screeched to a halt when Dunne hailed it. He got out a block from his apartment building and smoked a cigarette in the doorway across the street. No sign of a tail. He walked the three flights to his apartment. As he put his key in the lock and thought of that other key and the possibility that it was what Miss Lynch's killer had been looking for, the reason he'd searched her jewelry box and cut her open, he became aware of footsteps; not ordinary footsteps, but the relentless clump of a heavy-set flatfoot, the registered trademark of Robert I. Brannigan.

"Hi, Fin." Spoken over his shoulder, directly into his ear, the words were simultaneously accompanied by the descending *whap* of a leather slapjack, several ounces of lightly cushioned lead, crashing down on the right side of his head. Another part of the trademark. He came to in his own bathroom. Matt Terry, Brannigan's sidekick and deputy goon, held him lightly by the shoulders so he wouldn't fall off the toilet. Brannigan put his fist under Dunne's chin and raised his head.

"You came home drunk and fell down the stairs. Lucky for you we were passin' by and found you. You mighta' lay there all night," Terry said.

"Thanks. You're regular Good Samaritans."

Brannigan removed his fist, took a pail from beneath the sink, filled it with cold water, and dumped it over Dunne's head. "There, a little dousing and you'll be like new."

"Already been baptized."

"Keep jerking me around, it'll be the last rites." Brannigan shook the last drops from the pail and threw it in the tub. The clatter sharpened Dunne's sensation that a hot spike was embedded in his skull. Terry gave him a towel. Dunne touched the towel to the side of his head. What he thought was water dripping down behind his ear was blood. It blotched the towel. Terry grimaced when Dunne handed it back to him.

"What's with you, Fin, that you have to go and make it hard on everybody?" Brannigan stood with his legs spread wide, jacket hanging open. "Matt and me are done in from trying to find you."

"You're a little fatter, that's all. Otherwise you look nasty as ever."

Matt Terry stepped between Brannigan and Dunne. "You know better than to keep the Chief waitin'."

Brannigan shoved Terry aside and grabbed Dunne by the tie. Dunne knocked his hand away and tried to stand, but the instant onset of dizziness made him fall back on the toilet seat. Brannigan seized his tie again, twisting it around the thick knuckles of his fist. "This is your last warning." He twisted tighter and lifted Dunne off the seat. "You ever get in my way again, I'll make sure . . ."

"Chief," Terry interrupted, "I don't think he can breathe."

Brannigan loosened his grip. Dunne took a deep breath. As he let it out, he vomited. Above, the black sky was interwoven with swirls of light. A storm approached.

When he came to, his head was in the sink. Terry poured another pail of water over it. "Gotta be more careful, buddy, seems you're accident prone."

"Nice to know I got you to rely on." Once Terry had been a friend, decent, if always a little too willing to please the higher-ups. They'd been pals together in the regiment, in France, in 1918. Now, half driven by fear of Brannigan and half seduced by basking in the glow of his boss's power, he was nothing more than the hireling who swept up behind Brannigan like one of those circus workers who followed the elephants on their annual parade up Eighth Avenue from Penn Station to Madison Square Garden.

Brannigan bent close. "Sorry about this, Fin. But it's your own fault. Mrs. Babcock said you knew nothing about her intent to kill her husband. So, you see, there never was no reason to put Matt and me to all this trouble." He patted Dunne's shoulder. "Which means everything is square between us." Brannigan's voice fell to a whisper, harsh and intimate. "Just don't let me hear any more about you poking your nose into the Grillo case. It's over and done. *Finished.*"

The impact of Brannigan's fist against the side of his head sent Dunne off the toilet onto the floor. In the night sky, the constellations waltzed in electric circles. Mister Moon rose over the horizon. He had Charlie Chan's countenance. Beyond Mister Moon, a star bore the impression of Roberta Dee's face. The star directly behind had a face too. He couldn't make it out. There was a rumble of thunder. The storm was getting closer. The wind picked up. A wave broke over Dunne's head. He felt himself sinking into a lightless, noiseless void. Charlie Chan was laughing. So was Roberta Dee.

ABWEHR HEADQUARTERS, BERLIN

He'd slept no better the previous night than those before. In the morning, as soon as he appeared in his office, Gresser reminded him that a foreign visitor, another Englishman, was scheduled to arrive in a few minutes and inquired whether tea should be served. Canaris shook his head. This wouldn't be a long interview. He agreed to it only because he'd been asked by the Minister of Propaganda himself, Dr. Göbbels. The occasion was a reception for foreign journalists hosted by Göbbels several nights ago on Peacock Island, a pristine enclave on the outskirts of the city that Göbbels first used for entertaining during the '36 Olympic Games. Staying just long enough to satisfy protocol, Canaris was in line to retrieve his hat when he heard a scraping sound on the gravel path behind.

"There you are!" Dr. Göbbels rapidly approached, his lame leg dragging over the small stones. He took hold of Canaris's wrist. "I need a favor of you. This time instead of trying to avoid the press, I wish you to talk to one of them. My office will arrange it." In the hope of encouraging Anglo-German amity, Göbbels explained, he wanted Canaris to speak with an English journalist who was writing a book about the naval engagements in the last war.

Göbbels interrupted Canaris's protest that he'd just met with the British naval attaché. "The British love to talk."

"It's not my practice to give private interviews to journalists," Canaris said.

"I understand," Göbbels said. "Yes, they're all part-time spies, these journalists, but I'm confident you'll impress him with the soldierly dedication of the German military, and I'm sure you won't give any secrets away!" He poked a finger in Canaris's shoulder, playfully, as though giving him an injection, and laughed. "You know what the penalty is!" A flashbulb popped as a staff photographer took their picture. Göbbels let go Canaris's wrist and shuffled away with the same scuffing hobble.


The interview went smoothly. Possessed of the typical nonchalance of an English gentleman, reinforced by a wry grin, the journalist spoke impeccable German as well. He'd done his homework and knew the strategic context of what had happened to the *Dresden* and the rest of Admiral von Spee's South American squadron. Canaris enjoyed reminiscing and talked longer than he planned. Finally, to signal an end, he stood.

Instead of rising, the Englishman took a pipe and tobacco pouch from his pocket. He scooped the bowl full and packed the tobacco down with his thumb. "Last time I was in Berlin, I was working on a book about 'the new Germany,' and I met your adjutant."

"Which one?"

"Colonel Oster."

"Your research is wide."

"It wasn't research alone. I was referred to him for help in facilitating the emigration of acquaintances of mine from Germany. They're both doctors. The wife is Jewish."

Canaris looked down at the card the Englishman had handed him at the beginning of the interview. He had no recollection of Oster ever mentioning the name printed on it—*Ian Anderson*—but knew full well of the assistance Oster gave to those leaving Germany. "That's Colonel Oster's affair."

"It was an act of personal kindness, not official business. I'm told that you've also been of assistance to those encountering obstacles to their desire to leave Germany, Jews among them."

"Emigration isn't a concern of this office. I believe our discussion is over." It was possible, of course, that the Englishman was a British agent. Göbbels was only half-joking when he'd said they were all spies. But the British were usually too subtle and experienced to attempt an approach as clumsy as this. There was also the more remote chance that he was an SS plant, there to smoke out disloyalty.

"I was a soldier once myself. But no longer. I work out of New York now, as a professional scribbler."

Canaris reached beneath his desk to push the button that summoned Gresser. "Then your duty is done, and mine too. Good day."

As he rose to his feet, the Englishman simultaneously tucked his notebook in his pocket. "But duty isn't the same as willful blindness, do you think?"

"Duty is the fundamental requirement of a soldier, in your army and ours."

"Must every order be obeyed, even if it involves the death of innocent civilians?" The Englishman struck a match and lit his pipe. Smoke rose in a thick, lazy coil.

"There's a duty to defend one's country, and my country, unlike yours, isn't an island and doesn't have an empire to fall back on. We have only ourselves, and unless the *Volk* stands united and strong, we will be overrun and oppressed by the hostile peoples on every side of us."

"Inferior peoples, to be turned into chattel or removed, one way or another. Isn't that the Führer's view?"

Canaris pushed the buzzer several times to summon Gresser, who was apparently away from his desk. "My orderly will show you out."

"I've told my former colleagues in intelligence that there are still decent men in Germany who, if they see a willingness on the part of the British and French to go to war in defense of the Czechs, will do whatever necessary to prevent their government from provoking such a war."

"Please, I won't listen to such drivel."

"That's what they said."

Gresser entered the room. "You summoned me, Herr Admiral?"

It wasn't until later in the day that Canaris rediscovered Anderson's card beneath a sheaf of reports on the secret aid being given to Nazi agitators in the Sudetenland. He was about to throw it out when he noticed four carefully scripted lines on the back:

*We looked for peace*
*But no good came;*
*For a time of healing,*
*But behold, terror.*

He stuck the card in his drawer. The New York address, he told himself, was a secondhand souvenir of his long-ago visit, and the stanza of doggerel, a reminder to do no more favors for the Minister of Propaganda.

July 1938

# 4

"There exists today a widespread and fatuous belief in the power of environment, as well as of education and opportunity to alter heredity, which arises from the dogma of the brotherhood of man, derived in its turn from the loose thinkers of the French Revolution and their American mimics. Such beliefs have done much damage in the past and if allowed to go uncontradicted, may do even more serious damage in the future. Thus the view that the Negro slave was an unfortunate cousin of the white man, deeply tanned by the tropic sun and denied the blessings of Christianity and civilization, played no small part with the sentimentalists of the Civil War period and it has taken fifty years to learn that speaking English and going to school and church do not transform a Negro into a white man. Nor was a Syrian or Egyptian freedman transformed into a Roman by wearing a toga and applauding his favorite gladiator in the ampitheatre. Americans will have a similar experience with the Polish Jew, whose dwarf stature, peculiar mentality and ruthless concentration on self-interest are being grafted upon the stock of the nation."

—MADISON GRANT, *The Passing of the Great Race*
*or The Basis of European History*

WALL STREET, NEW YORK

UNDERNEATH THE MAIL that accumulated while Donovan was away was a large brown envelope, Ian Anderson's name and return address scrawled in the left corner. He removed two books from inside and ran his hand across the luxurious black leather cover of the top one. The title, *Racial Hygiene,*was embossed in gold. He scanned the introduction. The text was an English-language reprint of a 1921 German book with a foreword by Nazi bigwig Rudolph Hess. "National Socialism is nothing but applied biology," stated the opening line of his introduction.

Donovan turned to a chapter entitled "Human Rubbish." The opening paragraph was as blunt as the title: "The Aryan race is faced with an end as certain as the dinosaurs' unless it can stop the endless multiplication of racial defectives. Sterilization is an important tool in this struggle and must be wielded mercilessly, with the full coercive power of the state. Yet sterilization by itself will never be sufficient. Any adequate answer to the growing burden of disease, deficiency, and racial degeneration requires us to move beyond humanitarian sentimentality and religious superstition and face this most ancient truth of nature: either the strong destroy the weak or vice versa."

He put the book back in the envelope with its companion, a thinner volume that appeared to be some sort of Nazi handbook. What little he'd learned of eugenics had repelled him and left no desire to know more. Years ago, soon after he'd returned from the war, at the Saturn Club in Buffalo, a scion of one of the city's leading families gave him a copy of Madison Grant's *The Passing of the Great Race.* "Everyone's reading it," he said. "It's a clarion call to all concerned and civilized men." Donovan found it alternately tedious and hysterical. He stopped reading after reaching Grant's description of Ireland as a country in which "the mental and cultural traits of the aborigines have proved to be exceedingly persistent and appear especially in the unstable temperament and lack of coordinating and reasoning power, so often found among the Irish."

At first he thought the book might have been intended as an insult but then realized the gift giver was too thickheaded to have read beyond the first chapter and merely assumed anyone wealthy enough to belong to the Saturn Club was racially fit and would be edified by Grant's eugenical affirmation of Anglo-Saxon superiority.

His secretary returned to announce Mr. Anderson had arrived for his appointment.

"Do me a favor: If I press the intercom, let me know that my next appointment has arrived."

"You want me to lie?" she said with mock horror.

"Act."

"As in, 'Dinner is served in the main dining room'?"

"Tea would be better."

Sitting across from Donovan, Anderson looked like an Englishman out of Warner Bros. central casting. Slender, long-legged frame draped over the chair with an air of polished indifference, he planted the elbow of his rumpled linen suit on the armrest to support the pipe he moved in and out of his mouth. He seemed hardly to have aged in the two decades since they'd last met. The only feature Donovan didn't remember was Anderson's grin, a subtle curve in his mouth reminiscent of Leslie Howard in *The Petrified Forest*. He concluded he wasn't alone in that appraisal when his secretary served them tea and lingered by the desk, visibly taken with the looks and mannerisms of the visiting Englishman, not unlike Bette Davis when Leslie Howard entered her desert café. She exited, however, without attempting a speaking role.

Anderson added milk and several sugar cubes to his tea, stirred and gestured at the surroundings with the spoon. "You've done quite well since we last met. I'm told among your clients is the House of Morgan. As I remember, your intent was to return to your home out west, in Buffalo, and be a hometown lawyer. This is quite a leap." He ceased grinning long enough to take a sip of tea.

Donovan gulped plain, unsweetened tea. "Buffalo is in New York, in the western part. I did return there and practiced law but eventually came here."

"'*In sh'Allah,*' as the Arabs say. 'God wills it.'" Anderson dropped another sugar cube in his cup.

"I've taken my lumps." Donovan heard the sharpness in his own voice. He flushed at the imputation that a mick from Buffalo's First Ward had landed as a partner in his own Wall Street firm through the benevolent dictates of fate.

Nodding agreeably, Anderson sipped his tea. Donovan knew instantly that he'd inferred a meaning to Anderson's remark that was unintended. "I see you've taken up journalism," he noted, more gently.

"I dabble as a freelancer, which supplements my pension and provides a reason for traveling. I came to New York several years ago on a temporary assignment for the British Information Office. My chums in the British Passport Office, in Rockefeller Center, let me keep a desk. It's as close to a home as I have. Most of the time I'm on the road. Been all over, but there's never a dearth of places left to visit."

"You mentioned your travels in your letter. The role of journalist is a wonderful cover, no doubt."

"Cover?"

"For your work in the Secret Intelligence Service."

"Right to the point, Colonel. The American style. In Europe it would take hours, at least, before we could touch upon such matters. In the Orient, it might take a lifetime."

"I have a very busy schedule."

"Then I shan't keep you. I haven't come as a representative of anyone other than myself and with no purpose other than to renew our acquaintance."

"Consider it done." Donovan gently touched his cup to Anderson's, an ersatz toast. "What about your article?"

"Are you following events in Czechoslovakia?"

"I thought you were writing about the war?"

"I'm thinking more of the one to come."

"Most Americans believe it's a question for Europeans to settle and that we should stay out of it. I agree."

"You may wish to leave the world alone but the world won't leave you alone. There are forces at large that, if left unchecked, will reduce civilization to a state of undiluted barbarism."

"I presume you're referring to the New Deal."

Anderson's grin, which hadn't changed since he arrived, made it impossible to tell if he was amused by the remark. "I'm aware of your Republican loyalties," he said, "and of the opinions your party has about Mr. Roosevelt's policies."

"And Mrs. Roosevelt's," Donovan said.

"But the threat arising out of Germany dwarfs any differences between the political parties in this country. You cannot make peace, because the present regime's whole existence is predicated on waging war."

"Not according to John Foster Dulles. Are you aware of the articles he's written on the subject?"

"Aware, yes, but I haven't read them."

"He contends that the National Socialists are 'wild in word but conservative in deed.' Twenty years from now, he says, the Nazis will be nothing more than a German version of the Tories."

"Possibly, I suppose, if in twenty years the Tories have become a mass movement of fanatics led by homicidal gangsters."

"Which is pretty much what the Labour Party thinks, no?"

"Democracies are perpetually rife with rhetorical excess." Anderson put down his cup and lit his pipe. "However, I'm not employing politically inspired exaggerations. I've been to Germany. What is unfolding there is of a different order."

"The Germans have a legitimate grievance. The Sudetenland as a German majority. Self-determination was one of President Wilson's Fourteen Points, remember?"

Anderson shifted in his chair, as if in search of a comfortable position. "If only the world were so neat, in which borders are perfectly congruent with ethnic groups. Few borders, however, are so clear. Listen, the Sudetenland is a prelude rather than a conclusion, a confirmation of the naïveté of his opponents. No offer by the Czechs, however generous, will be acceptable."

"If the British and French won't fight, the Czechs will. They've built their own version of the Maginot Line."

"Not alone, they won't."

"Stalin will never allow Hitler a free hand in the East."

"Russia has no direct access to Czechoslovakia, nor any treaty obligation to defend it unless the French do so first."

"Your government seems not to share your bleak opinion. According to the newspapers, Britain and France might press the Czechs to make concessions."

"Quite right." Anderson puffed on his pipe.

Donovan brushed away the smoke. "If you're seeking some insights into the position of the American government, I'm afraid I can't be of much help. I'm a Republican, and the Democrats are calling the shots, at least until the next election. We're the last to know what's on the mind of the present administration." During his business trips to Chicago and Detroit, Donovan had found unanimous agreement against American involvement in the unfolding crises over Czechoslovakia. At dinner with a group of corporate lawyers in Grosse Point, a former assistant secretary of the Treasury under Hoover said loudly, "If Roosevelt tries to take the country to war, he'll be removed, by hook or by crook!" His colleagues nodded in agreement.

"I admired you as a soldier, Colonel."

"And I you."

"It seems far longer than just twenty years ago. I suppose you've forgotten everything we discussed."

"I remember your pessimism," Donovan said.

"I'm known to some of my acquaintances as 'Reverend Gloom.' They think I'm a frustrated theologian, clothing the ordinary contests among nations and men in the motley of good and evil. Perhaps they're right. Do you believe in prophecy, Colonel?"

"Can't say I've been to any fortune tellers lately."

"That's not the kind of prophecy I had in mind." Anderson's eyelids fluttered, as if calibrating the thinking going on behind them. "The last day before the armistice I was posted with a regiment of Welsh Fusiliers. We knew the war was about to end and the men were relaxed. Toward dusk, one of the subalterns, a devout Methodist chap and biblical scholar, decided to sit atop the parapet. He was working on his own translation of the Bible. Been at it for several years, having mastered Hebrew and Greek. He worked in the quiet twilight, eerie in its quietness, when a sniper drilled him in the eye, a marksman's shot. He was among the very last of the ten million killed in the war. I was smoking my pipe only a few feet away when he was hit. I retrieved the papers he'd dropped. There, splattered with blood and brains, was the last verse he'd translated."

Anderson took out of his pocket what at first appeared to

Donovan to be a business card. But printed on it, instead of a name and address was a biblical verse:

*"We looked for peace*
*But no good came;*
*For a time of healing,*
*But behold, terror."*
—JEREMIAH 14:19

Donovan went to his desk, put Anderson's card in the drawer and picked up one of his own, touching the intercom button as he did. He handed the card to Anderson. "We should stay in touch. Perhaps we could continue this conversation over dinner sometime."

The intercom buzzed. Donovan reached and flicked it on. His secretary's voice had a helpful hint of urgency: "Colonel, it's almost time for your next appointment."

"Do you suppose my friends are right?" Anderson said. "Maybe I'm straying into theology. If that be the case, I suppose what I'm really interested in is your soul."

"It's not for sale." Donovan leaned back on his desk, half-sitting.

The grin on Anderson's face no longer reminded Donovan of Leslie Howard but of other faces from another time: the antic smile of men who'd been in combat too long. Concussed by incessant shelling, overwhelmed by the ubiquity of death, they went slowly mad, holding it in until that expression of perpetual amusement impressed itself on their lips, the imprimatur of a man whose mind had become unhinged. Some threw themselves into an attack, inviting certain death. Others dissolved into shaking, weeping invalids and were shipped to the rear before their insanity turned infectious. A few simply carried on, jumpy, isolated, grinning.

"I wasn't intending to buy your soul," Anderson said. "Merely borrow it."

"'Neither a borrower nor a lender be.' Advice I've always followed, especially when it comes to souls." Donovan pushed off from the desk and moved to the door, positioning himself to show Anderson out.

Anderson slouched deeper in the seat. "Have you followed the *Yezhovschina* in the Soviet Union, the purges, confessions, executions? The latest estimates I've seen are that the number of executions is approaching a million, with another five million confined to labor camps."

"The Bolsheviks are barbarians," Donovan said.

"Quite the contrary. Barbarism is personal and inefficient. Stalin has created a highly oiled machine, the type only civilized men could create, men with the organizational skills required to carry out their plans efficiently."

"One man doesn't make a system."

"That's the point. In a henchman such as Nikolai Yezhov, Stalin has found a homicidal gnome who can read his master's mind and anticipate his wishes without even being told. But it's not the individual lackey who matters. Once the machine is in place, the parts are movable, thousands and thousands of apparatchiks who will perform their assigned roles as though working on an assembly line."

Donovan's impatience had turned into annoyance. He gripped the doorknob. Anderson seemed to take the hint. He knocked the smoldering remnant from his pipe into the ashtray and stood. "I hope we can continue our conversation some other time," he said. But instead of moving toward the door, he veered to the far wall and began to examine the bookshelves.

"There's nothing of interest there, only law books," Donovan said.

Anderson took a book from the shelf and paged through it idly. "I've sent you two books, Colonel. They should arrive soon. A present for your library. Something besides legal tomes to read in your spare time."

"*Time* is the one thing I can't spare."

"And I've already taken too much of it." Anderson snapped the book shut and returned it to the shelf. "The Germans have put in place even more efficient machinery than the Russians," he said. "They have both the motive *and* the method."

"You spoke earlier about their military prowess, if you remember."

"I'm not speaking exclusively of the armed forces. Their ambitions go beyond the battlefield to a wider struggle against

*Lebensunwertes Lebens,* 'life unworthy of life,' a radical cleansing of Germany, Europe, wherever the Reich can extend its influence."

Donovan's secretary pushed the door open and was slightly startled to find him directly in front of her. "Colonel, you're next appointment has been waiting." She smiled at Anderson, apparently believing the grin on his face was for her.

"You see," Anderson said, "the combination of eugenic theory, industrial efficiency, and political tyranny endows Germany with a unique advantage when it comes to murder on a mass scale."

"I didn't mean to interrupt your discussion." Minus her smile, she retreated into the outer office and pulled the door shut behind her.

Donovan immediately opened it again. "Even the bitterest critics of Hitler and his regime haven't leveled such a charge."

"I'm merely raising certain possibilities. Hear me out. Step A, let's say, is the theoretical identification of 'unworthy types'; both the categories of 'degenerate individuals'—the feebleminded, retarded, insane, epileptics, cripples—and of 'degenerate races,' beginning of course with the Jews."

"No civilized person endorses the current treatment of the Jews in Germany."

"Yes, but few seem terribly interested in doing much to stop it. Step B is the legal isolation of these people, stripping them of their legal rights and exposing them to 'treatments' not applied to the general populace. This is a crucial step because it indicates the willingness of the citizenry to endorse, or at least not oppose, the application of medical theories on entire categories of people who are, by definition, lacking in human status. Step C entails following this course of treatment until the 'diseased elements' are eliminated. A trickier proposition."

"Eugenics is a medical question. My business is the law, and I'm afraid I can't avoid attending to it any longer. We'll continue these discussions some other time." Donovan stepped into the outer office.

"Quite right. I've been shamefully self-indulgent in taking up so much time." As Anderson walked past, he muttered something that Donovan had trouble hearing. Anderson stopped and repeated it. "How," he asked, "would you recognize a murderer?"

Standing behind Anderson, Donovan's secretary pointed her finger at her head and made wide circular motions.

"Murderers here in New York are the concern of the district attorney," Donovan said in a soft, reassuring voice. "Our present one, Mr. Dewey, has developed quite a reputation for not only identifying them, but bringing them to justice."

"What if the murderer doesn't look like one of the villainous thugs Mr. Dewey and his fellow racket busters are continually bringing to justice?" Anderson asked. "What if he belongs to a group of professional men, reasonable, serious, intelligent? And what if he's motivated to murder not by ordinary passions, greed, revenge, lust, but by cold, impersonal theories? Moreover, suppose he doesn't think of himself as a murderer but as a scientist eliminating a threat to the future of the racially fit and wellborn. What would it take to see such a person for what he is?"

"An interesting theory. You should write about it."

"There's plenty written already. You can read for yourself in the books I've sent. Superstition dressed up as science and made a basis for murder. Better yet, I've some friends I'd like you to meet. They've recently arrived here from Germany. If I could bring them here to talk with you, I believe . . ."

"The Colonel's calendar is jam-packed for the immediate future," Donovan's secretary interrupted. It was obvious that if she still saw in Anderson a resemblance to a British actor, it was Boris Karloff, not Leslie Howard.

"There are decent men within Germany, as there are here," Anderson said. "But unless they act together to stop it, the world will be dragged into the abyss."

"I'll have to check and see when I have some time available."

"I'm no longer at my previous location. I'm officially retired now and been tossed out of my office altogether. Soon as I'm resettled, I'll call and let you know. Thanks for your time. Sorry to have imposed on your hospitality."

His secretary poked her head into the corridor outside her office, making sure their guest was truly gone. "What rock did he crawl from under?"

"The worst wounds can be to a man's mind. Some never heal."

She held the books Anderson had sent. "He's not a Nazi, is he?"

"Quite the opposite."

"I took a peek at these books. They belong in the garbage."

"I think I owe it to my guest to give them a look."

Donovan waited until after lunch to leaf through the smaller of the books Anderson had sent, the one he'd previously ignored, an English version of *The Nazi Primer: Official Handbook for Schooling the Hitler Youth*. He flipped to a section titled "Heredity and Race Fostering," where Anderson had placed a bookmark. Several paragraphs were underlined. He glanced at one: "The more serious of the hereditary diseases, especially the mental diseases, make the carriers completely unworthy of living. Those so afflicted have neither the capacity to reason nor any feeling of responsibility. They contribute nothing. Yet these worthless ones are allowed to multiply without restraint and spread their sickness everywhere." There was a special section devoted to the Jews, entitled "Not Different in Quality but Kind? Our Greatest Menace."

Donovan's secretary brought him the file for his next appointment. He put the two books together and passed them to her.

"Shall I put them on the shelves or file them away?"

"File them."

"Where?"

"Wherever you wish."

"How about under A for *Auf Wiedersehen*?" She dropped them in the wastebasket beside the desk.

Donovan made no protest, nor did he retrieve the books. Though he didn't doubt Anderson's sincerity, he hadn't forgot the shameless exaggerations—often as effective as they were outrageous—with which the British had painted Germany during the last war, portraying the conflict as a struggle between light and dark, the defenders of civilization versus a horde of evil "huns."

*In the spring of 1916, he's in London as a neutral civilian on a humanitarian mission for the Rockefeller Foundation. An army officer with a thick Scottish accent strikes up a conversation in the lobby of their hotel. After some friendly banter, the Scot invites him* to sit with him at dinner. By the time dessert arrives, he's completed an impassioned catalogue of the depredations visited by the Germans on Belgium and on "us Catholics."

"All I ask," he says, "is that as ye travel across the Belgian-German border put down a notation for every infantry unit and artillery piece. It'll be a small but significant contribution to removing the heel of the Hun from the neck of the brave Belgians."

At the end of the war, in 1918, during an Anglo-American military reception in Paris, a circle of British and U.S. officers stands around bantering and laughing. Donovan has the feeling that he's met one of the British officers before but can't place where.

"Maybe this will help," the officer says. He cocks his head to the side, closes one eye and says in a chanting burr, "'Tis guid to be merry and wise. 'Tis guid to be honest and true. 'Tis guid to support Caledonia's course. And bide by the buff and the blue! Do ye no remember me, laddie?" The British officer resumes his normal English tone. "You were easier to seduce than I imagined. I was hopeful a Yank would be softened by the sweet words of a Scotsman, and an Irish Yank by that Jacobite twaddle about 'us Catholics.' And it worked, didn't it! Did as you were asked, my fine bonnie lad!" The officers throw back their heads and have a good laugh.

Donovan doesn't join in.

## THE UPPER EAST SIDE, NEW YORK

The morning after his encounter with Brannigan, Dunne had come to with a fuzzy recollection of crawling out of the bathroom and lifting himself into bed. He attempted to stand but his head ached so badly he fell back on the pillow and stopped trying. He slept a long time. Finally able to get up, he showered, changed, and forced himself across the street to Doctor Finkelstein's office.

The old man gently poked at Dunne's head with his fingers. "What the hell happened to you?"

In the mirror above the Doctor's sink, a raccoonlike face, puffy with two black eyes, stared back at Dunne. "The moon fell on me."

"Must have been a full one." The Doctor sutured a line of black stitches into Dunne's head. "Probably got a concussion," he said. He gave Dunne a prescription and told him to stay in bed with his eyes closed.

Back home, Dunne took the phone off the hook and crawled under the covers. He woke up sweating the next morning. It was going to be a scorcher. He phoned the Medical Examiner's and asked to speak with Doc Cropsey. "Hang on," a voice said. A moment later, the voice came back on. "He wants to know who's calling."

"His mother."

There was another pause. "He says he doesn't have a mother."

"He does now."

Doc Cropsey came on the line, gruff and annoyed, but amused when he discovered it was Dunne taking him up on the offer to stay at his place in Southold.

Dunne mopped up the blood and threw out the bloody towel, sheets, and pillowcases. He looked through his suit for the envelope Elba had given him. Brannigan had performed his magic. *Abracadabra:* it had disappeared. He took the coffee can out of the refrigerator and removed the bulk of the money he'd stashed there. He threw some clothes in a canvas grip and was about to leave for Penn Station when the phone rang.

"May I please speak to Mr. Fintan Dunne." A woman's voice.

He thought he recognized the honeydew tone. "Depends who this is."

"It's Doctor Sparks's office, Mr. Dunne. Please hold a moment."

Sparks came on. "You're a hard man to reach, Mr. Dunne."

"Now I'm not."

Sparks paused. "This is difficult for me, but I need to see you on a matter I'm not comfortable discussing on the phone. Could you come to my office?"

"Who said I make house calls?"

"Please, Mr. Dunne. I'll reimburse any expenses you might incur."

"Cab fare?"

"Certainly. This won't take long. I promise."


Sparks's secretary was stouter and older than the slither-hither quality of her voice suggested. Her immaculate white dress was crisp and freshly pressed. The knot at the back of her head held her hair in tight, stringent order. She directed Dunne through a waiting room across a thick, richly textured Persian rug into Dr. Sparks's office.

Sparks didn't get up. He indicated the chair next to the desk. "Please, Mr. Dunne, have a seat." He wore a yellow linen jacket and a green silk ascot, the same color as his pants. If he owned one of those white coats beloved of meat cutters and medical men, it was nowhere in sight. "You look as though you've had a rather bad accident."

"Jack fell down and broke his crown."

"Head injuries should never be made light of. It's important to rest."

"I'm on furlough soon as I leave here."

"I like your style, Mr. Dunne. Very direct."

"You're in a distinct minority."

"Today's minority is tomorrow's majority. Isn't that what history teaches?"

"The Republicans hope so."

"Let me get to the point. I want to hire your services."

"I'm booked."

"Last time we talked, Mr. Dunne, you seemed eager for work. 'Whatever it takes to stay afloat' was, I believe, the phrase you used."

"My ship came in."

"At the risk of sounding unduly skeptical, I can't imagine a cut-and-dried case like the Lynch murder could have occupied much of your time."

"Things aren't always as cut-and-dried as they first appear."

"The police thought they were, and the judge and jury, and the Court of Appeals."

"Grillo won't be the first innocent man to go to the electric chair."

"There's another thing I like about you, Mr. Dunne, your persistence. In difficult situations, when it appears there's little chance of success, the instinct of the intellectual is to give up. But men like you pursue what they want, no matter the odds or opposing forces, and more often than not it's their will that triumphs."

"I work on a per diem. Don't persist, don't get paid."

"If you persist on my behalf, you'll be paid promptly and well." Sparks opened a leather-bound register and lifted a pen from the marble stand on his desk. He poised the pen above a page of corn-colored bank checks. "What do you require as a retainer?"

"What makes you think you need a private detective? Most times what people need is a lawyer, not a snoop."

"I'm being blackmailed."

"Then you need the cops."

"I can't risk the publicity. For a physician, reputation is everything. I need someone trustworthy and discreet who can deliver my message in person; someone whose whole demeanor conveys how serious I am and how final my answer."

"If you need a goon, your chauffeur, Bill What's-his-name, seems a natural."

"Bill Huber? Reliable in his own way, but he lacks discretion."

"That's not all he lacks."

"This has been a difficult time for me: a woman who worked for me is savagely murdered. Along with my name, one of those vile newspapers even published my picture. As a result, I'm approached by blackmailers who threaten to expose an embarrassing incident from my youth. My sense of security has been badly shaken, so if Bill on occasion acts in an overprotective way, I apologize. I feel required to have someone like him around. Unfortunately, I can't trust him with an assignment like this. He has no capacity for subtlety."

Sparks scratched the pen across the open page of checks. He pressed a blotter on it that was encased in the same leather as the register and detached the check along its perforated edges. "I suppose a retainer of a thousand dollars might suffice." He laid the check directly in front of Dunne.

*Pay to the Order of Fintan Dunne.* Drawn on the Corn Exchange Bank, its three zeroes were aligned in happy sequence, like the cherries on a slot. Sparks's florid but legible handwriting spilled across the face of the check and helped give it the same impressive feel as the framed diplomas and certificates on the walls, a document to be preserved and enshrined instead of cashed. *We hold these truths.*

"I didn't know a doctor's hand could be so clear."

"I despise sloppiness in all its forms."

"You might not like my style as much as you think."

Sparks pushed the check closer to Dunne. "Aren't you interested in why I'm being blackmailed?"

"If it involves a criminal matter, I'd prefer not to know. That way, there's no chance the cops can get it out of me."

"It's personal, not criminal, but could be used to hurt my practice. I made a payment with the understanding that would be the end of it and the blackmailers would go away. Now they're back and want more."

"That's the way the game is played."

"I'm willing to make one more payment but no more after that. I need to locate where these bloodsuckers are hiding and have my decision delivered in a calm and convincing manner."

"Sorry, I got a train to catch." Those zeroes: no small-time tip, two-bit exchange, the New York version of hello. But real money.

"What about when you return?"

"I don't play with blackmailers. Either you go to the cops or they'll keep coming back. It's that simple." Dunne slid the check toward Sparks. He remembered his father's refrain, while he was still Big Mike, before he shriveled into a wizened, exhausted wreck: *Learn the difference between being paid and being owned. A slave is bought. So is a scab. A taint no bath or shower could remove.* On the way out, the secretary handed him an envelope. "This is for today's expenses," she said. "I trust we'll see you again soon."

"You never know." He laid down the envelope and left.


It was a decade since he'd last been to Southold. Doc Cropsey had taken him and two other detectives for a summer's weekend.

They fished in the day (and caught nothing). At night they played cards by the light of a kerosene lamp and listened to the regular drone of the launches circling in from the ships parked outside the territorial limit to land illegal booze on Shelter Island.

Doc had fixed it so that Clem Payne, a sour, leather-skinned, tight-lipped, East-Ender, was waiting for Dunne at the Southold station. They stopped in a general store for provisions. A woman with a constipated frown filled a large cardboard box with milk, bread, eggs, crackers, jam, and other staples. Clem loaded the box on the back of his beat-up Ford truck. Dunne sat next to him on a torn seat. In several places the springs had popped through, their sharp, menacing corkscrew tips sticking straight up. They traveled east on the highway for a mile or so and turned onto a dirt road. Clem held the wheel tightly in his denim gloves as they jolted over the cratered, rutted surface, raising a cloud of dust that filled the cab.

Doc's place hadn't changed much. Inside were the same ripped screens and cork walls; same collection of secondhand furniture. The only noticeable improvements were the light bulbs that hung from the ceiling and the radio above the icebox. Outside, east of the small house, was an expanse of Sweet William. Closer in, the delicate leaves of a patch of Maiden Pink covered the ground like a mat. To the rear, by the fringe of trees that shielded the shack from the potato fields, a spread of lupines thrived. Peconic Bay was a hop, skip from the drooping screened-in porch.

It wasn't till he'd stored away the provisions that Dunne realized he forgot to bring any booze or cigarettes. He could walk to town, but it was getting dark and he was tired. He lay down and was quickly asleep. In the morning, he went for a swim and dried off on the front stairs. The sun, like the bay, was at flood tide. The trees swayed in the breeze off Peconic Bay.

The flowers were as fragrant as in the garden of the Catholic Protectory where Brother Flavian had tried his best to make them learn the names and characteristics of everything they grew. It was a prized position to be on his "garden squad." Unlike the Brothers who ran the laundry, the printing office, and the machine shop, big-handed, short-tempered Irishmen who didn't hesitate to cold-cock a kid, Brother Flavian was an old Frenchman who never raised his hand or voice. As tough as the boys of the Protectory insisted they were, as unafraid, they loved his gentleness and competed to be around him.

"Pleeze, repeat again ze names after me," he said, his accent thickened by the red wine that stained his teeth and sweetened his breath. Plants without a true stem. *Names that sound like Italian saints.* Narcissus, Hyacinth. Plants with stems twenty-four inches or above. *Names from a burlesque marquee.* Canass, Lily, Blackberry Lily. Flowers irregular, unsymmetrical. *Prizefighters' monikers.* Canna, Gladiolus, Anthonyza.

Brother Flavian strolled through the garden as they hoed and weeded. He wore a white duster over his cassock. After a short while, he sank into the chair with the canvas webbing, his mumbled speech becoming a snore that needed no translation. A moment later they were over the fence, across Unionport Road, down the hill with the high grass. They stripped as they went, hanging clothes on branches and bushes, tripping one another, till they reached the sprawling pond and jumped, naked, into the murky water. No one carried a watch, but somehow they always knew when it was time to go. The race reversed itself, clothes on, over the wall, back to their garden chores.

When Brother Flavian woke from his nap, he always found them where he left them. *"Bien, bien,"* he muttered as he pushed himself from his chair and, oblivious to their wet, tousled hair, resumed his flower talk.

Dunne followed a routine for the next week, rising early, going for a swim, taking a late morning nap, and, in the afternoon, setting out on a long, leisurely walk. At night, he stretched out on the grass and watched the crowd of stars, unobscured and vivid. *Star light, star bright, what's your wish tonight, Fin?* He thought about Elba and Roberta, two such different women joined together to save the same man. Elba's motive was clear. But Roberta's?

Out of provisions, he was about to walk to town when Clem Payne showed up with a box of supplies. "Doc Cropsey says to make sure you don't perish from hunger. 'City folk don't know how to feed themselves.' The doc said that, not me, though I'd be fibbin' if I says I disagree." He put the carton of food on the front porch and went back for a fresh block of ice wrapped in burlap, which he deposited in the icebox. Seeming in no hurry to leave, he slipped one hand in the bib of his overalls, and with the other pushed his faded, battered fisherman's cap to the side of his head. "Interested in some fishin'?"

"Never had much luck in that department."

"Ain't a matter of luck but knowin' where the fish are. Be by in the mornin', 'bout six. Poles, bait provided, cost of two dollars." He took off his work gloves and put out a gnarled hand minus two fingers. It reminded Dunne of a lobster claw. "Deal?"

"Deal." His handshake was powerful and firm, despite the missing fingers.

In the morning they went fishing on Peconic Bay. The weather was serene. Diamond-faceted water mirrored a sky so bleached with sunlight that the glare made Dunne's eye sockets ache. On the sixth or seventh morning, as the boat chugged toward Shelter Island, Dunne asked, "Ever rain out here?"

"Plenty," Clem said.

"Not this summer, I guess."

"Weather's got a will of its own, no tellin' what it'll do next, specially this summer, showerin' one week, scorchin' the next. You never know. Take, for instance, a great storm, like in '15. Nobody seen more than spit from May through August when, from nowhere, the Good Lord sends a deluge old Noah would recognize."

"Hurt your fishing business?"

"My business?" A thin smile spread across his dry, cracked lips. "I'm talkin' about *eighteen fifteen*. Old as I may seem, I ain't that old."

It was their last exchange of the morning. The rest of the time was spent wordlessly hooking a variety of fish, some as flat as cardboard, others round and full. Dunne had no idea what they were and didn't expose his ignorance by asking. When they were gutted and cleaned, he took home a supply of fillets for dinner, cooking them the way Clem told him, in a frying pan with butter and salt, boiled potatoes on the side. Nameless as they were, he relished their taste.

The weather turned cloudy and wet. Dunne skipped fishing and walked the several miles to Southold. He went to the pharmacy and sat in the phone booth. He picked up the receiver and hesitated. Brannigan's warning: *It's over and done.* Then again, maybe not. He placed a long-distance call to SP-3-1000, the general exchange at police headquarters. After several minutes, he reached Detective Tommy Hines.

"Dunne? What the hell do you want?"

"A favor."

"I don't owe you any."

"Ever hear of a Roberta Dee?"

"This a joke?"

"I'll let you know when I find out what the punchline is."

"Word is, Chief Brannigan gave you a few punchlines of his own."

"Told me to behave. I'm trying."

"You're not so bad, Dunne. I known worse, that's for sure."

"How about Roberta Dee?"

"Is it an alias?"

"Could be. Probably a sheet on her, if you wouldn't mind looking." As a cop, Dunne had used the files of the Bureau of Investigation, which cross-referenced every dip, thug, yegg, thief, murderer, pimp, and party girl by name, profession, and modus operandi, from auto thieves to zoo workers, first-story burglars to roof-top jumpers. A criminal *Who's Who, Who Was* and *Who Wants To Be*, it cataloged the race, height, sex, eye color, distinguishing features, aliases, and arrest records, of every felon and perpetrator who'd come under the jurisdiction of the NYPD. More often than not, even if an alias was used, it had some semblance to the real name, and if those patient enough to toil through the list were lucky enough to be guided by the surly clerks who oversaw it, they found what they were after.

"I got other matters on my mind. Dewey wants to retry my uncle."

"They don't call Jimmy Hines 'The Silver Fox' for nothing." The operator broke in and asked Dunne to deposit more coins. He ran to the counter to get change. *Come on, Tommy, let's not waste time on Uncle Jimmy. The whole city knows he's been on the take for years, a partner with the mob in operating the Harlem numbers racket, all those dimes sucked out of hopeful negroes producing riches for those who run the game and peanuts for those who play it. Sooner or later, Dewey will hunt him down.* "Tammany will see to it there's another mistrial or maybe even an acquittal."

"Hope you're right, Dunne."

"Now, about Miss Dee?"

"Not for free."

"Never entered my head."

"See what I can find. No promises. Got it?"

"Got it, Tommy."


Clem Payne deposited him at the station. He bought the New York papers, a pack of Lucky Strikes, and a roll of assorted LifeSavers. He sucked a succession of Pep-O-Mint, Wint-O-Green, Molas-O-Mint, so that the roll was half gone by the time the train pulled in. The windows on the train car were dust-covered and almost impossible to see through. Not much to see anyway, dull, flat potato fields, same empty landscape he remembered from Camp Mills, in Hempstead, where he'd trained under Major Donovan with the 69th Regiment in the summer of 1917, tents pitched in the sandy soil, a siege of rabbits, skunks, flies, gnats, mosquitoes. Eventually, it was a tent city of 30,000 men, the Rainbow Division. Most of the city boys were permanently cured of ever wanting to see the countryside again.

The lead stories in the papers all concerned Europe, the Germans' growls about Czechoslovakia, war games near the border, a repeat of what he'd heard on the radio plugged into the single porcelain outlet above the ice box, music interrupted by the urgent, self-important tones of newscasters who went on about "gathering war clouds" and "a drumbeat of aggression." He flipped through the sports pages. As much as he liked to watch a fight or horse race or ballgame, he got no enjoyment from reading about them. He rested the paper on his lap.

*War.* They were welcome to it. Blow themselves off the map. Good riddance. He wrestled with the window, managing to open it just a crack. Outside was a continuous smear of telephone poles, fences, farmhouses. The train's rock-a-bye motion made him drowsy. The odor from the countryside was musty and unpleasant, heavy with salt air and manure, a smell reminiscent of the wire.

*They don't believe it at first, when the limey sergeant major tells them that barbed wire has a smell. On their way to the front, they mingle with the English troops being relieved. The limey sergeant's cigarette looks pristine and unblemished in his begrimed hands.*

*"How far to the Front?" Dunne asks.*

*"Not far at all, Yank," the limey laughs. "You'll know you're there when you 'ad a sniff o' the wire." He repeats the phrase "sniff o' the wire" and laughs again, a hot, foul stench passing through teeth the color of rusted wire.*

*They don't smell anything at first, not until after the first leave and the return to the trenches. Sniff, Fin, sniff: the wire. The limey wasn't gibing some gullible Yanks. It's there, in the air, unmistakable. The wire is directly overhead. It's pitch dark. They can't see it but can definitely smell it. The artillery is supposed to blast a path straight through to the village of Landes-St. George. All it does is rearrange the wire, in some places making it even more tangled and impassable.*

*Major Donovan gives three long blasts on his whistle. He's off to the right somewhere. A flare scorches the night sky white. The entire unit rises and pitches itself into the wire. The whistle blows constantly, making itself heard over the growing sound of German machine guns. When dawn comes, bodies are hung on the wire like crumpled, discarded puppets. The whistle has stopped.*

*There aren't many bugles, not after Camp Mills, and no drums, not after they land in Southampton and the limey band plays a welcoming concert, banging away at hymns and Broadway tunes. Only gradually do they notice that the limey musicians are all in their fifties and sixties, a band of old codgers. There are no*

*young men in sight. There's an all-horn band when they land in*
*France. That's the end of the serenading, a froggy version of*
*"Camptown Races" and "The Star-Spangled Banner." From then*
*on it's all whistles' thin ear-pricking screech as sharp and uncom-*
*plicated as a bayonet.*

*Get up, you sons of bitches! Up and into the wire!*


"Sorry, bub, if I spoiled your nap."

From above, the open flap of a double-breasted suit rested on
Dunne's shoulder. The gut inside hung down like the underside of a
cow.

"This is too good to miss." Leaning over Dunne, the man in the
double-breasted suit gripped the metal latches on the railcar's window. He heaved, grunted, and jerked it open. "There, now we can
hear better." He stayed where he was, looming, big and bent.

The blare of bugles and drums seemed to piggyback on the
heavy, wet air that flooded through the open window.

"Yes, sir, whether you like the heinies or not, gotta give it to
'em. Sure know how to set a fella's feet to marchin'." His voice was
as oversized as his frame. Erect, at full height, the top of his straw
hat almost touching the disabled fan in the middle of the car, he
moved his feet up and down.

"Wanna march, they should go march in Germany. Kraut bastards." The bantam-sized conductor, dwarfed by the would-be
marcher, stood next to Dunne's seat.

Lined up by the tracks, in precise formation, were several
squads of ten across and five ranks deep. The one to the east, at the
rear of the train, was made up of teenage girls in dark blue ankle-
length skirts, white blouses, and red and white kerchiefs around
their necks. A handsome, big-boned girl with blonde hawser-like
braids was in front with a long pole, a limp flag hanging from it.
On the west flank were teenage boys in khaki shorts and shirts,
knapsacks on their backs, with the same kerchiefs as the girls. A tall
muscular boy held another flag.

The middle formation, men in brown trousers and shirts but
with black ties instead of scarves, wore brown legionnaire-style

caps and armbands on their right sleeves, white circle on a field of red, black swastika in the center. The all-male band, also in uniform, was several yards behind, in front of the black-lettered station sign: YAPHANK. Farther back, in the parking lot, was a casual mix of blank-faced spectators and what appeared to be proud relatives, smiling, pointing, applauding.

The conductor took off his hat and swiped the leather sweatband with his thumb. "Nazi cocksuckers," he said. "Maybe they got the trains runnin' on time in Germany but here on Long Island, they got us runnin' ten to fifteen minutes late." He shouted to make himself heard over the music.

On the front page of the newspaper in Dunne's lap was a picture of a Nazi parade in the Sudetenland. Three shades of black and gray. The spectacle beside the track had noise, color, action, as though the photo had popped to life. The conductor pulled on a gold chain hooked around the belt loop of his pants and lifted out a gold watch. He flipped the filigreed lid, an embossed tangle of Madeira vines, and looked at the face. "Longer we stay here, longer the cocksuckers will be waiting for their Führer to arrive."

"Ain't he still in Berlin?" The flap of the double-breasted jacket waved in front of Dunne's face as the giant once more leaned across and tried unsuccessfully to get his massive head through the window.

"Not Hitler but that Kuhn character, the clown that heads up the Bund." The conductor put his watch away and pointed at a line of cars snaking toward the station. "Here they come now. A greeting party of muck-a-mucks to welcome the kraut-in-chief. They're all nested together out there at Camp Siegfried, a regular Nazi Coney Island, full of beer bums and their fat-assed wives."

The procession of cars entered the parking lot, the first two nondescript sedans, the last a black Cadillac touring car, small swastika flags mounted on either side of the engine. The band stopped playing. The three formations came to attention.

"We won't move till we're sure all our passengers are aboard, and that means the eastbound Camp Siegfried special can't pull in till we're outta, here." The conductor walked to the rear of the car, took hold of the metal handgrip by the door, and swung the upper part of his body out over the crowd. "All aboard!" he yelled.

The ranks beside the tracks drew tighter. They raised their right arms in a single, synchronized motion. *"Sieg heil!"* they answered in unison, a phrase they kept repeating.

Retreating to the middle of the car, the conductor shook his head. "Give an inch, they want a mile. Here the railroad hands 'em their own special train every Saturday mornin', right from New York to Yaphank, a regular Nazi express, and how do they show their gratitude? By holdin' up the west-bound train with all this hoopla."

The train's sudden jerk sent everyone forward in their seats. The giant plopped down next to Dunne, turning the seat into a see-saw that sent him several inches in the air. The conductor kept his balance, jumping back and forth on his feet like one of those wish-bone-legged sailors on the Atlantic convoys who moved around the decks steady and nimble in the worst ocean howler. "Here we go!" he said.

The train stopped again after a minute or so. The Cadillac pulled up several yards behind it. The driver popped out and opened the rear door of the car. Two men emerged. The first wore black boots, black jodhpurs, Sam Browne belt over white shirt, and a swastika band on his arm. The second, the larger of the two, was in khaki slacks and a white shirt. He leaned over and looked down the tracks. Dunne got a view of his face as he stood with his hands on his hips, turning slowly but not casually, the way a bouncer scouts a barroom to pinpoint where the troublemakers might be. He nodded as his companion whispered in his ear, his mule-sized jaw moving up and down. A face you don't forget, no matter how hard you try. *Stand back, unless you wanna start a pushin' contest with this car.* Doctor Sparks's chauffeur, Bill Huber.

The train jolted forward, moving in herky-jerky fashion until it gathered speed. It stopped at the station in Riverhead. Dunne climbed over the giant, who had his straw hat over his face and was snoring loudly, and stood on the iron-decked entryway.

"Well, the schedule's gone to hell now." The conductor was behind him with his watch out. A train whistle sounded. "Here she comes, the Camp Siegfried special. They'll be squawkin' about being late, which the krauts can't abide, but it's their own friggin' fault. Was them who held us up at Yaphank."

A moment later, the eastbound train clattered past. People hung out the windows and waved the Stars and Stripes and swastika flags. As the last car came into view, a lone figure appeared on the rear platform, which was draped in red, white, and blue bunting. Seeing the two figures watching him from the train on the siding, he sucked in his gut and stretched out his arm in a stiff salute.

"*Herr Bundesführer* himself," the conductor said. "Been my misfortune to ride that special in the company of Fritz Kuhn and crew. He excels at two things. Givin' orders and grabbin' girls' asses, and not necessarily in that order."

The *Bundesführer* stayed where he was and maintained his salute. The conductor put his left hand in the bend of his right arm, and lifted them up. "Up where I was raised, in Italian Harlem, a half Jew, half mick kid on a block full of wops, we used to call this the 'Second Avenue salute.' He makes a fist with his right hand and raised his arm higher. "Hey, Fritz, *sieg heil* this!"


Dunne exited Penn Station through the cavernous, dingy waiting room onto Eighth Avenue. There'd been a shower, and while the rain had stopped, the air was still gray and dank, rife with engine fumes. He fell in with the sodden, wilted column of pedestrians moving north.

Sun or no sun, a horde of kids splashed in the spray of a fire hydrant, their mothers leaning out on the fire escapes above to keep watch. Tommy Scanlon had been from around here. Irish mother, Italian father, *Scanzoni* was his real name. For the sake of surviving among the micks of Hell's Kitchen, he called himself Scanlon. He was killed the same day as Francis Sheehy, a single bullet in the head while helping to remove the wounded. His old man had a vegetable pushcart in the old Paddy's Market on Ninth Avenue, beneath the El. Tommy's death knocked the life out of his old man, but he stayed doing business until the city started building the

Lincoln Tunnel and drove the street peddlers away. A grateful nation's way of saying thanks.

At Forty-second Street, Dunne went west, halfway down the block, to Holy Cross rectory, beside the church. He rang the bell and wiped the perspiration from his face. He was about to ring again when a short, prim housekeeper, her apron perfectly starched, opened the door. He asked to see Father McNevin. She said that the Father didn't see anyone without an appointment, unless it was an emergency. She didn't move out of the doorway when Dunne said he had an appointment.

"Made no mention of it to me." She was about to close the door, but hesitated. "Yet that's the way today, isn't it? No sense of doing things properly, not even among them who should be models for the rest of us." She motioned him in and led him to the parlor. "Wait here. I'll tell Father his appointment is here."

Dunne sat in a stiff-backed, horsehair chair, suitably uncomfortable for a parish-house parlor. Above the mantle was a picture of Father Duffy in helmet and uniform, looking pious and severe, two things he wasn't. Colonel Donovan said Duffy had been a noted theologian and scholar till he wrote something they didn't like in Rome and was banished to a parish. That didn't matter to the men in the regiment; what did was that he was a different kind of priest, unafraid to laugh aloud at the raunchiest choruses of "Mademoiselle from Armentieres." After the war, half of them— Donovan included— kept coming to him at Holy Cross for confession, every Saturday, right up until he died. *Bless me Father, for I have sinned.* Didn't matter what the sin was, Duffy never scolded or made the penalty too stiff: "For your penance say two Hail Marys."

The ormolu clock beneath Duffy's portrait ticked loudly. Dunne paged through a magazine with pictures of American nuns running an orphanage in some corner of China. The caption said the invading Japanese had killed the kids' parents. There were a hundred kids for every nun. Father McNevin entered with a cigar in hand, medicine-ball stomach protruding against his cassock.

In France, Private Aloysius McNevin had been known as "Old Grumbles," on account of his constant griping and complaining.

McNevin was the cautious, reliable type that others stuck close to in combat. They knew he'd never do anything silly, cowardly, or heroic. He seemed to have the natural temperament of a patrolman, which is what everyone predicted he'd be. But God works in strange ways, even in New York City. Dunne wasn't the only one surprised by the news that McNevin had entered the seminary. They'd stayed in touch after McNevin was ordained.

A curate in Sacred Heart Church, McNevin succeeded Duffy at Holy Cross, spending his whole career as a priest in the parishes of Hell's Kitchen, a neighborhood of tightly packed tenements crammed with dock workers who shaped up every morning on the West Side piers. Mixed in were the professional thugs and gangsters, and behind them, the ranks of minor criminals angling for a way into the majors. McNevin's prime clientele were the wives and mothers of the workers and roughnecks, an army of cleaning ladies, maids, cooks, and the usherettes who handed out programs in the Broadway theaters and made sure Father McNevin had the best seats for any show he cared to see. He kept on top of their kids and sent their husbands home from the bars, as much patrolman as priest, and they were grateful to him for that.

"You lied," McNevin said. "You told Mrs. Egan you had an appointment." He puffed on the cigar.

"Been eating fish all week. Don't I get any points for that?"

"It's not Friday. You can eat any damn thing you want." McNevin pulled his cassock over his knees and crossed one thick leg over the other. "Something tells me you're not here on matters of faith."

"Trying to track down somebody by the name of Lynch."

"Several families in the parish by that name. None have been in trouble before, least not the jail-time variety. This personal?"

"Professional. I need to talk to him."

"What's his baptismal name?"

"Don't know."

"Any last address?"

"I was told he lived in the Hoover Flats, other side of Twelfth."

"The men in those shanties are from all over, farmers from Tulsa, Oklahoma, factory hands from Cleveland, Ohio, or from the city itself. Some keep on the move, jumping freights. Some give up and surrender to the bottle. Most show up at the soup kitchen we run. We don't ask for names and they don't give 'em. Once in a while, I get a call to administer the last rites. Can't remember anyone named Leary."

"*Lynch*. The brother of the nurse who got murdered on the Upper West Side."

"Yeah, I remember. Bernie McElhone, a classmate of mine from Dunwoodie, anointed her. The boy who did it was Italian, if I remember correctly."

"Cuban."

"Close enough."

"Anybody you can think of might have some idea whether Lynch is in those shacks or where he might have gone?"

"These men don't have much else in this world save their privacy, so they don't take to people sticking their noses in. But I'll be on my afternoon rounds and there's a knockabout named Toby Butts might be able to help you, if he's where I think he'll be. Wait here till I change." McNevin returned in a badly rumpled white linen jacket over his black clerical vest and Roman collar, and an aging yellow-white straw hat. As soon as they reached the street, he began mopping his face with a handkerchief.

A block north, under the Ninth Avenue El and past the dime-a-dance places near Forty-second Street, the sidewalk was crowded with people shopping amid the outdoor stalls selling fruit and vegetables, fresh-killed poultry, and fish packed in chips of rapidly melting ice. Grocery boys hugged cartons of food for delivery and made a point of saying hello to the priest. Leather bag bulging with quarters collected from the meters he'd visited, a gas man stopped McNevin to thank him for visiting his mother. They went into a tenement on Tenth. In the lobby, an insurance agent was tallying up the dimes and quarters he reaped from those determined to avoid the parting indignity of a pauper's grave and have their own cemetery plot. "Irish real estate" was what they called it when Dunne was a kid. Once his mother died, there was nobody to pay those installments, so brother Jack went where he did.

They walked up three flights of crazily sloping stairs and down a dark hallway. An ancient, bent woman opened the door. She led McNevin to a sagging bed by an open window overlooking Tenth. The woman in the bed, who bore a striking resemblance to the one who'd opened the door, was taking deep, labored breaths. She took McNevin's hand and kissed it. Dunne stood in a corner, next to a bureau that was one of the few pieces of furniture in the spare but immaculate apartment. Atop the bureau, on a lace runner, was a statue of the Blessed Virgin.

McNevin spoke in whispers with the women. He traced the sign of the cross over them both. Outside on the stoop, he removed a half-smoked cigar from his jacket pocket and lit it. "The Murphy sisters are typical Irish. I keep telling 'em that Marion, the one in bed, should be in the hospital. But to them 'hospital' sounds the same as 'morgue,' the last stop when your time is up, and not a moment sooner. Probably got their life savings hidden in that statue of the Virgin. Be the first thing to disappear if they die in that place and the cops get there first."

At Forty-fifth Street, they turned east, past a stand-up eating joint and a print shop that specialized in putting any headline tourists wanted on fake newspapers. McNevin pushed open the door of a bar & grill packed two deep. He stood in the entryway and bellowed, "Lunchtime is done, boys!" The din at the bar subsided. A few of the patrons downed their drinks and left. Slowly, except for a handful, the others straggled out. He greeted most of the departing patrons by name. "Pay day," he said to Dunne. "Before long, the money is all gone and they go home with a load on. The wife complains, she gets a black eye, maybe worse. Sometimes bringing in the sheep won't suffice. Sometimes you gotta give 'em a boot in the rear."

They headed north on Broadway. Around the next corner a crowd of two or three dozen men stood around in small groups. The words on the metal sign above them were faded but still legible:

SAM STONE • PROMOTER • AGENT • MANAGER
ALL ASPECTS OF THE PUGILISTIC ARTS

"Ever know Sam Stone?" McNevin asked.

"Only by reputation as the promoter the promoters looked up to."

"Always looking for an angle, Sam was. Had a great dislike for, as he put it, 'uncertain outcomes.'"

"Let no fight go unfixed."

*De mortuis nil nisi bonum.* Of the dead say nothing but good. I can't speak about Sam's habits as a promoter, but I baptized him when he changed his name from Stein to Stone, gave up being a Jew and became a Catholic, account of his wife. After they divorced, Sam married a Protestant girl and moved uptown. Next time I hear from him, he's in the Presbyterian Hospital and sends word he's dying and wants to see me. I get there and Sam's sitting up in bed, a minister on one side and a rabbi on the other.

"'Sam,' says I, 'what is it you want from me?'

"'Fireproofing.' Like I said, Sam didn't like uncertain outcomes. He's been gone awhile now but this is where part of the fight crowd still gathers to make deals and arrange matches, mostly local stuff, Brooklyn, the Bronx, Jersey City."

McNevin snaked through the crowd, shaking hands and exchanging a succession of short greetings. The cops referred to this stretch of pavement as "The Stone Yard," a place they went when they had no real suspects in a stick-up or heist but wanted to pinch somebody who at least looked the part and was probably guilty of something anyway.

McNevin stopped to talk with a short, bulky plug whose squashed, sideways nose looked as though it had been run over by a bus. "This is Toby Butts," McNevin said. "Just who I hoped to find."

Dunne put out his hand. Butts held it in a tight grip. He shuffled his feet, shifting his weight and bobbing his head back and forth. "You smell like a cop," he said.

"Must be the aftershave."

Butts increased the pressure on Dunne's hand. "Cops don't smell like aftershave. They stink like dead fish been lyin' around in the sun."

McNevin put his arm around Butts. "Toby's the best fighter Holy Cross parish ever produced. 'The Manhattan Mauler' was what they called him. Got on the wrong side of the law and was sent to Sing Sing. Isn't that right, Toby?"

"A frame-up deluxe, Father. Cops railroaded me for a heist I'd nothin' to do with. Seven years in the can for nothin'. My best fightin' years."

"I'm a private eye, not a cop." Dunne winced from the pain of his squeezed fingers.

"Fintan Dunne is an old friend, Toby, a buddy from the war."

Butts released his grip, put his fists up, and threw a short jab that stopped an inch shy of Dunne's jaw. "Wish they'd stick me in the ring with a different cop every day, wouldn't stop till I'd smashed up the lot of 'em."

"Toby lives down by the river, in Hoover Flats," McNevin said.

"Beats the Bowery or the flops on Tenth. Less chance of gettin' your throat slit."

"Dunne here is trying to find a pal of his he thinks might be living down there. Lynch is the name."

"Pat Lynch?" Butts asked.

"Always knew him by Lynch. Didn't use any other moniker," Dunne said.

"Gotta be Pat. Gettin' a word outta him was like wringin' water from a rock."

"Still there?"

"Cops showed up one day and took him in. For what, I don't know. Pat wouldn't say. They banged him around. Then he skedaddled. No forwardin' address."

"Where'd he go?"

"Maine, California, somewhere in between. That's his business, not mine." Butts tipped his cap to McNevin and said he had to be going. He threw another practice jab at Dunne. "Wasn't for Father McNevin, I'd swear you was a cop."

McNevin exchanged small talk with a few more of the men. On the way back to Holy Cross, he stopped at the 18th Precinct House, on West Forty-seventh Street, "I'll ask about Pat Lynch while I'm here," he said. Dunne waited in the vestibule. A sporadic influx of patrolmen went by without noticing him, their attention focused on the hoodlums they had in tow, mostly punks who'd dropped out of school to practice the neighborhood arts of rolling drunks, pilfering from the docks or staging nickel-and-dime holdups, the small timers who'd spend their lives keeping the cops busy and causing them to hate their jobs.

"I talked to the captain," McNevin said when he returned. "He never heard of Pat Lynch. He said it was probably the boys from Headquarters brought him in."

"Headquarters usually lets the local captain know when they operate in his territory."

"I don't think he'd lie to me. I hear his confession every Saturday."

"Didn't say it was a lie, just that it's odd they'd go around him like that."

"That's why he's a captain. He knows how to play the game, especially when to keep his trap shut." McNevin put on his hat and gave it a gentle tap. "It's same as in the church. Best parishes go to the best politicians."

The housekeeper greeted Dunne with undisguised displeasure. Learning he'd been invited to stay to dinner, displeasure gave way to distress. She disappeared into the kitchen, grumbling to herself. McNevin took Dunne into the back parlor and made highballs. He did most of the talking, the bulk of it about their time in France, and seemed to appreciate Dunne's company. The heavy meal of potatoes and lamb chops, served by the silently hostile housekeeper, left Dunne drowsy. McNevin had a cigar and a glass of port, which Dunne declined. Afterwards, he took his leave. The tropical wetness on Forty-second Street did nothing to revive him.

He followed the street west, toward the river. An attractive blonde in a low-cut red dress smoked a cigarette in the entrance of a taxi-dance hall on the corner of Ninth. She smiled at Dunne, an inviting, suggestive smile, the smile of all the girls in the red dresses in the taxi-dance halls around Times Square, the too many halls and too many girls. Oversupply, too many goods, not enough demand, that's what the papers said drove the country into such a long Depression: the more people out of work, the lower the demand; the lower the demand, the more people out of work. The girls in the red dresses knew all about it. They got only a nickel on every dime ticket, often less, some places as little as two or three cents. Too many girls in red dresses meant she'd be working all night.

"How about a dance, handsome?" The white lights on the marquee shone on her pale skin. She had the complexion of a farm girl raised on milk and cream in one of those cold, northern places where the kids were bundled up most of the time, till they grew up and moved away to find their fortunes in the big city, their uncovered flesh as clear and unspotted as snow. Didn't take too long before the city turned it to slush.

"Some other time."

"I'll be waiting for you." She licked the tip of her cigarette.

The cobblestones on Twelfth Avenue were slippery wet. The hum of the highway overhead flowed like an electric current down the iron supports into the street. Behind a frayed, corroded wire fence was a huddle of tarpaper shacks; beyond, on the mist-shrouded river, the gigantic bulk of a passenger liner glided slowly toward the harbor's mouth. The sudden, explosive blare of its horn momentarily drowned out the heckle of horns, whistles, bells, the argument of the New York waterfront.

Dunne was through the fence when a hand took hold of his shoulders with the force of an iceman's forceps, twirled him around, and tossed him against the wall of a darkened shack, his right arm twisted upward into the hollow between his shoulder blades. He tried to turn and look behind, but his arm was jerked higher. He yelped with pain. "Keep your trap shut," a voice whispered in his ear. The sugary, chemical smell of cheap wine blew into his face. Another pair of hands patted him down from armpits to ankles and lifted his wallet from his back pocket. Suddenly, his arm was let go and a flashlight shone directly into his face.

"This is private property, no trespassers allowed."

"I'm looking up a friend." Dunne could make out two forms behind the light.

"Who'd that be?"

"Toby Butts."

"Toby Butts ain't no friend of yours." The flashlight turned upright, its beam giving Toby Butts's lumpy, boiled-potato face a weird glow. "Figured you'd show here sooner instead of later. Ol'

Toby knows the way cops think. Rats with cheese. Once they get a smell, can't stay away."

"Already told you, Toby. I'm not a cop."

"Then you was or maybe is plannin' to be. Save your breath denyin' it 'cause ol' Toby ain't gonna be convinced otherwise."

"Forty bucks in his wallet," said a voice from behind Toby.

"Here, gimme that." Toby put the flashlight beneath his arm, held the wallet in front of him and removed four five-dollar bills. "A fine of twenty bucks for trespassin' and wastin' my precious time." He handed Dunne back his wallet. "Now get lost before Jimmy here applies the battin' style got him three seasons with the Cleveland Indians."

"Four seasons, Toby. *Four.*" Vaguely illuminated by the nearby beam of Toby's flashlight, Jimmy crouched in a hitting stance and swung a nail-studded bat. "My best season, I hit .289."

Dunne took the remaining twenty out of the wallet and held it out. "Tell me what you know about Pat Lynch and you can have this too."

Butts chuckled. "Could have it anyways, without tellin' you nothin', if I wanted."

"I'm trying to help somebody been framed, probably with the help of some cops, so if you're really interested in sticking it to 'em, tell me what you know."

The beam left Jimmy and encircled a small patch of ground strewn with bottle caps and cigarette butts. "Hell, you was a cop, you'd never come alone. Cops are like nuns. Always travel in pairs." Butts turned off the flashlight. "All right, follow me."

Butts led Dunne into the camp, with Jimmy in the rear. At the end of a ramshackle lane of tarpapered shacks was a campfire, bean cans suspended above it from an iron spit. The men sitting around looked up but didn't say anything. Toby stopped in front of a shack. He pulled back the blanket that served as a door. "Go on in," he said.

Dunne choked back the urge to gag at the warm, repellent scent of grease, sweat, cheap wine processed into piss. Butts lit a kerosene lamp and sat on a small stool. He pulled up a stool for Dunne. Jimmy sat on the floor.

"Now let's see Handy Andy's happy face," Butts said.

Dunne handed him the twenty. Butts kissed General Jackson's engraving. "This don't change what I said. Pat Lynch left here without a word where he was headed."

"Say why?"

Butts picked at his scalp with a cracked, blackened fingernail. "He didn't have to. We all seen him get pinched on his way up to Holy Cross for a bowl of soup. Two squad cars. Woulda' thought they was liftin' Charlie Luciano instead poor ol' Pat. Anyways, he didn't come back till the next day, and it was obvious what the bulls done to him."

"Yeah," Jimmy said. "He was missin' a few more teeth."

"You wouldn't have a cigarette?" Butts asked.

Dunne found an unopened pack in his pocket that he'd forgotten was there. He tossed it to Butts. "Say why they'd brought him in?"

"Nope." Butts opened the pack, put a cigarette in his mouth, leaned over the lamp and lit it. "He didn't say, we didn't ask." Butts tossed the pack to his companion. "That's the way it works around here. Right, Jimmy?"

"Right, Toby." Jimmy lit his cigarette in the lamp, same as Butts.

"We don't stick our snouts in each other's doin's. Pat got knocked around by the cops. One time or another, happened to every man here. Then he came back, packed up and left without a word. We all done that, too. Could be I'll run into him some day maybe up north or out west. It's a big country. Most likely, I won't."

"Did he mention a sister?"

"Never mentioned nobody."

"Ever go off to visit somebody?"

"Funny you say that 'cause that was somethin' special about Pat." Jimmy squatted next to Butts, beside the lamp. Dunne got his first full view of him. Except for a raw diagonal scar that crossed his nose and split his eyebrow, he had the square, handsome, athletic face seen in ads for cereal or cigarettes. "When he was flat broke and shakin' so bad you'd think he was about to come apart, he'd disappear for a spell. Day or so later, when he comes back, he's on his feet, and here's the part what's special, he spread what he got, stood us all to drinks, smokes, whatever."

"Pat was an old-school hobo, from the days when 'boes was 'boes," Butts said. "Mighta' been down on his luck but he weren't no bum runnin' Sterno through a sock to squeeze out the grain alcohol or, worse, hoardin' the good stuff for his own use. No, with Pat it was share and share alike, which ain't the way with the trash inhabits this place. Nowadays, it's every man for hisself."

"Say where he got it?"

"Look, pal, I already told you, he didn't say nothin'." Butts threw his cigarette on the dirt floor and stomped on it with his laceless shoe. He pulled a dented metal flask from his pocket, twisted off the cap, and took a long swig. He handed it to Jimmy.

"What'd he take with him?"

"For somebody who ain't a cop, you got a habit of sounding like one." Butts took the flask back and had another long swig. He wiped the dribble off his chin with his sleeve. "Pat took what he had. What we all have. A gunnysack filled with clothes, a blanket, maybe an extra pair of shoes."

"Burned stuff, too," Jimmy said. "Stuff he didn't take, which was kinda' peculiar. Insisted on lightin' a fire right in the middle of this warm day and throwin' paper on it. Poked 'em with a stick till they was nothin' but ash."

"Any idea what they were?"

"Never seen 'em before till he took 'em out to be burned."

"Nothin' left to show." Butts had another significant swallow from the flask.

"Well, there's one thing." Jimmy went over to a corner of the shack and searched beneath a wooden crate. He came back with a square, cream-colored folder that he handed to Dunne.

Butts had the flask to his mouth again. "Hey, Toby," Jimmy piped. "Share and share alike, remember?"

"Yeah, yeah." Toby put the cap on the flask and gave it to Jimmy.

Dunne opened the folder and held it beneath the lamp. Inside was a picture of a man in a sailor's hat banging a plump, large-breasted woman. Underneath were more pictures of the same couple copulating in various poses.

"This belong to Pat?" Dunne asked.

"The pictures is Toby's. Was the folder that was Pat's." Jimmy had a prolonged gulp from the flask.

Butts grabbed the pictures from the folder with such force that he almost fell off his stool. "How'd they get there?"

"Put 'em there for safekeeping," Jimmy said. "I found the folder in Pat's place after he went, when we was scourin' for anythin' useful he mighta' left. Was stuck between a bench and the wall. Weren't nothin' in it. Whatever was musta got burned with the other stuff."

On the file tab that protruded from the folder's edge was a neatly typed label: SEKTIONEN 1-30.6.37/1-10. "Any idea what this means?" Dunne said.

"Got me," Jimmy said.

"Mind if I take this with me?"

Butts wobbled slightly as he stood. "Lookin' is free, takin' ain't."

"How much you want? I'll come back tomorrow with what you ask."

"*Tomorrow?*" Butts roared with laughter. "Hear that, Jimmy? *Tomorrow!*"

Jimmy smiled broadly. "Yeah, Toby, I heard."

"Tell you what, Mr. I-Ain't-No-Cop. We'll keep that file, and how about throwin' in them shoes and that jacket. You know, as collateral."

Jimmy moved in front of the blanket that served as a door. He leaned lightly on the nail-studded bat. Somewhere nearby a freighter or passenger liner gave a blast of its horn, a thunderous jolt that seemed to make the tarpapered walls flinch. Dunne put his hands to his ears. Butts said something but a second blast drowned him out. Butts moved closer. Dunne leaned back, lifted his leg and slammed his foot into Butts's groin. He sprang across the room headfirst into Jimmy, who went sprawling into the dirt lane, taking the blanket with him.

Dunne leaped over Jimmy, who lay stunned on the ground. The faces around the campfire barely looked up as he ran by. He scaled

the sagging wire fence and bolted across Twelfth Avenue, falling
once on the slippery cobblestones. He didn't stop running until he
reached Ninth. He leaned against a lamppost to catch his breath.
He'd lost his hat. He ran his hand through his hair and wiped the
sweat from his forehead. He turned to see if there was any sign of
Butts or Jimmy. There wasn't.

"Where's the fire?" The girl in the red dress was having another
cigarette in the entrance of the dance hall.

Dunne fanned himself with the folder. "Out for a stroll, that's
all."

"Come upstairs," she said. "Give you all the exercise you want
and you'll never break a sweat. Guaranteed or your money back."

"Sorry, just spent my last dime."

"Tell you what, you're good looking enough to get a free spin.
Like what you feel, you can come back tomorrow and pay for it."

"Some other time."

"Yeah, sure." She walked inside. Her skin faded to gray
beneath the feeble hallway light. She swiveled on the stairs. "That's
what all the fairies say."

# 5

Sometimes dreams are pure fantasies. More often, they are realities viewed through the lens of the subconscious. Occasionally, they are prophecies.

—MANFRED STERN, *Landscapes of the Imagination*

## ABWEHR HEADQUARTERS, BERLIN

OSTER WATCHED AS CANARIS read the copy of the memorandum. Over several days, Oster had worked with General Beck to get the words right. Beck's instinct was to indirection and nuance. Oster kept stripping away the verbiage, sharpening what Beck left vague. By now, he knew the text practically by heart. *History will indict these commanders of blood guilt if, in the light of their professional and political knowledge, they do not obey the dictates of their conscience.* He guessed from a sudden arch of Canaris's eyebrows that he had reached the gist of Beck's appeal. *The soldier's duty to obey ceases when his knowledge, his conscience, and his sense of responsibility forbid him to carry out a certain order.*

Canaris removed his glasses. "Has he sent it to anyone?"

"To General Brauchitsch."

"Brauchitsch concurred?"

"He's sympathetic."

"'Sympathetic'? That's a woman's word, not a soldier's."

"He said he'd share it with officers he felt he could trust."

"This is beginning to sound more like a sewing circle than a conspiracy. So far it seems to me that Beck stands alone. If he refuses to carry out his orders as chief of the General Staff, the Führer will find someone who will, and if Brauchitsch decides that, as commander of the army, he stands with Beck, he'll be replaced too. That's if he's lucky and the Führer doesn't smell a plot and sic Himmler and the SS on them."

"Beck is trying to build a consensus among the senior commanders to refuse to carry out an order for an attack on Czechoslovakia."

"A mutiny?"

"A strike."

"Oster, be serious. The generals have stood by as the high command has been emasculated and now, suddenly, you think they'll band together to defy the Führer? On what grounds?"

"Because Hitler will not be deterred by rational argument. He is determined to plunge Germany into a war we can't win."

"They've known his intent for almost a year." Canaris excused himself and went into the bathroom. He poured a packet of headache powder in a glass, filled it with water, and drank the mixture. The froth left him with a white, Führer-like mustache. Looking in the mirror, he wiped it away. He sat on the toilet and massaged his forehead with his fingertips. The hangover he was suffering from was the result of too much wine, which followed an argument with Erika. Oster had made it worse. It was one thing to grumble and grouse in private about the regime. There was a lot of that, especially when it involved the arrogance and lavish excesses of high-ranking Nazis. But to propose in writing a military defection, a strike, an open refusal to carry out an order, was treason.

Exiting the bathroom, Canaris hoped Oster would be gone, but he was still there, in the same chair. "Beck will not be cowed."

"That, if I remember correctly, is what you said about General von Blomberg." Canaris opened a file on his desk and pretended to read. He didn't say anything when Oster got up and left. He sensed Oster had been momentarily deflated by the reminder of the speed and ease with which the Führer had turned his would-be puppeteers into puppets. Tall, cultivated, sure of his abilities, Blomberg had exuded the army's confidence that it held final say on Germany's future. "Why quibble over political details when the appropriations for the armed forces outpace our ability to spend them?" he asked Beck. He raised no objection when the soldiers' oath was altered from loyalty to "people and fatherland" to "the Führer and the people." He took it upon himself to stop referring to "Herr Hitler" and address the Chancellor as "My Führer."

It wasn't until the previous November, in 1937, when Blomberg returned from a conference summoned by the Führer at the Reichschancellery, that Canaris saw the first cracks in the War Minister's façade of confidence. Blomberg attended along with the service chiefs and Foreign Minister Konstantin von Neurath. Two days later, he gathered his senior commanders and intelligence chiefs to report on the meeting with the Führer. Eyes fixed on the tabletop, Blomberg recounted the monologue with which the Führer had harangued the military chiefs and Neurath. The time had come for military action, the Führer declared. Within a few years, England and France would be rearmed and ready to fight. Austria and Czechoslovakia must be seized as soon as possible, before the Allies even knew what happened. The Polish question would be resolved soon afterwards. The Soviets were a tiger without teeth. There was no danger of a two-front war.

"Obviously, gentlemen," Blomberg said, "the Führer is the final arbiter of Germany's diplomatic goals, and no one here would argue with him." Behind Blomberg, stretched across the wall, was a large map of Europe. The room's shadows made the vast pink-colored splotch of the Soviet Union appear almost purple. "But there are tactical questions that can't be answered by constantly invoking the word *destiny*."

Beck marched to the center of the map and swept his hand eastward, over Czechoslovakia. "Germany is not in a position to run the risks involved in seizing Austria and Czechoslovakia. A further pursuit of this idea on the part of the army cannot be justified. Told of the Führer's speech, Oster flew into one of his tirades, denouncing the "cowards and toadies" who would drag Germany to ruin out of fear of spoiling their own careers. Canaris busied himself with paperwork, looking up only once to find Oster staring at him with a look that reminded him of Heydrich's inquisitive expression.

*What is it they are looking for?*

As it turned out, General Blomberg's duty to advise on military matters was soon ended. He fell in love with a woman young enough to be his daughter. Oster observed them dancing in the Kadaker Cabaret to the American song "O You Doll." Buxom, long-legged, and blonde, she was an irresistible target for the general who won her affections and rushed her to the altar, unaware of her professional credentials as a former whore. The SS and Gestapo couldn't hide their glee when he was forced to resign in disgrace. General von Fritsch, the next highest soldier, soon followed. Confronted with a trumped-up charge of homosexuality, cleverly framed by the SS, the general wavered between challenging Himmler to a duel and asking the army for its support. In the end, embarrassed and broken, he resigned.

Blomberg and Fritsch out of the way, the military command in disarray, Hitler used the opportunity to step in and take direct and personal control of the armed forces. The ministry of defense was abolished and replaced by the high command of the armed forces. The hapless, talentless General Wihelm Keitel was made its chief.

Sitting beside Canaris at an official rescreening of the newsreels of the Führer's triumphal entry into Vienna, Oster pointed out Keitel in the car behind Hitler's. Like the SS men and regular soldiers around him, like the crowds in Vienna and the millions throughout the Reich, Keitel beamed with satisfaction.

Canaris leaned close and whispered, "I'm told the Führer regards Keitel as endowed with 'the brains of a movie usher.'"

"The Führer insults the Reich's movie ushers," Oster whispered back.

The headache powder hadn't helped. Oster's wistful thinking in the face of the generals' previous inertia only added to the lingering anger Canaris felt toward Erika. It had been simmering all week, since Sunday, when Erika talked him into accompanying her to church. On the way out, still groggy from having napped through much of the service, he was greeted by a woman who acted as though they'd met before. He thought perhaps he recognized her attractive, middle-aged face and exchanged a few pleasantries. Before she walked away, she slipped a pamphlet in his hand, which he presumed to be some pious religious tract until he threw it on his desk at home and saw the title: *Concerning the Situation of the German Non-Aryans*. It was a mass-produced version of the memorandum of the Confessing Church, an indictment of all those who participated in the persecution of the Jews, as well as those who condoned it or were silent. Penciled in the margin was a question: "Admiral, are you one of these?"

He tore the pamphlet into small pieces, bristling with angry resentment at the insufferable sanctimoniousness of those who ignored the brute realities of rebuilding and defending the Reich. Aware of what had transpired and unwilling to let it drop, Erika had raised the issue of the Jews the evening before, ruining what he had hoped would be a quiet, romantic supper. At first, he restrained himself from commenting on her description of the abuse endured by several Jews of her acquaintance. He would do what he could, he said, to expedite their departure from Germany, if that's what they wished.

He turned the conversation to the larger context of contemporary events. He reminded her of the chaos that had followed Germany's defeat and the need to restore order, stability, and love of fatherland. More than ever before, Germans needed to be united as one people. The Jews had never been truly accepted as part of the fatherland. For better or worse, it was too late to change that. "Wouldn't everyone be better off if they went somewhere they were welcomed and felt at home?"

"Most of them have been here for centuries. They feel at home here. At least they *did*."

He reached across the table and took her hand. *What was the use of trying to explain?* "Look, my dear," he said, "let's order dinner and leave such matters to those entrusted with the nation's destiny. Besides, politics is bad for the appetite, or so my doctor tells me." He wanted to make her smile.

She withdrew her hand. Her green accusing eyes sharpened into an aculeate glare: *What is it that drives you besides ambition and duty?*

Instead of culminating in lovemaking, as he'd expected, the night ended with him staying in the guest room. Sleep had been elusive. He summoned Gresser and instructed him to hold all calls and turn away any visitors, particularly Oster. He pulled the curtains shut, lay on the couch, closed his eyes, and waited for sleep, a few moments free of doubts, dread. Trying not to think, he sank into the dark, momentarily unsure if he was awake or asleep.

*"Hush, you bastards! Look what I've caught!"*

*An oil slick glides across the black water of the Landwehr Canal, a herring-shaped membrane. The gray monochrome landscape of Berlin in the aftermath of the Spartacist revolt. In the bleak, influenza-ridden winter of 1919, the Freikorp troops hold the whole city in their grip. They tease the navy man in their midst. "Was you salts got the revolution underway. Took the likes of us to turn the tide against the Reds." The sergeant is as drunk as his men. The warm, revolting taste of their spit seasons the schnapps-filled canteen they pass around. The soldiers are searching the canal for the corpse of Rosa Luxemburg, the diva of the Left, who'd helped lead the unsuccessful attempt of the radicals in the Sparatacist League to seize control of the infant Republic and ignite a Red revolution. The buildings across the way, once prosperous counting houses, are abandoned, windows boarded up, sad, deflated façades of Berlin in the first winter after the surrender.*

*The soldiers troll their grappling irons like fishermen's hooks. Only recently, their commander had tossed Red Rosa in the canal after smashing her skull, but now the government wants the corpse in order to try the murderers. They laugh as they go about their work, knowing that the real purposes are to make sure the Reds don't get hold of any relics of their "Saint Rosa" and the gathering of evidence doesn't provide anything to be used against her murderers. They banter with each other, finally ignoring the reserved but fidgety naval officer who supervises their work.*

*A soldier yells once more for them to hush. "Look, you bastards, I've caught us a fish!" He tosses a rope to his fellows on the bridge who wrap it around a cast-iron newel and haul a dripping*

*hulk out of the water into the air. As it twists about, arms still tight-*
*ly bound behind its back, a mix of silt and spoiled brains pours*
*from the gaping hole in the right side of its head. The soldier reach-*
*es up and stops the body from revolving by sticking a bayonet in its*
*crotch. "What have we here?" he says. He pokes some more with*
*the bayonet. "Not Rosa, but one of her boyfriends, it seems." He*
*jams the bayonet farther in. "And what do you know, our Red*
*friend has an iron dick. Won't the whores of Berlin be glad to wel-*
*come him back from the dead!" The platoon of inebriated, war-*
*hardened men joins in the laughter. They play with their catch.*
*They've forgotten the naval officer, who slips down an alleyway*
*beside the counting houses to a place stranger still, a ruined, sul-*
*furous landscape that looks as though swept by fire. Shattered*
*bricks and the smoldering carcasses of horses and men are every-*
*where. The entire city seems to have been blown apart except for*
*the squat, concrete, bunker-like structure directly ahead. A crowd*
*of emaciated people in tattered clothing waits to get in. Their*
*shaved heads make it hard to tell if they are men or women. They*
*push and shove their way into a windowless room. Wet tingle of*
*concrete floor beneath bare feet. Look down: instead of feet, legs*
*end in rodent's paws, curled about them what seems a slimy rubber*
*hose.*

*It can't be removed or discarded. It's attached, this rat's tail!*

*Don't tell me my brave soldier boy is scared!*

*O Gresser, usher me back from the sleeping nightmare to the*
*waking one. My loyal corporal, get me out!*

A distant voice, a gentle nudge.

"Admiral, wake up. It's time for your lunch."


## THE HACKETT BUILDING, NEW YORK


Dunne stayed away from the Hackett Building until he was sure
Brannigan wasn't about to pick up where he'd left off. Deciding it
was safe to pay a visit, he searched the closet for a suit that was pre-
sentable. The nearest he came was a dark-blue poplin that Lily had

picked out on one of those rare shopping trips she'd shanghaied him on. He pitched everything out of his traveling grip except shorts, sweat shirt and canvas shoes. He stuck the folder he'd rescued from Toby Butts beneath his gear and caught a cab.

For an instant, he thought he was in the wrong place. The lobby had been reborn, walls and ceilings re-plastered and painted, marble floors steam-cleaned and polished, a new brass-framed directory mounted by the entrance. There was no trace of the jerrybuilt receptionist's stand. An attendant wearing a red-trimmed gray uniform and a floorwalker's smile blocked the way to the elevator. He asked if he could be of help. His happy-to-serve-you face evaporated as soon as Dunne introduced himself.

"The landlord's been trying to reach you, Mr. Dunne, for some time," he said. "Arrears in rent are remediable, if a payment schedule can be arranged, but visits from the police are disruptive to the other tenants and physically destructive of the premises. Regretfully, the landlord has decided to seek an official order of eviction." The attendant backed away as he spoke, as if afraid of being grabbed by the throat, an outcome he might have already met at the hands of those to whom he'd given similar news.

Jerroff was on the phone with his door open. An electric fan was pointed in his face. He hung up when he saw Dunne and waddled into the hallway. A notice of eviction was stuck to Dunne's door and there was a dent in the jam where Brannigan and crew had pried their way in. Dunne pushed the door open with his foot. The contents of the desk and file cabinet had been emptied on the floor.

"I tried to warn you," Jerroff said from behind. "I called you at home several times but never got an answer."

"I took a vacation." He ripped the eviction notice from the door.

"The landlord wants us out. I got a notice, too. Only a month or two behind in the rent. Since when is that a crime?"

Dunne walked over to open the window, leaving a trail of footprints on the carpet of files and papers. He started scooping them up and piling them on the desk.

"I listened for your phone when I could," Jerroff said. "But I probably missed more than I answered. The messages and your mail are in my office." He darted next door and returned with a stack of papers held together by a rubber band.

"Miss Corado was most anxious to reach you."

There were a dozen "please call" messages from Elba, several from Roberta Dee, a few from bill collectors, the landlord, and one from Tommy Hines. The mail consisted of fliers and bills, and the envelope that he'd mailed himself after visiting Miss Lynch's apartment. He ripped off the end, shook the key into his hand, and put it in his pocket. Jerroff prattled on about the tenants who'd already been evicted and the jacked-up rents the landlord was demanding. Finally, he excused himself and went back to his office.

It took almost an hour to gather all the papers, put them in proper sequence, and refile them. He called Tommy Hines several times before he reached him. Hines had Roberta Dee's sheet. He said that it took a bit of searching—the name turned out to be an alias—and agreed to meet at Rostoff's at 3:00 P.M. Be a "service charge" of twenty bucks, which was "cut-rate cheap" compared to what he'd normally get, Hines said. "But you bein' an old acquaintance, I'm lowerin' the price."

Dunne barely had the phone back in its black-sprocketed cradle when the doorknob rattled, as though someone were testing to see if the door were unlocked; it swung open with enough force to make the glass panel shake. Roberta Dee entered wearing a black dress and a black saucer-style hat with a half-veil of crisscrossed lace.

"People with manners knock," Dunne said.

"I was afraid you might turn out to be a snake. I was wrong. You're a lot lower."

"Let me guess. You paid the pipsqueak downstairs to call you when I came back."

"Reprehensible, isn't it, spying on people like that?"

"You're in the wrong business. Should've been a private eye."

"I couldn't stoop that low."

"Have a seat."

"I'd rather not. Let's get this over quick as possible. Elba can't believe you betrayed her. Wish I could say the same. Giver her money back or I go to the cops."

"The money is gone, and you won't go to the cops because you know better."

"I thought I'd already met the worst scum this city has to offer. Until now."

"The cops stole Elba's money."

"Come now, a major-league liar like you can do better than that."

"They made it clear they don't want me near the Lynch murder, six stitches and a concussion clear."

"You look tan and fit to me."

Dunne bowed his head and pushed away the hair covering where Dr. Finkelstein had removed the stitches. "Believe it or not, I didn't do this to myself."

Roberta lowered herself onto the edge of the chair, gingerly, as though it might be septic. "You're serious, aren't you?"

"Figured the best thing was to lie low and let 'em think I was scared off."

"Meanwhile Wilfredo is a lot closer to being electrocuted."

"Just have to work faster."

"Why should I believe you?"

"Because it's the truth and because I'm already on the case and the next dick you go to will probably take you for a ride."

"That's the best you can say for yourself?"

"Don't like it, there's the door. I'll mail Elba back her money as soon as I can raise it. Sorry if I've disappointed her. She's a sweet kid."

"So sweet you took her to City Island to watch the sunset. Do you think I don't know what that was about?"

"I wanted her to tell me about Wilfredo. She did. That was it."

"Just because a snake didn't strike doesn't mean it wasn't poised to." Roberta lifted the veil from her face, plucked a silver cigarette case from her purse, lit one, and threw the matches on the desk.

"Suppose you tell me your real interest in this case," Dunne said.

She put the cigarette to her lips and took several short puffs. The chair made a loud cracking noise as she leaned back in it. "You need new furniture."

"Don't change the subject."

"I'll do whatever I can to help her save her brother."

"Too bad he won't do the same for himself. I went to see him. The state won't have to pay anybody to strap him into the electric chair. He'll do it himself." Dunne picked up the matchbook. The cover was embossed with a champagne glass. Above it was a pair of dice showing a five and a two, lucky seven; beneath, in fancy script, BEN MARDEN'S RIVIERA, FORT LEE, NEW JERSEY.

"Play it straight, that's all I ask." She crossed her legs. Her ankles and calves, hosed in black silk, were every bit as shapely as Elba's.

He pushed up his sleeves. "No tricks, see."

"Wasn't your sleeves I was thinking of."

"How about I buy you dinner?"

"Where?"

He handed back the matches. "Ben Marden's."

"You can read." She dropped the matches in her purse. "But can you drive?"

"Seems you can."

"My last time to Ben Marden's was with Clem Babcock. His chauffeur drove."

"Mine's on vacation."

"Pick you up at eight."

"Your car?"

"No, but I'm resourceful. I know where to get one."

"One other thing," Dunne shuffled some papers on his desk. "I need an advance."

"So you can take me out to dinner?"

"That and some other things."

She opened her purse and laid several bills on his desk. "Do me a favor. Try to hold on to them until tonight."

"Thanks." He folded the money and stuck it in his pocket. "Hope you don't mind me saying so, but you look like you're on your way to a funeral."

"Coming from. There was a memorial service for Clem Babcock at St. Thomas's Church on Fifth Avenue. The funeral was private, so friends and acquaintances could say goodbye. Clem's secretary was decent enough to call me. I'm glad I went. There were eleven people in the church."

"Not a lot of regard in this town for the dead."

"Or the living." Softly, Roberta closed the door behind her.


Rostoff's was almost deserted, the post-lunch lull disturbed only by the rattle of dishes as the tray boy cleared the tables. Tommy Hines was in the back, hands around a glass of iced tea. He surveyed the room as Dunne took a seat.

"Got the money?"

"Nice to see you too, Tommy."

"Yeah, sure. Only doin' this as a personal favor 'cause you were a cop. Can't be sure who to trust nowadays, with Dewey and his crowd pokin' their noses everywhere. My uncle goes on trial soon. Gettin' harder and harder to make a decent livin'."

Dunne reached in his back pocket to get his wallet. A hand grabbed his knee.

"Under the table," Hines said in a harsh whisper, "put it under the table." Dunne passed the money to him. Hines lowered his eyes and counted the bills. Only a ten and two fives but it seemed to take him a moment to tally. He slid the file into Dunne's hand. "Don't pull it out till I'm gone. Fifteen minutes, I'm back and the folder is right here on this table, where I forgot it. After that I'm thinkin' to myself, 'Ain't that a coincidence, bumpin' into Fintan Dunne again?'" He jabbed Dunne's shoulder. "Fifteen minutes. Over that, there's an extra charge, and no discount."

The name on the filing tab, Rosalinda Dorsch, was followed by a trio of AKAs: Linda Doors, Rosa De Marco, and Roberta Dee. Dunne recognized the story inside as interchangeable with thousands of other files filled with crimes and misdemeanors. *Born Rosalinda Dorsch, November 22, 1901, on Essex Street. Mother's occupation: seamstress. Father deceased. Charged in Brooklyn Magistrate's Court with vagrancy and truancy, September 1916. Arrested March 1917, after having run away from the reformatory for loitering for the purposes of prostitution. Charges dismissed. Defendant ordered returned to Cedar Knolls. Arrested April 1920*

*while riding in a stolen vehicle with Lenny Moskowitz (AKA Lenny
Moss). Pled guilty to being an accessory. Sentenced to 60 days in
the Women's House of Detention. Arrested November 1923 on the
premises of Georgia Hurfritz's boarding house at 420 Sterling Place
on suspicion of prostitution. Gave false identification to arresting
officer, using alias of Linda Doors. Charges reduced to disorderly
conduct. Sixty days in the Women's House of Detention. Arrested
July 1926, in Mickey Luria's Angel Club, 370 Ludlow Street, an
unlicensed nightclub serving illegal alcohol on the premises. Gives
false identification to the arresting officer, using alias of Rosa De
Marco. Charged in Manhattan Magistrate's Court with resisting
arrest and soliciting for the purpose of prostitution. Pleads guilty
to reduced charge of disorderly conduct and loitering on the premises of an illegal establishment. Ninety days in the Women's House
of Detention. Arrested December 1930, on the premises of Rita
Vander's at 112 Water Street. Gives false identification to the
arresting officer, using alias of Roberta Dee. Charged in Criminal
Court with being employed in a house of prostitution. Case tried
March 28 & 29, 1931. Disposition: acquittal.*

As far as Dunne could tell, Roberta's story was only different in
two ways. First, she'd managed to go through a trial and be acquit-
ted, which meant that the madam, Rita Vander, had either hired a
good lawyer, pulled some strings with a Tammany judge, or both.
Second, although she hadn't left the profession, she'd apparently
managed to go off on her own and not be arrested since 1931. The
way Lucky Luciano had taken control of the prostitution racket
and the massive crackdown that Dewey had undertaken to break
his hold, both pointed to a single conclusion: She was neither a
helpless victim nor the gold-hearted whore of popular legend, but a
tough, independent player who refused to end up like so many of
her co-workers, used and tossed aside.

Besides the rap sheet, the file held two separate fingerprint cards,
dated 1920 and 1926. Mug shots were glued tenuously to them. In
both, Roberta had the same lean, girlish face, glum in the way most
faces in mug shots are. But downcast mouth and hostile gaze didn't
hide how pretty she was. Her face had matured since the mug shots
were taken, lost the gauntness that was undoubtedly exaggerated by

the harsh lighting of the police photographer. Despite that, there was an unchanging, ageless quality to her face, defiance as well as beauty. It flickered in her eyes, something that couldn't be extinguished by cops or johns or the makers of mug shots.

Dunne wrote down some dates. They jibed with the picture he'd formed of Roberta Dee, the lines that connected the dots, like the lines drawn across the sky on the ceiling of Grand Central. *Star light, start bright.* Staring at you all the time, Fin. Tommy Hines reappeared in front of Rostoff's. As Dunne went out the door, Hines passed without a word, went straight to the table in the back and found his file, right where he'd forgotten it.

Searching in his pocket, Dunne found several of the slugs that Hubert had given him. He ducked in a phone booth and called the Shack. He took the lack of an answer as a convincing clue that the Professor was off enjoying some afternoon refreshment. He rode the subway downtown.


Tending a patronless bar, the newspaper spread out before him, McGloin grunted a hello and jabbed the paper with a forefinger stained pale gold by nicotine.

"Look here," he said. "Numbers don't lie. The stock market is comin' back. All those Reds and Commies screamin' about an end to capitalism was wrong. Jacks like myself who held on through the crash in '29 and again in '37, them that didn't panic and sell, our reward is on its way. Just like Jesus said in the Sermon on the Mount, 'All things come to him who waits!'"

A voice from a high-backed booth in the corner, whose occupants Dunne couldn't see, yelled, "Longfellow, my dear man, not Jesus!"

"Whoever it was," McGloin shouted back, "he knew what he was talkin' about!"

Dunne sidled to the middle of the room to get a view of the booth. The Professor was sitting between Corrigan and a young man Dunne didn't recognize. The instant he saw Dunne, the Professor directed the young man to move over and make room. He called to McGloin for another round of beer and whiskey.

"I'm not used to drinking this early," the young man said. Dunne put his bag in his lap and slid in beside him.

"It's not early at all," the Professor said.

"It's four twenty-five." The young man extended his wristwatch.

"I speak poetically, my dear boy. We're at the end of an age." The Professor put an arm around Corrigan. "Look at us. A classical duo. The Herodotus and Thucydides of Gotham's homicides, chroniclers who together have spent three quarters of a century recording the murderous misdeeds of those who prey on the citizenry of our great polis. While in you, Mr. John Mayhew Taylor, we have the avatar of the new."

Taylor looked around with a half-silly, half-sick grin. He reached over and shook Dunne's hand with a soft, uncertain grip.

"Mr. Taylor," the Professor said, "is a graduate of Rutgers University and was editor of the student newspaper. For the past six months he's been working as a copy boy at the *Standard*. Now he's been dispatched to 'assist' me. Isn't that so, Mr. Taylor?"

"What the hell is a 'student newspaper'?" Corrigan said.

Taylor looked at them, unsure whose question to answer first.

The Professor didn't wait for him to answer. "Some would rejoice in the opportunity to work under such tutelage. Mr. Taylor, however, regards it as a 'detour.'"

"I didn't mean it to sound like that. Just that, like I said, I was hoping to be assigned to Europe and cover what's unfolding there. Be the story of the century."

Corrigan plunked his glass down. "The public never gave a hoot about foreign stuff, and thanks to the last war, it gives less of a hoot than ever. Maybe it's a headline at Rutabaga University, or wherever the hell you went, but take my word for it, the people in Canarsie don't give a rat's ass."

"Well, they will. Sooner or later the whole world is going to be dragged in, America included."

"Mr. Corrigan is correct," the Professor said. "When it comes to extraterritorial events, one must never underestimate the pococurantism of the Republic's hoi polloi."

Corrigan scratched above his ear. "Say again."

"The indifference of the common man, the forgotten man. Call him what you will, our dear reader has no interest in the opinions of the Roumanian foreign minister or the grievances of the Ruthenians. He is interested in events only so far as he perceives that they directly touch his life, or to the degree that our noble profession can convince him they do. Thus our enduring emphasis on crime and murder. The screaming headline tells him, THIS COULD HAVE BEEN YOU! Once his attention is focused, he reads on with a mixture of one part fear, *My God, a fiend is on the loose!* . . . and one part curiosity, *Where will he strike next?* . . . and one part relief, *At least it wasn't me.* The more his imagination is fed with gruesome detail, the greater both his relief at being spared and his fear of being next."

"Excuse me, Professor," Taylor said, "but when war comes, it'll not only dwarf the last but we'll inevitably be drawn in. Mr. and Mrs. Canarsie will have more curiosity and fear than they dreamed possible."

"Who cares what those dunces do to one another?" Corrigan turned and shouted for McGloin to hurry with the round the Professor ordered.

"In his own vulgar style, my venerable colleague, Mr. Corrigan, has touched on the truth. In the case of the European situation, the element of fear is missing. Should the citizens of Bay Ridge wake one day to see a horde of plunderous Huns steaming through the narrows, their interest will be greatly piqued. Absent that, especially given the bad taste left from the last fracas, you'll have a hard time selling your war to the populace."

Taylor shook his head. "Like it or not, the next war will be on a scale still hard to imagine. They'll be nowhere to hide."

"Who's payin'?" McGloin stood beside the table with a tray of drinks.

The Professor and Corrigan stared at the checkered tablecloth with the concentrated gaze of chess players. Dunne threw a bill on the tray. McGloin put down the tray and made change from the pocket of his apron.

"Hey, we better get back." Taylor stood and swayed like a tree-top in a stiff breeze. "We're on deadline, remember?"

"Go ahead," the Professor said, "make straight the way. I'll follow shortly."

Taylor tacked an unsteady course across the barroom, using the backs of chairs for support. Finished with his own whiskey, the Professor took Taylor's. "The boy has a lot to learn. Foremost, the world will rotate without him having to turn it."

Corrigan grabbed Taylor's beer. "Once they go to college, they're useless. Can't teach 'em anythin' because they think they know everythin'. College has been the downfall of many a promisin' newsman."

"True enough. The company of coistrels is what I keep. A brood of varlets." The Professor raised Taylor's drink as if to make a toast. "But, by God, it's a vast improvement over the faculty at Princeton."

"What's the matter, Fin?" Corrigan pointed at the untouched drinks in front of Dunne. "Don't tell me you've turned teetotaler."

"On a deadline of my own."

"Good God," the Professor said, "you're not still pursuing that dreadful matter of Señor What's-his-name?"

"Walter Grillo."

"The 'West Side Ripper'?" Corrigan put the beer down without drinking it. "He's gettin' exactly what he deserves. May he rot in hell."

"Ever the bleeding heart, aren't you?" the Professor said.

Dunne groped in his bag, beneath the shoes and sweatshirt, till he came up with the folder he'd taken from Toby Butts. He handed it to the Professor. "This label, SEKTIONEN 1-30.6.37/1-10. Any idea what it means?"

"You know, Fin," Corrigan said, "I'm the one pinned Grillo as 'The West Side Ripper.' I seen firsthand what he done. Wish I was the one to throw the switch."

The Professor put on his glasses, looked at the label, and opened the folder. "It's empty."

"What'd you expect?" Corrigan said.

"Well, in my pre-war days, my reportorial duties sometimes resulted in my attending autopsies at the old Lutheran hospital on Avenue A. German was still in use back then, and since 'sektionen' was how the Teutonic medicos referred to such dissections, I assume that's the case here. The dating is done European style, day first, month second, so this would probably be for numbers one through ten, from June 1 through 30, 1937."

"What's this got to do with Grillo?" Corrigan said.

"That, I suppose, is what Fin is trying to find out. Where'd you unearth this?"

"In the Hoover Flats over by Twelfth Avenue."

"I was unaware that a German medical facility was among its amenities."

"Wasn't exactly a 'medical facility,' German or otherwise, where I found it."

"Wanna know what I think the problem with the Germans is?" Corrigan downed his beer and wiped the foam from his lips.

"No, though I gather we're about to," the Professor said.

"Heinies think they're better than everybody else. And it didn't start with Hitler. Always been like that. Stick together like gum and asphalt, tighter than guineas."

"You micks are no slouch in that regard."

"Yeah, but only to keep an eye on one another so nobody gets too far ahead of anybody else." Corrigan called for another round, and Dunne excused himself just as McGloin arrived with it. He rode the IRT uptown to Times Square and hiked the block to Danny Schwartz's gym, where he rented a locker. He changed into the clothes he'd brought with him. After jumping rope and pummeling a punching bag, his calves and shoulders were warm and aching. He dripped with sweat.

Finished showering, he exchanged a few pleasantries with the man shaving at the next sink and was struck by the similarity of their builds, same square shoulders, tight chest, roughly the same weight and height. Their lockers turned out to be adjacent. When the man went off for a massage, he inadvertently left his locker ajar. Sitting on a bench to put on his socks, Dunne extended his leg and toed it open. Inside was a handsome glen-plaid suit, clean white shirt, foulard tie, a pair of polished wing tips, and a soft gray hat. He recalled the words of Brother Flavian on the two types of temptation: those the sinner sought out and those he stumbled upon. "Premeditation," he said, "is the difference between venial and mortal sin, when will and intellect are in unison."

"You two share everything?" Dunne said.

"Everything but men." Roberta Dee had arrived at the Hackett Building in Elba Corado's car right at eight. She was a better driver than Elba. They went up the West Side Highway, across the George Washington Bridge, into New Jersey, then north. She pulled into the driveway of a large pillbox-shaped building. A valet drove the car into a parking area behind a high hedge.

"Nice suit," she said to Dunne. "New?"

"Sort of."

*Bless me, Father, for I have sinned.*

She walked ahead. There was a slit up the left side of her black dress that he hadn't noticed in the car. The red bolero jacket over it was fringed with black beads. She waited for him at the top of the steps and took his arm.

"You look special yourself," he said.

Upstairs, in the gaming room, a sparse crowd was scattered among the different tables. The window at the far end ran the length of the room, framing a panoramic view of the bridge and, farther south, the Manhattan skyline.

"Last time I was here," Dunne said, "I blew my rent money."

"I'll bring you luck."

Dunne purchased a stack of chips and went to the craps table. Roberta stood behind him, her hand on his shoulder. He doubled his money in the space of a few minutes. He switched to roulette. Roberta put her hand in the same position. He kept winning, drawing a cluster of onlookers. When he moved to the blackjack table, Roberta walked away. He lost half of what he'd won at the other tables in the space of a few minutes. He cashed in the rest of his winnings, which were substantial, and found Roberta downstairs, sitting alone at the bar.

"You took my luck away." He counted out five tens. "Here's your advance."

"I figured you'd stay till you broke the bank or, more likely, it broke you." She put the money in her bag.

"Figured wrong. I've always lived by the rule that the cats and dogs do okay, it's the pigs who get slaughtered." He showed her the roll of bills that he'd cashed in for his chips. "I'll get us a table."

"Right this way, Mr. Dunne, your table is waiting." The maître d' hurriedly pocketed the hefty tip Dunne gave him. He seated them on the terrace, next to the dance floor. The evening was so mild and clear that the awning had been rolled back. Dunne let the maître d' select a bottle of red wine for them.

"Here's to Lady Luck." Dunne touched the rim of his glass to hers.

"We're on the side of goodness and truth, remember?"

"Ever know that to be the winning side?"

"Elba thinks it is."

"Have you told her the truth?"

She took a cigarette from the crystal cylinder on the table. "About what?"

Dunne lit it for her. "About you, Wilfredo, everything. She'll figure it out for herself sooner or later. She's a smart girl, like her mother."

Roberta rested the cigarette in the ashtray. "Excuse me. I need a moment." She removed a tissue from her purse and touched it to the corners of her eyes.

"Take your time." He sipped his wine.

"You figured it out for yourself?"

"Should have known from the start."

"Why didn't you?" She put the tissue back in her purse.

"Detectives and dimwits. You're the one said they're hard to tell apart."

"What clued you in?"

He pointed upward. "The stars."

"What'd they tell you?"

"A story about a girl who learns early how to make her way in the world and wants to spare her daughter all the bitter lessons she's had to learn for herself."

"You're not such a dimwit."

"I didn't buy that bunk about 'goodness and truth' for a minute. There had to be another reason why you'd be so interested in Elba. In the end, I could only think of one."

"In the end there is only one."

"Let's have it."

"Long or short version?" She put out her cigarette.

"The truth, that's all."

The maître d' came to take their dinner order. Dunne said they needed more time. "If you wish," he said, "I could bring you our special steak." Dunne nodded. "Where were we?" he said.

"*Genesis*, chapter one, verse one. My parents met in the needle trade. She was a country girl from Sicily. He was a Jewish tailor from Polish Silesia. He died when I was two, and my mother moved us from the Lower East Side to a flat in Brooklyn, in East New York. She thought I'd follow her into the trade, meet a hard-working stiff like my father and save our money in a jar above the sink. I thought I'd go to college, become a Fifth Avenue doctor, have a penthouse overlooking Central Park, a country home on the North Shore, and sail first-class to Europe every summer.

"Neither of us got our way. I dropped out of high school after a year but there was no way I was going to schlep on the subway every day to Grand Street to sew dresses. I traveled with a fast crowd on Rockaway Avenue. Before long, some of them got arrested for possession of stolen property. They pinched the rest of us for vagrancy.

"Mamma went to the parish priest. He told her to pray harder. Then she went to see my father's brother, Uncle Manny, who was in with all the politicians. He had a talk with the judge in the Magistrate's Court, and I was sent to Cedar Knolls, the female part of the Jewish reformatory, up in Hawthorne. Far as I was concerned, might as well have been Alaska. 'Not to worry,' Uncle Manny told my mother. 'They got a better class of delinquents than you'd find among the goyim.'

"I made a lot of friends at Cedar Knolls. Two of the closest were from Allen Street, where all the brothels were, and they clued me in how working girls found a way to support themselves better than any seamstress or shop clerk could hope for. We escaped together from Cedar Knolls. I won't bore you with the particulars since I'm sure you already made it your business to see my record, except the part that isn't in there, when I got out of Cedar Knolls a second time."

She turned her wine glass slowly, breathed the aroma, and finished what was left. The maître d' quickly refilled their glasses. "One night," Roberta said, "some friends and I were at the Club Trocadero when this gorgeous Latin type sends over a bottle of champagne. He asked me to dance. He moved like no man I'd ever met."

"Enter Wilfredo."

"Yes."

"How old were you?"

"Sixteen, but I looked twenty. I was an early bloomer. Elba got that from me."

"Wilfredo was at Columbia?"

"How'd you know that?"

"Elba told me that much."

"He didn't do much studying. We ended up spending the next few months together. I told him I was an aspiring actress. He actually thought I was rehearsing for a part when I told him I was pregnant. He was shocked and horrified the way boys are when they get reminded of the connection between sex and babies. That's when he told me he was scheduled to go home the next week. I asked for money for an abortion. He begged me not to. Said he'd pay all the expenses and arrange to have the baby adopted. His conscience bothered him enough to stick around a few extra months. But not enough to stay for Elba's birth. I was alone for that.

"Few years later, I would have known what to do and done it pronto. But I was a kid. Immediately after the baby was born, she was sent to the Foundling Hospital, which Wilfredo had arranged, and then it was over. Wilfredo and the baby were gone." She leaned back her head, as if to see the stars. Dunne took another cigarette from the cylinder, lit it. and handed it to her. She took a long drag, then looked down and exhaled. "Did the stars already tell you any of this?" she said.

"Once I figured out why you were so hot to keep Elba from the clutches of the good-time Charlies, the outline was pretty clear." Dunne glanced up at the stars. It was a story repeated an endless number of times in an endless number of places. The philosopher-types called it "the human condition," which didn't quite describe the disparities in the way the worst parts of that condition were handed out, nor dull the pain when you got more than your share. In that case, Dunne knew, a cigarette offered more instant solace than any philosopher.

After a final puff, she rubbed out her cigarette in the ashtray. "Where was I?"

"Alone."

"Alone, yes, and faced with having to support myself, which I managed. I never imagined I'd hear from Wilfredo again, but he wrote me from Cuba and not just a now-and-then note. I got a stream of apologetic, remorseful letters. He sent me money but I sent it back. I told him to stop writing, told him I was working as a hooker and what I needed was clients, not pity. He stopped. Unfortunately, he's always been an incurable idealist. He also has a compassionate heart. Unknown to me, he arranged to have the baby brought to Cuba and raised by his aunt as a cosseted, privileged convent girl. That lasted until the political situation destroyed their privacy and safety.

"Meantime, I'd done what most desperate, lonely girls do. I got married. He was a shining prince, a decorated doughboy, blonde, blue-eyed, and full of fun. We moved to his hometown of Hartford. It wasn't long before I discovered the prince was a frog. Second time he knocked me around, I was on the next train back to New York. Looked up Lenny Moss when I got back. Fixed me with a job right away."

"Noticed right off that when you mentioned his trial, you left out he was a pimp," Dunne said.

"He never hit a girl or held anybody against her will."

"A regular Francis of Assisi."

"Compared to Charlie Luciano he was."

"How long you work for Lenny?"

"Not long. Set myself up in a couple of different houses. The madams were sensible and businesslike. Knew most of the girls were there only until they got the money to do something else. Some were on the greedy side, for sure, but there was no strong-arm stuff, and they always provided a doctor or a lawyer if you needed one."

The maître d' stood by as a waiter brought their dinner. Dunne ordered another bottle of wine, which was quickly delivered.

"That's when Lucky Luciano elbowed his way in?"

"Luciano and his crew ran over the madams, pimps, girls, all of us, forced us into one big combine and squeezed the life out of everyone, especially the girls, and when there was no work left in them, tossed them into the street, or into the river."

"You were working for Rita Vander at the time?"

"You remember Rita?"

"Remembered the name soon as I saw it on your sheet. She was murdered not long after I left the police department. Case was never solved."

"Murdered is too nice a description. Rita was tortured and mutilated. She'd run one of the best houses in the city and took guff from no one. When the combine moved in, she threatened to make a stink. Next day, they found her floating hog-tied in the East River with her tongue cut out. Nobody had to be told who was responsible, but somehow the police managed to be baffled and left it unsolved."

"That's when you went out on your own?"

"I probably should have applied to medical school, but despite all I'd learned about anatomy, I figured they still wouldn't take me. At first, myself and a few other girls simply dropped out of sight. I kept thinking about how to make the system work for us instead of the other way around. Figured out that if we set up ourselves as a system of independent operators, pooling a part of our money to retain a doctor, a lawyer, and our own central booking service, we could protect ourselves as well as keep the largest share of the profits. It would require being highly discreet, sticking to a select list of customers, preferably businessmen, and only taking those recommended by at least two other customers, but I was confident we could pull it off.

"We built up a dependable clientele. One or two of the girls got scared and ran back to the combine, but they never ratted on us. Before long we had a very nice business. Couple of the girls even married their clients. An executive at Time Inc. A congressman. By their own decision, the girls decided to give me an extra cut of the profits for overseeing the operation. The only customer I kept was my first, Clem Babcock. The money was good and, believe it or not, I was afraid I'd hurt him if I ended our arrangement. Funny thing is, now I suspect he kept seeing me for the same reason."

"When did Wilfredo show up again?"

"Two-and-a-half years ago. A phone call out of the blue. Thought it might be a joke at first, a heavily accented voice asking for Rosalinda Dorsch."

"How'd he find you?"

"Part luck, part effort. Wilfredo was a steady customer of the West Side cathouses. He knew I was in the business. I'd written him that much. He kept asking the girls he was with if they'd ever heard of Rosalinda Dorsch. One day, bingo, he found a girl named Lina Linnet, who had."

"That's when he told you about Elba?"

"We arranged to meet at the Bickford's on 34th and Eighth. I didn't recognize him when he walked in, a bloated man in an ill-fitting suit, so unlike the Wilfredo I remembered. The real shock was to hear about our daughter, and the kicker came when he told me that because of the political situation in Cuba, he'd brought her to New York. Had her in a Catholic girls' college in the Bronx but couldn't afford to keep her there and, besides, she wanted to get out on her own and open a dress shop."

"So you gave the money to Wilfredo to set her up in her shop?"

"Yes."

"Then became a customer and had your associates buy their clothes there too."

"Yes."

"Nice work if you can get it."

"At the start it was a charade, yet Elba ran a first-class business and built her own clientele. First time I saw her, I was struck by how much she looked like Wilfredo. Over time, as I came to know her, I saw how ambitious she is, how determined to make her own way, how sure that if she persists, things will turn out all right." She paused and rubbed the edge of her wine glass with her index finger. "I was like that once."

The maître d' reappeared to inquire if there was something wrong with the food they'd barely touched. They cut into their steaks. He poured more wine. They ate in silence for a few minutes before Roberta put down her knife and fork and wiped her lips with her napkin. "There's not a chance Wilfredo did what he's been convicted of. I've been with every kind of man, good, bad, the worst. Wilfredo was always a gentleman, and though he drank, he was one of the few who, the more he had, the quieter and more passive he became. The prosecution painted him as half man, half animal, and the reporters' only interest was in hurrying him along to the electric chair."

"Wilfredo helped in that regard."

"He wants to die out of shame at the monster the papers pictured him as."

"He's close to getting his wish."

"Elba can't let go. She's been torn apart by this. She hired one detective who took her money and tried to take her to bed. I straightened him out and got her money back. Then he disappeared."

"'Disappeared'?" Dunne pretended to look shocked.

"Left town. Leave it at that."

"And you figured me for another?"

"I hoped you weren't. It was as though fate sent you. There I am, standing at my window, waiting for Clem to show up, and I'm staring at this Joe on a bench across the street. He's taken off his hat and is soaking up the sun. I felt as if I knew him from somewhere. Soon as Clem pulls up, he's got his hat back on and is scratching on a notepad. Next week, same time, same story."

"So you turned the table and tailed me? I still find that hard to swallow."

"It was a cinch, really. I knew you'd never suspect a woman of following you. The moment I saw the name Fintan Dunne on the building directory, it fell in place. That cop from Lenny Moss's trial.

That well-built Irish cop with the wavy black hair and sky-blue eyes. The one who told the truth. Not easy to forget a mick like that."

"Why didn't you tell Babcock he was being tailed?"

"I planned to. That's the day he didn't show."

"And the day you sent Elba to see me."

"As soon as his secretary called with the news about Clem, I sent Elba to see you. I thought you'd be looking for new clients. I wanted her to get there before anyone else."

The Ernie Carero Orchestra was in place on the grandstand, a dozen Latin men, brown and good-looking, in white dinner jackets with red carnations in their lapels. Carero, the bandleader, came to the microphone. "This first song," he said, "is for everyone who's ever been in love, or is in love now, or wants to be." He turned to the band, tapped his baton rhythmically on the music stand and the orchestra began to play. A crooner with slicked-back hair and a pencil mustache replaced him at the microphone. He sang in a soft, understated voice, carefully articulating each word:

*Dancing in the dark till the tune ends*
*We're dancing in the dark and it soon ends*
*We're waltzing in the wonder of why we're here*
*Time hurries by, we're here and we're gone.*

Only one couple was on the dance floor. Carero returned to the microphone. "Come on, folks, where are all the lovers? Don't tell me they're all upstairs gambling!"

"Let's dance," Roberta said.

"Not exactly the dancing type," Dunne said.

"Tonight you are." She led him onto the floor, put an arm around his shoulder, and slipped her other hand into his. "Relax," she said. "That's the only secret there is to dancing. Listen to the music and follow me." He looked down at her feet.

"Forget your feet. Look at me."

He followed her graceful direction, the sure push of her body against his. The dance floor filled up. "There," Carero said after the next chorus. "I knew we had an audience full of lovers." The singer held the microphone in a close embrace:

*Looking for the light of a new love*
*To brighten up the night, I have you, love*
*And we can face the music together*
*Dancing in the dark, dancing in the dark,*
*Dancing in the dark.*

From the second floor of the Riviera, where the gamblers were busier than ever at the gaming tables, came a cheer and a burst of applause. "Sounds like somebody hit the jackpot," Roberta said. "It must be his lucky night."

"Must be."

They danced until their dessert was served. Roberta asked him about his life. "As soon as I get around to writing my autobiography, I'll see you get a copy," he said.

She smiled. "Or maybe I'll just wait until they make it into a movie."

He changed the subject, talking instead about meeting Wilfredo and his visit to Miss Lynch's apartment. He took the key he'd found beneath the highboy from his pocket and placed it on the table. "I think this is why Miss Lynch was killed," he said. "The murderer strangled her to death as he tried to force out of her where it was. Raped and stabbed her to make it look like a crime of passion. Probably cut her open to see if she might have swallowed it."

Roberta moved her chair back, putting an extra bit of space between herself and the key. "Any idea what it might unlock?"

"Maybe the motive for murder. I won't know until I find it."


A valet brought the car around to the front of Ben Marden's. Roberta seemed sleepy and asked Dunne to drive. As he got in the driver's seat, he noticed the gas gauge was almost on empty. He stopped at a station in Fort Lee. Roberta's eyes were closed. He rolled up his window and went to the men's room. Above the cracked and reeking urinal was a padlocked dispensing machine. THE YOUNG RUBBER CORPORATION OF CLEVELAND, OHIO. SOLD FOR THE PREVENTION OF DISEASE ONLY. He shook free the last few drops and buttoned his fly. The first time he used a condom was in France. The mademoiselle had to show him how to put it on. She laughed and said something in French about Americans that he guessed wasn't intended as praise.

Back in the car, the fragrance of Roberta's perfume was overwhelming, a scent different from Lily's, less sweet but no less alluring. He put his window down and started the engine. On the other side of the George Washington Bridge, he exited onto the Henry Hudson Parkway and drove north. Roberta stayed asleep and didn't notice that they were traveling away from Brooklyn. He turned off the Parkway, followed a winding road through Fort Tryon Park to the Cloisters, and steered into the parking lot on the west side of the building. The sole empty space was next to a large white sign with black lettering:

PARK HERE ONLY WHILE ENJOYING THE VIEW. NO PLAYING OF RADIOS OR CONSUMPTION OF ALCOHOLIC BEVERAGES ALLOWED.

He tapped her gently. She woke and looked around. "Where are we?"

"Fort Tryon Park, the Cloisters. Come on, let's get some fresh air."

He got out and opened the door for her. They sat on the low stone wall that faced the river. A few other couples sat on the wall, enjoying the light breeze. Radios played softly in several of the cars. In the rear of the lot, close to the looming tower of the Cloisters, a row of cars was tucked deep into the shadows. Satisfied with what they had, cool night air, stars, river, the moonlight on it, bodies at rest content to stay at rest, none of the river gazers bothered to peer or intrude.

He lit a cigarette and offered her one. She held hers to his, sucking on it until the tip flared red. She took his hand, and they sat watching the Hudson River in silence.

To the left, the bridge spanned the moon-streaked river, a looming latticework of steel and cable that was at once massive and graceful. South of the bridge was Palisades Amusement Park. Its searchlights played across the night sky as though it were the roof of a vast tent. From below came the steady *thrum* of tires on asphalt that could be mistaken for the faint echo of Palisades Park, a drone of laughter and screams, the monotone exhilaration of crowds sharing the same fright or thrill.

By the time they got back in the car, the lights across the river had been turned off and the park seemed to have magically disappeared. "You can drive to your place," Roberta said. "I'll take it from there."

He drove down Broadway. She was asleep again in a few minutes. He decided to let her sleep, drive her home to Brooklyn, and take a cab back.

As they crossed the Brooklyn Bridge, the horizon shaded toward blue. It was the moment Dunne enjoyed most when he'd worked the nightshift on homicide, the city momentarily balanced between night and day. Partygoers, bakers, printers, cops, office cleaners, insomniacs out of necessity or choice were getting into bed as the city's sleepers started to put aside the covers, stretching, scratching, trying either to remember or forget their dreams: a pause in the day's routine, when even the crime rate fell.

Dunne looked in the rearview mirror. A black sedan was some distance behind, two men in the front seat. He switched on the radio. A cheery voice hawked Ivory Soap, as a xylophone mimicked the happy ascent of soap bubbles. He slowed down. The sedan slowed too. He made a sharp left onto Atlantic Avenue, running a red light, and pulled over on Flatbush Avenue in front of Bickford's Cafeteria, which was brightly lit and filled with early-morning customers.

Roberta woke with a confused look on her face. "What's going on?"

The sedan pulled up behind them. Both men got out. They flanked the car. The one on Dunne's side produced a badge and said, "I'm Agent Lundgren of the FBI."

"Didn't know the FBI was in charge of red lights," Dunne said.

Another sedan pulled up behind the first. Two more FBI-types got out. One of them reached in, unlocked Dunne's door, and swung it open. "Please step out slowly." He cuffed Dunne's hands behind his back. Another agent did the same to Roberta. The agents hustled them into the backseat of the second car. Dunne leaned forward. The handcuffs were tight and uncomfortable. Agent Lundgren got in the passenger seat. When Dunne complained about the cuffs, Lundgren stepped outside. Dunne whispered to Roberta the address of Cassidy's Bar. "Call me there," he said. "No place else."

Camera around his neck, Sniffles Ott stood a few feet away as Lundgren adjusted Dunne's cuffs. "Made my night, Fin. Here's me sippin' a cup of coffee, thinkin' I wasted a whole shift without takin' a single worthwhile snap, and who rolls up to get himself arrested but you'se!" He readied his camera to take a picture.

Lundgren put his hand in front of the lens. "I'd ask that you stop, or I'll be required to detain you for interfering with an arrest by the FBI."

"G-men? What'd you do this time, Fin, rob a bank?"

"Worse, I ran a red light."

"That's a federal offense?"

Dunne inclined his head toward Lundgren. "Ask him."

Sniffles had his camera in position again. Lundgren put Dunne back in the car and aimed a finger at Sniffles. "I tell you to desist, I mean desist. Try again, I'll confiscate the camera."

Once Lundgren was in the passenger seat, the agent who took the wheel made a U-turn and headed down Flatbush, toward Manhattan. Lundgren used the hand receiver on the two-way radio to report that "the suspects had been successfully apprehended" and that they should be "returned shortly." As they merged into the traffic headed for the Brooklyn Bridge, he swiveled around and rested his left arm on the back of the front seat.

"You're under arrest, Mr. Dunne, for transporting a woman across state lines for immoral purposes."

Roberta seemed unsure whether she was truly awake or mired in an unpleasantly realistic dream. "Is this some sort of joke?"

"It's no joke, ma'am. There are any number of female inmates in the Federal Industrial Institution, in Alderson, West Virginia, who can testify to the seriousness with which the Bureau regards the Mann Act. Some of them have been put there by the Director himself, who's personally involved himself in apprehending violators."

"Since when is it a crime to take a car ride to New Jersey?"

"Miss Dee, let's not kid each other. I'm aware of who you are.

You know what the Mann Act is and, no offense, what's meant by 'immoral purposes.'"

"The only immorality was the price of the steak at Ben Marden's."

"The Mann Act doesn't require an 'overt act.' The crime was complete the moment you and your companion crossed the state line with immoral purpose. I'm afraid it won't take much to convince a jury what the two of you were up to."

The Manhattan-bound traffic was heavier than when they'd crossed the bridge earlier. An accident had slowed traffic to a crawl. In the distance, a small fleet of yachts, sails taut with wind, moved past Governors Island. Farther out an ocean liner proceeded with majestic certainty toward the Narrows and the open sea. The car inched forward. The ocean liner grew smaller.

Roberta looked away from the window directly at Lundgren. "This is ridiculous," she snapped. "For a car ride and dinner, you send people to the federal stir in Asshole, West Virginia? Law or not, it's goddamn ridiculous."

"If I was a lady, I certainly wouldn't talk that way."

"I was a G-man, I'd chase real criminals not act like a glorified truant officer."

"Save your breath," Dunne said. "He's only doing his job."

They rode in silence until they pulled up behind the Federal Courthouse on Foley Square. At the elevator bank, the other agent shepherded Roberta toward an adjoining corridor.

"I thought we were being booked together," she said.

"First, a female attendant will do a search and see to any personal needs," Lundgren said.

The elevator arrived. "Wasn't such a lucky night after all," Fin said. "Sorry."

Lundgren barked out a floor number to the operator and ensconced himself in the back. Poised and self-assured, without a trace of intimidation, Roberta paused to blow an imaginary kiss in their direction.

In a small room on the fifteenth floor, Lundgren removed the cuffs and left him alone. Except for a table, chairs, and a ceiling fixture that was both a light and a fan, the room was bare. The single window was covered with wire mesh. Below, the East River was busy with barges and ships. Midstream, a tug, struggling against a swift outgoing tide, appeared to be standing still as it inched upriver. Leaning close to the mesh, Dunne tried to look northwards, toward Drydock Street, the old neighborhood. His father turned that same corner every night. Sometimes Big Mike was singing loudly, not drunk, but lubricated enough to sing in a loud, pleasing way. A happy moment when he was like that.

He heard the door open and close behind him. "I wouldn't waste my time looking for a way out, Mr. Dunne. There is none."

He kept his face angled to the mesh. "Quite a view. You should sell tickets."

The fat slap of a folder sounded on the tabletop. "Enjoy it. Where you're going the views will be decidedly less expansive."

Dunne pulled a chair away from the table and sat. The man across from him jotted notes in the folder. "I'm Michael McCarthy, assistant U.S. Attorney." He didn't look up. "You're in serious trouble, Mr. Dunne. I suppose you realize that."

"If taking a date to dinner in Jersey is the charge, I plead guilty."

McCarthy closed the folder. He twisted the cap back on his fountain pen and placed it in his shirt pocket. "You were at Ben Marden's, a notorious carpet palace that serves as a hangout for gangsters and gamblers." He had the broad shoulders of a football player and a head of thick, reddish blond hair that matched one of the colors in his plaid bow tie. Nice combination of brawn and good looks, with just the right dose of boyish innocence. Juries probably loved him. "You were accompanied by a woman who has an extensive police record that includes several arrests for prostitution."

"If you want to frame me, you'll need to do better. How about tax evasion? Maybe I don't really put a quarter in the collection basket every Sunday."

"This office has never 'framed' anyone, and if the accusation came from a more reputable source, I'd resent it. But you're someone no prosecutor, no matter how unscrupulous, would have to frame."

"You didn't go to all this trouble just to nail me on a Mann Act violation. You know I'm not involved in transporting girls across state lines. The sooner you say what this is about, the sooner we can get to real business."

"Oh, this *is* real. And serious." McCarthy's folded hands had the same light sprinkling of freckles as his face. "But you're right. The Mann Act violation, serious though it is, is overshadowed by your involvement with a known swindler who's passed from mail fraud to arranging the transportation and disposition of stolen vehicles across state lines. Don't try to tell me that you've never heard of Emile Jerroff."

"He can't even pay the rent."

"I didn't say he was successful. He's new to this racket and hasn't been circumspect. But then, that building you inhabit is a rat's nest of pornographers, shysters, and con artists of every type. Once the FBI got Jerroff in their sights, it wasn't long before they noticed his close association with you."

McCarthy paged through the file until he found what he was looking for. "Agent Warren Tucker followed you from a meeting with Jerroff and an unidentified female. You spent the night in a bar that serves liquor after the legal closing hour. Next morning, after a trip to Foley Square, you rode the subway to Brooklyn. Agent Tucker was able to ascertain from the building's staff that you were visiting a Miss Roberta Dee. Upon leaving her building, you apparently caught on to being tailed, gave Agent Tucker the slip, and subsequently dropped out of sight.

"The Bureau maintained a close watch on both Jerroff and Miss Dee. During that time, the police undertook an examination of your office in an unrelated case concerning a client of yours." McCarthy glanced up from the file. "That client had committed *murder*. In your absence, the Bureau established that, like Jerroff, Miss Dee had an extensive criminal record. It was also observed that Jerroff made frequent use of your office and phone, regularly arranging for the transport of stolen vehicles to the Trust-tee Garage and Repair Shop in Bridgeport, Connecticut, where they're repainted and prepared for resale through New England."

"Let me take a wild guess where this all leads," Dunne said. "Either I stand trial on the Mann Act violation or turn informer on

Jerroff, help you get the evidence you need to put him away, and receive a slap on the wrist for myself."

"Without suggesting a formal offer and barring the possibility of other crimes coming to light, the U.S. Attorney's office might be open to some arrangement."

"And after Jerroff, I suppose, I could play professional informer full-time, maybe even incriminate the guy in the office on the other side of mine. Who knows? I might help put the whole Hackett Building behind bars."

"A far-fetched but not undesirable possibility."

"I got two words for you, McCarthy, and they're not happy birthday."

"I have two words for you, Dunne. *Think again*. Think about the certainty of not only losing your license but of doing hard time in federal prison." McCarthy put the folder under his arm and went to the door. "Think what it'll be like to emerge from the pen in five or ten years with no way to make a living."

"I thought in America the accused still got to make a phone call."

"I'll see about a phone. Meantime, think over what I said."

A wave of exhaustion washed over Dunne. He lay his head on the desk and fell asleep. When he woke, the sun was on the other side of the harbor, more than halfway through its daily commute from Brooklyn to New Jersey. He returned to the window. Except for the alteration in the light and the fact that the tide was now running in instead of out, it was the same scene as before. In a city precinct house, the cops could usually be relied on to make sure the most recent arrival wasn't left idle or bored. Work him over till either he spilled his guts, they got tired, or a more inviting prospect showed up.

Another hour passed before McCarthy reappeared. "We're sending out for food."

"Make mine steak."

"Ham salad or chicken salad sandwich, that's the choice."

"Forget the food. I need to make a call. No call, no deal."

"Your only ticket out of here is the deal I offered. You call a lawyer, better be a damned good one."

"For once we agree."

McCarthy led him to a small office. The framed diplomas on the wall testified it was McCarthy's. "One call," he said. "I'll be right outside the door."

*One call.* The secretary who answered at the other end did so in the way any good executive secretary would under the circumstances: "Sorry, sir, Colonel Donovan's unavailable, but I'll give him your message. Yes, Mr. Dunne, I'll tell him it's urgent." She hung up before he could start the next sentence.

McCarthy delivered Dunne to the same room as before. "Think some more." He grinned as he closed the door.

Dunne put the phone number back in his wallet. He had carried it there a long time. He'd copied it down without consciously believing he'd use it, keeping it less as a resource than as a reminder of a spontaneous decision to risk his life. Maybe all such decisions were spontaneous, but every soldier went into battle with his own expectations, and Dunne's didn't include jumping into a smoldering trench as the screech of the next shell retraced the trajectory of the first.

*He staggers badly under Donovan's weight at first. Donovan yells to put him down and run. Dunne hurtles several yards, Donovan's weight adding to his momentum, and falls into the nearest hole just as the shell strikes. He lies there for several minutes, struggling to catch his breath, unsure if he's been hit.*

*"You all right?" Donovan is stretched prone next to him. Their faces almost touch.*

*Dunne nods. He says nothing but thinks of the one expectation he'd brought to France: he'd take death before he'd desert his buddies; otherwise, he wasn't going out of his way, and that goes double for officers. Live and learn, Fin.*

McCarthy returned an hour later. Grimly silent, he escorted Dunne back to his office. The door was shut. "Your lawyer's inside." He turned and walked away.

Opening the door, Dunne was nonplussed to see a short, stocky man in a white dinner jacket pacing back and forth. He stopped immediately and shook Dunne's hand. "Please, take a seat," he said, pushing aside his hat and some files piled on the desk. He positioned himself sideways in the place he'd cleared. "You're in some fix." He took a gold lighter and pack of cigarettes from his jacket pocket. He offered one to Dunne.

Dunne stuck the cigarette in his mouth and inserted it into the lighter's flame. The lighter was engraved with the same initials as the man's gold cufflink, WJD. Some men made a practice of attending the regimental reunions. Not Dunne. It had been almost twenty years since he'd last seen Colonel Donovan. That final handshake at the end of the parade down Fifth, when the regiment disbanded. After, there'd only been a few phone calls. Yet, though grayer and stouter, Donovan hadn't changed that much. Recovered from his momentary mental scramble, Dunne didn't need any more prompting. "Colonel," he said, "I didn't mean to drag you here in person. I thought we could talk on the phone."

"I wasn't getting anywhere with Mr. McCarthy on the phone. Now he's fully explained what he intends to charge you with. Is it true?"

"It's a set-up."

"You're innocent of everything?"

"Innocent of what he accuses me of, yes."

"On your word."

"Yes."

"All right, I'll see what I can do." Donovan picked up his hat. "I'm on my way to a dinner. I'll talk with someone who might be of help. Still, no matter what happens tonight, you're going to need legal representation. Call my office in the morning."

"I'm very grateful to you."

Donovan started toward the door, then paused. "When I first identified myself to Mr. McCarthy on the phone, he volunteered that I was one of his heroes. When he learned the reason for my call, it was a great disappointment. Men hate nothing more than to lose their heroes. I'm counting on the fact that you're telling me the truth." He left without closing the door.

If McCarthy was surprised by the brevity of their meeting, he didn't say so when he returned. Nor did he express any curiosity about why a former assistant attorney general of the United States, U.S. Attorney for the Western District of New York, candidate for governor, winner of the Congressional Medal of Honor, and highly respected lawyer had involved himself. Donovan was right, Dunne surmised. Anything was better for McCarthy than discovering war heroes and paragons of the law were in the clutches of lowlifes and criminals.

Dunne didn't volunteer an explanation: two bewildered, frightened men in a blasted, smoking hole had reached an unspoken but inalterable estimation of each other.

It didn't lend itself to explanation.

McCarthy's face was slumped and pale. The undone bowtie hung around his neck like a loose thread that, if pulled hard enough, would make him unravel.

"My constitutional right to relieve myself has been violated," Dunne said.

"There's a public restroom at the end of the corridor." McCarthy nodded toward the open door. "Use it on your way out."

"I'm free to go?"

"For now. But don't imagine you're going to get away with anything. This inning goes to you. The game's still got a long way to go."

"Win some, lose some. What about Miss Dee?"

"She doesn't have the same friends you do."

"I didn't cross the state line with immoral purpose, neither did she. Last I heard, it wasn't a crime to grind your own organ. Or has there been a change of policy?"

"Since you've been direct with me, Dunne, I'll return the favor." McCarthy cleared his throat. "My father spent his career walking a beat in the Bronx and never took so much as a dishonest cent. He was an honorable, hard-working cop who managed to put three sons through Fordham University. But due to scum like you, men who drag the entire profession into the gutter, honest cops live under a shadow of corruption and suspicion. You disgust me. You're a walking disgrace."

"That's not a crime, either."

"Don't think I'm finished with you, Dunne, because I'm not."

"Next time I'll be sure to order the chicken salad."

WALL STREET, NEW YORK

Donovan spent the next morning working on the pile of legal briefs that had accumulated in his absence. He tried to put out of his head the memories that last night's visit with Fintan Dunne had stirred. Faces of the dead. Scanlon's startled expression. Three boys cowering at the moment before death. *Are you all right, Major Donovan?* Dunne was the last person in the world he'd expected to hear from. The evening before, when he'd finished dressing in his office for the Bar Association dinner and glanced at his list of unreturned phone calls, he almost skipped over Dunne's name, which was halfway down the list. A question mark drew his attention: *Fintan (?) Dunne.* He'd buzzed his secretary on the intercom and asked her to step into his office.

"Fintan Dunne," he said, "What did he want?"

"He wouldn't say. Just that it was urgent. Colonel, your bowtie is crooked."

"Did he say where he was?" He lifted his chin.

"He said hardly anything, except that he needed to speak with you and that you'd know who he was." She stood close and adjusted his tie. "Your car is waiting downstairs. You're sitting at the head table, with Mr. Dewey and Mr. Dulles."

"I wasn't sure about the first name of the gentleman on the phone. But he hung up before I could ask him to spell it."

"You got it right."

"He's from the regiment, isn't he?"

Donovan nodded. "Call him back, and let me know when he's on the line."

The person she had on the line, his secretary reported, was a Mr. McCarthy, and he'd identified himself as an assistant U.S. Attorney. Polite but distant, McCarthy was reluctant to discuss why

Dunne was in custody. When Donovan told him that he was acting as Dunne's legal counsel, there'd been a prolonged silence.

The Bar Association dinner had been more lighthearted than usual. Perhaps it was the effect of summer. In most cases, the men's wives were already gone to Maine or Cape Cod or Eastern Long Island, where they'd soon join them. The courts were in virtual recess. Tom Dewey was in particularly good spirits. He worked the room with a practiced bonhomie that seemed almost, if never quite, sincere. He was attentive to Donovan's request and summoned one of his assistants to call the U.S. Attorney's office immediately. After the speeches, the assistant returned and whispered into Dewey's ear. On the way out, Dewey put his arm around Donovan. "It's been taken care of," he said. "I offered my personal assurance that you'd see to it that your client would be available for further questioning. Your word is gold in our profession."

"I'm in your debt, Tom," Donovan said.

"There are no debts between friends." John Foster Dulles said as he joined them. "Just a mutual willingness to lend a hand when it's needed."

Donovan knew the risks to his own reputation if Dunne turned out to be the rogue the feds suspected he was. But Donovan believed, above all else, that men like Dunne were owed something. Huddled in muddy trenches, rats gnawing on the dead, clouds of poison gas filling the air, high-percussion shells raining down, up and over the top straight into the withering hail of machine guns, the wonder was that more hadn't gone mad. The military cemeteries in northern France and Flanders, planted thick with dead, were barely two decades old. Hospital wards still tended to the mental and physical cripples. Anderson was only one of a myriad still befuddled by what they had endured. For what? A troubled peace, a wrecked economy, forebodings of another war.

He'd made it a point to stay in touch with as many of the men as he could. Some sought financial help, and he did what he could, particularly for those with families who'd been thrown out of work by the Depression. A few he never heard from again. Several contacted him only once, usually for some special assistance when they were in trouble with the law, phoning him at the office, or that one time when he'd been called at home, in the fall of 1919. He was just settling back into the routine of his life in Buffalo. The maid called him to the phone in an agitated state. The man on the other end insisted he'd served in the war under Colonel Donovan in France and needed to talk with him right away. He'd called back three times and wouldn't be dissuaded.

He'd taken the receiver reluctantly but, in an instant, placed the name: Dunne. Fintan Dunne. A sullen, wisecracking, skeptical recruit whose truculence in training became bravery on the battlefield, he'd been the one who'd come back into the trench after the others were blown to bits; risked the same fate pulling out his commanding officer before the next round landed and acted as a messenger the rest of the day, running from position to position, in constant danger of being shot. When it was over, he'd dismissed the idea of being recommended for a medal. "Only award I want," he said, "is to get back to New York alive." A boy who'd become a soldier. A soldier who'd seen his own bravery as nothing out of the ordinary.

Dunne plunged into his story without any preliminary niceties. He said he was calling from the State Hospital in Buffalo. His sister had been sent there several years before after being diagnosed as a "feeble-minded epileptic." The clerk in the superintendent's office wouldn't tell him anything except that she'd been released the previous autumn. Dunne put up a fuss and demanded to see her records. The clerk returned with a doctor who insisted the regulations were designed to protect the patients and couldn't be ignored. Dunne said he was heading back to New York City that afternoon and asked Donovan if he could find anything and write to let him know. He ended the same way he'd begun, brusquely. If he said thanks, Donovan didn't hear it.

It was a week before Donovan got around to calling the superintendent and another week before he paid a visit to the hospital's records room, where the file of Maura Dunne was waiting for him on a large oak table. "You may not take notes or remove any portion of the file," the chief clerk told him. There wasn't much to copy. Soon after she'd been admitted, a course of treatment had been decided: *In the case of a patient in Miss Dunne's category, both imbecilic and epileptic, sterilization is as much required as recommended. She is clearly a potential bearer of mentally inadequate offspring, and therefore, a salpingectomy is directed.* A few more pages filled out Maura's subsequent career at the hospital. In March 1915, a physician noted that Maura wasn't dumb, as had been previously thought, but was quite capable of speech. *Patient demonstrated a capacity for reasoning and cogitating beyond what had previously been thought possible.* By September 1918, the file indicated, she no longer seemed to suffer from seizures. Given her marked improvement and asexualization, she was released to her own custody and provided with the fare back to her place of origin. There was nothing more.

He wrote Dunne, reporting Maura's sterilization and eventual discharge, and informing him there was nothing in her file to indicate her present whereabouts. It was several months before Dunne wrote back. This time he offered his thanks and reported that he'd been appointed a patrolman in New York City. He'd been looking for Maura but had no luck.

Until last evening, Donovan had suspected he'd never hear from Dunne again. The number of men who contacted him grew fewer each year. But no matter how much time passed, the memory of the Great War was a tie that didn't weaken. Forged in the blood and mire of the Western Front, their time in hell, it would always bind Donovan to his men.

August 1938

# 6

The shelves in Professor Gerhard von S.'s Munich lecture hall are partially filled with medical tomes and reference works. Interspersed among the books are human skulls that the Professor has collected in his research as a racial anthropologist. An advisor to the SS, the exclusive guard that has superseded the rowdy street fighters of the SA, or Brown Shirts, the Professor has earned a reputation for his vigorous, single-minded pursuit of anthropometry, the comparative study of physical measurements which, supposedly, distinguish the races. In addressing his attentive, note-taking students, the Professor prefaces this day's discussion of Jewish racial characteristics with a philosophic note. The ultimate enemy of science, he declares, isn't ignorance but sentiment. "Consider, for example," he says, "that the average citizen of the Reich will readily acknowledge the demonstrably poisonous effects of the Jew on normal society yet, practically in the same breath, will acquit Jews of his acquaintance as 'good Jews,' unlike the rest of their race." The Professor holds up a skull but finds in it not a stark and universal symbol of our shared human destiny, the way Hamlet did with Yorick. Instead, he describes the cranial details that make this a Jewish skull and put it in its own racial category. "Science allows us to describe the disease," he concludes. "What remains to be seen is whether we have the will to apply a cure."

—IAN ANDERSON, *Travels in the New Germany*

## ABWEHR HEADQUARTERS, BERLIN

GRESSER'S FACE WAS as blank as ever. The expressionless mask every lifer wore. "Herr Admiral," Gresser said, "Doctor Arnheim is here to see you."

"*Arnheim?*" Canaris struggled to control his temper. "Who told you to schedule a meeting with Arnheim? I told you quite the opposite, didn't I?

"Yes, Herr Admiral."

"Then are you purposely acting like a dolt, or does it come naturally?" Instantly he regretted his derisive tone, the bullying style of the martinet that he loathed.

"He has been phoning for several weeks, Herr Admiral, and each time I've told him you were unavailable." Gresser's neutral countenance was unchanged. "But now he has arrived unannounced, with no appointment, and says he has business that cannot be postponed. I'll send him away, if you wish."

"Never mind. It sounds as though he'll pester me until he gets his interview. But we'll make it quick. Poke your head in after a few minutes and remind me that I'm scheduled to be at a briefing upstairs."

A few moments later, Arnheim hunched forward in the chair, as if unsure whether to stay. He held his thin briefcase in his lap. "You look tired, Herr Admiral."

"I'm feeling fit. I had a nap. Perhaps I still look a bit sleepy."

"Naps provide refreshment for the brain. I recommend them to all my patients." Arnheim eyed Gresser. As soon as the Corporal exited and pulled the door shut, Arnheim moved his chair closer to Canaris's desk. "Admiral, I am a loyal German. Have you ever doubted that?"

"Why would I?"

"That's my point. You know my record as a deputy leader of the German Medical Association and the assistant head of the Party's Physicians League."

Canaris was almost certain what was next: request for a letter of recommendation for some position or promotion or honor. Perhaps all three. The purpose of the visit—*the business of great urgency*—revealed itself: a toady's tale. "Doctor, before you go any further, I'm sure there are others better acquainted with your record than I."

"Mind if I smoke?"

"I didn't think you had such a vice, Doctor."

Arnheim took out a cigarette case, removed one for himself, and offered one to Canaris. "I do now."

Declining a cigarette for himself, Canaris snapped open his gold lighter, flicking the flint wheel with his thumb, and held out the flame. Arnheim craned his neck forward, the cigarette held between his lips, inserted it in the flame and puffed. Suddenly, he gripped Canaris's wrist. "Do you know I have a daughter?"

For an instant, Canaris imagined Arnheim intended to take his pulse, but the tight, clammy pressure of Arnheim's hand felt as though he were clinging. After a second, he let go. "Get to the point, Doctor, and do so quickly. I'm due at a briefing shortly." This time Canaris didn't regret his curt tone.

Arnheim sank back in the chair. "I'll be direct, Herr Admiral. My daughter is my only child, a beautiful, gifted girl, a brilliant student, a magnificent musician. During her first year at university, her mind became clouded, she heard voices. I thought it was some fleeting neurasthenic disorder, a symptom of overwork. Students are notoriously inclined to such. I ordered her to take a term off, which she did, but the condition worsened. She drifted into her own world for days at a time, and the lucent periods became increasingly intermittent. I took her to the best doctors. The diagnosis was schizophrenia. Several treatments were tried. Nothing worked. It was as if I were standing on shore watching her drown and there was nothing I could do."

The door opened and Gresser's head popped in. "Herr Admiral, I apologize for intruding, but the briefing is about to begin."

"It'll have to wait," Canaris said. Gresser's look of befuddlement as he closed the door was perhaps the first discernable emotion Canaris had ever seen cross the corporal's face. "Forgive the interruption, Doctor. Please continue."

"A year after she was committed to the mental institution at Kaufbeuren-Irsee, in 1933, the Racial Hygiene Laws went into effect. She was subject to the same compulsory sterilization regulations as the other inmates. My wife pleaded with me to have our child spared. I suppose I might have intervened. But how could I support the medical crusade to save the German people from eugenical suicide, a cause I'd been part of my entire career, and spare my own daughter? If one was spared, why not all? I did nothing. She was sterilized, with the others. A salpingectomy was performed. Her fallopian tubes were cut."

Arnheim sighed and exhaled cigarette smoke in the same breath. "Next time I visited her she had entered one of those periods in which she was in possession of her faculties. She turned away and wouldn't look at me. She has never talked to me since." He slipped a folded piece of typescript from the briefcase on his lap. "Admiral, I'm not here to seek your sympathy, nor do I wish to involve you in matters that don't concern you. I know you are a loyal soldier of the Reich but I thought you should be alerted to certain facts." He laid the paper on the desk.

"Medical matters are totally outside my jurisdiction," Canaris said. The sheet was plain and nondescript, a simple piece of paper. Or perhaps not. Bait, perhaps. To either not report the doctor's breach of security or to express sympathy or approval, both courses would be treason. The rats' attempt to lure the recalcitrant cats to expose their true stripes, bit of fish, whiff of herring, *here kitty,* a few nibbles, a solid bite, *snap, swoosh, crack,* last sounds you hear as the metal bar breaks your felid neck.

"This goes beyond the purely medical. It involves the whole nation."

"If it concerns internal security, it should be brought to the attention of General Heydrich. That's his bailiwick, not mine." Oster's opinion: *Himmler and Heydrich presume the overwhelming majority of the officer corps is entirely seduced and the rest too cowardly to do more than grumble. That gives us the crucial advantage of surprise.* Heydrich's warning: *We will show no mercy to such scum, even though they wear a German uniform.*

"The leadership is aware of what's involved." Arnheim squashed his cigarette in the ashtray. "That's why I've come to you, Herr Admiral. I presume you don't know but believe you should. Reichsleiter Bouhler himself said it would eventually touch the whole nation, that it is, in his words, 'central to the historic destiny of the Third Reich.'"

Canaris smelled a slight lingering trace of lunch, hint of smoked herring that had sat too long on his desk. "When did he tell you about this?"

"Reichsleiter Bouhler invited me to a reception at the chancellery shortly after the Führer's return from Vienna. I thought it was to be a celebration. The mood of the whole country seemed to be of unadulterated joy. But there was only a handful of us. Dr. Karl Brandt, the Führer's physician, Dr. Werner Heyde of the SS, and a few others, mostly medical men. We had a round of drinks. The atmosphere was somber. Bouhler soon asked us to retire to a near-by conference room, where he closed the door and said he had a vital and highly confidential matter to share.

"Bouhler said war is inevitable. Austria is only a prelude. The great struggle against the globe-engirding hydra of Jewish Bolshevism is immediately ahead. Inevitably, this will put such great strains on the nation's resources that a dramatic and rapid purification of the Reich will be required. Up to now, he said, we had recognized that the scientific dictum of 'life unworthy of life' necessitated sterilization of the unfit. They mustn't be allowed to reproduce. But now we face a deeper, harder question: What was to be done with the 'useless eaters' filling our asylums and hospitals at a time when the healthy would need every possible ounce of strength to defend our race and secure its future? In the event of war, how could we best make room for wounded soldiers and prevent the drain on precious supplies of food and medicine by the legions of mental and physical defectives?

"Bouhler asked that we give careful thought to these questions. The principle at stake was clear enough. Kindness to the weak is subversion of the strong. Compassion toward the unfit is treason to the race. Victory belongs to the merciless. What was left to determine was an efficient means of carrying it out. The Führer looked to us to show the way. He said that at least one bold practitioner had been carrying on an experiment in involuntary euthanasia for several years. He didn't reveal the location but said the experiment was still proceeding secretly and successfully. Soon, he told us, the doctor who'd conducted it would be 'back in the Reich' and school us in the lessons he'd learned from his experience. Bouhler warned against any discussion or mention of what he'd told us outside our circle. Nothing should be committed to paper. Not yet."

Arnheim pushed the paper toward Canaris. "I have written down what was said as best as I can remember. Perhaps you think me disloyal. I'm willing to take that risk."

"You're touching on private discussion that, however theoretical, would have grave ramifications if made public."

"'Trust yourself, and you will know how to live.' Goethe wrote that. Mostly, Admiral, I have trusted others to tell me what to do. Our whole nation has been expert at taking orders. Today, however, I trust myself, my own feelings and instincts, and in that trust I find that I'm no longer a eugenicist dedicated to abetting the triumph of the fit and the strong and willing to carry out any order to that end. I'm the father of a young woman whose suffering has been increased because of my callousness. I will not under any circumstances become a willing party to her murder. I will kill myself first."

"It's merely a conversation you were privy to, Doctor. Talk, that's all. No action has been taken."

"Not yet."

"Who else knows you came here?"

"No one. I'm sorry to involve you. I realize it's outside your jurisdiction. It's just that the supply of decent men seems to grow shorter by the day. I think you are one. I couldn't think of where else to go. I'm grateful to you for hearing me out. I hope, perhaps, when you've given it some thought, you might offer some advice about the best way to proceed."

An instant after Arnheim showed himself out, Gresser returned. "General Heydrich's secretary called. The General wishes to know if you'll be riding with him in the morning."

"Convey my regrets. I'm indisposed." Canaris stood in front of the mantel. He ran his finger along the hull of the *Dresden*. On the voyage back to South America from Baltimore, they had been caught in a monstrous storm off Bermuda. The wind-driven swells beat the *Dresden* so relentlessly her engines choked. It seemed she might capsize but the crew got the engines fixed and the captain set her right. They rode out the rest of the storm without further incident. The next morning the navigator was incredulous at their position. "Foul weather or not," he said, "it seems impossible we could have been blown this far off course."

Canaris took the paper into the bathroom. Scanning Arnheim's typed summary of the meeting and the proposed extermination of

Germany's mental and physical defectives, he held the paper over the toilet, put his lighter beneath, and set it afire. As the flame raced up, he turned it sideways, making sure it crumpled and burned, and dropped it in the toilet just before the fire reached his fingers. He flushed long and hard, then again.

He returned to his desk and smoked. After a few minutes, there was no longer any scent of herring. Only smoke.

# 7

Geographically, the Bronx is the odd man out amongst the five boroughs that comprise the metropolis of New York. Unlike Manhattan or Staten Island, which are enisled by water, and Brooklyn and Queens, which are part of Long Island, the Bronx is on the mainland of the United States. It is a stolid place of apartment buildings and modest homes, crowded in its southern and western regions, adjacent to Manhattan, still rural in the north and the east, but everywhere characterized by the aspirational plodding of its hard-working, if Depression-chastened inhabitants, most of whom are only one or two generations removed from the old world villages of their immigrant ancestors. Possessed of a first-class zoo and botanical gardens, several colleges and universities, one of which houses the American Hall of Fame, and a baseball stadium made famous by sports titan Babe Ruth, the Bronx has only one hotel worthy of the name. Rare is the visitor to New York who will spend more than a few hours in the Bronx, though those who do are often rewarded by the discovery of unexpected attractions.

—IAN ANDERSON,
"New York, Home to the Next World's Fair,"
*World Traveler Magazine*

## UPPER EAST SIDE, NEW YORK

DUNNE LAY LOW before he made a sortie to Cassidy's. There was an old message waiting from Roberta: the Feds had let her go. He knew they had. There'd been nothing in the papers. Besides, the fish they wanted was Jerroff. Roberta was an incidental catch that could be thrown back at only a small loss or put on ice for future use. He dropped one of Hubert's slugs to call her back. No answer.

He waited until Red Doyle and his cadre of transit workers were through with their meeting, then went back and spent the night at Cassidy's. Time was running out for Wilfredo. The outcome was guaranteed by New York State. Next morning, after going home to shower and change, he headed to Dr. Sparks's office. He stayed across the street until the car with Bill Huber at the wheel picked up Sparks for his tennis match. There was a different doorman on duty, older and stouter, a Santa Claus build, topped by a round, florid, clean-shaven face.

Dunne went over to him as soon as Sparks's car was out of sight. "Excuse me," he said, "has Dr. Sparks left yet?"

"Just miss him."

"His office still open?"

"Closed too." The doorman's manner matched his jovial, open face. He lacked the guard-dog ardor of the area's native-born knob-pushers; also, his hand wasn't out.

Dunne thought he detected an accent. German, maybe. "Can I leave a message?"

"For sure."

"It's for his chauffeur, Bill Huber."

"You're friend of Huber?" The doorman scrutinized Dunne, displaying the suspicion he hadn't exhibited earlier.

"Didn't know he had any friends?"

"Ja! That the truth."

"I'm with the Health Department. I've been sent to check why Mr. Huber has stopped his syphilis treatments."

"Syphilis! Didn't I know that lug be the one to spread it!"

"You must know him pretty well."

"Don't know him hardly at all. I'm Bohemian, mister, a Czech. The less I have to do with Huber and them Nazi bastards, the happier I am!"

A maid exited the building carrying a tiny white poodle that looked as if it had been coifed and primped at the beauty salon in the Savoy Plaza. "Better watch the language, Jan. Get yourself fired if you're not careful." She put the dog on the ground.

Jan glared at her as she moved down the block with the dog in tow. "Busybodies. Maids is all busybodies, every one the same."

"He tell you he was a Nazi?"

"Did who tell me?"

"Huber."

"He don't tell me nothin'. I see for myself." Jan turned his attention back to Dunne. "When Hitler started trouble over Sudetenland, the Bund march to Bohemian National Hall, break windows, shout and yell. The people inside, at a dance, are made to feel terror what might come next. Next night we Bohemians march on Yorkville Casino, and the Bund bastards are there in their *Sturmabteilung* uniforms waitin' for us. Before fight begin, the police show up and put themselves between us. And who I see with those Nazi bastards? Huber!"

"What time you expect Huber to bring the Doctor back?"

"No time soon. After the tennis, Huber usually drops Doctor at asylum and somebody drives him back later. But I tell you, mister, you want to see Huber tonight, try the Yorkville Casino. A big Bund rally is there this evening. We Czechs will be outside. Go up to that Huber in front of all them Nazi bastards and remind him about his syphilis! Ha!"

"See what I can do. Tell me, if I also had a message for Doctor Sparks, what asylum could I find him at?"

"*His* sanatorium, the one he runs. You tell him about Huber's syphilis, no?"

"I guess it wouldn't hurt."

"Stay one minute." Jan went into the vestibule and came back with a small package. He put on his glasses. "Look here." He pointed at the return label. "This is the place you find him." He read the address aloud: "Hermes Sanatorium, East Tremont Avenue, Bronx, New York."

"A hospital?"

"A home the Doctor runs, an asylum. He's quiet about it. He don't want attention."

"There a street number?"

"You know the Bronx?"

"Enough."

"It's east of Westchester Square, some blocks east. I asked him about it once. He say only it's for them defective or sick in the head."

Dunne tried to slip a bill into Jan's hand, but he pushed it away. "Get rid of that Huber and be me who pay you! Doctor Sparks is a German too, but a generous one. Twenty-five dollar he tip every Christmas! The reason he have a swine like Huber around, I never understand!"

"No accounting for taste."

"But such rotten taste in such a fine gentleman!"


A handful of people were on the subway platform. Dunne bought the papers at the newsstand. He put a penny in a gum machine bolted to an iron pillar. The machine swallowed the penny but didn't dispense any gum. He gave it several hard bangs with the heel of his hand, but still no gum. He got on the first train that pulled in and jumped off as the doors closed. No one else did. It didn't seem he was being tailed.

The next train was crowded. After several stops he got a seat, buried himself in the newspapers, and didn't look up again until 138th Street, in the Bronx. Directly across the car was a woman in a cheap housedress and a small red hat. She had a kid on either side. The smaller one, who looked about six or seven, rested his head in her lap. The other, a gangly, skinny teenager, stared at his shoes. Both boys wore yarmulkes. The woman had a tired face, not old, not homely, just tired.

She caught Dunne looking at them. He went back to the papers, skimming pages he'd already read. The train idled in the station. The lights dimmed. There were places in the city where the Depression mood was lifting. A World's Fair in Flushing, new roads and housing being built, a revived sense of hope, the promise of change, any change. But not in the subway. Here, the accumulated pain and despair of the past decade had been sucked down with the exhaust from the streets. Broken dreams and discarded ambitions mingled with the debris of candy wrappers, apple cores, and half-chewed pretzels rotting in the filthy, stagnant water in the troughs between the tracks. The lights went out completely, then came on again.

The woman across the way rested the back of her head against the green metal wall of the car. She appeared to Dunne to be asleep. *Sweet dreams, lady:* a momentary respite from a lifetime of pennies put away with no effect, gobbled up by the machinery of history, by high-sounding theories that couldn't erase the ordinary miseries of lost jobs, savings, aspirations, an unemployed husband who sat around the house for years until one day he put on his hat and coat, went out the door, and never came back. Sleep was the cheapest escape of all, as long as your dreams took you to a better place. The train left the tunnel at Whitlock Avenue and rattled on elevated tracks high across the Bronx River. The woman woke and gently nudged the sleeping child on her lap. She and the two boys got off at Elder Avenue.

The train was almost empty when it pulled into the Hugh Grant Circle station. It idled once more. Dunne got up and stretched. The Catholic Protectory, which used to be clearly visible from the station's height, was gone. So, too, were the thick forest that bordered it on the east and the pond where the Protectory boys swam. A fleet of bulldozers was busy leveling the ground. Great clouds of dust swirled around them. New streets were being carved out. A parade of tall redbrick apartment buildings marched off into the distance.

To the right, two bulldozers were flattening the hill above where Brother Flavian's garden had been. They went back and forth, erasing the spot where he fell asleep each day after lunch. Chair turned south, toward the sun, he'd sit slack and still, except for the one time he rose from his chair, shielding his eyes, shouting something in French that the boys didn't understand. He gathered his cassock in his hand and ran in the direction of Walker Avenue and the Morris Park Racecourse. They dropped their hoes and rakes and called after him, but he kept running until he reached the crest of the hill. He pointed at the sky and shouted, *Voila! Voila!* Then they saw it too, a speck that rapidly grew larger as it approached. It circled above, drew near, and came so close they could make out the bushy mustache, goggles, and high-laced boots of the man at the controls. Round and round he went. The uproar of the engine that drove the propellers on his double-winged aeroplane drowned their cries and cheers.

That night, in their dreams, instead of sex with naked, willing girls, there was the sensation of hovering above the earth, soaring above the clouds and leaving the Protectory forever. Day after day, they searched the sky for that aeroplane. Vinnie Coll swore he'd find where it was kept, steal it, fly out west, and start a gang. "Swoop in and out in my aeroplane," he bragged. "Them hicks will never know what hit 'em."

Not long after, the New York Aeronautic Society rented the abandoned racecourse at Morris Park for the city's first "air show." More than 20,000 people attended. Biplanes and triplanes filled the sky above the Protectory. The smell of gasoline was everywhere. A plane was forced to make an emergency landing and ran over Brother Flavian's prized roses. "No good will come of such machines," he fumed. "They are the devil's invention!" By the time the air show was over, they barely looked up when an aeroplane passed over. Didn't take much notice again until France and the Argonne offensive. The German planes spit bullets everywhere. American and British planes counterattacked, and the sky was smudged with the black smoke of wounded and dying aircraft. The devil's work. In the trenches below, there were no more dreams of flying but of sex with naked, willing French girls between clean, dry sheets.

Dunne descended from the El at Westchester Square. He thought there might be a cab waiting but there wasn't. Behind the fountain in the drugstore on the corner, a fat, pockmarked teenager in a paper service hat didn't look up from his comic book when Dunne asked about a cab.

"Won't be none till after five, when people come home from work."

"What about the trolley?"

"Comes every forty minutes, except when it don't." He wet his index finger and turned the page.

"When was the last one by?"

"'Bout two hours ago."

Dunne ordered a Coke. "Ever hear of the Hermes Sanatorium?"

"Yup." The kid kept reading as he jerked the soda.

"Is it within walking distance?"

"Depends on who's walkin'." The kid held up his comic book. Underneath the title, *Visitors from Outer Space*, was a creature with a half dozen eyes and a matching number of legs. "Two legs gets you there in about twenty minutes. Six legs, you'd be there a whole lot faster." He chuckled and buried himself back in the comic.

Dunne slung his suit jacket over his shoulder and started walking. The area east of the El was flat and sparsely populated, the sun strong and relentless. He shielded his eyes. Way off, beyond St. Raymond's Cemetery, an aircraft climbed into the sky. According to John Mayhew Taylor, the Professor's understudy, it wouldn't be long before the Germans or Japs could attack America's coasts. As the plane circled over the Sound and headed out to sea, another appeared and flew off in the same direction. The air traffic, Dunne realized, was part of the growing fleet of planes coming in and out of the North Beach Airport. Their mission wasn't military but commercial and recreational. They were carrying businessmen and wealthy vacationers to California and the Orient, whisking them in a day to places that had once taken weeks or months to reach.

At almost the same moment Dunne reached the pitted, crumbling sidewalk in front of the Hermes Sanatorium, the Tremont Avenue trolley rumbled past. There was no sign on the surrounding wall, but it was the only structure on the entire block. A towering Victorian pile of turrets and dormers, it had obviously been built in the days when this section of the Bronx was still part of Westchester and its fringes—hinterlands once deemed as distant from the metropolis as the Indian territories out West.

The latch on the wrought-iron gate lifted easily. He donned his jacket and walked leisurely up the gravel driveway that curved across a well manicured lawn. The slight movement of the lace curtain next to the front door alerted him that his arrival was being watched. The door opened as soon as he set foot on the porch. A trim, youthful man emerged in white tennis shoes, white pants, and a collarless white shirt tight enough to show off his rock-hard build. He grasped Dunne's hand. "I'm Louis, Mr.

Waldruff. We spoke on the phone. Dr. Sparks told us you'd be driving up."

"I took the train. It seemed easier," Dunne said. Obviously mistaken for someone else, he decided to play along and use the opportunity.

"Miss Loben is expecting you." Louis led him into the foyer. It was far cooler inside. He put Dunne's hat in a closet beneath the stairway. Dunne craned his neck and looked up. The walls were painted the same sky blue as those on the first floor. A cascade of sunlight poured through an arched window at the top of the stairs.

The house was airy, cheery, bright, the opposite of how it appeared on the outside. Flanking the stairs were two large, gold-framed watercolors of blossoming plants, yellow nasturtiums, blue larkspur, and a cluster of red bleeding hearts. "I'll let Miss Loben know you're here." Louis went down a corridor to the right, his rubber-soled shoes moving noiselessly across the thickly carpeted floors, and disappeared.

The soft click-clack, click-clack, click-clack of the ceiling fan slowly revolving above Dunne's head was the only noise. He listened for voices, footsteps, any sound of movement. Nothing. The place felt more like a funeral home than a refuge for those whose minds were feeble or disturbed.

Louis returned and said Miss Loben was ready to see him. Dunne asked to use a bathroom first. Louis's smile instantly soured. "Miss Loben doesn't like to be kept waiting."

"I think I'd rather be late than have an accident in her office."

"All right." Louis directed Dunne to a door close to the stairway. "I'll let her know you're delayed a minute." Louis went off in the same direction as before.

Dunne examined the inside lock on the bathroom door. He cracked the door open, reached outside, and removed the key. The door could only be locked or unlocked from outside, a precaution, Dunne supposed, to prevent the inmates from locking themselves inside. He took the change from his pocket, picking through it until he found a coin that fit into the keyhole. It turned out to be the last of Hubert's slugs. He flushed the toilet and stepped out into the empty hallway. He locked the door, removed the key, and stuck the slug in the hole. He buried the key in the dirt of the potted palm next to the door.

"Welcome." A blonde woman, short but well proportioned, approached. Louis was directly behind her.

"I'm Irene Loben." She took her hand from the pocket of the yellow smock she was wearing and extended it to Dunne. "Louis told me you were driving up. Now he tells me you came by train."

"That's what Dr. Sparks's office told me," Louis said.

"Mr. Waldruff, I apologize that no one was at Westchester Square to meet you, and I appreciate your arriving exactly at the appointed time. If only the whole country were run that way, we'd all be better off."

Louis had an unhappy look on his face, like a dog who'd just been scolded. "But Miss Loben, it wasn't my fault. That's what Dr. Sparks's office . . ."

"Not now, Louis," Miss Loben snapped. "We'll settle this later."

"Actually, I enjoyed the exercise," Dunne said.

"I'm glad to hear it. But be assured that Louis will drive you back to the train." Miss Loben dismissed Louis with a few curt words and guided Dunne to a sunny corner office that had her name on the door. A large desk was catty-cornered between two casement windows that looked out on a playground, which contained a slide and a set of bars for climbing and swinging. The ground beneath was covered with what appeared to be a mixture of sand and ash, meticulously raked, no sign of any footprints. To the rear, the high weeds of the Bronx swamplands stretched off toward Long Island Sound.

Miss Loben sat behind the desk, Dunne in the chair directly in front of her. She lifted a pair of wire-rimmed glasses from the breast pocket of her smock and removed a crystal paperweight from atop the lone file on the empty expanse of the desk. "The paperwork is all complete. We just need your signature." Her stare was made more severe by the glasses.

Dunne gestured at the window behind her, where another plane could be seen ascending. "It must be nice to be on one of those planes headed to some lush resort."

"I suppose." Miss Loben didn't bother to look. "But our work doesn't permit such frivolity." She turned the paperweight to face him, as though she wanted him to read the motto incised on it:

STRENGTH IS THE HIGHEST WISDOM

"Of course." Whoever Miss Loben thought he was, he didn't want to say anything that might tip her off he wasn't.

"Dr. Sparks has undoubtedly covered most of the particulars with you."

"He was pressed for time, a tennis match on Long Island that he was late for."

"Yes, the doctor takes his tennis quite seriously."

"He said you'd go over everything."

Her eyebrows lifted above the wire rims. "*Everything?*"

"Dr. Sparks wanted to be sure there are no misunderstandings."

Her jaw tightened visibly. She removed her glasses. "As the director of a public institution, you're correct to pay careful attention to what happens to those committed to your care. But, at the very least, you're acquainted with our reputation for the care we provide to a wide range of defective children—idiots, imbeciles, morons, mongoloids, the feeble-minded, epileptics, those with hydrocephalus. That's why you're here, isn't it?"

"Yes, but you can never be too careful. Wouldn't you agree?"

"Very well, then, let me put your mind at rest." She flashed her flawlessly straight smile, perfect except for a fleck of blood-red lipstick on the top right front tooth. "The twin boys you're requesting be transferred here are both chronic defectives, bereft of parents or close relatives, and have been resident with you for almost a decade. We understand your dilemma all too well. The state legislature of Vermont cuts your funding and at the same time insists you take more inmates. The situation grows worse each year. Even compulsory sterilization seems to make no dent in the increasing crop of mentally diseased defectives.

"The same story, in one form or another, is repeated across our country, which is why this sanatorium was founded. Thanks to private funding, we're able to take a select number of patients off the public rolls and offer a level of care they could find nowhere else.

That's why it's so important to be utterly discreet about the transfer. Otherwise, we would be overwhelmed with requests." She placed a pen on the open file and pushed it toward him. "All we need is your signature, Mr. Waldruff. It's as simple as that."

He closed the file and turned it sideways. An ordinary file, standard size and color, available in most stationery stores, identical to the one he'd rescued from the Hoover Flats. "My one concern is, well, if something happens to the twins."

"Happens?"

"What if they die?"

"In that eventuality, after examining the body for any clues to the eugenic origin of its defects, the cremated remains are properly disposed of. In ten years, there's never been a single question asked. Remember, we only take those cases where there are no close family members, or contact has been broken."

"I have one more problem, Miss Loben."

"Which is?" She gripped the pen tightly.

"My stomach's giving me trouble. I need to use the bathroom again."

She jabbed a buzzer on her desk. Louis must have been right outside her office, because he reappeared immediately. "Please escort Mr. Waldruff to the bathroom."

"Again?" Louis asked.

"I'll be as quick as I can," Dunne said

"Please do." She put her glasses back on and read, or pretended to read, the file on her desk.

Louis led him to the same bathroom as before, and was about to walk away when Dunne called him back. "The door seems to be locked," he said.

"Here, let me give it a try." Louis jiggled the doorknob. "The key's missing."

"It was there when I went before. Please get it open. I *really* have to go."

"It's okay. I got the master." Louis tried to slide the key chained to his belt into the hole but it wouldn't go. "Damn," he said. "Feels like something's stuck in there." He knelt on one knee to peer inside.

Dunne hopped from foot to foot. "God, I can't wait anymore."

Louis stood and pushed his shoulder against the door. He twisted hard on the knob. "Shit," he muttered.

Arms round his stomach, Dunne let out a moan.

"All right, quick, follow me." Louis hurried up the stairs. Dunne followed, still moaning and bent over. Louis pushed open the first door on the right. "In here."

Dunne slammed the door shut. He flushed the toilet and moaned again, but softly, as if in relief rather than desperation.

"You all right, Mr. Waldruff?"

"Yeah, thanks, just made it. Be a few minutes, I'm afraid." He flushed the toilet several more times. He sat and listened. There was no sound from outside. He opened the door a crack and peeked out. Louis was gone. Tiptoeing into the hallway, he pulled the door gently shut. One after another, he tried the doors that lined the corridor, but they were all locked. He stopped and listened. The house was enveloped in silence. The last door he tried, next to the servant's stairway, swung open.

He entered a handsomely appointed office. The furniture was heavy and oaken. The bookcases lining the walls were filled with leather-bound volumes, gold-embossed titles in Latin or German on their spines. He sat behind the desk, its leather blotter stamped with a gold caduceus, and opened the deep, capacious drawers. A few sheets of stationery and some medical forms were all they contained. He was about to close the bottom left drawer when he noticed how shallow it seemed. There was a small indentation on the bottom of the drawer. He used his penknife as a lever. The bottom lifted like the lid on a box. Beneath was a honeycombed box; each cell held a sealed vial. The drawer on the other side had the same trick bottom and arrangement of sealed vials. He stuck one in his pocket, restored the papers to the desk, and closed the drawers.

He crossed to the door set between the built-in bookcases, which opened to a large closet. He pulled on the cord that hung from the ceiling and turned on the light. The closet contained six oak filing cabinets, three on either side. He took the key from his pocket, the one he'd rescued from beneath Miss Lynch's highboy. It went smoothly into the lock. The key opened all the filing cabinets.

They were stuffed with files similar to the one he'd taken from Toby Butts—hundreds of them. The same word, *Sektionen*, and the same numbering system deciphered by the Professor were on each. Inside were photos of children as well as adults, detailed drawings and measurements of skulls and facial features, and pages of medical observations transcribed in both German and English.

He opened one to a picture of a boy who looked about seven or eight. There was an index card stapled to the cover sheet with a notation written in a clear hand: *Maria Savati, age 10, Caucasian (Mediterranean), polio, spastic idiot. Luminal dose administered 21.2.34, 8:30 A.M.*

After he put the file back and relocked the cabinets, he pulled the cord and turned off the light. He was about to step outside when he noticed an electric glow leaching through a razor-thin slit at the base of the far wall. He put his palm against the wall and patted it. There was no latch or keyhole. He kept his hand pressed to the wall and moved it to the right. The wall slid sideways, gliding noiselessly out of the way.

He entered a glistening, fully equipped operating room, shoes tapping loudly on the tiled floor. He toured the large, windowless space. The stainless steel cabinets were all locked. Two steel tables were in the middle of the floor. On one was a neatly arranged row of injection needles and a single syringe, a glass jar filled with cotton balls, a rubber tourniquet, and a bottle of clear alcohol. An immaculate white towel covered the other. He lifted it and exposed a precisely laid out row of surgical knives and instruments. Nearby was a steel basin and, above it, a shelf with a large jar filled with cloudy liquid. He drew closer to peer at its contents. Inside was a brain, pink with white and gray ridges. Typed on an index card beneath: *Thomas Packett, age 20, Negro, epileptic, low-grade moron. Luminal dose administered 9.7.38, 1:00 P.M.*

He slid the panel door shut and was ready to step into the office when he heard the outer door open. He froze where he was. A voice said, "There's nobody in here," and the door closed again. He waited several minutes before he ventured out. Once in the hallway, he turned left and ran down the servant's stairway into the kitchen and through the pantry. The door to Miss Loben's office was directly in front of him. He entered without knocking, sat in the same seat as before, picked up the file from her desk, and dashed off a nearly illegible signature with her pen.

Miss Loben burst into the room just as he finished. Louis and another attendant were directly behind her. She uttered a small yelp when she saw him in the chair. "My God, where were you?"

"Where Louis took me." He handed her the file. "I've signed it."

"You *weren't* there when I checked," Louis said.

"I came down the back stairs."

The other attendant spoke up. "I went up and down them and never saw nobody."

"I made a wrong turn in the kitchen and got lost. I could've used your help."

Miss Loben turned to Louis. "How many times must you be told to stay with the guests?"

"I did," Louis protested.

"You weren't there when I came out," Dunne said, "or I wouldn't have got lost."

"I was gone a minute, but *just* a minute. I waited a while before I knocked to see if he was okay and that's when I discovered he wasn't in there any more."

"If you wish a break, you must ensure your position is covered by a replacement. This is the last time I'm going to tell you, Louis! Do you understand?"

Miss Loben's cold, contained fury made Louis hang his head. "Yes, ma'am."

"Good, then get out." She stood behind her desk and produced a pack of cigarettes from her smock. "Doctor Sparks frowns on smoking in the building but the frustrations of this job sometimes makes that impossible. Do you mind if I smoke?"

"Be my guest."

She cranked open the casement window behind her desk and blew the smoke outside. He came around the desk and stood beside her.

"Sorry for all these mix-ups," she said.

"It happens."

"It's thankless work we're in, Mr. Waldruff. Even those who

grasp the principles of racial hygiene are often either too weak or too scared to follow through."

"Call me Woody," he said. "That's my nickname."

"Thank you, Woody." Her smile revealed that the spot of red lipstick was gone from her teeth. "Please call me Irene." She hugged herself and her shapely breasts protruded against her smock. "It can get very lonely living and working here."

"It must take a lot of dedication."

"What it takes most of all is the strength to do what must be done and to carry the struggle to its end. To do anything less is to surrender the future to the unfit." The puff of cigarette smoke that she let out became a lone cloud in an otherwise empty sky. "But given the proportions of the challenge we face, how can we be anything less than brutally, even pitilessly, strong? The defective population grows and grows. Eugenic sterilization is at best a stop-gap. The great mass of defectives goes on reproducing, constantly multiplying their number and infecting the healthy. The kind of experiment we're carrying out here cannot be replicated widely. Political conditions make it impossible in the United States. But in other places, in a more eugenically advanced nation, conditions are becoming ripe."

"Dr. Sparks is lucky to have you, Irene."

"You're generous to say that."

"It's only the truth."

"We all need to hear the truth, even if only occasionally." She took hold of his bicep. "So many of our visitors say all the right things but they're afraid. You can smell their fear. For all their rhetoric about the survival of our race, they have no capacity for action. They're moral and physical weaklings who've never tasted real struggle. But you have, Woody. I sense it. I hear it in your voice. You're hard. Come, let me show you the sanatorium. Perhaps you might like to stay to dinner." Her gem-blue pupils were softened by a watery mist. "I'd love if you did. I really would."

The sound of tires on the gravel driveway caught her attention. "If that's Dr. Sparks he's awfully early." She let go of his arm, thrust her head out the window, and tossed her cigarette on the ground below.

Dunne quietly turned, went directly to the closet beneath the stairs, and retrieved his hat. He exited onto the porch. Louis was already outside, next to the car with Vermont license plates that had just arrived. The driver, a spectacled, mousy man in a gray-brown suit, got out and offered Louis his hand. "I'm Peyton Waldruff," he said. "I have an appointment with Miss Irene Loben. Sorry to be so late."

Louis looked at him but didn't take his hand. Dunne rushed down the stairs and shook it. "Welcome to the Hermes Sanatorium!" He patted Louis's brawny shoulder. "Louis here will show you inside. Miss Loben is eager to meet you."

"I'm glad to be here at last," Waldruff said as Dunne continued to pump his hand.

"Who *are* you?" Miss Loben was on the porch. She seemed slightly dazed, and it was unclear to whom the question was directed.

Waldruff removed his hat. His darting glances betrayed his confusion. "Is that Miss Loben?" he asked Dunne.

"Yes, I forget that you've never met." Dunne bowed in her direction. "Allow me to introduce Miss Irene Loben."

Looking up at Miss Loben, Waldruff's face brightened. "Ah, Miss Loben, Dr. Sparks has spoken very highly of you. I'm Peyton Waldruff. Sorry I'm late, but I got a little lost. The Bronx is a confusing place."

"You're not the only one who thinks so," Dunne said.

"Who *are* you?" Miss Loben repeated her question. This time there was no doubt it was directed to Dunne.

A trolley sounded its bell as it came over a small rise and clattered along the tracks toward Westchester Square.

"I'd love to continue our conversation, Irene, but there's my ride." Dunne walked rapidly down the driveway. As he neared the open gate, he trotted onto Tremont Avenue and waved to the trolley driver, who slowed the car to a crawl. He swung himself aboard and the car picked up speed. He dropped a dime in the fare box. In the window behind the driver, Dunne saw Miss Loben alone on the top step of the porch stairs. She had her hand on her throat, as though choking back a scream.

* * *

Dunne exited the subway at 86th Street and went into Child's, where he nursed a cup of coffee. A warm, light drizzle fell on the throng of pedestrians flowing toward the Yorkville Casino. The crowded sidewalk had the same anticipatory air usually encountered outside Madison Square Garden, commencing in October with the Six-Day Bicycle Race, continuing through the Horse Show, college basketball, boxing, and the Rangers, and culminating the following May with the circus.

The crowds lined up behind the police barricades were rapidly thickening. A contingent of mounted police stood guard in front of the Casino. Alert to the noise and animation of the crowd, the horses snorted and stamped their hooves. Across the street, on the north side of 86th Street, an assortment of protesters was packed together. The largest contingent was gathered behind the banner of the Young Communist League, fists raised in the air, chanting "To hell with Hitler!" The mounted policemen pulled hard on their reins and stroked the necks of the horses, trying to calm them.

Dunne came out of Child's just as the music of the approaching band began to surge through the street. The protesters grew louder. A large Czechoslovakian flag was suddenly draped from the parapet of the building directly across from the Casino. The group next to the Young Communists, a loosely organized collection of children in Bohemian folk costumes, chanting students and older, grayer Czechs, let out a roar that momentarily drowned out the Communists. Pressed against the barricade, his face red and contorted from shouting, was the doorman from Sparks's building.

The honor guard and band of the German-American Bund turned the corner of Third Avenue onto 86th Street. Following the men carrying the Stars and Stripes and the swastika flag was a line of tall, stocky troopers in brown shirts and riding boots. Several more units of brown shirts and Nazi youth came past. There was no sign of Bill Huber. Dunne thought about trying to cross the street and ask Sparks's doorman if he'd seen Huber, but the size of the crowd and the barricades made that impossible.

He retreated to a brownstone stoop and stood in the doorway, out of the drizzle and high enough to see over the crowd. A good-looking kid about fifteen or sixteen with slicked-back hair and prominent cheekbones came up the stoop.

"Wanna buy a paper?" he asked.

"Got all the papers I need."

"Bet you don't got a copy of *Social Justice*. Give you the *real* truth, the way Father Coughlin tells it." He moved next to Dunne in the doorway, pulled a paper from the stack beneath his arm, and held it out. "Only three cents."

"No thanks."

"You a Jew?" The kid hooked his thumb on the belt of his black trousers, which were tucked into laced-up boots. His shirt, the color of tarnished silver, was embossed with an eagle holding a cross in its talons. His black tie bore the same emblem.

"None of your business what I am."

The kid put his papers down on the doorstep and took a pack of cigarettes from his shirt pocket. "Got a match?"

"Thought the Boy Scout motto was 'Be Prepared.'"

"I ain't no Boy Scout." The kid's front tooth was chipped and discolored. He was better looking with his mouth closed. "I belong to the Christian Front."

Dunne tossed him a pack of matches. He hung a cigarette from his lower lip, lit it, and sucked in the smoke. He exhaled through his nose and kept his eyes half-closed. He had the tough guy's way of lighting a cigarette down pat, the standard movie routine.

Another line of American and Nazi flags came past. The kid stretched out his arm in a Fascist-style salute. A large number of people in the crowd did the same. A chorus of "Heil Hitler!" started up. For all the hubbub, it was a sterner, flintier gathering than found at sporting events. Burly men in groups of two or three prowled the edge of the crowd. Beneath their canvas rain slickers they wore quasi-uniforms, with brown and silver shirts. Sprinkled about were unescorted older women, thin and gray, in cheap dresses that had been laundered one too many times; they had faces to match, worn and washed-out. Clutching their handbags, eyes trained on the ground, they seemed desperate to make sure they didn't step on any toes.

A brawl erupted down the street, closer to the casino. Three brownshirts descended on a man who held up his middle finger as the honor guard went by. They knocked the demonstrator to the ground and began kicking him. The cops waded into the crowd, swinging their billies indiscriminately. The mounted police trotted over to reinforce them. The kid started toward the spreading melee but Dunne grabbed his arm.

"I'd stay where I was, I was you."

The kid tried to twist his arm free. "Lemme go!" he shouted. Dunne tightened his hold. In the space of a few minutes, the cops chased away the brownshirts and brought the crowd under control. Dunne let go. The burned-down butt still hanging from his lower lip, the kid picked up his papers. "What are you, a friggin' cop?"

"Let's just say I give advice to people who need it. If you were going to help your friends, forget it. Was already three against one. And if you were going to fight the cops, you'd get your ass kicked and wind up in jail. You're still young. Plenty of time for that later on."

"Keep your friggin' advice. Who asked for it?" He flicked the butt and sent it spinning in a high arc over the sidewalk and into the gutter. "People had enough of bein' pushed around by sheenie bankers who own everythin', includin' the Jew-lover-in-chief in the White House. Hitler's been the only one with balls enough to put them Christ-killin' bloodsuckers in their place. Now it's America's turn. The day of reckonin' is comin'. The Jew is gonna get his. Just wait and see."

"What part you gonna play?"

"Part?"

"Yeah. Chief bully or assistant stooge, like you are now?"

The kid darted down the steps. "Go kiss a Jew's ass. It's you who's the stooge. Bet you've had a lot of practice at it."

*Not a lot, really, just that once. He meets Tommy Bellows and the others on his way home from sweeping the floor in Koening's Butcher Shop and putting enough fresh sawdust to soak up the thick, red-black blood. They invited him to tag along to the East River to see who can throw a stone the farthest. It's Tommy who spots two boys in yarmulkes across the street, lets out a holler, and chases after them. The pack follows, shouting and laughing. It seems at first the boys will get away, and most of the pack begin to* slow down, satisfied with the fun they've already had. But the boys take a wrong turn, down a dead-end alley, and are instantly trapped.

"Kneel!" Tommy yells. When they don't, he punches one of them and the whole pack falls on them, pulls the book bags off their backs, and dumps their contents on the slime-slicked cobblestones. Tommy picks up one of the books. It's filled with the same indecipherable characters as on the signs outside synagogues and Jewish stores. "Here, Hymie," Tommy says to the boy he's punched, "Sing us a Jew song."

"This isn't a song book," the boy said. "It's a prayer book."

"Then pray us some Jew prayers." Tommy laughs, and they all joined in, even the ones who don't feel like laughing, who see in the boys' eyes a painful, familiar fear of being outnumbered, overpowered, mocked, beaten, and humiliated. Human fears. Their own. They silently wish it would stop.

Tommy hits the boy again and this time blood begins to spurt from his nose. He pulls off the boy's skullcap and sticks it on his own head. "Sheenie, sheenie," he chanted, "who's got your beanie?" He drops the skullcap on the ground.

The laughter rises again, then stops. A shadow appears over the alley, as though a cloud has crossed the sun. Fin is about to turn when a hand takes hold of his collar, lifts him off his feet, and hurls him against the adjacent wall. Lying stunned, left shoulder roaring with pain, face on the wet, greasy, foul-smelling pavement, Fin watches as the cluster of shoes around him backs away and flees down the alley.

"Get up." The bush of his father's mustache protrudes from beneath his small, round nose. His eyes are shaded by his cap. He tells Fin to help the two boys gather their books and pick up the yarmulke. When they're finished, he walks a pace or two ahead of Fin and doesn't turn around until they've reached the corner of Drydock. Fin puts his arms over his head, sure of what's next. But his father only talks. "There are only three types of men in this world. Bullies, their stooges, and them who refuse to be either. A bully or a stooge, Fin, is that what you want to be?"

*Fin puts his arms down. "Wasn't my idea. Was Tommy Bellows'."*

*"So you're Tommy's stooge, is that what you're telling me? Then you're the first among us Dunnes. We never put our foot on another man's neck or aided them who did. You're better than that, Fin. Never let me—or yourself—down like this again." Big Mike goes into the tenement where they live. He never speaks about it again. He doesn't have to.*

By the time the rally ended and the people inside started leaving the casino, most of the protesters had drifted away. The *Bundesführer* himself, Fritz Kuhn, came out a side door surrounded by a guard of beefy brownshirts. A small crowd of news photographers started to shoot. The pop of flash bulbs brought a beamish smile to the *Bundesführer's* face. He ordered his bodyguards to step aside so the photographers could get a shot of him with his arm outstretched in the Hitler salute. He entered a waiting limousine in that same position. There was no sign of Bill Huber anywhere.

The kid Dunne had encountered earlier was among the last to leave the casino. He joined other boys in the same get-ups loitering outside. Dunne watched as they pushed and jostled one another. Loud and playful, they could have been coming from a dance. Instead, they'd been treated to two hours of Jew-baiting and race mongering, the milk of human meanness.

Drink up, kids, it's on the house.

## THE GENDARMENMARKT, BERLIN

Erika left a message with Corporal Gresser informing her husband she had a severe headache and wouldn't be able to accompany him to the special performance that evening. Canaris wasn't surprised when he returned from putting on his dress uniform in the bathroom to find Gresser's note on his desk. Any invitation from General Heydrich usually resulted in Erika developing a headache and being unable to attend. Heydrich invariably feigned disappointment, but since he made no effort to include Erika in his conversations and focused all his attention on her husband, he got over her absence almost instantly.

Heydrich's Mercedes arrived promptly at seven. His only response to Canaris's apology for Erika's indisposition was a slight nod. They rode in silence for several minutes. Heydrich stared ahead, betraying no emotion except for the constant torsion of his gloves, twisting and untwisting the fine kid like a poultry farmer wringing the necks of chickens. They stopped at a light. Heydrich slipped open the glass separating them from the chauffeur. "Faster," he said.

"Shall I use the siren, Herr General?" the chauffeur said.

"Do what is necessary to get us there on time." Heydrich shut the panel and sank back into the seat. The siren went off. The car moved rapidly ahead, the traffic parting to make way, the driver no longer paying attention to the traffic lights.

"If it were up to me," Heydrich said, "I'd do what Stalin does with his generals. I'd have Beck taken out and shot. One, two, three." Heydrich put down his gloves and brushed his hands together, as though cleaning off some residue.

"I doubt that would do much to help the situation."

"The 'situation'?"

Canaris turned his head away from Heydrich and watched the pedestrians stop and stare at the speeding limousine with its flags and siren, trying to guess which of the regime's leaders was inside. "The nervousness of the commanders over war with Britain and France," he said, "Who knows what Russia and America would do? We've been down this road before."

"Beck called a meeting of the army commanders on his *own*, without consulting the Führer. That's the 'situation,' my friend, and the proper word to describe it is *treason*."

Heydrich retreated back into silence for the last few minutes of the ride. When they arrived at the Gendarmenmarkt, an SS orderly ran alongside to open the door, Heydrich bounded out of the car, smiling broadly, his arm half raised in a casual salute. The Schauspielhaus was draped in German and Italian flags, which announced the special salute to the fifty-fifth birthday of Benito Mussolini, the Führer's faithful ally, a tribute inspired by the Duce's endorsement of the Reich's recent takeover of Austria. Dr. Göbbels, ever the stage master, had especially chosen the Gendarmenmarkt for the occasion because of its intentional resemblance to Rome's Piazza del Populo, a gesture to make the Italians feel at home in a city for which they expressed, often vociferously and indiscreetly, nothing but dislike.

The celebration, occurring a week after the Duce's official birth date, was supposed to have been attended by the Führer and Count Ciano, the Italian Foreign Minister. But when Ciano announced he was indisposed and couldn't travel to Berlin, the Führer decided he wouldn't be there either, which set off a cascade of cancellations among the Nazi hierarchy that left Heydrich among the top officials to attend. A trio of children dressed in the attire of peasants from the Italian Tyrol greeted Heydrich at the top of the stairs. The girl in the middle, very blonde and very shy, presented him with a bouquet. He patted her on the cheek, handed the flowers to an orderly, and proceeded down a receiving line of Italian diplomats and military officers.

Canaris followed, shaking hands with a succession of officials and exchanging a few pleasantries in Italian. Inside, he was escorted by an SS officer to the private champagne reception for the V.I.P. guests. He stood awkwardly for a moment, looking for someone to converse with, when Dr. Max de Crinis approached with two glasses of champagne, one of which he handed to Canaris. An officer in the *Sicherheitsdienst*, or SD, Heydrich's security force, Crinis was both a well-known doctor of psychiatry and neurology and a bon vivant who rarely passed up an invitation to an official function.

On other occasions, Canaris avoided him. Tonight, he welcomed his company: Crinis's talent for monologue—a mastery of small talk characteristic of his native Vienna—relieving him of the need to make conversation. Looking around the room, Crinis narrated a bit of gossip about almost every guest, implicating each in various acts of adultery, debauchery, and financial chicanery and making it all sound amusing rather than immoral. He was interrupted by a hubbub on the other side of the room. Foreign Minister von Ribbentrop arrived to pay his respects. Since Ribbentrop couldn't stay for the performance, Bernado Attolico, the Italian ambassador, offered a toast to the enduring friendship of the German and Italian peoples. Ribbentrop responded with a toast to the Duce's birthday, followed by a long-winded paean to the Führer's leadership, in German, which left the Italian guests looking bored and indifferent.

On his way into the performance, Canaris was stopped by an Ambassador Attolico's aide, who conveyed the ambassador's invitation to join him. Canaris politely declined, but Attollico came over, slipped his arm into Canaris's, and guided him to his box. "We must talk," he said.

"I wouldn't want to disturb your enjoyment of the music," Canaris said.

Attolico shrugged, "They play Wagner in the Duce's honor, why? Are there no great Italian composers? Wagner gives me a headache. Better to talk than listen."

True to his word, as soon as the music began, Attolico began a hushed but fervently animated reiteration of everything that his boss, Count Ciano, had said to Canaris three months before, during the Führer's visit to Rome. From across the way, in a box directly opposite, Heydrich spent much of the time staring at them through a pair of opera glasses he'd dispatched an SS adjutant to fetch for him.

"I talked to Count Ciano tonight by telephone," Attolico said. "He instructed me to give you his special regards. 'The Admiral,' in his words, 'is a gentleman, which cannot be said of all his countrymen.'"

At their first meeting, several years before, Canaris had been prepared to dislike Ciano, a slick charmer, blessed with olive skin and Latin good looks. Like Ribbentrop, who'd used his marriage to the daughter of a champagne-company proprietor as a lever of career advancement, Ciano was the beneficiary of an advantageous marriage, to Mussolini's daughter. Publicly, Ciano was a second-hand version of his father-in-law, whose pugnacious gestures and scowling facial poses he slavishly imitated. In private, Canaris found Ciano a charming, intelligent conversationalist undeceived by his government's pretensions to a revival of the Roman Empire.

The previous May sitting in his magnificent office in the Palazzo Chigi, its three great windows facing the Piazza Colonna, Ciano had told Canaris that the Duce was disturbed by Ribbentrop's constant refrain about "the imminent showdown with Britain and France." The Duce didn't want to believe that the Führer shared that desire. "Hitler is a statesman in the Duce's eyes," Ciano had said, "and Ribbentrop a clown." Sotto voce, he had added that the king, who was playing host to the Germans at the Quirinale Palace, couldn't wait until they both were gone. "He regards Ribbentrop as a cross between a head butler and a pimp, and Hitler as a sort of psycho-physiological degenerate."

"You're a Latin, aren't you?" Ciano asked.

"Partly. My father's family was from around Lake Como. Canarisi was the name, but that was several centuries ago."

"No matter." Ciano waved his hand dismissively. "A man's blood isn't altered because he changes seats." He confided that he didn't share the Duce's opinion of the Führer. He thought Hitler, *well . . .* searching for the right word, he finally chose an English one: *odd.* Bluster, bluff, intimidation, the annexation of weaker states and acquisition of colonies, these were all part of the game played by the great powers, and Italy had every right to participate. But to deliberately plot another war like the last, which wrecked half of Europe and set loose the forces of chaos, only a lunatic could contemplate such a thing.

Ciano warned Canaris not to be deceived by martial displays staged for the benefit of the German visitors. It was all a masquerade. Italy lacked the economic muscle to create anything close to Germany's military machine. The army was short of ammunition, its artillery outmoded and tanks poorly armored; the air force was small and the country's air defenses negligible. "With a military like ours," Ciano said, "we can safely declare war only on Peru." The miserable state of the armed forces was matched by the people's morale. "Except for a few fanatics, there's absolutely no appetite for war."

He left his desk, which was overshadowed by a larger-than-life portrait of a helmeted and belligerent Duce, and escorted Canaris to one of the windows that looked down on the piazza. "Czecho-slovakia isn't Austria. Unless responsible men take charge, we may find ourselves drawn, in Dante's phrase, 'Into the everlasting dark-ness, into fire and into ice.' War is like a runaway train. Once it starts, no one can know where or when it'll stop. There must be men in Germany with sense enough to prevent it from leaving the station, no?"

Ambassador Attolico concluded his conversation with the same metaphor Ciano had used in Rome. "This train is headed for a wreck, unless somebody stops it. Surely, there are those in the army high command who understand this."

Canaris said little, nodding occasionally, trying not to notice the opera glasses trained on them from the other side of the house. On the way out of the box, Crinis reappeared and accompanied Canaris to the post-performance reception on the balcony. "I could see our Italian friend had taken you prisoner, so I decided to come to the rescue. Except for the Duce, they're all defeatists. We'd prob-ably be better off if they joined the French and British and added a further measure of cowardice to the Allies."

Producing a finely tooled leather case from his pocket, Crinis extracted two maduros. He bit off the end of one, spit it over the railing, and rolled his tongue over the tightly packed tobacco. He offered the other to Canaris.

"I don't know if I should," Canaris said. "It's quite a while since I had a cigar."

"Go on. If war comes, these will be at a premium. *Carpe diem*." Crinis lit his cigar and held out the match for Canaris. A white-gloved orderly brought them two glasses of champagne. "The thing about war is that it heightens the senses in profound ways, and pleasures we might ordinarily take for granted acquire new inten-sity." As a statuesque woman in a black gown came out on the bal-cony, Crinis ogled her.

"Pain and pleasure both increase in wartime." Canaris gently puffed on the cigar. The taste was intense.

"The weak feel the pain. The strong find the pleasure." Crinis took a sip of champagne. "You've heard about Werner Arnheim, I suppose?"

"Dr. Arnheim?"

"Yes."

"He's my physician. I saw him last month. A routine physical. Has something happened to him?"

"A tragic case, I'm afraid. He had a nervous collapse, or so it was thought. He was brought to me for examination at the beginning of the month. He proved to be a congenital psychotic, afflicted by periods of severe delusion and paranoia. Though he'd managed to mask it for most of his career, in the end, as always happens, it overwhelmed him. He had a daughter with the same affliction, but hers manifested itself earlier." The woman in black passed by again, and Crinis made a polite bow.

"I'm sorry to hear that. He seemed the nervous type but, still, a competent physician." Canaris detected no hint that Crinis, whose gaze followed the attractive passerby, knew anything of Arnheim's visit or allegations.

"He's out of his misery now. He committed suicide last evening in the institution where he was being held. He hung himself in the shower."

Unthinkingly, Canaris inhaled the cigar as if it were a cigarette. A rush of hot air scorched his throat. His eyes filled with water.

"Are you all right?" Crinis patted him on the back. "Smoking a maduro is an art, you know, to be enjoyed slowly, like lovemaking." He held up his cigar and gazed at it admiringly. "I've made sure I have an adequate supply. I don't intend to let the British navy come between me and a good smoke, the way it did in the last war."

Canaris gulped his champagne. He would have thrown the cigar over the balcony into the street if Crinis wasn't standing there.

"One can feel sorry for Arnheim, of course, yet his fate is a reminder of the poisonous effect of degenerate bloodlines. There's no cure, I'm afraid, other than elimination." Excusing himself, Crinis walked over to the woman who'd held his attention and struck up a conversation. She laughed at the first thing he said.

\* \* \*

It was nearly 1:00 A.M. before the reception ended. Max de Crinis and the woman were nowhere to be seen. Canaris rode home with Heydrich. He felt dizzy and a little nauseated; Heydrich, whom he'd presumed to be a teetotaler, had seemingly made an exception in honor of the Duce's birthday, becoming relaxed and chatty. "You know, Wilhelm," he said, "the generals may grumble but in the end they're soldiers, and they'll obey. The Wehrmacht will make short work of the Czechs and, seeing their ally defeated and annexed, the British and French will have no choice but to acquiesce."

"The Czechs have 34 well-armed divisions dug into heavily fortified positions," Canaris said. "If an attack bogged down, the French could easily overrun our western defenses, which are pitifully weak."

"Come, Wilhelm, you're beginning to sound like General Beck and the weak-kneed tin hats around him."

"Facts are facts."

"Facts are paltry things in the face of destiny. The Führer understands that, even if the generals don't." Heydrich leaned forward, pushed the glass back, and instructed his driver to get them home as fast as possible. They rode down the Unter der Linden in silence, west and south toward Wannsee, through the warm, dark, preternaturally quiet streets of Berlin.

## FOLEY SQUARE, NEW YORK

The two rows of chairs in the FBI waiting room were lined in military order. The first visitor of the morning, Dunne was the sole occupant. In front of him, on a table with dachshund-sized legs, were neatly arranged issues of *Time* and *Reader's Digest*. Aside from the fact that the magazines were new, rather than six months old, and the two receptionists wore neat gray suits rather than medical whites, it could have been a doctor's office. The younger receptionist, whose wholesome Sonja Henie-like face indicated she was probably a Norwegian from Bay Ridge, had taken Dunne's name and told him to have a seat. She'd been curt and cold, more North Pole than South Brooklyn.

A quarter of an hour's worth of page-flipping sent Dunne back to the receptionist's desk. There'd been no thaw. "Have a seat, please," she said without looking up. "You'll be called at the appropriate time." The receptionists typed away non-stop on their Underwoods. The tinny tap-tap-tap was reminiscent of toy Tommy guns, perfect accompaniment to the framed photo of J. Edgar Hoover behind them, his bulldog face set in a perpetual scowl. A parade of agents came in and out. They traded helloes with the receptionists, who addressed each by name.

Dunne had hopped in a cab without having a cup of coffee or reading the papers. Hurry up and wait. A time-honored police tactic: Never let a civilian dictate the pace of work. It was about the only policelike feature in the orderly, spic-and-span room. The Best & Co. pair at the front desk turned from typing to filing. The agents coming past seemed to be dressed out of the same catalog as the receptionists, all in gray, brown, or blue suits, starched white shirts, sharp creases in their pants, jackets pressed and clean. They had the earnest air of salesmen going out on their rounds. The receptionist who'd spoken to Dunne stopped her filing. Without looking at him, she said, "Agent Lundgren will be with you in a few minutes."

Two well-scrubbed agents emerged from inside and bantered for a moment with the receptionists. They fitted their hats to their heads and snapped their brims, Knights of the Gray Fedora, and exited into the hallway with a purposeful stride.

"Mr. Dunne, would you please step this way." The receptionist opened the door behind her desk. "Agent Lundgren will see you." Lundgren's office was directly across the hall. She motioned for Dunne to go in.

Jacket draped around the back of his chair, tie pulled down from the open collar of his shirt, Lundgren scribbled on a yellow legal pad. Beneath each armpit was a crescent of perspiration. He was the closest thing to a real cop Dunne had seen all morning.

"Sit," he said.

"Should I give you my paw?"

Lundgren glanced up, a tight, disdainful grin on his face. "Don't bother. I'm out of dog biscuits." He stopped writing and put down his pencil. He cleared his desk, tossing a folded copy of the *Standard* and a paper coffee cup in the wastebasket. "Just so we understand one another, I grew up in Flatbush, so don't think I'm impressed by your wise-ass routine. I knew a slew of Irishers like you. Half of them are in jail."

"And the other half put them there. I called for an appointment because I've got an urgent matter to discuss."

"Before you say anything, you should know your buddy Jerroff confessed. We don't operate like the police department and beat it out of people. We talk in a reasonable way. Unfortunately, sometimes it can go on a long time."

"You turn him into an informer?"

"That's none of your business." Lundgren rubbed his eyes. "Listen, Dunne, I've been up all night. I'm tired and want to go home. Jerroff swears up and down that you've never been part of his schemes. He's pretty much got me convinced, so why don't you go and ruin somebody else's day before I change my mind."

"I want to report a murder."

"Then go to the police."

"This involves transporting people across state lines."

"Kidnapping?"

"In a sense."

"By whom?"

"A doctor."

"For ransom?"

"For experiments. He puts them to death and then dissects them."

"*Them?*"

"The inmates of his sanatorium." Dunne didn't—wouldn't— say it. It was his business, nobody else's: there was no reason to believe that Maura, his sister, had ever been an inmate there, but it was her face that came to mind, blue eyes, sad and fearful.

"Which ones?"

"All of them."

"*All?* But nobody's reported any?"

"One tried. She was killed before she could talk. An innocent man's been framed by the police. He's on his way to the chair for a murder he didn't commit."

"A regular crime wave." Lundgren ripped the page off the pad and put it in the pocket of his jacket. His attempt to suppress a yawn came out sounding like a sigh.

"He's got help. A staff. A goon from the Bund acts as his bodyguard."

"Spies too? This is quite a case. Undetermined number of people killed, but none reported, and no witnesses except a woman who gets killed to shut her up. And the motive of the police in framing the man accused of murdering her? I missed that."

"I didn't say. I'm not sure."

The intercom buzzed. Lundgren picked up the receiver. "Tell him not to leave. Tell him I'll be right out." He pulled his tie tight around his neck and put on his jacket. "I got a detail in the Jerroff matter to attend to. Be right back."

He returned shortly with Michael McCarthy. "Well, well," McCarthy said. "Peck's bad boy returns." He forced a smile as he leaned against the file cabinet in the corner. "What do you think, Lundgren, should we order a cake and throw a party?"

"Soon as he leaves." Lundgren retook his seat.

"Agent Lundgren tells me you've stumbled on a mass murderer. Coming up in the world, aren't you? Last time we met you were focused on more prosaic concerns. By the way, how's Miss Dee?"

"Why don't you call and ask. I'm sure she'd love to hear from you."

"Has she gone into the detective business? Or is she in her usual line of work?"

"Which line interests you?"

McCarthy blushed.

"He says he also wants to turn in a Nazi spy," Lundgren said.

"I never said a spy. I said he was in the Bund."

"We have a unit dedicated to the Bund. How about I put you in touch?"

"What really brings you here, Dunne?" McCarthy seemed taller than Dunne remembered. Legs crossed, hands in the pockets of his pleated pants, he had the athletic trimness of somebody who'd run track in college. It looked to Dunne as though he bought his clothes at the same stores as the Ivy League boys: A Fordham kid and cop's son doing his best to make it look as though he were from Yale or Harvard. But what to do about the reddish hair and the spritz of freckles across the nose and cheeks? A mick's mug. Try again, Mike.

"Business brings me here, just like I said. Don't want to listen? Well, sometimes it's inconvenient to listen when you're parked in a government job and can suck the public tit no matter what you do or don't do."

"Listen, you five-and-dime grifter," Lundgren said, "we don't have to take that guff from you."

"Let him talk," McCarthy said. "Let's hear what he has to say. Go on, fill us in."

"I've been on a case, a murder, and it's put me on the trail of a high-class doctor. I didn't like him from the minute I met him, and I liked his chauffeur even less. At one point, he tried to hire me to scare off a blackmailer, but it felt as though he had some other purpose. Anyways, it was the chauffeur I was suspicious of, at first."

"You're getting ahead of yourself. "What's the doctor's name?" It was hard to tell from McCarthy's blank expression if he was taking seriously anything he'd heard.

"Dr. Sparks."

Lundgren's head jerked up. "Who?"

"Dr. Joseph Sparks."

"Of the Hermes Sanatorium?"

The instant Dunne said yes, Lundgren broke out laughing. McCarthy settled for a faint, mocking smile.

"You've no shame, have you?" Lundgren reached into the wastebasket and rescued the late city edition of the *Standard* he'd thrown away. "What do you think, we're so dull we don't read the papers?" He spread the front page open on the desk and turned the headline toward Dunne:

INFERNO IN THE BRONX
HERMES SANATORIUM BURNS AND A SCORE
OF IDIOTS PERISH IN FIRE

DR. JOSEPH SPARKS LOSES LIFE IN
RESCUE ATTEMPT
HAILED AS SAINT AND HERO
By John Mayhew Taylor

Beneath the headline was a photograph of a structure totally engulfed in flames. A tongue of fire protruded from the widow's walk atop the roof and jutted into the night sky. Dunne skimmed the story. What it lacked in facts it made up for in high-flown prose. "Merciless flames, cruel and insatiable, consumed the innocent lives of an undetermined number of feeble-minded inmates. . . . The same kindhearted doctor who had taken them into his care stayed with them to the end. . . . He laid down his life in a selfless but unsuccessful attempt to lead his childlike charges to safety."

"I wonder, Gus, if you wouldn't mind letting me talk to Dunne alone? Only be a  few minutes," McCarthy said.

"Be my guest." Lundgren got up and left.

McCarthy took Lundgren's seat. He picked up the pencil that Lundgren had left, turned it slowly between thumb and forefinger like a spit. "I owe you an apology," he said. "I've done some digging, and it turns out Colonel Donovan isn't alone in his opinion of you. You have a number of admirers in the NYPD, especially among the ranks of the most reliable, honest men. They all say you were a good cop."

Dunne studied the newspaper picture, trying to find some hint of a human form. The building and the soaring, all-consuming fire yielded no secrets. He read the caption to himself: *The building collapsed less than an hour after the fire was first reported. Three firemen were treated at Westchester Square Hospital for smoke inhalation.*

McCarthy put down the pen, reached across the desk, and covered the picture with his hand. "Listen to me."

"I'm listening."

"I'm on an important case. My office is involved in an investigation of certain members of the NYPD. We're working in cooperation with the D.A.'s office. It was Dewey's office helped get you off the hook in the last matter. Donovan called his office and their investigation had already turned up your name in a favorable light. The man we're after is Borough Inspector Robert I. Brannigan."

McCarthy sat back. He picked up the pen again and held it in the same position as before, rotating the spit. "We believe he's a top player in a prostitution racket that moves girls up and down the East Coast in a condition close to indentured servitude. Brannigan not only provides protection but shares in the proceeds."

"Brannigan's been a rotten cop for years. It never hurt him before."

"Times change. There are honest officials running the department now. Brannigan and his kind aren't going to be tolerated any longer."

"Except when they help get convictions."

"Under Brannigan, the Homicide Squad has a splendid record in terms of nabbing perpetrators. But now it's been discovered he's also been a friend to racketeers, gamblers and pimps. Unfortunately, he's got a lot of people afraid of him, including many of his colleagues in the department. I'm told, however, that you're not one of them. You have more admirers in the department than you know."

"They're good at hiding it."

"I want him put away, and I want your help."

"I'm busy with a case. Ever hear of Water Grillo?"

"Grillo? Sure, 'The West Side Ripper.'"

"He's innocent."

"Tom Regan tried the case. He's a friend of mine and a fine prosecutor."

"Brannigan handled the investigation."

"He's a dishonest cop, not a stupid one. As venal as he appears to be, I know of no evidence that he's ever tampered with the truth in a murder case."

"Maybe you forgot to look. He framed Grillo."

"Tell you what. You help put away Brannigan, I'll see what I can turn up on Grillo." McCarthy jammed the pen in its holder, stood, and came from behind the desk.

"You got it backwards. Grillo first. He's the one with the dead-line."

McCarthy paced back and forth, as though addressing a box full of jurors. "I'm the one who'll decide that. Grillo's chances, to be honest, are slim. Meanwhile, Brannigan and his fellow rogues are a running sore on the body politic of this city. Soon as he catches wind of an investigation, he'll pull out every stop to derail it. There's no time to waste." He turned away from the imaginary jury. Fearless gangbuster, scourge of dishonest cops, incorruptible prosecutor, he was on the verge of shedding his boyish good looks and acquiring a more substantial and experienced presence. Add a few pounds, mix in a little gray, and he'd have the kind of face that stared with firm determination from campaign posters plastered on walls and pinned to telephone poles.

"More mileage in convicting a crooked detective than in rescuing a spic janitor from the electric chair. See, what makes you so sure that Brannigan didn't railroad half of those supposed murderers he brought in and manufactured the evidence needed for conviction? That would make for a very busy situation in the appeals courts, wouldn't it?"

"Don't get high and mighty with me, Dunne. It doesn't suit you."

"Sorry, I'm not ready to sign on with your campaign. The way I see it, it's fine with you if Grillo goes to the chair so long as you get Brannigan's scalp. Then you ride that victory to the bench or congress or the governor's chair. But the system hasn't changed. Soon enough it'll produce a new Brannigan, somebody who makes so many arrests that stick the higher-ups turn a blind eye to his less reputable hobbies."

"You're not crooked. You're just crude. You should learn some manners and try acting like a gentleman. You might enjoy the sheer novelty of it."

"You should learn to hide your ambitions better, Mike. Right now they're as plain as the freckles on your nose."

The flush in McCarthy's face turned the bright crimson of a bad sunburn. "I've had enough of you. Get out. You'll regret this. I promise you."

\* \* \*

Dunne found the Professor and Corrigan in the back booth at McGloin's. John Mayhew Taylor was wedged between them. Dunne sat beside Corrigan.

"Mr. Taylor is moving me toward his point of view," the Professor said. "If the Germans move on the Czechs, surely the French and British will move on the Germans and be joined by the Soviets. The Japanese will then move against the French and British colonies in the Orient, widening their war against China. It will be an even grander conflagration than in 1914. Should it last long enough, we may well be embroiled."

"Any president who tries to rush us into war will be impeached," Corrigan said.

The Professor looked around for McGloin, who was nowhere to be seen. "I don't believe I solicited your views," he said to Corrigan. McGloin appeared out of the long-unused and dust-covered kitchen, and the Professor signaled for a round of drinks.

Corrigan finished his drink almost as soon as McGloin served it. "I got quite a thirst today," he said.

"You were born with a Niagara of a thirst," the Professor said. "I acquired mine at Princeton. Mr. Taylor, on the other hand, has the imbibitional disposition of a dromedary. A drink a month can keep him going."

"I'm not in the mood, that's all." Taylor slid his glass toward Corrigan.

Corrigan pushed it back. "Go on, Taylor, it'll cheer you up."

The Professor lifted his glass. "If last evening caused tragedy for some, it brought triumph to one. The byline of John Mayhew Taylor has appeared for the first time on the front page of the *New York Standard!*"

"Wait," Corrigan said, "I need a drink to toast with."

"I'm no coolie," McGloin said. "I'll bring another round, but I ain't shuttlin' single drinks."

"Another round it is, *propre*, if you please," the Professor said.

Taylor pushed away his drink once more. This time Corrigan took it, raising it to toast with the Professor. "What about you Dunne?" he asked.

"I'm on the same wagon as Taylor."

"Very well." The Professor tapped his glass to Corrigan's. "Though only half the present company is participating, the good cheer is shared by all:

*"See, the conquering hero comes!*
*Sound the trumpet, bang the drums!"*

"The inmates were all hopelessly feeble-minded. They couldn't save themselves. The whole area was blanketed with the stench of their burnt flesh. It was horrific." Taylor leaned away from the table. "There's nothing to celebrate."

"What kind of war correspondent recoils at the sights and smells of death?" The Professor tipped the glass on his lower lip and swallowed its contents.

"Maybe you're one of 'em be happier on the society beat," Corrigan said.

"I was up there all night after I rushed that skeleton copy to the paper last evening. The old place was a tinderbox. A huge amount of rubbing alcohol and medical supplies was beneath the stairs. The firemen think that one of the staff ducked in there for a smoke and set the whole thing off. The building became a virtual crematorium. Just because I'm not jumping up and down with joy doesn't mean I didn't do my job."

"You submitted a fine story. Good writing done under a tight deadline," the Professor said. "The mark of a true reporter."

"Lord have mercy on those morons and idiots." Corrigan consumed the whiskey he'd taken from Taylor. "And especially doctor what's-his-name."

"Sparks," Taylor said.

"You sure he was inside?" Dunne asked.

Taylor gave him a quizzical look. "Of course I'm sure. You can read the full story in the copy I filed for today's paper. Sparks arrived just as the fire was breaking out. He ran upstairs to help evacuate the patients and was almost instantly trapped."

"Destiny put you in the vicinity," the Professor said.

"Duty not destiny. I was covering a bank robbery on Tremont Avenue. I didn't get on the scene till the worst had already happened."

"You were close enough to get the scoop. Destiny saw to that, and it's destiny that separates the great reporters from the good, and puts them where they need to be."

"I was lucky, that's all."

"Luck is merely a demotic appellation for destiny."

"If nobody survived, how do you know Sparks died that way?" Dunne said.

"There was a witness. That's *how* I know. His chauffeur was waiting outside in the car. They'd just stopped off on their way back from Long Island. Dr. Sparks was a remarkable man. Built a swank East Side practice, but also operated this place out of his own pocket. He was constantly traveling up there to take care of them."

"A true physician and, apparently, a fellow classicist. He used the name of Hermes for his institute, the Greek god whom the Romans called Mercury, he of winged foot who carried the caduceus, the entwined snakes, the symbol of the physician." The Professor raised one of the refills that McGloin had just delivered. "He deserves a special toast."

"Christ, it's not even noon," Corrigan said. "It's too early for a lecture."

"What happened to the chauffeur?"

The Professor put down his glass without taking a sip. "My, my, Dunne, you sound as though you're still a cop."

"Curious, that's all."

"It's okay," Taylor said. "I'll tell you what you want to know. When the chauffeur saw the fire, he tried to get inside, but the flames beat him back."

"Where's he now?" Dunne asked.

"I've no idea."

"Didn't get his address?"

"The cops did. That's *their* job. And the fire marshals'."

"What about Miss Loben and Mr. Waldruff?"

"Who?"

"She worked there. He was a visitor."

"How'd you get so well acquainted with the sanatorium?" Taylor seemed impressed rather than bothered.

"I get around. That's *my* job."

"Remarkable," the Professor said. "No quarter of Gotham seems immune from your fossorial expeditions."

"I'd appreciate your telling me anything you know about it," Taylor said. "The police are still trying to identify exactly who and how many were in there at the time of the fire. Dr. Sparks's secretary gave them the files from his East Side office, but she said the only fully up-to-date and complete records were kept in the sanatorium."

"What about next-of-kin?" Dunne said.

"None has come forward yet."

Dunne excused himself to go to the bathroom. He passed McGloin, who was on his way back with another tray of refills, and left without returning to the booth. He rode the uptown IRT to Sparks's office. It was closed. Outside, photographers and reporters attempted to interview anyone leaving or entering about the saintly but unobtrusive, ever elusive, now deceased Doctor Sparks.


The doorman winked and raised two fingers to the visor of his cap when Dunne arrived at Roberta's building, testament to the legacy of good will a generous tipper can create. He shrugged when asked if she were home. "She went out the day before yesterday without sayin' goodbye. Next thing you know, the movers come to put her stuff in storage. Landlord's already got the place for rent. Take a look if you want. The door's open."

The doorknob turned at Dunne's touch. The empty hallway and room beyond looked smaller than he remembered. The apartment had been swept clean. On the wall above where the couch had been was the faint outline of the picture that had hung there, sea at night, moon glow, angry waves working themselves into a rage.

The doorman stopped Dunne on his way out. "I hate to lose a tenant the likes of Miss Dee," he said. "If you see her, tell her Frank Morello sends his regards."

Flatbush Avenue was hot and fume-choked. Dunne stopped in a bar. A knot of patrons was gathered around a radio at the far end. The Dodger game was on. The bartender served Dunne a beer. "I can't listen to anymore of that," the bartender said. "The Bums are in a depression of their own." He went on about how this hot shot McPhail thought he could save them from the National League cellar with gimmicks like having Babe Ruth coaching at first. "Too bad the Babe ain't ten years younger and fifty pounds lighter, but when you're past your prime, you're past your prime. Ain't nothin' can be done about it." The game ended with the Dodgers losing to the Cardinals. A news report followed on the worsening crisis over Czechoslovakia and an emergency meeting of the British cabinet. "To hell with the limeys and the frogs and the krauts. They deserve each other." He snapped the radio off.

Dunne studied the patrons in the mirror behind the bar. He didn't recognize any faces, but he knew the type. Unraveled from around the radio and perched on the row of stools, they hunched over their drinks like birds too tired to fly, heads tucked inside their exhausted wings. Men past their prime, their dreams KO'd so long ago they had to be drunk to remember them, they rented furnished rooms by the Navy Yard or in Park Slope, taking whatever work came their way as part-time token clerks or movie-ticket sellers. Though they scavenged their daily newspapers out of trashcans and dined on baked beans five times a week at the Automat in order to have money for drink, they hadn't fallen as low as the residents of the Hoover Flats. Yet, if and when the boom times came back, it'd be too late for them. From now on, they'd do the only thing they knew how to do, get by.

The mirror was adorned with a dust-covered set of Christmas lights and three green, wilted cardboard shamrocks, reminders of holidays past, omens of ones to come, moments not worth remembering or looking forward to. Dunne stared silently at their reflections, backward images that couldn't distort the straightforward question in eyes as impassive as those of drowned men lolling in the weightless embrace of the waves: *Mirror, mirror, on the wall, who's the loneliest of us all?*

From outside, through the open door, the rumble-bumble of Brooklyn flowed with the steady rush of a fast-moving river. Dunne pulled himself off the stool and left a full glass of beer on the bar. He joined the current of people and vehicles moving downtown; tributary streets and avenues pouring in more all the time, the roar-

ing, hustling, honking stream pulling him along, carrying him to the
bridge and over, and depositing him sometime later on the doorstep
of Cassidy's Bar & Grill.

Cassidy served drinks to the transit workers who couldn't fit
into the back room, where Red Doyle's agitated brogue regaled the
crowd with a non-stop denunciation of the shift bosses and the bus-
line owners. Without a word to his customers, Cassidy raised the
hinged service board and stepped out from behind the bar. A howl
of protest went up.

"Workers of the world," he shouted, "be patient!"

He came over to Dunne and led him to the corner by the phone
booth. "In trouble again, aren't you?" he said.

"Was I ever out of it?"

"Brannigan was in here last night askin' if I knew where you
was." Cassidy produced a slip of paper from the pocket of his
apron. "And this woman's called for you several times, always with
the same message 'bout how important it is she reaches you. Last
time wasn't more than twenty minutes ago. Said she needs to get in
touch right away." He handed Dunne the slip. "Wants you to call
her at this number if you come in anytime soon, which you have."

"Give her name?"

"Good barman never asks. But I got an idea you know who
it is."

The crowd clamored for Cassidy to return. "Better get back,"
he said. He returned to his post at the dignified pace of a priest
ascending to the altar, he retied the cincture on his apron and
draped a towel over his forearm, like a priest's maniple. "Now, gentlemen," he intoned with mock solemnity, "who's first?"

The patrons congregated on the other side of the rail answered
in chorus, "Me!"

Dunne dialed the number on the slip. It had a West Side prefix.
Between the noise outside the booth and the hushed tone of the person who answered, he barely heard the indistinct "Hello."

"Who's this?" Dunne said.

The same murmurously low voice said, "Who you want?"

"Roberta Dee."

There was a wordless pause. Dunne sensed the phone being

handed to someone else. "Fin?" The new voice was as understated as the last, but he knew immediately from one syllable, as personal and identifiable as any fingerprint, it was Roberta's.

"Where are you?" He couldn't make out the answer. "Speak up," he said.

She spoke just loudly enough for him to catch an address on the Upper West Side. A muffled background conversation indicated she was talking to the person who had picked up. With clear urgency, she said, "Come right away." Then she hung up.

The address turned out to be off Riverside Drive, a turn-of-the-century limestone mansion discolored by soot and pigeon droppings and cut up into a dozen apartments. Dunne peered through iron latticework that guarded the glass in the front door. The vestibule and hallway were dimly lit. A shadow stirred at the end of the hallway and moved along the wall, furtively. The door opened. Roberta held the inner door ajar with her foot as she let him in.

She pressed her forefinger to her lips. Radio music came from upstairs. Hugging the shadows, they went silently to a room in the back. A single red-fringed lamp made it brighter than the hallway, but not much. A lone red chair, covered in the same red plush as the bed, was beside a shuttered window.

"Stay here," she said. "I'll be right back."

He blocked the door. "Wait a minute." Dunne didn't bother asking where they were. The stale odor of nicotine mingled with the wet, thick residue of a thousand-odd couplings: Whatever name they stuck on it—cathouse, notch spot, joy palace—didn't take a veteran of the vice squad to figure it out. "What brought you here?"

"I'm not working here, if that's what you're thinking."

"I had no idea where you'd gone, that's all."

"Once the feds let me go, I knew I'd soon have a visit from Brannigan. I had no choice other than to make a fast, clean break and drop out of sight. It also made it easier to look for Lina Linnet."

"Who?"

"That night at Ben Marden's, you asked who'd put Wilfredo in touch with me. Soon as I said Lina Linnet, it occurred to me Wilfredo had been a regular of hers and maybe they'd still been in touch at the time of the murder. A wild card, but I figured there was nothing to lose by playing it. Turned out, she was at the same address."

"She's here now?"

"She's scared, Fin. Very scared. Stay here. I'll be right back."

Dunne helped himself to a cigarette from the pack on the table next to the bed. He almost knocked over a butt-filled ashtray but caught it in time. There was a knock. Roberta entered with a black-haired, buxom woman in a tight black dress who took a heavy drag on a cigarette and drawled out a smoky, insubstantial veil that hung across her heavily made-up face. "Roberta says you're a friend and that you'll help me get away from here," she said. "Right up front, so there's no mistake, I'll tell you what I told her. I'll give you what I know. Use it any way you want. But I don't intend to end up in the river. No way am I testifyin' about anythin' whatsoever."

"Tell me what you know, and I'll do what I can to get you away from here."

"Far away, where they can't find me?"

"Far away, I promise."

"Tell him who runs this place," Roberta said.

"Well, Sally Hoffritz is the madam. Roberta and me both worked for her sometime back. That's when we got friendly."

"Tell him who *really* runs it."

"Head of the local precinct, Captain Jim Morris, he takes a large cut. That's why this place is still runnin' when so many others been shut. Hardly a cop in the precinct don't got dibs on a girl."

"But Morris isn't alone. Biggest share goes to the person who supplies the place with girls and makes sure the vice squad steers clear. Right, Lina?"

Cigarette held between her lips, Lina used her hands to adjust her too-tight dress. "Yeah."

"Go ahead," Roberta said, "give him the name."

Lina looked down at her shoes. "I never ratted on nobody before."

"The real rats are the ones that keep you and the others terrified," Roberta said.

"You want to stay here?" Dunne rubbed out his cigarette in the ashtray.

One arm crossed on the flat of her stomach, Lina rested the other elbow on it and removed the cigarette from her lips. She shook her head.

As Roberta prodded her, Lina became more reticent. "Tell him about Walter Grillo," she said. "About that night."

"Walter Grillo had been comin' round for years. First time, I was workin' in Gertie Bohan's place on 68th Street. That's when he asked me if I ever knew Rosalinda Dorsch and I told him about Roberta. Anyways, he stayed a customer when I came here. Lotta' times he was tipsy but this once he was the other side of loaded and after we was done, there was no wakin' him up. I tried everythin', believe me.

"Finally, I go to tell Sally Hoffritz, who hates hearin' this 'cause she's always tellin' us that if a john is really hooched either don't take him or do it standin' up. Easier said than done. Anyways, I go to tell Sally, who's in the upstairs parlor havin' a drink with one of Brannigan's boys."

"Which one?" Dunne asked.

"Matt Terry. Know him?"

"Sorry to say, I do."

"Sorry is right. He's a regular here and thinks this whole thing with Grillo is hilarious till Sally tells him to go down and carry him outta' the room. He says he's no whorehouse porter, so Sally says she'll call Brannigan, who's the one really in charge here. Terry stops laughin' and does what he's told."

"What time was that?"

"'Bout seven-thirty." Lina took another cigarette from the pack on the table and lit it with the one she was finishing. "Anyways, I help Terry carry him out, and we leave him in the back parlor. Grillo was still there when I finish with the next john, but next time I come through, after nine, he's gone."

"You sure about the time?"

"It couldn't have been much later than nine. Business was the slowest we ever had 'cause there was a murder that same night a block or so away. Cops flooded the neighborhood. Nothin' scares the johns away like that."

"Where was Matt Terry?"

"I didn't see him again till the next evenin'. I was all excited 'bout havin' spotted Grillo's picture in the papers. I figured when I tell him the guy in the picture is the same one he helped carry outta my room, he's gonna get flustered 'cause they pinched the wrong guy. He don't even look at the picture. 'Stead, he gives my cheek a pat and says, 'Keep to your business, Lina, and we'll keep to ours. We got who we want.'

"I went to Sally Hoffritz and told her 'bout Grillo. Said it didn't seem right to let a man get fried for a crime that was committed while he was here. She mentioned it to Brannigan. He told her I was mistaken. Then he came to my room. Stayed the night. Didn't say anythin' about Grillo. He didn't have to. I got the message."

There was a sharp rap on the door. Before anyone could react, Matt Terry lurched in; swaying unsteadily, he squinted in the dimness and gaped directly at Roberta. "Hello, gorgeous, where they been hidin' you?"

"Hello, Matt." Dunne advanced toward the light.

As Terry groped clumsily for his sidearm, Roberta swept her hand out of the pocket of her linen jacket and pressed a compact, silver-plated, snub-nosed pistol to his temple, the trigger already cocked.

"What the hell's goin' on here, Lina?" The pink, boisterous coloration of alcohol drained from Terry's face.

"You're the cop. Figure it out for yourself."

Dunne took Terry's gun. "Have a seat."

Terry sank on the bed. Roberta uncocked her gun and dropped it to her side. Dunne guessed from the expert way she wielded it that this wasn't the first time she'd pointed a gun at someone's head. That detective who'd tried to seduce Elba, for example, and then "disappeared." It could be she'd also used it.

Color returned to Terry's face. "Can't stop steppin' in shit, can you?"

"This time you're the one's stepped in it. A whole pile," Dunne said.

"So I like gettin' laid. Sue me."

"Was that why you were here the night of the Lynch murder?"

Terry glared at Lina. "I wasn't near here. I was with Brannigan, down at headquarters. Why not call and ask? He'd love hearin' from you."

"You help carry anybody out of Lina's room?"

"Helped carry plenty of people outta Lina's room. Dead drunks is her specialty."

Lina landed her open palm on his cheek. "You *never* carried nobody outta' my room, 'cept that once, less it was yourself."

Stunned, he rubbed the side of his face. "Okay, maybe I helped lug out some drunk that night. I did Sally a favor, that's all."

"No idea who it was?" Dunne said.

"I'm not in the habit of tryin' to tell one drunk from another. Like tryin' to tell Chinamen apart. Or flies."

"A man is sentenced to the electric chair for a crime he didn't commit. Maybe you could save him the trip."

"When did you go off and join the Salvation Army, Fin?" Terry stood. "Use that gun on me, you and your hooker friends will beat Grillo to the electric chair." He stepped toward the door. Dunne spun him around, impaled the loose flesh beneath his jaw with the barrel of his gun and pushed it up until the back of Terry's head slammed hard against the door.

Terry's eyes bulged wide. He emitted a small, strangled moan.

Roberta put her hand on Dunne's arm; pressed gently until he lowered the gun from beneath Terry's chin. "Stop, Fin," she said. "Let him talk."

Terry sagged on the bed. He sat silently, not moving, covered his face with his hands for a second or two, like someone about to go to confession. He sighed and folded over at the waist, as though he were an inflated doll that had suddenly sprung a large, irreparable leak. "Christ, I need a smoke," he said. Lina handed him hers.

"Was Grillo you carried out that night, wasn't it?" Dunne asked.

"Yeah."

"Whose idea was it to pin the murder on him?"

"Whose the hell do you think?" Terry inhaled until the gray-red tip almost touched the yellow stain between his fingertips. He ground the butt in the ashtray and wiped the perspiration from his face. "Not long after I hauled Grillo out of Lina's room, I got a call to report to Brannigan who was workin' a homicide a few blocks away. When I get there he tells me that he's lookin' for the super, Walter Grillo, who's missin'.

"Right away, I tell him about Grillo and where I left him, and I think the Chief will laugh. But he tells me to go get Grillo and bring him back. Don't let anybody see me and make sure Grillo don't wake up. Once I got Grillo, we poured more liquor down his throat and dumped him in the boiler room, with the knife nearby. A little while later, we go lookin' for him, with some reporters in tow. Bingo.

"The Chief had the whole thing figured out in a matter of minutes. He knew the murder would generate a lot of attention from the D.A. as well as the papers. Longer it went unsolved, the more they'd be pokin' their noses where they don't belong. He wanted the case closed quick as possible. From then on, he took personal charge. It was like Grillo was made for the part. The papers dubbed him 'the West Side Ripper.' Best of all, he'd apparently been so soused, he'd no memory of bein' here at Sally's. He never even brought it up. All he remembered was goin' for a walk."

"He remembered," Roberta said. "But there were people he thought would be embarrassed or hurt by the truth, and he didn't want to let them down."

Terry shrugged. "Each his own. Me, I'd rather hurt somebody's feelings than go to the chair."

"It never bothered you that he was innocent?"

"I'm a cop, lady, not a judge or jury. Grillo had a lawyer and the chance to defend himself. Besides, I never got called to the stand."

"Brannigan did," Dunne said.

"That's Brannigan's problem."

"Now it's yours too." Dunne made Terry stretch out on the

floor. He tore the cord from the blinds and knotted it around his hands and feet. "Where can I find Brannigan?"

"You're not serious, are you?"

"Humor me."

"The Chief always said your problem's mental. 'Dunne lost his mind in the war,' he says to me more than once."

Dunne pulled the cord tight. "Where can I find him?"

"All right, go ahead, be my guest. He's at Joe O'Brien's card game. You was smart, you'd drop this while you still can. Skip town for a while. I won't say a word 'bout this to no one, not even the Chief. Promise."

"I'll tell Brannigan you said hello."

"Stop bein' such a jerk, Fin. Stick with us, we'll stick with you. That's how it works, how it'll always work. Look after your own, they'll look after you."

"I look after myself. It's less complicated." Dunne shoved his handkerchief in Terry's mouth and tied the sash from the curtain around it. He dragged him into the closet and closed the door.

He sent Roberta and Lina to wait in the drugstore on the corner and sat on the bed until Terry began to kick hard against the wall. He opened the closet door and put the gun to the tip of Terry's nose. There was no more kicking. Dunne stayed a few moments longer, before tiptoeing out and closing the door gently behind him. Roberta and Lina were waiting for him. He handed Roberta the vial he'd removed from the Hermes Sanatorium. "Take it to Dr. Cropsey," he said. He gave her the address as well as Agent Lundgren's phone number. "Call him soon as I leave."

"Think he'll take a call from me?" Roberta said.

"Tell him I'm stealing a case right from underneath his nose. Tell him I'm in the George Washington Hotel, on Lexington, beating the FBI at its own game and grabbing the credit."

"Will he believe me?"

"He'll believe that."

Except for Joe O'Brien at the front desk, the lobby of the George Washington Hotel was empty. Wavy-haired and pencilstached, with a close resemblance to the actor William Powell, O'Brien was the hotel night clerk as well as host and proprietor of the East Side's longest running poker game. Initially, a pickup among O'Brien's fellow veterans from the 69th Regiment, whose headquarters was just up the avenue at 27th Street, the game became a regular stop for seasoned night prowlers and the lobster-shift crowd. For some, there was the added advantage of knowing that the presence of high-ranking police officers was a safeguard against the mob-run holdup artists who knocked over poker parlors with the regularity and precision of a Swiss clock.

Dunne dropped two dollars on the counter. "Been a while," O'Brien said.

"Turned over a new leaf."

"I liked the old leaf better." O'Brien pocketed the money. "Just so you know, Brannigan's in there." He pushed a buzzer beneath the counter and Dunne went through the door behind him. Nothing had changed in the year or so since his last visit: same four round tables situated close to one another and a well stocked bar in the corner. The smoky, stale air smelled as though it had been around since the armistice.

Brannigan was at the nearest table, the only one that was occupied, facing the door. John Mayhew Taylor and Tommy Hines were on either side. Dunne didn't know the names of the other two players, but he'd seen them here before. Long-time residents of the hotel, they were financial hucksters who ran hand-to-mouth boiler-room operations that peddled worthless stocks to the gullible and desperate, an endless line of dupes looking to strike it rich. Once upon a time, they'd been highfliers, nesting in the upstairs bar at the old Waldorf-Astoria. The Crash and the birth of the SEC had brought those days to an end. The old Waldorf was knocked down to make way for the Empire State Building. Like swallows to San Capistrano, they winged it back to the second-rate hotels in which they'd been hatched.

"Well, look what the wind blew in," Tommy Hines said.

Brannigan lifted his eyes from the cards. He was squeezed in a captain's chair, the handles of his midsection pressing against the armrests. His massive shoulders bulged tightly against the seams of his shirt. "Join us?"

"Just watching."

"Lost your nerve?" Brannigan asked.

"Somebody swiped my cash," Dunne said.

"Report it to the police?"

"Think it'd help?"

Brannigan shifted in his chair. "Think it'd hurt?"

Somebody else his size might have looked fat and ungainly. But Dunne had come to see in Brannigan a close resemblance to the tigers in the Bronx Zoo who sprawled in roly-poly repose until feeding time, when they sprang up with savage agility, lax skin turning taut and murderous. Brannigan's smile did nothing to diminish the catlike intensity of his stare.

"If you want, take my chair." Taylor threw down his cards and left the table. "I should have listened to the Professor. He warned me against coming here."

Hines folded his hand. "If luck was water, I'd be dead of thirst." The two others also folded. Brannigan swept the pot into his pile of winnings. From the size of it, if luck was water, he was having a bath. He shuffled the cards for a fresh hand.

Joe O'Brien brought in a box full of sandwiches wrapped in wax paper. Right behind was Red Doyle, who took off his hat and tossed it on one of the empty tables.

"Well if it ain't Leon O'Trotsky himself," Hines said.

Doyle slipped off his jacket and hung it over the back of the chair that Taylor had just vacated. "Deal me in."

Brannigan dealt. Hines arranged his cards. "Surprised to see you, Red. Last I heard you was learnin' Russian for your next trip to the Workers' Motherland."

The others laughed. Doyle picked up his cards. "Why don't you tag along. Stop in Berlin and give 'em some tips on beatin' confessions out of defenseless prisoners."

"Shut up and play cards," Brannigan said.

"Hey, Joe," Doyle said, "do me a favor and pour me a Scotch."

"Thought vodka would be the beverage of choice for Comrade Doyle." Hines chuckled to himself.

"And bring these Christian Fronters here some beers," Doyle said. "Good German beer if you have it, the kind the Führer has pissed in. Put it on my tab."

After several more hands, Brannigan's winnings, if not as large as when Doyle arrived, were still substantial. It was Hines's turn to deal. He swept up the cards. "Where you rabble-rousin' nowadays?" he asked Doyle.

"Organizin', you mean. The doorman and maintenance workers are unionizin', and I'm givin' a hand."

"Next, it'll be hookers and dope fiends," said the player across from Brannigan.

"Give everybody an equal start and offer a basic measure of security, maybe we won't churn out hookers and dope fiends the way we do today," Doyle said.

Brannigan was back on a winning streak. "This is the last time I'll say it. Shut up or leave the table."

The player across from Brannigan threw down his cards and quit the game. He picked up a newspaper from the bar. "Look at this." He whacked the tabloid with the back of his hand and held up the headline: HITLER TO JEWS: GET OUT.

"Ten to one, those sheenies will be headed here." Another of the players tossed in his cards and went to the bar.

"Just what we need, more sheenies." The player at the bar handed him a drink.

"You guys are a regular font of human kindness," O'Brien said.

"More like a urinal." Doyle folded, too.

Brannigan gathered in his winnings. He left his chair, stretched, and yawned. He joined the others at the bar and poured himself a Scotch. "Why so quiet, Fin?" he said. The glass was almost invisible in the curl of his hand.

"Sometimes you learn more by listening," Dunne said.

"Sure, and it's a lot safer than driving hookers to New Jersey." Brannigan threw an arm across Dunne's shoulder. "Believe it or not, despite all your shenanigans, I still got a soft spot for you. Maybe I can steer some clients your way. Save you from having to scrounge in the gutter." He dropped his arm and clapped Dunne on the back, a friendly pat, if also a little harder than that.

"Lately, I've been listening to Matt Terry. He's been shooting his mouth off at Sally Hoffritz's place, telling everybody how Grillo got framed."

"I meant what I said about helping you find work, Dunne. Once a cop, always a cop. You stop being a pain in the butt, I'll help make sure your business goes right." Brannigan lit a cigar.

"Be quite a scoop if what Terry said is true," Taylor said. "But who framed him and why? Did Terry say?"

"Matt Terry never said any such thing." Brannigan rested the cigar on the edge of the bar, spread his feet apart, and brushed his chin with the side of his hand.

"Sure he did. Still at Sally's, blubbering his head off. Don't believe me, come on, we'll go over right now."

Brannigan eyed the floor as if he'd dropped something. Dunne recognized the feint: same slouch of the shoulders and swivel of the head Brannigan used to deceive scores of suspects, guilty and innocent alike. For an instant, they were sure he was ready to walk away, satisfied or at least not displeased with whatever answers they'd given, utterly off-guard for the hammer blow that would send them across the room.

Dunne's hard, well aimed punch preempted Brannigan, smashing into the bridge of his nose and knocking him backward into Taylor, who lost his balance and tumbled to the floor. Dunne popped in close to Brannigan and hit him again, squarely on his jaw. The immediate and ferocious pain that shot up his arm telegraphed to Dunne that, whatever damage he'd done to Brannigan, he'd also broken his right hand.

"Hold it, Dunne!" Tommy Hines reached for his revolver, but before he could unholster it, Red Doyle pinned his arms behind his back.

"Don't anyone interfere," Brannigan used his sleeve to wipe the blood flowing from his nose. "Now it's my turn."

The sharp pain in Dunne's hand became a paralyzing ache. He tried to reach into his belt and grasp the gun he'd taken from Terry, but his fingers wouldn't close. Brannigan charged at him. With his left hand, Dunne hooked the handle of the pitcher of beer on the bar and, taking a wide swing, delivered it into Branngian's face.

Brannigan reeled back on his heels, tripped over Taylor, who was crawling on hands and knees to get out of the way, and crashed into the table where they'd been playing cards. It collapsed under his weight, scattering cards, drinks, and winnings across the floor.

Dunne took a second pitcher of beer and poured it over a prone and unconscious Brannigan. "Here, Chief," he said, "I owe you a dousing." He used his left hand to pick up the bills from Brannigan's winnings and stuff them in his pocket. He got Terry's pistol from his belt and dropped it on Brannigan's stomach. Brannigan moaned but didn't open his eyes. Dunne removed the cigar from the bar and stuck it in Brannigan's mouth. "Now we're even, Chief. Almost."

Taylor huddled in a corner with Joe O'Brien and the others. "You want a scoop, better come now," Dunne said.

Rid of Doyle's grip, Hines went to aid Brannigan. "You won't get away with this!"

"We'll see who gets away with what, Tommy."

Outside, Doyle went into a crouch and threw a battery of shadow punches. "Nice sock to the nose," he said, "but you missed a perfect chance with the left." An unmarked sedan pulled up. Lundgren hopped out of the passenger's side. "Where you think you're going, Dunne?" he said.

"Brannigan's inside. All primed to spill his guts. Meantime, I'm helping Taylor here with a story."

"Better not be pulling my chain."

Taylor hailed a cab. "*Au revoir*," Dunne said. He gave the cabby the address of Sally Hoffritz's place, and they sped away.

THE OLD BUDAPEST INN, BERLIN

Although he betrayed no sign of it, Canaris was nonplussed by the sight of General Beck in civilian clothes. The usually well tailored soldier, who always looked trim and smart in uniform, wore a gray suit and white shirt, buttoned to the collar and no tie. He seemed to have shrunk and grown older in the few days since Canaris had last seen him.

Beck picked at the veal stew. He put down his fork and took a drink of water. "I had to resign," he said. "If I wanted to preserve even one shred of self-respect, I could not do otherwise."

The waiter returned to the private room that Canaris had reserved in his favorite Hungarian restaurant, a block from military headquarters. He and Beck said nothing while the waiter filled their glasses with Tokay. "That will be all," Canaris said.

"The Führer is determined to attack the Czechs, sometime between September 21 and October 1." Beck stared at his food. "It was my hope that when others saw the Chief of the General Staff had resigned to protest against such unwarranted aggression, they would follow."

"Your decision is widely admired."

"But not imitated."

"Soldiers are soldiers. Obedience is in our blood."

"There comes a time when even a soldier must think with his brain and not just listen to his blood."

Canaris pushed away his plate. Neither he nor Beck had done more than nibble at their food. He had hoped that dinner with Beck might lift his spirits, as his intellect and straightforward conversation usually did. Instead, Canaris felt himself further deflated by Beck's forlorn appearance.

"Oster is furious with me, I suppose," Beck said.

"He was, well, surprised that you allowed the reason for your resignation to be kept private."

"I sat in the same seat as great soldiers such as Moltke and Schlieffen. I couldn't cooperate with a band of criminals determined to set loose a war, but neither could I act in the fashion of a prima donna, turning an act of conscience into a public spectacle."

Using the small silver bell by his plate, Canaris signaled for the waiter, instructing him to take away their dishes and bring a check.

"You weren't pleased with the food?" the waiter asked.

"I haven't much of an appetite today, that's all." Canaris lit a cigarette. The intemperate monologue he'd endured from Oster that afternoon had put him in a black mood. He told Oster to lower his voice. Oster ignored him, railing against Beck's decision to go quietly and allow the Führer to credit the resignation of his Chief of Staff to "ill health."

Beck folded his hands and bowed his head, as though ready to pray grace after meals. "Have you heard anything from England?"

"Nothing very encouraging, I'm afraid. The attitude of the Foreign Office seems to be that any disagreements within the regime are internal squabbles of no consequence to His Majesty's government. Their overriding desire is to reach some accommodation that will avoid another war." Canaris turned his head to exhale the smoke away from Beck, who made no secret of his dislike for cigarettes. The door to the room was half-opened. Outside, the waiter was writing in his order book, totaling up the bill, perhaps.

"Franz Halder came and spoke with me as soon as the Führer named him successor as Chief of Staff. He's a good soldier. He, too, is afraid of another war. He thinks that, as a new voice, he might be able to reason with the Führer."

"He'll learn quickly." Canaris caught the waiter's attention and signaled for the check.

The waiter approached with the check in both hands, as if he were about to read from it. "Pardon me, if this appears rude, but you are General Beck, are you not?"

Beck nodded. His mouth was slightly ajar.

"I was sure it was you. Admiral Canaris I have seen here many times, but I recognize you from your picture in the newspaper." He smiled and put down the check.

Canaris examined it, pretending to make sure the addition was correct. He tried to reassure himself that the sensitive parts of his conversation with Beck had been out of the waiter's earshot. "That will be all." He signed the check and handed it back.

"Yes, Herr Admiral." The waiter stuck the check in his order book but made no motion to leave. "I hope this doesn't seem too forward or out of line, but I know that you gentlemen were talking about the situation with the Czechs."

Beck's mouth opened wider. He seemed about to speak but no sound came out.

"Well, you should know that among us Magyars there is a growing cadre determined to replicate the success of the Third Reich in our homeland. We are ready to stand with Germany against the Czechs, the British, and all the willing dupes of Jewish-run Bolshevist subversion and degeneracy."

Canaris and Beck rose simultaneously. Beck walked to the door without saying anything. "Your expression of support is appreciated," Canaris said.

"A new order is coming to Europe," the waiter said, as Canaris followed Beck out of the room. "Those who aren't for it are against it, and those against it are doomed!"

Gresser informed Canaris as soon as he arrived at his office that Lieutenant Colonel Piekenbrock had requested to see him. Following a cup of coffee and a glance through the morning paper, Canaris had Gresser summon Piekenbrock. When he arrived, Canaris sent Gresser on an errand and shut the door.

Canaris poured himself another cup. "Would you care for some?"

"No, thank you, and I apologize for the delay," Piekenbrock said.

"What delay?" Canaris motioned for him to sit.

"The information on the SS agent in New York you requested." Piekenbrock undid a button on his tunic and took from the inner breast pocket a thin sheath of papers. He unfolded it on the desk and smoothed the sheets with several strokes of his palm.

"Of course, yes. I'm afraid I've been distracted."

Piekenbrock rebuttoned the tunic. "I went about my inquiries 'discreetly,' as you instructed. It took longer than I'd hoped, but I believe I avoided raising any suspicions, at least above what is normal. Mostly, it required drinking with my SS counterparts and listening to them brag, which takes only a modicum of encouragement. That, and the occasional bribe."

"Wait a moment while I ask Oster to come in. He brought this to my attention."

Oster came immediately. He spread out on the couch, arms across the tops of the leather cushions.

"Forgive any sloppiness or errors. I was allowed to look at Hausser's SS dossier but not retain it."

"Hausser?" Canaris said.

Springing from the couch, Oster reached over and took the papers Piekenbrock had placed on the desk. "Yes, if you recall our conversation of several weeks ago, that's the agent's name." After a quick examination, he abruptly handed them to Canaris, ignoring the latter's visible irritation at their interception.

Canaris put on his glasses. The handwriting was small, cramped, difficult to read. He gave the papers back to Piekenbrock. "What's the gist?"

"The SS wants to take over the Abwehr." The scorn in Oster's voice was undisguised. He lifted the lighter from the desk, thumbed the flint, and leaned the cigarette in his mouth into the flame. "That's become the gist of about everything around here."

Although annoyed at Oster's obtrusion and impertinence, Canaris acted as if unaffected. "In outline, what have you discovered?"

"Gregor Hausser is an American," Piekenbrock said. "At least he was born there, in the city of Hoboken, in 1901. His parents were East Prussians, from Königsberg. His father, a chemist, brought the family back to Germany shortly after the outbreak of the war and served with distinction on the Western Front. He was killed at the Somme in 1917. Hausser left school in 1918, at the war's end, and joined a Freikorps unit in Berlin. He settled there, working as a butcher's apprentice, until 1925, when he returned to America. There, he worked in a meat-packing plant in Chicago, until 1929, when he lost his job and returned once more to Germany."

Oster went back to the couch. "The fellow's a regular gypsy."

Fumbling for a moment, Piekenbrock marked the place he was looking for with his forefinger. "Here's the gist, I suppose: he joined the Nazi Party in 1930; the SS in '31. He assisted in the purge of Röhm and the SA in 1934 and was assigned as an aide to Eicke, at Dachau. On Eicke's recommendation, Hausser was sent to the SS Officers Academy at Bad Tolz and was subsequently appointed to its training staff."

"The American background explains why he was judged suitable for a mission to the United States," Canaris said. "But what's the purpose of the mission?"

"There was no hint in his file, but there are facts I discovered not in the official documents. You should know that these cost me—or, more accurately, the Abwehr—a case of fine cognac and a pair of the best English riding boots."

"That's all?" Oster pretended to be disappointed. "If it were worth anything to those bloodsuckers in the SS, they'd have charged you a hundred times that."

"Let's find out what it is before we worry whether we under-paid." Canaris no longer felt peeved at Oster's behavior. He knew it was rooted in frustration with the manner of General Beck's res-ignation and the wobbling resolve to mount a coup if and when war broke out. He merely wished for his sake and everyone else's that Oster would try to do a better job of hiding it.

"Hausser has a police record," Piekenbrock again shuffled the papers until he'd pinpointed a paragraph with his finger. He read aloud: "Arrested in Munich, in 1934, for the near fatal beating of a prostitute. Charges quashed by order of the State Minister of Police. Repeat arrests in 1935 and '36, same charges, same out-comes. Detained in the stabbing, strangulation death of a prosti-tute in Berlin, June 1937. Further prosecution of the case was stopped by order of Reinhard Heydrich, Chief of the Security Services."

"Even by SS standards, an odd choice for a secret agent, wouldn't you say?" Oster lit a new cigarette with the burned-down remnant of the old.

"There's more. When Hausser served with the Death's Head Unit at Dachau, he earned the nickname 'The King of Spades' for on-the-spot executions of prisoners in his work detail with a sharpened shovel. They were recorded as 'accidental deaths.' It's all here." Piekenbrock handed the sheet he'd been reading from to Canaris.

"Have you made any inquiries with our Abwehr agents in New York?"

"Yes, Admiral, they already knew of Hausser, who's hardly kept a low profile. He's hung around the Bund in New York and been a loudmouth participant in some of their rallies. He bragged to fellow Bundists of a personal acquaintance with General

Heydrich. Our agents figured him for either an FBI plant or a hollow-headed braggart."

"The incurable arrogance of the SS. They all suffer from it. Worse, it's highly contagious." Oster was on his feet again, pacing back and forth in front of the door.

"You instructed our agents to keep a watch on him, I trust," Canaris said.

"I planned to, but before I could, I was informed he'd disappeared."

"Disappeared? You mean, recalled to Germany?"

"It's unclear. I'm still receiving information from New York. It seems he's been working as a chauffeur, and his employer died in a fire."

"Is Hausser suspected in it?"

"It doesn't appear so. But our agents in New York tell us that he's vanished from sight."

"What do your SS contacts tell you?"

"They're being untypically tight-lipped. Either they don't know or won't divulge. I don't want to do anything that would indicate too deep an interest on my part."

Canaris smiled, slightly. "Perhaps, he's gone underground and joined up with the gangsters who run New York."

"In New York, the gangsters rule the underground." Oster shot a fulgurous glance at Canaris. "But in Berlin they run the government."

September 1938

# 8

The Jew, as seen through the eyes of the ordinary non-Jew, is a study in contradictions. He is at once communist subversive and capitalist exploiter. He is an unhealthy creature, lax in matters of personal hygiene and poorly conditioned, yet an extraordinary seducer of wholesome, attractive gentile girls. He is the modernist par excellence, the enemy of tradition, but a stubborn adherent to the practices of his ancient faith. He controls the newspapers and the movies but the little attention paid him in these venues is often in the form of disparaging stereotypes. The Jew is a peddler and small businessman, a scrounger and a scavenger; and he is plutocrat and millionaire, overlord of the factories and department stores that drive the peddler and small businessman out of business. He is a coward and a pacifist, afraid of war because it often results in pogroms directed against himself and his tribe, and he is a scheming warmonger eager for the profits that war will bring. Attempts to reconcile these opposing perceptions of the Jew will invariably fail unless one understands that they have little to do with the perceived—i.e., the Jew—and everything to do with the perceiver, the non-Jew. Perhaps the best way to think of it is to imagine the Jew as a movie screen, a blank surface, upon which society projects its submerged fears, resentments and lusts, allowing them to flicker through the filter of everyday perceptions. Pity the poor Jew, if you wish. But beware the projectionist, you must.

—MANFRED STERN, *Landscapes of the Imagination*

## THE RIVER CLUB, EAST 52ND STREET, NEW YORK

DONOVAN LOWERED THE newspaper. The account of the reopening of the Grillo case had absorbed him so thoroughly that he hadn't noticed that most of the other breakfasters in the River Club had finished and left. A waiter poured him another cup of coffee. He lifted it—a silent, solo toast. *Here's to Dunne. He'd come through.*

Donovan almost congratulated himself on never doubting that he would; but he knew there'd been moments when he had. How couldn't there have been when he'd stuck out his neck on such little evidence?

"What's got you looking so happy?" Jim Forrestal stood on the other side of the table, hat at his side. He was smiling, or what passed for a smile with Forrestal, one corner of his mouth turned up at a wry, sarcastic angle. "Every time I read the papers, I want to puke."

Donovan pointed at the headline. "This murder case that's being re-opened, and the exposé of the crooked cops who were involved."

"What about it?"

"An acquaintance of mine is responsible, Fintan Dunne, an ex-cop and private investigator. He served with me in the 69th."

"Catch one rat today. Tomorrow another brood is born. That's the way of the world." Forrestal put his hat on the table and pulled up a chair. "Mind if I sit?" He sat before Donovan could say anything, looked around for a waiter and snapped his fingers at one he spotted in the corner. "Bring me a cup of tea."

"I thought you'd still be out on the North Shore," Donovan said.

"I'd rather die from heat then boredom." Forrestal brushed his finger beneath his flat and slightly tilted nose, a reminder of a knockout blow he'd taken in his days as a college boxer. He turned in his chair. "Where's that tea?"

Donovan laughed at Forrestal's impatience. He'd never been put off by Forrestal's abruptness, which others found unmannerly and abrasive. He considered it part of the sales pitch by the brokerage house of Dillion, Read, a firm headed by arrivistes like Clarence Dillon (born Lapowski, he'd done a nuptial reverse and taken his wife's maiden name) and Jim Forrestal, who, though he did his damnedest to avoid any reference to it, had never entirely erased the taint of his Irish working-class origin up the Hudson River, in Beacon, New York. Outsiders perceived Dillon, Read as part of the Street's blue-blood club. Insiders knew that Dillon and Forrestal had climbed up from below and snickered among themselves at Hymie and Paddy's efforts to pass as Anglo-Saxons. Yet they were often more likely to trust their money to men who were born without it and knew its true value than to those fed from a silver porridge bowl with a silver spoon.

The waiter brought Forrestal a cup, saucer, and pot of tea. "Do you wish me to pour, sir? Or do you prefer to let it steep?"

Forrestal didn't look at him. "Steep."

"How was your trip to Washington?" Donovan didn't expect that Forrestal would resent being questioned about his invitation to the White House. It was common knowledge that, after six years of unremitting animosity, F.D.R. was trying to repair his relationship with the financial community and had summoned men he perceived might be sympathetic, Forrestal among them.

"You think it's hot here? Washington is a hell hole."

"Did it go well?"

"My trip?"

"Your meeting with the President."

"Fine." Forrestal poured himself a cup of tea.

"Did he cast the famous Roosevelt spell over you?"

The corner of Forrestal's mouth angled up in a sardonic smile. "He said I had a reputation as a tough, short-tempered son of a bitch."

"I suppose that's better than being 'a malefactor of great wealth.' The government doesn't hound every son of a bitch over his income taxes."

"He meant it as a compliment. He said he was looking for men who know how to get things done, especially how to organize and finance large-scale industrial enterprises."

"Too bad he didn't think of that six years ago, before he plunged the country into a failed experiment with socialism. He's only got two years before his time is up."

Forrestal shrugged. "He's thinking about the country's defenses. The threats from overseas are becoming too powerful to ignore. He said he wants to bring the whole country behind an effort to make sure we're armed and ready for whatever comes."

"Come on, Jim. The man will say whatever he thinks will bring you over to the Democrats. If ever there was a living embodiment of Dr. Johnson's dictum that 'Patriotism is the last refuge of a scoundrel,' it's F.D.R. He's failed to end the Depression, and he and his party know the political tide is turning against them."

"I like him."

"That's not the issue. The fact is, you can't trust him."

"*Trust?*" Forrestal poured himself a cup of tea, blew on it, and took a gulp. "Who said anything about trust? I think he'll do whatever's necessary to ensure we don't end up at the mercy of our enemies."

"You're about half right, Jim. He'll do whatever is necessary to ensure he can outfox his political adversaries. War is about the last card he has to play."

"He asked about you."

"Me?"

"Yeah, you. Apparently, he knows we're neighbors on Beekman Place."

"And cut from the same green cloth. He knows the Irish in the country are overwhelmingly opposed to bailing out the British a second time."

Forrestal ignored Donovan's reference to their shared Irish Catholic background. "He asked if I ever saw you, and when I said we often bumped into each other, he said to send his regards."

Donovan ignored the message from the president. "This time it's not just the Irish who are opposed. The vast majority of Americans are against sending our boys overseas again."

"It's different this time," Forrestal said.

"Yes, this time instead of an insufferable moralist like Woodrow Wilson for our president, who couldn't accept any fact that didn't fit his ideals, we have Franklin Roosevelt, a thoroughbred opportunist who has no ideals other than ensuring his own political survival. Did he reminisce with you about the time he and I spent together at Columbia and our mutual love of football?"

"No. All he said was that Bill Donovan is a patriot. 'When the time comes,' he said, 'I know I'll be able to count on him.'"

"Now that he's got that rogue Joe Kennedy as ambassador to London, he'll try to add a few more Irish names to his administration to keep the Paddy vote loyal in case he decides to try for a third term. He's a shameless politician."

"I wouldn't want to be led by a shameful one." Forrestal finished his tea. He picked up his hat and stood. "I better be going."

"I'll walk with you on the way out." Donovan signed for his breakfast and accompanied Forrestal to the street.

"This Czech business is just a start." Forrestal snapped the brim of his hat to protect against the glare of the morning sun.

"It's also none of our business. It's for the Europeans to figure out."

"For now maybe. But not for long."

Donovan's driver pulled up in front of them. "Can I offer you a ride downtown?"

"Thanks, but no." Forrestal slipped his hands into the pockets of his crisply pressed, handsomely tailored suit. "I'm going to stop at my gym."

Donovan guessed Forrestal had the suit made by a Savile Row tailor. Like most on Wall Street who weren't born to the upper class, Forrestal was careful to always dress as if he were.

"You're not going to believe this," Forrestal said, apparently aware Donovan was admiring his suit, "but a few weeks ago, some louse stole one of my suits while I was working out at the gym. He left my wallet and keys but took everything else, including shirt, tie, and shoes. Maybe I should hire that private eye friend of yours to look into it."

"Dunne? I'm afraid he's got bigger things on his mind. But you're lucky, because it could have been worse."

"How?"

"If the thief was a New Dealer, he'd have taken the wallet, too."

Forrestal wasn't amused. "Whoever he was, if I ever get my hands on him, I'll break his neck."


Delayed by the downtown traffic, Donovan hurried into his office, giving his secretary a quick, perfunctory hello. She followed behind and placed a file on his desk. She held several phone messages in her hand.

"Damn traffic," Donovan said. "Pretty soon it's going to bring the entire city to a standstill." He took his jacket and tossed it over the arm of a chair.

She picked it up, smoothed it with her hand, and draped it carefully over her arm. "Which would you like first, the good news or the bad?"

He sat behind the desk. "Good."

"There's no need to rush. Your ten o'clock appointment is canceled. Mr. Pennoyer from Morgan's is indisposed. He'll have to reschedule."

"And the bad?"

She laid five phone messages on his blotter as though they were a poker hand. "Take your pick. They're all from the same person."

He picked one out and read the name aloud, "Ian Anderson."

"He called twice after you left last evening and three times this morning. The last was about twenty minutes ago."

"Did he say what he wanted?"

"Only that it was urgent."

"Next time insist that you need more information."

She shifted his jacket to her other arm. "I'm afraid the bad news gets worse. He's nearby and intends to stop here in hopes of catching a few spare minutes with you. I told him you have none to spare, but I don't think I dissuaded him."

Donovan looked at his watch. "Well, I suppose now that the ten o'clock appointment is canceled, I can give him a few minutes. But don't close the door." By the time he returned from a trip to the bathroom, Anderson had arrived. His visit turned out to be mercifully brief. He explained that he'd read in last night's paper about the sudden re-opening of the Grillo case and wondered if Donovan might not use his connections with the prosecutor's office to put him in touch with the chief investigator.

Pleased at such an easy request to fulfill, Donovan didn't pry. He told Anderson he could do even better than put him in touch, since he was a personal acquaintance of the private detective being celebrated in the papers. They'd served together in the war, and though Donovan kept mum about his role in getting Dunne out of jail, he promised Anderson that Dunne would gladly provide whatever help he could. He dialed Dunne's number several times but only got a busy signal. He summoned his secretary and asked her to keep trying.

It was only when Anderson had taken Dunne's number to try himself, and was about to leave, that Donovan asked him about his interest in the case. "Last time we talked," he said, "you seemed interested in bigger matters."

Politely evasive, Anderson said the case was of concern to friends of his. Once he gathered more information, he'd have more to say. For now, he was simply grateful to be pointed in Mr. Dunne's direction. "You wouldn't mind if I use your name with Mr. Dunne, would you?" he asked.

"Not at all. He can phone if he has any questions. But I doubt he will."

"One hand washes the other, is that it?

"Something like that."


THE HACKETT BUILDING, NEW YORK


Dunne removed his hand from beneath the cardboard cup. Lukewarm coffee slowly dripped from its bottom. A single drop made a direct hit on the week-old front page of the *Standard*, splattering Brannigan's face and the detectives on either side. The brown blot might have obscured his angry disbelief at being in the perpetrator's position, flash bulbs almost blinding him while shouts came from all sides—*Say 'cheese,' Chief, say 'thirty years to life'*—except Brannigan's heavily bandaged nose and jaw were fixed with the blank numbness of a broken-down prizefighter direct from a final trip to the canvas.

The chief's vacant face reminded Dunne for the first time in a long while of the Brannigan he'd met when they'd both been rookies. Brannigan had come across as decent enough, even a notch above most. He hadn't been in the war. Instead, he'd spent a year at Manhattan College studying to be an engineer. When his money ran out, he became a cop. But it hadn't taken long for casual corruption to turn habitual, and for the poison to spread throughout his system.

His acolyte, Matt Terry, pulled the cork the minute they dragged him out of the closet in Sally Hoffritz's place, gushing his story to Taylor with the unplugged contrition of a drunken driver who comes to in the middle of the fatal pileup he'd caused. True to the Professor's formulation that one man's tragedy is another's triumph, the Brannigan exposé brought Taylor his second headline in the *Standard*.

TOP COP IMPLICATED IN PROSTITUTION RACKET SCANDAL

COULD TOUCH MANY IN THE RANKS: DEWEY PROMISES

'NEW WAR ON CORRUPTION' FEDS ALSO LIKELY TO ACT

By John Mayhew Taylor

The reader had to turn the page to find a piece by John Lockwood headlined:

BRANNIGAN ARREST RAISES NEW QUESTION ON

GRILLO CASE: STAY OF EXECUTION LIKELY

The Professor pointed out that Brannigan's record of success as the head of homicide had apparently won him a degree of immunity when it came to his other activities. As long as Brannigan didn't flaunt his involvement in illicit sidelines, the attitude of department higher-ups seemed to be, why endanger the acclaim he won from the press, the public, and prosecutors for catching murderers? Now, however, with the extent of his corruption exposed, the mayor, police commissioner, and D.A. were unanimous in calling for the Chief Inspector's head.

The Professor gave prominent mention to the role of private investigator and former policeman Fintan Dunne and reported it was Dunne's involvement in the case of convicted killer Walter Grillo that caused him to look into Brannigan's alleged crimes. A spokesman for the D.A.'s office was quoted as saying that all of the recent cases Brannigan handled would be reviewed. Since Grillo was so close to being executed, his would be first. Inspector William Hanlon, the new Chief of Homicide, pledged a full reexamination of the case.

The *Mirror* made no mention of the D.A.'s decision to reconsider the Grillo case. Later, rather than sooner, Corrigan would write it up. For now the paper was full of the cop scandal and in no hurry to remind readers of its role in dubbing Grillo the "West Side Ripper." Dunne ripped off the front page of the *Mirror*, wrapped it around the leaky bottom of his coffee cup, and tossed it in the wastebasket. The mention of his name in the papers and on the radio was enough to keep his phone ringing most of the morning. The calls were all from people who wanted to hire him to help prove a friend/lover/relative innocent of the murder/heist/forgery for which he/she stood accused/convicted. *Oh, please, Mr. Dunne, you're our last hope.* He took their numbers and said he'd call them back. That morning, even the usher in the lobby of the Hackett Building had been fawningly polite, his welcome free of any mention of impending eviction.

He rang Elba Corado's shop several times. There was no answer. He was about to leave when the phone rang and kept ringing. Thinking it might be Elba or Roberta, he picked up. A voice with one of those high-hat-and-tails English accents asked, "I wonder if I might speak with Mr. Fintan Dunne?"

"He's unavailable."

"Perhaps you have a number at which he can be reached."

"This is the number."

"Might I leave my name and number?"

"Try later."

"If you wouldn't mind, tell him Colonel William Donovan advised I call."

"What'd you say your name was?"

"I didn't. It's Ian Anderson."

"Can you give him time to clean up some business?"

"I'm at his disposal."

"Leave a number. Mr. Dunne will get back to you. It's no emergency, is it?"

"Tell Mr. Dunne that remains to be seen."

## WORTH STREET, NEW YORK

Doc Cropsey was eating a tuna fish sandwich at his desk and reading the *Standard* when Dunne appeared at his door. He peered over the top of his glasses. "I see the politicians finally woke up to the fact that Brannigan's a crook. Only took 'em ten years to acknowledge what the rest of the city knew the day he got the job." He turned the page. "And I see you managed to squeeze some ink for yourself out of poor old Lockwood."

"Good for business."

"Now you're famous, I suppose I'll have to stick a plaque on my place in Southold: 'Fintan Dunne Slept Here.' But tell me, before I do, did you sleep alone or did you have those two women you sent here?"

"I was wondering if they made it to see you."

"Stop wondering. When the guard wouldn't let them in, they caused quite a stir."

"Did they give you the vial?"

"I sent it to the toxicological lab at Bellevue. They already got back to me."

"What do I owe you?"

"It'll cost you five bucks." Cropsey finished his sandwich. He took a pad from the drawer of his desk and insisted on giving Dunne a receipt. "Phenobarbital," he said, "that's what was in it."

"Not Luminal?"

"Luminal's a trademark for Phenobarbital."

"Can it kill?"

"Depends on the age, weight, and the physical condition of the person it's used on. Also, if there was already a sufficient buildup of Luminal in the bloodstream, dose as strong as what was in there would cause pulmonary depression. Lungs fill up with water. Death's inevitable."

"So someone with an adequate supply of Phenobarbital and a way of administering it could kill at will?"

"That's why you need a prescription."

"But a doctor could pretty much get all he wants, no?"

"A doctor determined to commit murder has plenty of means at his disposal, if that's what he wants, and there's been the occasional lunatic who's done so. Last century, Dr. Thomas Cream in London killed seven women with strychnine injections. Herman Mudgett in Chicago, a former medical student and pharmacist, confessed to twenty-eight murders by various means, including gas, poison, and strangulation. I'm sure there've been other cases. But it goes against a doctor's whole training to willfully destroy human life. Besides, can you think of a better way for a doctor to put himself out of business than killing all his patients?"

"What if a doctor had an endless supply of patients and the means both to kill and dispose of them?"

"He'd still need a motive."

"Human sanitation. Free the world of misfits. Preserve the purity of the race."

"What'd he do with the remains?"

"The bodies are used as specimens. They're dissected or experimented on, then incinerated, the ashes mixed with sand and made the soft bed of a playground."

"How about their relatives?"

"What if they were without families? Orphans? People who'd been abandoned?"

"He'd still need a good deal of help."

"What if there were plenty of people who believed what he believed and considered it a duty to assist?"

"He'd never be able to hide it. Somebody'd snitch or catch on."

"What if somebody did catch on, by accident, and tried to gather evidence but was killed before it could be revealed?"

"Fin, I've been in the bone trade long enough to know that when a normally sensible person detects ghouls and murderers round every corner, it's time to give the gray matter a breather. Overwork is the enemy of a clear mind. Alcohol's no friend either. My day, I knew plenty of both, but since I've given up the booze and spend every spare minute fishing on Peconic Bay, I'm thinking clear as the purest spring in Paradise. Come out soon. Doctor's orders."

"Soon as I can."

"You're always welcome, long as you come alone."

When Dunne arrived at the Hackett Building, the only one in the lobby was a lanky pipe smoker examining the wall directory. The back of his badly wrinkled linen suit jacket had a perspiration stain shaped roughly like the Chrysler Building. His straw hat was white as milk, the way new straw is, and he wore slender, hand-crafted English shoes that cost a bundle but, if properly cared for, last a lifetime. Hearing someone behind him, he turned quickly. "Good day," he said, a greeting that exposed him as a foreigner, as much for his noticeable accent as his woeful unfamiliarity with the New York rule of never acknowledging anyone waiting for the same conveyance. His tie was thinner than was stylish but had those blue, gold, and red stripes beloved of British officers and the American private-school crowd who couldn't imagine anything nobler or more desirable than being taken for one.

"Mr. Anderson?" Dunne thought it was a safe bet that this was the Englishman he'd talked to earlier on the phone.

"Why, yes." He grinned and extended his hand. If he was surprised at a total stranger addressing him by name, he didn't show it.

Dunne introduced himself and invited him to his office. They rode the elevator in silence. The office, like the day, had become smotheringly hot. Dunne flipped the switch for the ceiling fan, but it stayed motionless. The building's refurbishment apparently hadn't included the wiring. He pushed up the window as far as it would go. A pygmy puff of wind blew in and, with it, the stench of two-day-old garbage from the rear of the beanery across the alley.

"Mind if I smoke?" Anderson was already stuffing the pipe from the tobacco pouch he'd removed from his pocket.

"Be my guest."

"I'm thankful your assistant was able to get hold of you. Did Colonel Donovan reach you as well?"

"I didn't know he tried."

"He called several times. He's very proud of you and your new-found fame."

"Wasn't for him, I'd be serving old-fashioned jail time."

"And Mr. Grillo would have been executed for a crime he didn't commit."

"You know about Grillo?" Dunne asked.

"It's why I'm here. I've an interest in one of the peripheral figures in the investigation. His name came up in the newspaper account I read of the D.A.'s intent to re-examine Mr. Grillo's conviction."

"Who's that?"

"The late Dr. Sparks. When I contacted Colonel Donovan to inquire if he might put me in touch with someone in the prosecutor's office who could assist me, he quite enthusiastically suggested that, instead of the prosecutor, I talk to you."

"How do you know Colonel Donovan?"

"Like you, I served with him in the war." An abundant plume of smoke rose from Anderson's pipe.

"I served *under* him." Dunne resisted the urge to stick his head out the window. "You a friend of Sparks's?" he asked.

"Never met the man."

"Insurance?"

"Pardon?"

"You investigating a claim?"

Anderson laughed. "Hardly."

Dunne considered picking up the phone to call Colonel Donovan and get the full story on the grinning Englishman he'd sicced on him. But with a debt the size he owed Donovan, he didn't want to even hint at ingratitude.

"I know of Sparks only through a book he wrote some years ago and through two acquaintances of mine who used to live in Germany but now reside in New York. I was out of the country at the time, but they alerted me to the news of his demise. They believe Sparks is alive. Do you?"

"Let's just say he disappeared at a convenient moment."

"I believe very strongly that Sparks is alive, and I also believe that if he's caught and exposed, it's a chance to compel people to confront the larger reality he embodies. In that regard, I wonder if I might introduce you to the two I spoke of before? They are most knowledgeable about Sparks and his connections. I think they'll help resolve any questions you might have about who he was, or rather, is." Anderson looked around the office as though he didn't know where the smoke had come from. "At worst, it'll be a chance to get some fresh air."

The air in Yorkville was rank with the slightly sour smell of roasted hops from the Rupert Brewery, every bit as stale as the smoke left behind in Dunne's office. The address Anderson directed the cab driver to was an as-you'd-expect uptown tenement, indistinguishable from the other dun-colored buildings on the block. But the vestibule was meticulously kept, cracked tile floor mopped and scrubbed, light fixture and mailboxes polished to an out-of-place elegance.

"I should warn you that the couple we're visiting are Germans *and* doctors," Anderson said. "They're in the habit of lecturing. But unlike some of their countrymen, they're worth listening to." He led the way up three flights and knocked on the apartment door nearest the stairwell. What sounded like a grunt came from inside. A heavy, jowly man in tweed pants, suspenders draped by his sides, and his white shirt hanging out in front, opened the door. He looked to be in his fifties, but his girth probably made him seem older than he was. He had a head full of closely cropped white bristles and a mustache like the Kaiser used to wear, with the ends brushed up. He and Anderson spoke in German as they went down a narrow hallway into a small living room in which the shades were drawn and the lamps on either side of the couch turned on.

"I should like to introduce you to Dr. Franz Ignatz," Anderson said.

Franz Ignatz gripped Dunne's hand. "My friend informs me you're a detective."

"A private eye."

"Like Sherlock Holmes?"

"I don't smoke a pipe."

"But Mr. Anderson does. Perhaps he's Holmes and you're Dr. Watson!" Franz Ignatz smiled broadly. He spoke with only a slight

German accent. In the doorway behind him, which led to the rear of the apartment, a thin woman appeared, a bathrobe pulled tightly around her slight waist. Her silver-veined brown hair was drawn back from her pale, delicate face in a loose braid, partly unraveled.

Anderson made a small bow. "Dr. Ignatz, I'm glad to see you up and about."

Franz Ignatz took her hand. "Mr. Dunne, allow me to introduce my wife, Dr. Mathilde Ignatz. Unlike her husband, Mathilde is a *famous* physician, a fellow at the Kaiser Wilhelm Institute whose research has often been cited for a possible Nobel Prize."

"Please forgive my husband," she said. "He is given to exaggeration. I'm no longer a fellow at the Institute, and I've neither won nor expect to win a Nobel Prize."

"Ach, what do you medical researchers know about the practice of medicine? Where would a doctor be if he couldn't exaggerate? How could he frighten his patients into taking care of themselves?"

"I'm sure our visitors aren't here to hear us debate the difference between researchers and practitioners. Would you gentlemen care for some coffee? I was brewing a pot when you arrived."

Anderson accepted enthusiastically for them both. They sat on the couch. Franz Ignatz pulled up a straight-backed chair so close to Dunne their knees almost touched. Anderson loaded his pipe and lit it. "I've spoken to Franz and Mathilde about your interest in Dr. Sparks," he said.

"Did you know him?" Franz Ignatz asked.

"Met him twice, but only briefly."

"Long enough to know that he remains among the living," Anderson said.

"Did you ever talk to the police about him?" Dunne said.

"The police?" Dr. Ignatz clapped his hands on his knees. "The police are worse than useless!"

Mathilde Ignatz laid a tray on the small table behind the couch. She handed around cups of steaming coffee. "Franz, I think it would be easier for Mr. Dunne to understand all that's involved if you told him how you know Sparks."

"'Understand all that's involved'? That's something no American can seem to do, at least when it comes to Germany!"

Coffee sloshed about in Franz Ignatz's cup, spilled into the saucer and overflowed onto his pants.

"Franz, be careful!"

He put his cup and saucer on the floor. "*Huns!* That's how Germans were thought of in America, no? The British and French, the world's two greatest imperialist nations, were excused of any blame for the war. At Versailles, in 1919, it was all laid on Germany. When the end came and the army collapsed and the monarchy along with it, we had looked to America and President Wilson to support the new German republic. Instead, we had 'Huns' thrown in our faces. You Americans allowed the chances for lasting peace in Europe and democratic change in Germany to be poisoned by reparations and a humiliating treaty, and then you walked away as if the outcome was none of your concern!"

"Lower your voice," his wife said. "You'll disturb the neighbors." Her green eyes were sunk in dark, sallow-edged orbits.

"To hell with the neighbors!" Franz Ignatz clapped his knees again. "They should hear this too. Once, perhaps, you Americans, Mr. Dunne, had an excuse for your ignorance. Now there's no excuse! It's been written down for you in *Mein Kampf*. Hitler makes no secret of his intents. War against the weak. The vilification of the Jews. Purify the race, whatever the cost. It's no great mystery, Mr. Dunne, that if Hitler has his way, this marriage of medicine and murder will come about. The only question is when."

He picked up a book lying atop a stack of newspapers and shook it in the air. "It's in here, *Die Rassenhygiene*, by Josef von Funke. The American version, *Racial Hygiene*, was published with the help of the Eugenics Record Office in Cold Spring Harbor. I gave my copy to Mr. Anderson."

"And I've already passed it on in hopes it will help awaken more people to what's already occurring," Anderson said.

Franz Ignatz paged through until he reached what he was looking for and handed the open book to Dunne. "There, look at those photographs. Page after page of sick, injured human beings turned into specimens of 'racial degeneracy,' a burden on the fit that must be removed. Just past the pictures is the chapter on involuntary sterilization. It was published in America in pamphlet form in

1926, as part of the campaign to introduce the practice into every state. I heard the president of Stanford University speak at the Kaiser Wilhelm Institute and boast that the state of California performed more involuntary sterilizations than any nation in the world."

"You see, Mr. Dunne, our German eugenicists are by no means alone," Mathilde Ignatz said as she took a pack of Mexican cigarettes from the pocket of her robe. The coarse yellow paper flared brightly as she lit it. She sucked in the smoke and sucked again, as though to drag it down into her stomach. "They belong to an international movement that insists there are millions upon millions whose very existence endangers the healthy and fit."

"*Lebensunwertes Lebens*," Franz Ignatz said. "Life unworthy of life. Even before the Nazis took over, it was much discussed. I was a vice minister in the Department of Health in the Weimar Republic when the Depression struck. As financial conditions worsened, the eugenicists gained new influence. They pointed to how America had restricted immigration on the basis of race and practiced compulsory sterilization. They said Germany could do no less and must do more."

"Let's not overwhelm Mr. Dunne," Anderson said. "This is quite new to him."

"Not all new. I knew a girl once." He stopped himself from mentioning Maura, his sister. The old code. A reflex. No complaining. No crying. *Offer it up.*

Mathilde Ignatz rested her cigarette on the saucer beneath her cup. "At the Kaiser Wilhelm Institute, some of my colleagues held discussions with the Society for Racial Hygiene. Gathering scientific support for a systematic program of enforced sterilization was part of their agenda. But only part." She reached over, took the open book from Dunne's lap, and flipped to the back pages. She marked the place with her thumb and handed the book to him. "See the title of the last chapter: '*Tötung der Vollidioten.*' In English, 'Killing the Mentally Retarded.' This was another topic of discussion."

"When Hitler took power, all debate ceased," Franz Ignatz said. "Compulsory sterilization became national policy. I resigned my position before I could be fired. My wife was summarily dismissed."

"I'm a Jew, Mr. Dunne," Mathilde Ignatz said. "I was not only dismissed but restricted to treating only those 'racially diseased' like myself." She took a final drag on her cigarette and dropped it in the dregs of her coffee cup. "Forgive us, Mr. Dunne, for our digressions. In all this time you've yet to hear about Sparks."

"I'll tell you what we know," Franz Ignatz said. "I first met him after the war, at medical school in Munich. Though he came from pure German stock, he was an American, a graduate of Yale. At a time when most in Germany were struggling to eat, he was wealthy and well fed. Resented by us students, he was equally a figure of fascination.

"He claimed he was descended from a Margrave who'd been an early patron of the Teutonic Knights. He introduced himself as Josef von Funke and though friendly to almost everyone, save the smattering of Poles and Jews, he became particularly intimate with the members of the *Deutsche Gesellschaft für Rassenghygiene.*"

"The German Society for Racial Hygiene," Anderson interjected. "Remember, Franz, Mr. Dunne has no German."

"Of course. I'm sorry. In Europe, nearly every educated person speaks German. Here it is different. The students of whom I speak came to see themselves as the avant-garde of Germany's world-leading scientific community, a cadre of medical pioneers possessed of knowledge that the rest of the racially fit, including most Germans, were too riddled with the residue of Judeo-Christian moral superstitions to carry into action. They styled themselves the 'Brotherhood of Hermes Trismegistus,' evoking the myth of the Greek god Hermes, 'thrice greatest,' who bestowed on his adepts the secret of human regeneration."

"Hence the Hermes Sanatorium," Anderson said. "A first step in testing how the theory of 'racial healing' could be translated into practice, quietly, protected from public scrutiny. The magical healing properties of the caduceus are replaced by the murderous power of a hypodermic."

Mathilde Ignatz lit another cigarette. "Funke made a stir in 1921 when he published *Die Rassenhygiene,* with its insistence that the true physician must be executioner as well as healer. Isn't that right, Franz?"

"Yes. Though much of it was a rehash of *The Release and Destruction of Lives Not Worth Living*, a far more massive work co-written by a lawyer and a physician who argued that the state should kill defectives, Funke wrote in a more mystical style. He mingled a pitiless program of enforced euthanasia and social Darwinism with a passionate appeal for raising up a race of Aryan *übermenschen*, or supermen. In the summer of '23, a nurse in an asylum outside Munich claimed a doctor had dispatched several inmates by fatal injection. The doctor in question turned out to be Josef von Funke. There were charges and countercharges. But it was a confused time in Germany. Inflation was out of control. In November, Hitler attempted his putsch.

"It was reported that Funke was among those who marched with Hitler during the putsch, in 1923, and was at the Feldherrnhalle when the troops opened fire. He supposedly wasn't far from Heinrich Himmler, locked arm-in-arm with a student and salesman who were both killed instantly. They dragged Funke down with them, saving his life but breaking his collarbone. This is the story he told the doctor who treated his fracture. Whether it was true, I have no idea, but he most certainly used the ensuing confusion to vanish. His disappearance prevented him from being enshrined in the Nazi martyrology of those killed or wounded that day."

"A pity those soldiers hadn't better aim," Mathilde Ignatz, said as she rolled the cigarette between her thumb and forefinger as though it were a bullet, "The fact that Hitler was spared reinforced his belief that destiny is on his side."

"For his part," Franz Ignatz said, "Funke returned to America. Here the failed putsch was barely noticed. He built up a practice with an enviable list of patients. I almost skipped over his name when I read the news account of Miss Lynch's murder. But then I saw his picture. It triggered the connection: *funke* in English is spark. I still wasn't certain until I looked up Dr. Sparks in my medical directory and, sure enough, he'd been at the same school as I, and at the same time."

"Franz and I decided that the facts about Sparks might not be known and could have bearing on the murder. We felt the police should know."

"I made the call. I said I had information that might be relevant to the investigation of the murdered nurse. Two detectives came to see me."

"Let me guess," Dunne said. "One was big and unfriendly."

"Not so much unfriendly as uninterested. I told him Sparks's history. He only shrugged and said thousands of German Americans had chosen English versions of their names as a result of the last war. He said the Lynch case was about murder and rape, not politics. 'Besides,' he added, 'we already have the man who committed the crime.' He didn't take a single note."

Mathilde dropped the cigarette in the same cup as the previous one. She coiled a loose strand of hair around her finger. "Several days later the FBI came. They were very polite, unlike the detectives. They questioned me about my immigration papers."

"It is thanks to Mr. Anderson that we got out of Germany," Franz Ignatz said.

"I was writing an article on life under the Nazi regime, and the name of Dr. Mathilde Ignatz came up on every list of outstanding scientists who'd been forced into retirement," Anderson said. "After making her acquaintance, I was able to offer assistance in leaving Germany."

"Franz and I refused to leave at first. We were convinced Hitler would be tripped up by his vulgarity and ignorance. But he moved from triumph to triumph, and the people gladly followed, even some who'd been our friends. When it became clear my science was as despised as my religion and my people, we decided to leave. My politics, however, caused some difficulties, but Mr. Anderson used his connections to facilitate our departure. We went to Cuba and Mexico, and then to the United States."

"Mr. Dunne, you should know that my wife was a Communist but made no mention of it when she entered the country."

"I was a member of the Spartacist League, during the uprising of 1919," she said. "We hoped at the time to bring about a true social revolution in Germany. I was arrested by the Freikorps."

"And tortured," her husband added.

"But not murdered, as several colleagues were. I stayed in the Party, a largely inactive member, until 1930, when the Nazis began to explode in popularity. The Communists made it clear they were as intent on bringing down the Republic as the Nazis. They thought that if Hitler assumed power, it would be a step forward. I protested that policy, yet I didn't formally resign, and my husband is correct: I didn't mention my Party membership when I entered the country. We were afraid of being sent back."

"Somebody here in Yorkville informed on her," Franz Ignatz said. "It could have been a Bund member or maybe an active Communist seeking to punish a former comrade who had the audacity to question the Party. The FBI said the omission was a very serious matter."

"There was more trouble after that," Mathilde Ignatz continued, playing with the lock of hair, curling it in the same nervous, distracted way as before.

"This time, I'm afraid, it was my fault. I acted on my passions, not my intellect."

"It wasn't a question of being at fault. Before we are doctors, we are human beings. It is wise never to forget that, Franz." She put her hand over her husband's.

"I posed as a pharmaceutical salesman and went to see Sparks. I saw him as a manifestation of all our misfortunes, and here he was enjoying comfort and success. It was stupid of me. Once I got in to see him, I started yelling and threatened to expose him. He tried to quiet me down, even wrote a check, which I ripped up and threw at him. I left just as his chauffeur arrived, a thuggish-looking *Sturmabteilung* type. He tried to grab me, but I pushed him aside and left."

"A *Sturmabteilung*," Anderson said, "is a Nazi Storm Trooper. They were the vanguard of Hitler's takeover but have since given way to the SS."

"Yes, Mr. Dunne, I'm sorry. Here in Yorkville we often mistakenly assume that everyone understands what is taking place in Germany."

"I'm learning," Dunne said. "I had my own run-in with Bill Huber, Sparks's chauffeur."

"Huber, that's him! Unfortunately, my encounters with him didn't end at Sparks's office. Several nights later I was on the dais of an anti-Nazi meeting at the Moravian Church. A squad of Bundists broke in and a fight ensued. Huber was with them. The lights were extinguished. Several shots were fired. One grazed my neck."

"My husband barely escaped with his life, Mr. Dunne." Mathilde Ignatz leaned forward until her head almost touched her husband's knee. She seemed in pain. "It's as though we can't get beyond their reach, even here in New York."

Anderson made a small smacking sound as he sucked on his exhausted pipe. He relit it. "At that point, I advised the Ignatzes to withdraw from public view. Their lives, I believed, were in danger, and involvements in any violent incident could only aggravate their troubles with the immigration authorities."

"You didn't report it to the police?" Dunne asked.

"We didn't want to bring more attention to ourselves."

"Sparks tried to hire me to find you. He claimed he was being blackmailed."

"A lie!" Franz Ignatz stood.

"It's obvious that Mr. Dunne didn't take the job," Anderson said. "Once he located you, Huber would have undoubtedly killed you, then done the same to him. Or perhaps Sparks would have tried to make it seem as though Dunne was the murderer. I suppose there were those in the police who'd have welcomed that."

"One for sure," Dunne said.

Mathilde Ignatz pulled the hair so tightly around her finger that the tip turned red. "You don't believe Sparks is dead, do you, Mr. Dunne?"

"Not till I see the body."

"I'm glad to hear that. You are free to share with anyone what Franz and I have told you. But, please, no mention of our names. We want to be left out of this. *Please.*"

"My wife's family is still in Germany. Two sisters and a brother."

"We're trying to get them out of Germany and mustn't endanger their exit."

"Mr. Dunne can be trusted to do the right thing." Anderson

knocked the bowl of his pipe on the table for emphasis. "I wouldn't have brought him if I believed otherwise."

"We understand that, of course. But time is so short now. It's as though destiny itself is marching in step with Hitler, as though no one has the will to stop him." Mathilde Ignatz grimaced and bit her lip. She lit another cigarette and inhaled. Her face relaxed. Whatever pain had seized her seemed to abate.

"The Czechs won't let him get away with his bullying and bluster." Franz Ignatz thumped his fist into his palm. "They'll stand up to him, just watch."

They sat in silence. A thin, lonesome breeze fluttered the window shades. The room's shadows seemed to protect it from the ovenlike temperatures that had the rest of the city on broil. In the kitchen, a cuckoo left his clock and called out the hour.

"My God, look at the time!" Franz Ignatz went over and switched on the radio. He moved the dial around. "Listen! CBS is carrying it live. Hitler's speech at the Party Congress in Nuremberg." A high-pitched voice screamed in German. There was a thunderous roar of approval. Franz Ignatz translated. "Hitler is warning the French and British not to support the Czechs. He says Germany isn't afraid of war!"

Mathilde Ignatz dropped the stub of another cigarette in her coffee cup. "I can't bear any more of that man's ravings. Excuse me, gentlemen, I'm going to lie down."

Anderson and Dunne left Franz Ignatz alone, sitting next to the radio, head bowed beneath a transatlantic uproar of *Sieg Heils*! In the lobby, before they stepped into the street, Anderson said, "I should like to hire you to help find Sparks."

"No need. I've hired myself. But if we're going to work together, you better tell me who you work for."

"Myself."

"And you've never met Sparks?"

"Not face to face, not yet. But I've watched what he represents grow and grow while decent, intelligent men fail to recognize it for what it is. I've witnessed terror take over an entire government. If Sparks is exposed, it will become harder for America to keep its eyes closed."

"Tall order."

"Then let me add a short one. Mathilde Ignatz is the most brilliant person I've ever encountered. Her research, which might have advanced our knowledge of the human brain several decades, was confiscated and destroyed. Her job was given to a certified quack. She's been hounded out of her own country. People she thought were her friends have turned their backs. And now she's been diagnosed with stomach cancer. If I can do anything that gives her hope that one day the man and movement that have taken away her home, family, country, and livelihood will be overthrown, I will do so."

"Come by my office in the a.m."

Dunne walked up 86th Street. The Yorkville Casino was shut tight. Not a Bundist in sight. The sidewalks were filled with people out for a drink, a stroll, a breath of air. He found himself searching their faces the same way he had when he'd first learned that his sister Maura had been discharged from the state hospital in Buffalo. She must have come back to the city, he thought. It was the only place she knew. Unable to find any paper record of her, he sometimes walked aimlessly, on the distant possibility he might encounter her. It didn't happen, not then, not now.

He kept looking at the faces. Few took notice of his stare. Those who did ignored it. A typical mix—delivery boy, mechanic heading home, swarthy sailor with a plump blonde on his arm, Jew at his newsstand, traffic cop with the red, scoured face, woman with the shapely gams—they passed in anonymous pursuit of ordinary ambitions, sex, food, sleep, fun, the need to make a buck.

Life in the ceaseless hustle of a New York evening.

Busy. Noisy. Horny. Unequal. Unfair. Unfinished.

Life worthy of life.

# 9

"The world is made of iron, you can't do anything about it, it comes rushing up at you like a steamroller, nothing to be done about it, there it comes, it rushes on . . . and nobody can escape."

—ALFRED DÖBLIN, *Berlin Alexanderplatz*

ABWEHR HEADQUARTERS, BERLIN

"COLONEL OSTER IS INSIDE waiting for you." Corporal Gresser stood at attention by his desk. Canaris handed him the notes he'd taken in his meeting with General Wilhelm Adam, commander of Germany's western defenses. Canaris had transcribed in outline the facts that General Adam had laid before the Führer during his inspection tour of the so-called West Wall. He omitted Adam's summation of the Führer's character: *I saw this man's lack of education, his inability to face reality, his lack of knowledge of foreigners, his fanatic mentality and his mendacity.*

Oster sat behind the desk, smoking.

"I see I've already been replaced," Canaris said.

"It's not you who's about to lose his place, but him." Oster nodded at the requisite picture of the Führer on the opposite wall. He put out his cigarette and stood.

"Stay where you are." Canaris went over to the window. A breeze rippled across the tree tops along the canal. Below, an elderly gent with a soldier's bearing consulted his watch and scanned the street for a tram.

"It's on," Oster said as he sat once more. Canaris could see that Oster was acting out of exhaustion, not impertinence. Pale and slightly rumpled, an uncommon sight, he had the look of someone who hadn't slept in several days.

"Another strike?"

"A coup."

Canaris said nothing. He thought for a moment he recognized the old timer waiting for the tram. But when the man removed his homberg to wipe his bald pate with a handkerchief, Canaris realized he was mistaken. The man consulted his watch once again and tapped his walking stick against the curb, impatiently.

"You're skeptical."

Oster's tone was that of a schoolboy wounded by a teacher's cutting remark. It annoyed Canaris, the way Oster looked for his approval. He kept his gaze out the window.

This morning's summary of the foreign press contained a recent editorial from the *Times* of London raising the possibility that Czechoslovakia might be made more homogeneous "by the cessation of that fringe of alien populations who are contiguous to the nation to which they are united by race." If the *Times* was reflecting the thinking of His Majesty's Government, which it often did, it seemed British resolve was rubbery, at best. Canaris guessed that Oster had been too preoccupied to read the summary.

"You are right to be so, I suppose, but the pieces are falling into place this time." Oster reported that General Erwin von Witzleben, commander of the Berlin military district, had signed on. He would guarantee that the Führer's special bodyguard, the Leibstandarte-SS Adolf Hitler, was neutralized, and he would order the Potsdam Division to take control of the city's police stations, radio transmitters, and telephone installations. Halder, Beck's successor, was also on board and would see to it that the government quarter was sealed off. Göbbels, Himmler, and Heydrich would be arrested, and the offices of the SD and Gestapo occupied.

"I believe you've omitted one person," Canaris said.

"An elite force under Captain Friedrich Heinz will secure the Reichschancellery and take the Führer into protective custody."

"Heinz is a thug."

"He's bitter over the murder of Ernst Röhm and the purge of the SA. He's hungry for revenge."

"He'll kill his prey."

"Perhaps."

"And then you'll have to kill him."

"When it's done, and Germany is rescued from war and the corruption of the regime exposed, the nation will be grateful."

The papers on the desk were almost scattered by a wayward gust from outside, but Oster caught them in time. He used Canaris's lighter as a paperweight.

"What if the rat decides it's not the right time to fly?" Canaris asked.

"What?"

"Remember the fable you told me? The cats rebel at the last hour, when the rat tries to lead them over the cliff. Suppose there is no war. Suppose the Allies offer him what he wants. What then?"

"He will give the French and British no way out. He intends to march into Prague and nothing will stop him."

Oster continued to catalog the details of the planned coup. Canaris was impressed by its thoroughness. The precise timetables for deployment and execution had been carefully worked out, nothing left to chance, except of course the yet-to-occur mistakes, misinterpreted instructions, muffed signals, missed schedules, which, along with the immeasurable, inevitable human elements of fear, stupidity, and betrayal, couldn't be factored in. If it went badly, they would all share the same fate, no matter the degree of involvement. The lucky ones would be able to take their own lives. The rest would face interrogation, torture, and a death sufficiently gruesome and humiliating to discourage other would-be conspirators.

Down in the street, the old man stopped a policeman. He shook his walking stick in the direction from which the tram should be approaching. Canaris sensed his frustration, even surprise. How was it possible that the inviolable timetable should suddenly be violated? Such irregularities were not supposed to happen, not in Berlin. The policeman watched with the old man for a moment, then shrugged, as if to say, Nothing is for certain, not even in Berlin. He resumed his patrol.

\* \* \*

As soon as Oster was gone, Canaris stuffed his briefcase with papers, knowing all the time that he'd never get around to reading them at home. At best, they'd help put him to sleep, distracting him from the showdown Oster had described. He felt a wild rush of fear. Taking a deep breath, he struggled to control it. Most times he succeeded. His subordinates on the U-boat he commanded in the last year of the war were impressed by his icy calm as they were almost blown apart by British depth charges. So too, during his service on the *Dresden*. The surface never cracked. No nervous twitches. No hint of the panic tearing at his stomach or the scream held in by the practiced compression of his lips.

Only very rarely did it ever show: That once, years before, an age ago it seemed now, in the summer after the inflation had been tamed, when the Republic seemed to have found its balance, he ran into Paula, an old girlfriend, at an official reception. He didn't recognize her at first. She was bereft of her former mane of curls. Her hair was cut short and straight, in keeping with the new style of the Weimar Republic. The romantic idealism of the German merchant's daughter he'd met as a cadet at the naval academy was also gone; in its place, the sardonic sophistication of a woman whose wits had been sharpened by the financial ruin her family had undergone in the post-war inflation. She had nothing left but a talent to charm and seduce. They began an affair.

On a sweltering July day, Paula talked him into a visit to Luna Park, the sprawling amusement grounds on Halensee Lake, at the edge of the Grunewald. They swam in the great pool, with its artificially produced waves and hordes of squealing, splashing children. They drove a miniature electric car around a small oval, rode in a gondola that was propelled by their own pedaling and listened to a jazz band composed entirely of American Negroes. He enjoyed himself more than he thought he would.

Just before they left, Paula saw the House of Terror. She begged him to go with her, kissed him on the lips when he said no, and promised a larger reward if he changed his mind. They had to wait in a long line that stretched beneath a billboard painted with the face of a hideous green-faced ghoul. Inside, they stumbled through

crooked hallways and dark rooms, across wildly pitched floors that
sent them crashing into walls. Luminescent skeletons popped out
and mechanical bats swooped close to their heads. She clung to
him, alternately screaming and laughing. At the final turn, they
were confronted by two doors, each marked EXIT. A sonorous, dis-
embodied voice informed them that behind one was the park, the
world they left behind, lights, noise, happy crowds—behind the
other, the ghoul pictured on the front of the building, face half rotted away, one eyeball hanging down on his cheek.

*Choose*, the voice said.

Paula squeezed his arm. *Willi, go ahead!*

The mild claustrophobia he sometimes felt deepened into something else. He tried to move but couldn't.

Paula bent close. Her breath touched his cheek. *Willi?* There
was surprise and playfulness in her voice, and a slight but unmistakable intimation of mockery: *Don't tell me my brave soldier boy
is scared!*

He left the office early and waited beneath the building's portico for his driver to arrive. Though Berlin was in the last days of
summer, the light was already autumnal, a suffusion of faded gold,
weak and pallid as it filtered through leaves edged in red and yellow. Motes swirled amid sunbeams like tiny snowflakes. The sun
dipped lower in the west, caught fire in the windows of the build
ings on the east side of the canal, and filled them with an incendiary glow. Summer was retreating and winter closing in. Soon
enough, reinforced by relentless battalions of gray Baltic clouds,
the cold he despised would overtake the city. *Into the eternal darkness, into fire and ice.* Ciano was right. Latin blood still ran in his
veins.

Perhaps Oster and his fellow putschists would succeed.
Perhaps they'd bring the cats to their senses and drive the rats
away. Or perhaps they'd fail and be disgraced and shot. Or perhaps there would be no war and no putsch. The snag in the conspirators' plan was that it depended on what others did. On the
French. On the British. On the Czechs. Fate had to be on their

side. But fate seemed to be with the Führer. *My destiny is out of human hands. It is written in the stars.* It had yet to be revealed where that destiny would take them. The only certainty was that spring would arrive. Nature depended on no one, required no conspirators to carry out its designs. Seasons changed whatever men and nations might decide. Winter would have its turn, then April. His driver arrived. Canaris got into the car buoyed by that thought.

## THE HACKETT BUILDING, NEW YORK

Dunne stopped at the furniture store around the corner from the Hackett Building and purchased a Philco Deluxe Table Radio, a floor model on sale that fit on top of the filing cabinet as though built to. He turned the dial away from the bulletins about Prime Minister Chamberlain's imminent address to the House of Commons on the Czech situation, until he found a station content to interrupt the music only for the occasional commercial. Most of the tunes were from movies and Broadway shows. A duet sang:

*You say 'either' and I say 'either'*
*You say 'neither,' and I say 'neither'*
*'Either' 'either,' 'neither' 'neither'*
*Let's call the whole thing off . . .*

The phone rang. He picked it up. Her voice at last: "Fin?"

His voice, as casual as he could make it: "Let me turn the radio down."

The couple on the radio sang:

*Oh, let's call the whole thing off*
*Oh, if we call the whole thing off*
*Then we must part and oh*
*If ever we part, that would break my heart . . .*

He turned the volume to a notch above a whisper. "I guess you didn't hear. The D.A. is reopening Wilfredo's case."

"The whole city's heard. I didn't call sooner because I was busy."

"Back in business?"

Her silence: *That hurt, Fin.*

His: *Like it was intended to.*

"Is that what you really think?"

He thinks: *The time waiting for you to call. The resentment when you don't.*

"What else am I supposed to think?" he said.

"I've been with Elba. I told her everything. She knows who Wilfredo and I are to her. She's having a tough time dealing with all this at once."

"Hard to believe that a smart girl like that never figured it out for herself."

"Even smart people do stupid things." She paused.

The diminished voices from the radio filled the void:

*Sugar, what the problem?*

*Oh, for we need each other so . . .*

"Elba and I want you to know, whatever you charge, no amount can repay you."

"Try my per diem plus expenses, minus the retainer. Stick it in the mail."

"That's why I called, Fin. I need your help."

"Another case of the good and the true?"

"Lina Linnet."

"She's got nothing to worry about. Brannigan and his crew are locked up."

"She's afraid his friends will do what they can to see she never testifies."

"The D.A. will make sure she's safe."

"She's fearful he can't."

"Tom Dewey might not be Mr. Ball O'Fun, but he's one person she can trust."

"She needs to get away for a while. Her nerves are shot."

"Send her on a trip."

"I'll *take* her on one, but I need a few days with Elba first."

"Put her in a hotel till you're ready. That's the best advice I can give, Roberta."

"She thinks they might find her there."

"Are you asking what I think you're asking?"

"Just for a few days. You can stay at Cassidy's. You're accustomed to that."

"Seems like you already have it all arranged."

"You promised her, remember?"

"I said I'd make sure she'd get away from here, *not* live in my apartment."

"Not live, just stay a few days. That's all, Fin. I promise."

The song on the radio came to its conclusion:

*We'd better call the calling off off*
*so let's call it off, oh let's call it off*
*Oh, let's call it off, baby let's call it off*
*Let's call the whole thing off.*

He told her he'd leave his apartment key with the lobby attendant and went down the hall to the men's room, relieved himself, and washed his hands. He sang to the mug in the mirror:

"If ever we part, that would break my heart

So, I say 'ursta' you say 'oyster'

Oh, let's call the whole thing off . . ."

ABWEHR HEADQUARTERS, BERLIN

Canaris invited Oster to lunch. Gresser fetched it for them, and they ate in Canaris's office. Canaris expected Oster to be crestfallen that the next day British Prime Minister Chamberlain would take his maiden plane trip to meet with Hitler at his mountain retreat, Berchtesgarten. But, though saturnine, Oster wasn't ready to admit defeat.

"Chamberlain will try to reason with Hitler," Oster said. "When he learns that's impossible, he'll be back where he started. He'll have to fight. When that moment arrives, we're ready to move."

Oster left his half-eaten lunch to attend a briefing. Shortly after, Piekenbrock arrived and asked Gresser if he could see the Admiral on an important matter.

Canaris was glad for the company. "Come in," he said, "and let's hear what vital secrets you've uncovered."

"It concerns that SS agent in New York."

"I'd almost forgotten about him. We've had far larger things to be concerned with, I'm afraid."

"The SS hasn't forgotten. They've demanded the navy dispatch a U-boat to bring him back."

"A U-boat to violate American waters and return a single agent? Admiral Dönitz is vehemently opposed to the use of U-boats on such missions!"

"The request—or, more accurately, the directive—was received by the admiralty last evening. The Admiral has been overruled, and it's unclear how many are to be picked up. It seems more than one person is involved."

"It will take a U-boat two to three weeks to reach America."

"No, it won't. There are a number already waiting off Iceland in case of war. The SS wants one of them to rendezvous with their man in one week, on September 21." Piekenbrock laid an index card on the desk; on it, in block letters, was hand-printed a single word: MONTAUK.

Canaris glanced down at it. "What's the meaning?

"The U-boat's destination."

"In America?"

Piekenbrock turned the card over. On the back, he'd drawn a crude map. On the left, a star was labeled "New York City." A long two-pronged island jutted to the right. At the end of the southern and longer prong was another star, marked "Montauk." He moved his finger from one side to the other. "Montauk is about 140 miles northeast of New York City."

"Is it a city?"

"A fishing village, popular in the summer as a tourist resort but left to fishermen the rest of the year. American coastal defenses are paltry and this place seems remote. But, still, it seems a big risk for the navy to rescue one SS small fry, don't you think?"

"No doubt. But you've done well in sticking with this and uncovering these facts. It's old dogs like you who make me confident in the future of this department."

"If you'll permit me to say so, that's the first time anyone called me a dog and intended it as a compliment."

Oster seemed to have regained his spirits when Canaris told him of Piekenbrock's discovery. Canaris supposed it would have that effect—a distraction from the consternation caused by Chamberlain's parley with the Führer. "I've put in a call to Heydrich," Canaris said. "This time he's clearly crossed the line, not only interfering in foreign intelligence matters, but drawing in the navy."

"Outrageous," Oster said. "And more and more to be expected."

The intercom signaled a phone call. "Line one, Herr Admiral," Corporal Gresser said. "General Heydrich calling."

Canaris nodded at Oster, who stood next to the phone extension by the couch. He picked up the receiver simultaneously with Canaris, a small, practiced, perfectly synchronized duet. The General's secretary confirmed that Canaris was on the line and asked him to hold. There was a click on the other end of the line. "Wilhelm, how are you?" Without waiting for an answer, Heydrich launched into a monologue about the coming assault on the Czechs and the need to follow annexation with a speedy roundup of Communists and German exiles before they had a chance to escape. "The Führer threw down the gauntlet at Nuremberg. There's no turning back." He seemed ready to hang up, either forgetful or unconcerned that he was returning Canaris's call.

"Before you go, Reinhard, I've a favor to ask."

"Whatever you wish."

"It's a question really. I've been informed of a request by your department."

"What request?"

"The use of a navy U-boat for an overseas operation directed by the SS."

"It was an order, not a request."

"From whom?"

"Reichsführer-SS Himmler."

"He has no jurisdiction over military affairs or foreign intelligence."

"He has jurisdiction over whatever the Führer says he has." Heydrich's voice was taut, as though he were struggling to control himself.

"But this transgresses established lines of command and violates the territorial waters of the United States, a nation with whom the Führer has expressed the desire to remain at peace."

"Who told you it was going to the United States?"

"It's my responsibility to know such things and, when they are withheld, to ferret them out." Canaris was careful to sound calm and matter-of-fact.

"Your responsibility is the same as mine and every German's: *to obey*. I suggest you remember that. Good day."

Oster put down the receiver. "Well done. You got under his skin. I don't suppose there are many who can do that anymore."

"We still don't know what's behind this mission. What requires the risk they're taking?"

"If war comes and our plan succeeds, this will be forgotten. If not, it will be remembered as only a tiny contribution to Germany's transformation from a law-abiding state to a gangster nation." Oster began to review the details of the plot, rehashing how Witzleben's troops would secure Berlin, surround the government quarter, and arrest the leadership. His initial animation descended into a flat monotone. "In the end," he said, "we must do what we can do and hope fate is on our side, not his."

NEW YORK

Dunne practiced the most ancient and well-known secret of the world's most thrilling profession, doling out baksheesh to a passing parade of janitors and doormen, a few surly and uncooperative even after they were paid, the majority willing to help as long as the basic ground rule was understood: *Look, pal, I don't want to get mixed up in any trouble.*

Where Sparks's secretary went, nobody could say. She'd kept to herself. Never hostile but not very friendly either, she'd made it clear to her neighbors that she wanted to be left alone. The doorman at Sparks's building had an idea she was originally from Canada but couldn't remember exactly where. Huber had vacated his furnished room on 90th and First Avenue—only a few blocks from the Ignatzs'—right after the fire at the Hermes Sanatorium. The dour Hungarian landlady let Dunne look at the stuffy, pigeon-hole room after they'd haggled over the cost. She wanted a week's rent for granting Dunne the privilege—"five dollars or no peek"—but settled for two. "Mr. Huber was no trouble," she said. "Quiet and sober. Some Germans aren't like that. They're loud and drink too much, but they're not dirty, like the Irish. Mostly, I rent to my own. Magyars know how to behave, and they're as clean as cats." Spare and small, the room had no trace of Huber or anyone else, not so much as a stray dust ball.

Irene Loben never existed, at least as far as the official records were concerned. Sparks's doorman had never met her, although he'd heard her name or was pretty sure he had. There was no entry for her in any of the phone directories for the five boroughs, no mention in the police files, no birth record as far as he could tell. After the fire, not a single inquiry was made with the police about her. Whoever she was, she apparently went up in smoke with the Hermes Sanatorium.

There was a memorial service in the lobby of the Bronx County Building. A crowd of about fifty oldsters, gray-haired and shabby, were dispersed amid four times as many folding chairs. Their motive for attending seemed a lack of anything better to do. Borough President Lyons offered several minutes of platitudes capped by a litany of the fine Bronx hospitals and medical institutions that hadn't burned down and were still in operation. A doctor praised the Hermes Sanatorium as an example of "the compassionate heart" of private physicians as opposed to the "coldness and impersonality of socialistic medicine." A minister ended the service by reading the Beatitudes.

People stood around for a moment or two as two court officers rolled away the podium. The Borough President shook hands and searched unsuccessfully for any reporters who might have attended. Dunne exited down the steps of the building's main entrance on 161st Street. The park on the other side of the street was named after Joyce Kilmer, who'd served with the 69th in France as the staff sergeant in charge of intelligence reports. Dunne remembered him as cordial in his own quiet way. He'd been killed at the Ourcq by the same sniper who drilled Tommy Scanlon in the head. They had been planted in nearby plots in the same military cemetery under identical crosses. But since Kilmer had a reputation as something of a poet, he also got a park named after him on the swank Grand Concourse. The Professor thought the honor excessive. "In view of the quality of Mr. Kilmer's work," he'd told Dunne, "Erato, the muse of poetry, would have been satisfied to see a fire hydrant named in Kilmer's honor, preferably in some quarter of the city with a large population of micturating canines."

The swelling sounds coming from Yankee Stadium two blocks west indicated that the home team was pulverizing another opponent in their routine of bringing the World Series to the Bronx. Dunne hurried to the subway before the game was over and the train filled with kids wielding pennants on long sticks expertly designed to poke somebody's eye out.

A special-delivery letter from the Vermont Welfare Commissioner's office was waiting for him at the Hackett Building. On behalf of the commissioner, some flunky offered thanks for the expression of condolences on the tragic death of Peyton Waldruff, superintendent of the State Asylum for Feebleminded Idiots (an expression Dunne had no recollection of making). As to the inquiry about Mr. Waldruff's relationship to the Hermes Sanatorium and the transfer of any of those under Mr. Waldruff's care to that facility, the records were sealed in order to protect the inmates. Any breach of that protection would require a court order.

The rest of the afternoon was expended once again in contemplating how smooth a wall appears till you stare at it long enough and the true surface reveals itself, a complicated terrain of bumps, depressions, cracks, nicks, and replasterings. The Hackett Building had gone up in the early Twenties. But the wall had an ancient texture, as if lifted from some centuries-old prison or monastery and, like the Cloisters in Fort Tryon Park, transported here so that those with too much time on their hands would have something to keep their minds busy. Once the wall stopped providing sufficient distraction there was always the radio.

It was hard to find any station without hearing the refrain, "We interrupt our regularly scheduled programming to bring you the latest news on the situation in Europe." The surprise announcement by Prime Minister Chamberlain that he intended to fly to Germany to meet Hitler had electrified the world press. It seemed certain Chamberlain and the French would pressure the Czechs to make the concessions needed to avoid a general war. The citizens of Munich cheered when he drove through their streets to reach the train that would take him to Berchtesgaden for his meeting with the Führer. When he returned to England, British crowds shouted their approval.

The previous evening, the London correspondent for CBS, Edward R. Murrow, had described the profound relief that overtook the city when Chamberlain came back with the hope of preserving peace. As one of the Englishmen interviewed put it, "Surely reasonable men can reach a reasonable compromise." Only a few, Murrow reported, thought that Britain was confronted by a regime whose ultimate purpose was war and conquest, not negotiation, and that it must resist. One of them was Winston Churchill, a member of parliament and former cabinet minister, who had once been considered as a potential prime minister but whose extreme views on the need for English rearmament had made him increasingly irrelevant. He'd issued a statement to the European press, declaring that "The personal intervention of Mr. Chamberlain does not at all alter the gravity of the issue at stake. We must hope it does not foreshadow another complete failure of the Western democracies to withstand the threats and violence of Nazi Germany." For the time being, Murrow concluded, Mr. Churchill remained in a distinct minority.

BERLIN

Canaris opened the middle drawer of his desk and rummaged through a disorderly heap of old memos, outdated schedules, and unused requisition forms. In the corner, beneath a sheaf of forgotten correspondence, he found what he was looking for: the card the English visitor had left with him the previous June. The U-boat was due at Montauk in less than a week. Oster was right. The failure of its mission wouldn't mean much in the scheme of things. But at least it would mean *something*.

He recalled how as a small boy vacationing with his parents on the Adriatic he'd written a letter on thick, important-looking stationery he found in the desk in their hotel room. He addressed it TO WHOMEVER FINDS THIS and included a childish message about having been captured by pirates. He stuck it in a bottle and threw it into the sea, wondering whether it would float to North Africa or perhaps into the Mediterranean and out into the Atlantic, across to America. On their last day at the shore, he found the bottle washed back on the very spot from which he tossed it. Water had seeped in and obliterated the message. Still, it was worth a try. A vote in favor of Oster's conspiracy. He'd never voted in an election. Never wanted to. A useless gesture, he'd imagined. Now, he experienced the satisfaction sometimes even a gesture can bring. Who could say where it would lead? A bottle tossed into the sea. Let the tides take it where they will.

On a plain index card, he printed:

SS-AGENT GUSTAV HAUSSER (HUBER)/RENDEZVOUS:
MONTAUK, 22.9.

He put it, along with the Englishman's card, in an envelope, addressed it, and attached a note directing it be sent express post, via air mail, to the addressee in New York. He then fit it inside a larger envelope. He summoned Piekenbrock, who arrived quickly. "I have an assignment for you," he said. "You've been working too hard. I want you to take a few days rest."

"Thank you, Admiral. I'm a bit tired, but so is everyone else. Besides, all leaves are canceled."

"I canceled them. In your case, however, I'm countermanding my order."

"You're very thoughtful. But I have neither the need nor the desire for a leave."

"No matter. *Mens sans in corpore sano* has long been a principle of mine. I'm *ordering* you to take a rest. More, I'm ordering you to take it in Copenhagen, immediately. The Danes know how to relax."

"This is most unnecessary, Admiral. I'm perfectly fine. I really am."

"And while you're there, I wonder if you wouldn't mind dropping this off with a former member of this department, a cryptographer. He's a partner in an import-export firm. It's a bit of personal business."

Piekenbrock held the letter in front of him. "Yes, I remember him," he said. "A good officer. I was sorry when he transferred out of the department; sorrier still, when I heard he felt compelled to resign from the service."

Canaris suspected for an instant Piekenbrock might put it up to the light and try to peer at the contents. Instead, he unfastened the next-to-top button of his tunic and slipped it in the inner breast pocket. "Is there anything else, Herr Admiral?"

"Yes, enjoy your leave. That too is an order."


NEW YORK


Half a bottle of bourbon helped put Lina Linnet to sleep. Roberta had packed the refrigerator with food and convinced Fin to hire a cleaning lady to tidy up his apartment before Lina arrived. There was a pile of old magazines next to the radio. But Lina didn't have an appetite and couldn't concentrate enough to do more than skim the magazines. She took a long bath and smoked cigarettes while listening to the radio. In the late afternoon, she had a nap. When she woke, she telephoned the liquor store on the corner and had a bottle delivered. By midnight she was asleep again.

She was roused by what sounded like someone fumbling with the lock. She lay still and listened. The clock next to the bed read 3:10. There were more sounds from the hallway. Tiptoeing to the door, she raised the peephole. Across the hall, a man swayed back and forth as he made one unsuccessful attempt after another to put his key into the lock. Finally, a woman opened the door. "You're drunk, Frank," she hissed. "You swore you'd stay sober, but you're drunk." She grabbed his arm and jerked him inside.

Lina sat in the dark by the window next to the fire escape and smoked a cigarette. High above the building opposite, a three-quarters moon shone brightly. She hummed to herself; a song from twenty years ago when she was fourteen; the night Jimmy Ryan took her to Bronx Park and they drank whiskey from the bottle he'd lifted from his father's bar on Tremont Avenue; her first time lying with a boy:

*"By the light of the silv'ry moon I want to spoon*
*To my honey I'll croon love's tune*
*Honeymoon, keep a-shinin' in June*
*Your silv'ry beams will bring love's dreams . . ."*

Jimmy turned out to be a rotten egg, like the others, a crate of rotten eggs. Getting laid, that's all that was ever on their minds. At least he got his, gunned down in the speakeasy he took over from his father for refusing to buy beer from Dutch Schultz's gang. She put out the cigarette and went back to bed.

The pressure of someone sitting down on the bed awakened her before the gentle jiggling of a hand on her shoulder. It took her several seconds to remember where she was. The clock indicated 5:15. She turned, expecting to see Roberta, but it was a man. He had a long face, not unattractive, and when she looked at him, he broke into a wide smile. He leaned toward her and said softly, "Where's Fintan Dunne?"

"Are you a friend of his?" She felt a delayed sense of fright.

"A good friend, very close."

She glanced at the phone. He followed her eyes. "No need for that," he said, and his smile grew wider, his red tongue poking for an instant over his teeth. "I'm not here to harm anyone." He opened his hands wide. "See."

"Come closer," she said, "and I'll scream."

With a swift, instantaneous sweep of his hands, he covered her mouth and pinned her throat against the wall. "Now why would you do that? All we're going to do is have a little fun, and then I'm going to leave a message for my friend, Fintan Dunne." He held her legs down with his knee. "You're trembling," he said, his smile turning into a tight grin, as he spoke through clenched teeth: "You whore bitch."


Anderson seemed neither surprised nor disappointed by the lack of success in unearthing a single lead about Sparks's whereabouts. He sat by the window, head resting on his palm, fuming pipe gripped between his teeth, and listened to the hurried, self-important commentary of H.V. Kaltenborn, the CBS commentator in New York, as he reported Chamberlain's startling visit to Hitler at his mountain retreat. Twice, Anderson muttered to himself, "He doesn't know what he's dealing with."

When the station went back to its regular programming, Dunne switched off the radio. Anderson tilted his head back, his eyes directed out the window at the blue rectangle of sky atop the shaftway. "Since Sparks is *officially* dead, he can't risk traveling on his passport. He must hide somewhere until he judges it sufficiently safe to travel."

"Somewhere could be anywhere."

"What about his chauffeur?"

"Huber? He's vanished without a trace. He could be with Sparks or maybe he's on his own."

"He didn't seem comfortable in the background. He had a public presence in the Bund, even led the attack on the meeting at which Dr. Ignatz was almost killed."

"He liked to swagger." Dunne related sighting Huber at Yaphank among the Bundists from Camp Siegfried.

"There may be a chance to unearth information. I have contacts who make it a habit of following the Bund's activities."

"Contacts?"

"To the Intelligence Service."

"Whose?"

"His Majesty's."

"What'll it cost?"

"Cost?"

Dunne rubbed his thumb across the two opposing fingers. "How much?"

"That's not how gentlemen operate."

"I guess I haven't dealt with many."

Anderson nodded, as though in agreement. "Well, they don't betray confidences, that's for certain. But there are those who are willing to put moral principles ahead of professional duties, and several share my conviction that the response of the Intelligence Service to the German menace, like that of the present British Government itself, is hopelessly inadequate."

"Give them a call."

"That would be unwise. I'll see if I can arrange a meeting. Suppose we rendezvous near Rockefeller Center tomorrow afternoon. Pick a time and place."

"Three o'clock, at Schrafft's, on the corner of Madison, across from St. Patrick's."

"Schrafft's it is." Anderson nodded once more.

"You'll feel at home." Dunne said. "All the help is Irish."

The petite, freckle faced waitress in the black dress and white apron gave Dunne his check. He paid it and went out to the curb. He killed his cigarette on the top of a fireplug. Two priests walked hurriedly toward St. Patrick's. The one closest, beefy and flat-footed, gave him a once-over worthy of a patrolman. Just as Dunne was about to hail a cab, Anderson came around the corner.

"I was afraid you'd have already left," he said.

"I did. You're an hour late. I'm on my way back to my office."

"My foray wasn't entirely fruitless. They've got a bead on Huber. They've identified him as a German agent, although there's some confusion about which branch of the Nazi government he works for."

"Don't they only have one branch?"

"Almost."

"No notion where he's gone?"

"Not much interest, either. Their minds are concentrated on the Czech situation."

Dunne watched over Anderson's right shoulder as a patrol car pulled up at the curb. Bill Hanlon, the new Chief of Homicide, exited the passenger's side. His head-down, hands-in-his-pockets stride ruled out that he was there by coincidence or on a social call. "Thought you'd have stopped tailing me by now," Dunne said.

Hanlon gave Anderson a sideways glance. "I need to talk to you, Fin. Alone."

"Anderson is my associate. Say it to me, say it to him."

"All right, come inside." Hanlon led the way to the back of Schrafft's. The same Irish waitress appeared. He ordered a butterscotch sundae; Anderson ordered tea. She curtsied when she heard Anderson's accent and returned quickly with the tea and sundae. Hanlon pushed the ice cream around the metal dish with his spoon.

"It's your nickel, Chief," Dunne said.

Expecting a lecture on why private investigators should stay out of the way of the homicide squad, Dunne was momentarily dazed by a blunt account of how the police had been summoned to his apartment, where they'd found Lina Linnet's "butchered body." Roberta Dee, who'd discovered it, was in protective custody. Hanlon wagged his spoon at Dunne. "Been nice you'd let us know Linnet was holed up in your place."

"She was fed up with cops."

"She'd be alive if she trusted me."

"You here to book me?"

"You're not a suspect. You're a nuisance."

"Was the butchery similar to that inflicted on Miss Lynch?" Anderson asked.

"Only an animal would do what was done to her."

"You didn't answer the question," Dunne said.

"Very similar." Hanlon stood the spoon in the ice cream and shunted the dish aside. He folded his arms on the table and bent toward Dunne. "I know what went on under Brannigan, and I'm goin' see it don't happen again. But I'm off to a bum start. The brass will be down my throat. The papers will say Linnet was killed to protect Brannigan. Their only question will be whether I'm a crook or an incompetent."

"There are witnesses galore against Brannigan."

"You got a theory who killed her?"

"I prefer facts. They're hard to come by but more useful."

"I figured you'd keep what you know to yourself. Solve the case on your own. That's your business, Fin, I understand that. But I want an assist."

"What kind?"

"Drop out of sight for a period. Let me get my footing and start this job without gettin' beat over the head 'bout how the city would be better off with a private eye running the show instead of a cop."

"Roberta Dee comes with me."

"Sure." Hanlon slid out of the booth and slapped a dollar on the table. "I owe you." He nodded at the dish of ice cream. "Either of you want that sundae, feel free. I barely touched it."


"You were less than entirely truthful just then," Anderson said as he filled his pipe, put a match to the bowl, and took several puffs. "You undoubtedly have the same theory I do. Huber committed this crime. He was hoping to find you but stumbled on poor Miss Linnet instead, which means he must still be in the vicinity. That place where you saw Huber, what was it?"

"The Bund camp?"

"Yes, where exactly?"

"Yaphank, on Long Island, but Huber or Sparks would only go there if he was interested in being caught. It's got lots of visitors, most of them in love with beer and speeches, and it's a good bet the FBI has a close eye on the place."

"It can't hurt to visit. Detective Hanlon would be grateful for your absence."

"How'd you propose we get there?"

"Didn't you tell me you passed it on a train?"

"It's after Labor Day. Be one a day, if you're lucky, and then you'll have to take a taxi to get to the Camp. Might as well tele-graph ahead to say you're coming."

"We can drive."

"You know how?"

"Surely you must. All Americans do."

"Can't operate the shift, not with this." Dunne held up his right hand in its plaster cast. "Even if I could, I don't own a car. Most New Yorkers don't."

"Who's Roberta Dee? Is it possible she does?"

September 20-21, 1938

# 10

The human and economic toll was measurable. The deepest impact of the hurricane [of 1938] was not. The swiftness and totality of the disaster were so stunning as to defy reason, logic, credulity. Social change evolves. Dunes and beaches and shorelines are shaped over a century of wind and wave. Lives and landscape require years of patient building, grain upon grain. They cannot be redrawn in two or three hours. On September 21, 1938, what couldn't happen did, and even for those who had been cushioned from the ravages of the Depression, life seemed suddenly fragile.

The vagaries of nature shook the status quo and weakened its underpinnings. On that rough September afternoon, wealth, social position, and property provided no buffer from the fury of wind and water. The comfort zone they had ensured would never seem quite as insular again. The hurricane has been called "a savage leveler." Chaos blew in, and in some ways it stayed on after the hurricane left town. The well-ordered life with distinct rules and classes came to an end, replaced by a world with new rules, new liberties, new equalities, and a new tempo. Some line had been crossed and nothing would ever be quite the same again.

—R.A. SCOTTI, *Sudden Sea: The Great Hurricane of 1938*

## THE HACKETT BUILDING, NEW YORK

ROBERTA HAD ALREADY LEFT police headquarters when Dunne arrived. He reached her at the number she'd left specifically for him. She was composed and unemotional. "Lina was murdered by the same person as Miss Lynch, wasn't she?" she said.

"That's a good guess," he said. He asked about the car. Elba, it turned out, had taken the train to Sing Sing to see Wilfredo, the first time she'd face him as her father. Roberta was watching the shop, but business was slow. There'd be no problem closing it for a day.

He said he'd explain where they were going and why, "when you pick us up."

*"Us?"* she asked.

"I can't get into it on the phone." He was sure Roberta was alert to the possibility that the FBI had taken the precaution of having Elba's phone tapped in case she was somehow connected to the interstate prostitution ring they'd nailed Brannigan for.

"Meet you same place as last time," she said. "Noon. Don't keep me waiting."

Anderson got in the back of Roberta's car. Glancing up into the rearview mirror and seeing Anderson's reflection, Roberta presumed his grin was for her. She grinned back. "Since Fin doesn't have enough manners to introduce me, I'll do it myself. I'm Roberta Dee."

Anderson removed his hat and lay it beside him on the seat. "I'm Ian Anderson. I'm most appreciative of the trouble you're going to in order to transport us to . . ." He paused. "Where is it we're going, Fin?"

"Yaphank."

"Out in the boondocks of Long Island?"

"Unless you know another Yaphank." Dunne told her to turn onto Third Avenue and drive south.

"It'll take us half the day to get there."

"Yaphank," Anderson said, "has a bit of an Indian ring, don't you think?"

"Yaphank is so far out in the sticks, the Indians may still be there." Roberta raced through a light just before it changed red.

"It's not that out of the way," Dunne said. "In the war, Yaphank held 40,000 recruits and even got a musical in its honor, 'Yip, Yip, Yaphank.' Ever hear 'Oh! How I Hate to Get Up in the Morning'? That's from the show."

"Of course I've heard it. Every Tommy did. The Yanks taught it to us during the war." Anderson began to sing a soft baritone:

*"Oh, how I hate to get up in the morning*
*Oh, how I'd love to remain in bed*
*For the hardest blow of all*
*Is to hear the bugler's call—*
*You've gotta get up*
*You've gotta get up*
*You've gotta get up in the morning."*

Dunne joined in the next chorus:

*"Someday I'm going to murder the bugler*
*Someday they're going to find him dead.*
*I'll amputate his reveille*
*And stomp upon it heavily*
*And spend the rest of my life in bed."*

"That's just lovely," Roberta said. "But if we're going to Yaphank, how come you have me driving toward Staten Island?"

"Think we're being followed?" Anderson said.

"Been known to happen," Dunne said. "Make a right here."

Roberta drove west as far as Eighth Avenue, where Dunne told her to make another right. Back against the door, arm resting on the back of the front seat, he watched behind. They were quickly mired in a noontime traffic jam.

"At this rate, we should be in Yaphank by sometime next Saturday. Mind telling me why we're headed there?"

"It'll take a while."

"We're not exactly in a rush." Roberta nodded at the standstill in front of them.

Dunne told her for the first time about his visit to the Hermes Sanatorium, the fire that followed, and the supposed death of Sparks. In imminent danger of being implicated in the murder of Miss Lynch, Sparks and his henchman Huber had torched the place and staged their deaths. Huber, he speculated, had come looking for him and, finding Lina in his apartment, killed her instead, in the same way he'd killed Lynch. Huber was the reason they were headed to Yaphank.

"It all sounds so weird."

"Ah, Miss Dee," Anderson said, "you've gone to the root of the dilemma. The Saxon word for fate was *wyrd*, from which our word 'weird' is taken. Certainly, in the modern sense, there is a weirdness to the detached homicidal objectivity of a man like Sparks, more so than the traditional savagery of a thug like Huber. But when such weirdness is institutionalized, when it's accepted as truth by supposedly reputable scientists and medical men, when it's advocated as a political program and turned into a policy of state, such a concept approaches the meaning of *wyrd* in the ancient sense: a destiny we cannot avoid, a fate we won't or can't resist."

Roberta looked again in the rearview mirror. Anderson's grin made her unsure if he was joking or not. The traffic gradually thinned as they went north. They turned east on 125th Street and drove past the Apollo Theater, where a line of well-dressed Negroes waited to be admitted to a matinee. Once on the other side of the Triborough Bridge, they exited onto Astoria Avenue, in Queens, and followed it to Northern Boulevard.

It was almost two-thirty by the time they reached the uncluttered, open lanes of the Northern State Parkway. Roberta turned on the radio. H.V. Kaltenborn was reporting on the previous evening's joint British-French communiqué announcing that the two nations would accept Hitler's demands and insist that the Czechs return the Sudetenland to Germany. Prime Minister Chamberlain would soon depart for Bad Godesberg, in the Rhineland, for his second meeting with Hitler, at which the deal would be concluded and an orderly transfer arranged. "So far," Kaltenborn concluded, "mighty America refuses to speak. She seems primarily concerned with keeping out of war."

"If you wouldn't mind turning off the radio, I'd be most appreciative." Closing his eyes, Anderson fell asleep instantly. When they reached the end of the Northern State, the country opened into a flat vista of cultivated fields occasionally interrupted by single farmhouses and clusters of the weathered, tumbledown shacks used by migrant laborers. The air was seasoned with the sharp, rancid odor of duck farms, fertilizer and brine from the adjacent but invisible sea baked together through the long summer season.

Roberta rolled up her window. "Who says the city smells? Give me Fifth Avenue any day." They were a short distance beyond Smithtown when Roberta pulled over at a roadside beer garden. "Time for a break," she said.

They sat in a small grove beneath a latticed canopy. Dunne ordered hot dogs and beer for the table. Roberta asked for a root beer.

"What's the plan?" Roberta asked.

"Ask the general," Dunne said. "It's his expedition."

Anderson either ignored or didn't hear Dunne's comment. A cluster of brown and yellow leaves on the tree above were beginning to glide down one by one. He studied them, as if something significant was being revealed.

"Anybody know exactly where we go from here?" Roberta said.

"At this moment that's the general condition of humanity, isn't it?"

"I asked where *we're* going, not the world."

"Either case, the answer is, 'I am not sure.' I'm afraid that's the best I can do."

"Would you mind telling me what's your interest in all this?" Roberta said. She lit a cigarette. The day had turned sultry and close. The Englishman's philosophical air had begun to annoy her, and so had his grin.

"My interest is in seeing Sparks brought to trial. A proper exposé of his program of medical murder and its relationship to the greater ambitions of the Nazi Reich might help wake Americans from their sleep and stiffen their will to resist."

"Who do you work for?"

"Who pays me?"

"Last I heard, the two were related."

"I pay myself."

After only a puff, Roberta dropped her cigarette on the ground. "Let's not waste any more time. At this rate, we won't get back to the city before midnight."

The rest of the way, Roberta kept fiddling with the radio dial to find music and avoid the news bulletins. It was dark when they reached Yaphank. They stopped at a small grocery. Dunne came out with six bottles of beer and directions to the camp. "It's directly up the road. Turn left at the top of the hill. There's a dirt road that leads to it. Guy behind the counter says it's been pretty much deserted since Labor Day."

They reached the road in a few minutes. "We'll walk from here," Anderson said.

"Bet nobody thought to bring a flashlight," Roberta said.

"The moonlight will suffice." Anderson set off into the woods.

"Wait up," Dunne called.

Roberta slouched behind the wheel. "I'll stay here. Don't do anything stupid."

Beneath a partial moon half-hidden by clouds, Anderson stumbled over fallen trees and underbrush, his curses alerting Dunne where to tread carefully. They came into a clearing as the moon escaped the clouds and shone on a towering slab of concrete. They drew close to it. Atop was a bronze eagle, a wreathed swastika clutched in its talons. Beyond the meadow was a neat row of cabins. Anderson tried the door of the first. It was unlocked. Each side of a central aisle was lined with metal-frame bunk beds. The door on the other end was flanked by pictures of George Washington and Adolf Hitler. They stopped and listened. On the path of pebbles that connected the cabins, came the slow, cautious, unmistakable crunch of footsteps. Anderson pointed to the ground. He lay flat, and Dunne lay beside him.

The footsteps stopped. Dunne felt the thump-bump, thump-bump of his heart against the ground. A beam from a flashlight appeared in the window directly above, darted around the cabin and spilled through the floorboards. Anderson crouched, in a running position. Dunne got set to dash behind him. A second light appeared on the side of the cabin and approached rapidly. The instant the person carrying it turned the corner, Anderson jumped up, drove a forearm into his throat, and landed a hard punch to his stomach. The flashlight rolled on the ground. Anderson grabbed it, turned off the beam, and used it as a bludgeon. The blow made a distinct thud.

The backdoor of the cabin flew open and the beam of the other flashlight pinpointed Anderson astride the person he'd just clubbed into unconsciousness.

"Move, and I'll shoot!"

Dunne tucked his immobilized hand beneath his left arm, aimed his shoulder at the knees of whoever was standing directly above him on the cabin steps, and leaped forward. A shot went off as Dunne toppled him. Anderson was on him in an instant and hit him with the flashlight until he lay still.

"You weren't hit, were you?" Anderson said.

Dunne got up. "No, it was a wild shot."

Anderson pointed the light to the man at their feet. He was moaning.

"Turn off the light." Dunne knelt, put his head on the chest of the man, and took his pulse. "He's not dead. But, congratulations, you've knocked out two FBI agents."

"How can you tell?"

"This one's name is Agent Lundgren. We've crossed paths."

"It was self-defense. They made no effort to identify themselves. We should stay and explain ourselves."

"Self-defense? You beaned the first guy before he knew we were here. We should get the hell out of here before they haul us off to the federal pen."

They blundered their way through the woods, back to where Roberta was parked. She was visibly upset and fumbled with the choke. "I thought I heard a shot."

"You did. Let's go." Dunne jumped in the front seat.

The car didn't start. She tried several more times before the engine turned over. She pulled onto the main road. "Where to?"

"It might help if you could see the road." Dunne reached over and switched on the headlights. "Make it seem you know where you're going and aren't in any hurry. Anderson, get down on the floor. This way we're just a man and woman out for a spin."

They drove for several minutes in silence before Roberta spoke: "What happened back there?"

"Anderson decided to murder the bugler."

From the back seat came Anderson's muffled voice: "I didn't decide to *murder* anyone. It was pitch dark. I acted in self-defense."

"He knocked out two FBI agents. Lundgren was one of them."

Roberta put her hand to her forehead. "Oh, Christ."

"You helped, Fin. You tackled the chap on the steps," Anderson said.

"After you'd KO'd the first one, I didn't have much choice."

They drove on a narrow, winding road through a heavily wooded area that emerged in a treeless expanse of cultivated fields. They continued until they reached Riverhead. The town was deserted and closed up for the night.

"What now?" Roberta parked in front of a gas station that was dark and shut tight. "We don't have much gas left."

"Ten to one, Lundgren and his companion weren't by themselves. They've probably been found by now. If there's a roadblock, it'll most likely be west of Yaphank looking for cars headed back to the city. Best thing for us to do is keep driving east."

Roberta followed his instructions to drive slowly, as though returning from a church meeting or dinner with friends. Dunne watched the roadside. When he spied what he was looking for, a dirt road that veered toward Peconic Bay, he told Roberta to turn. The car jolted violently over the pitted, rutted surface.

Anderson popped his head up, "Have we lost our way?"

"I'd say so, but consult our navigator," Roberta said.

"Straight," Dunne said. "It should be right ahead."

The headlights rested on a one-story cabin with a sagging roof. "I hope you made reservations. Looks like it's all booked up." Roberta turned off the headlights.

Dunne switched them back on. "I need the light." He got out of the car and stepped onto the front porch. "Doc?" he said. "Anybody here?" He opened the door. Warm, mildewed air, wafted past. Doc Cropsey, it seemed, had yet to start his retirement. Dunne turned on the bulb that hung over the ice box and opened the windows. He went back on the porch and told Roberta and Anderson to come inside.

Anderson's eyes had a dazed, distant look. He seemed not so much unsure of where he was as oblivious. "Are we staying the night?"

"Got a better idea?" Dunne said.

"Not at the moment." He bowed slightly. "The day's activities have left me quite spent." He removed his jacket, draped it over a kitchen chair, and disappeared into one of the two rear bedrooms.

Dunne retrieved one of the beers he'd bought earlier. He took

an opener from the kitchen drawer. There was no sign of Roberta.
He presumed she'd lay down in the other bedroom. He sat on the
front steps and sipped the beer. The stars were visible and numer-
ous, but faded. A lone sliver of cloud nibbled at the lower edge of
the moon's half sphere and moved on.

"Star light, star bright, what's your wish tonight, Fin?" Roberta
was standing at the screen door behind him.

"Thought you went to bed."

"I can't stop thinking about what happened to Lina. I caught a
glimpse. It was sickening. I'd hate to see them get away with this."

"Sparks once told me that he admired my persistence. Well,
now he's going to find out firsthand."

"Where did Anderson come from?"

"Friend of a friend."

"Doesn't he seem a little strange?"

"Not after you get to know him."

"What's his real interest in this? One minute he seems so
removed. The next, he sounds as though he's out to save the
world."

"It's a long story."

"And sad?"

"One of the many. He's in love with a dying woman."

She came outside, sat on the bottom step and stretched out her
feet. "Doesn't feel like the last night of summer. Still seems like
July."

"Want a beer?"

"No thanks." Leaning back, she peered up at the stars. "They
look tired."

"Maybe they can't pay the electric bill. Join the club."

Without a word, she pushed herself up and strolled to the
water's edge. She dropped her dress, removed slip, garters, and
stockings, and stripped to her skin. She walked into the water up to
her buttocks, raised her arms above her head and dove in.

He waited for her to reappear, but the surface stayed still. He
put down his beer and called her name. Other than the gentle pulse
of the bay's insignificant waves, there were no sounds. He pulled off
his shoes and socks and ran to the water. He called her name again.

A breeze ruffled the vacant bay. Hampered by the cast on his hand, he tore off a button as he removed his shirt and was unbuckling his belt when, far from where she'd submerged, Roberta rose gracefully from the sea. The water cascaded off her hair. She swam several yards farther out, stopped and cried, "Come on, Fin, it's beautiful!"

He removed the rest of his clothes and walked into the water up to his waist. Roberta swam toward him. Still several yards away, she arched her body and resubmerged. Something brushed against his legs. Before he could turn, she came up behind. She tried to swim away, but he caught her ankle. Her body was slippery. It shimmered in the silver glow of the moon. He drew her close and kissed her. Her wet body angled into his, a neat fit.

They gathered their clothes and went back to the house. Despite the raucous protest of Doc Cropsey's bedsprings, unaccustomed to the prolonged and boisterous repetition of compression and release, Anderson's loud snoring in the next room continued uninterrupted. Rain pounded the roof and then stopped as suddenly as it had begun. Near dawn, she got up and covered them with a blanket. The birds screamed in berserk anticipation of the sunrise. Dunne nestled into the sinuous curve of her body. He whispered in her ear:

> "Oh, how I hate to get up in the morning
> Oh, how I'd love to remain in bed."

He draped his arm over her. She took his hand in hers and sang softly:

> "And then we'll get the other pup,
> the guy who wakes the bugler up
> and spend the rest of our lives in bed."

They left Doc's place late morning, amid a pale, motionless mist. Shelter Island was Roberta's idea. She found a road map in Doc's kitchen and pointed out that if they used the Shelter Island ferries, they could reach the south shore of Long Island and return to the city without retracing their steps or coming near Yaphank. They filled up with gas at the first service station they came to and drove to Greenport. The line for the ferry on Main Street was only two cars long. Anderson wanted to go into the restaurant next to the ferry line for a cup of tea. Dunne convinced him it would be better if they waited until they reached the South Shore. Anderson sat glum and unhappy in the back.

The ferry arrived in a few minutes. Once they were on, it left for Shelter Island. Cap pulled low over his eyes, a ferryman came to collect the fare. He held out a receipt in a hand missing two fingers.

"See that sky?" he said.

The morning mist was gone; a rising wind stampeded a herd of gray, dark-bellied clouds eastward, toward the open sea. "The clouds?" Roberta said.

"Nope."

Dunne sat motionless, staring down into his lap. He recognized the ferryman: Clem Payne, the man who had taken him fishing earlier in the summer. Anderson stuck his head out the window and quickly withdrew it. "No gulls."

"Yep. Mornin' like this, wind or no wind, they'd be swarmin' over them trawlers tied up at the docks, waitin' for the scraps be throwed 'em. Not today," the ferryman said.

"Could be, they went back to the city with the summer visitors," Roberta said.

"Gulls got more sense than city people. They know when bad weather is movin' in. From the look of things, I'd say we're 'bout to get ourselves a nor'easter. Maybe worse. Either way, seems Mother Nature might have somethin' up her sleeve." He put his receipt book in his pocket and readied to tie the boat to the pilings as it docked in the ferry slip.

Roberta waved at the ferryman as they drove off the boat. He nodded rather than waved. "Did you have to be that rude?" Roberta said. "You barely looked at him, Fin."

"We've met before. I wasn't eager to jog his memory."

"Unlikely," Anderson said. "He's a country person. They're the same the world over. To them, all city people look alike."

Shelter Island had the appearance of a deserted village. Many of the houses were already boarded up for the winter. The single road they followed from the north ferry to the south was only lightly trafficked. The boat ride was significantly shorter than on the north side, but the wind continued to pick up. They had to roll up the windows to keep from getting soaked by the spray from the choppy water.

Sag Harbor was as forlorn as Shelter Island. Only a few cars were parked on the main street. A wind-driven spiral of papers and leaves rampaged across it. When they reached the Montauk Highway, they turned west, toward the city. After a brief while, they stopped so Dunne could relieve himself. The clock in the office said 12:15. He looked at his watch. It was five after two. "Your clock has stopped," he said to the attendant.

The attendant laughed. "Only thing workin' around here today is me. Look at the barometer 'neath the clock. This mornin' was well over 29. Now it's down under 27.5. Ain't never been that low before. It's like the damn thing just up and died."

Anderson wasn't in the car when Dunne returned. "'Mutiny on the Bounty,'" Roberta said. "I told him to wait for you, but he said he couldn't wait any longer for his cup of tea. He's up the street in that greasy spoon." She pointed to a luncheonette several storefronts away.

"We might as well join him," Dunne said. "It's a straight drive west from here to the city. Guess it can't hurt if we eat first."

They left the car at the gas station. Roberta tied a silk kerchief over her head. The roiling black sky looked ready to burst. The wind came in spurts, dying down for a moment before a fresh, fiercer gust arrived. It almost ripped the kerchief off Roberta's head. She ducked into the doorway of a florist's shop to retie it. Dunne turned his back to the street, cupped a match in his hand and lit a cigarette. He did the same for Roberta. She lowered her head toward the flame. The small sign in the window behind her advertised END OF SUMMER SALE. EVERYTHING MUST GO. Except for a few pots of golden chrysanthemums and a box of sea lavender, everything had.

Roberta touched the flowers in the window box. "These are pretty," she said. "I wonder what they are." In the glass above the box was the weak reflection of street and sky. The clouds moved with menacing speed. A black car pulled up across the way. A woman got out, looked around, and ran to a pharmacy.

"Impatiens," Dunne said. "Their time is almost up."

"You're the last man I'd ever think would know anything about flowers." She dropped her cigarette and stepped on it.

The woman across the street rapped on the door of the pharmacy, which seemed to be closed. She turned and glanced about. Finally, the door opened and she went in.

Dunne gripped Roberta's arm with his left hand and held her back.

"Fin, let go! You're hurting me!"

He kept his grip. "Go to the car right now. Pull around to the front of the luncheonette. I'll get Anderson. Do it fast!"

"What's got into you?" When he released her, she rubbed her arm and stayed where she was.

He stared past her, into the window. "Look over my shoulder. See that car? It's being driven by Irene Loben, one of Sparks's accomplices."

"I'll be there in a minute." She ran back to the car.

He pulled down his hat, securing it against the wind, and rushed into the luncheonette. Anderson was at the far end of the counter. The counterman brought him his tea and buttered toast.

"I've been looking forward to this all day," Anderson said as he lifted the cup. "Cheers."

Dunne held the door ajar. The wind surged in behind him. "Let's go."

"Close that damn door," the counterman snapped.

Anderson sipped his tea. "What's the hurry?"

"Sparks's friend is parked across the street."

"Good God." Anderson dropped his cup. The contents splashed across the counter. He slapped a quarter on the cash register and followed Dunne outside. Miss Loben was exiting the pharmacy. Last time he'd seen her was on the steps of the Hermes Sanatorium, a look of horrified surprise on her face. Now, expressionless, she lowered her head and ran to the car, got in, and drove east, in the direction of Montauk.

Roberta drove toward them and made a screeching U-turn in front of the luncheonette. A bread truck just missed hitting her. The driver screamed and shook his fist. The car stalled. She started it again, slowed down enough for Dunne and Anderson to hop in, and sped away. Rain suddenly beat against the windshield in blinding sheets. "I can barely see."

"Just keep driving." Dunne opened the glove compartment and rifled through it. He reached to the back and removed a compact, silver-plated, snub-nosed pistol.

Roberta glanced at him. "How'd you know it was in there?"

He made sure the pistol was loaded. "Checked your clothes and your purse. Wasn't there, so I figured it had to be here."

"That's what I love most about you, Fin. You're such a romantic." The sky had turned pitch black. She turned on the headlights. The road ahead was layered over with leaves and broken branches. "We have to pull over," she said, "I can hardly make out the road."

Directly ahead, the red glow of tail lights was suddenly visible. "Damn it, stay behind those lights!" Anderson yelled.

"That could be anybody." Roberta erased the vapor on the window with a swipe of her sleeve.

Dunne helped her. "Won't know unless we follow it."

They trailed at a short distance. Several times they inched around giant elms that had been toppled by the wind. The car ahead picked up speed and skidded through a pond-sized puddle. Roberta stepped on the gas. A few yards beyond, the car veered off the highway, rode up on the shoulder, and smashed a picket fence. They could barely keep the tail lights in sight as it raced in the direction of the beach. Crossing over a small bridge, they encountered only darkness. The car had vanished.

"We've lost her," Roberta said. "We better go back."

"There!" Anderson pointed up a narrow lane that cut between a high hedge and ran toward the dunes. The lights rose as the car cleared a knoll, and then sank out of view. "Pull over!"

The wind pushed so hard against the car that it listed into the hedge. There was a lone shack up the road, on the bay side. "Maybe we'd be safer there," Roberta said.

"I don't think we should move anywhere at the moment," Anderson said. As he spoke, the roof of the shack lifted off in one piece, twisted in the air, and broke apart in an explosion of wooden shingles. A flock of them landed on the roof of the car, pounding dents in it. The wind peaked higher, then slowly began to wane in the way it had risen, powerful bursts interspersed by calm. Gradually, the rain tapered off with the wind. The clouds parted. Sunlight glistened on soaked fields and bushes.

Roberta sat up. "That was some squall."

"It was no squall." Anderson got out of the car. He reached down, lifted his pants leg, and removed a pistol strapped to his ankle. "I've been in the Tropics for these storms. This is a full-blown Cape Verde hurricane. We're in the eye of it."

"This isn't the Tropics. Those storms don't come this far north," Dunne said.

"Apparently, the Weather Bureau forgot to inform the storm of that. As soon as the eye passes, it will resume. We haven't much time. You two go back and alert the authorities. I'll make sure they can't drive away."

"Who should I call?" Dunne said. "The FBI?" Dunne handed the snub-nosed pistol to Roberta. "Back the car across the driveway. If anybody tries to get through . . ."

"Don't worry about me," Roberta looked at Anderson. "Just remember to shoot first." She returned to the car and put it in reverse, blocking the road. Anderson and Dunne walked through a palisade of high hedges. They climbed a small knoll. When they reached the crest, the sun was playing peek-a-boo with the clouds. The wind returned, this time from the south. The whipped sand stung their faces. In front, fifty yards or so, was a cottage tucked between the knoll and the grass-covered dunes. Loben's car was parked outside.

Clouds piled on one another and rapidly blocked out the sun. Anderson and Dunne lay down on the leeward side of a dune. Beyond the cottage, waves pounded the beach. Their plumes rose high in the air, over the far dunes, and scattered like shrapnel. Down the beach, the sea had already broken through and was surrounding several houses.

"We can't just wait here!" Dunne yelled.

"We don't have to! Look!"

Hatless, in a yellow rain slicker, white pants, and blue deck shoes, Sparks had exited the cottage. Irene Loben was behind him. The hood of her red pullover covered her head. They stood by the car, sheltering themselves by its side, but made no attempt to get in. Neither of them seemed surprised to see Anderson approaching. Dunne ran to catch up with him, tripped over a rotted log, and fell hard on his cast. He cried out in pain. The rain started again, coming in gray sheets laced with sand and the salted spray of the ocean. He struggled to stand.

Anderson neared the bottom of the hollow. He was close enough to see the smile on Sparks's face. He raised his gun, motioning for Sparks and Loben to return to the cottage when, from behind, the blade of a gardener's spade shattered his clavicle; a quick second blow sliced open his carotid artery, spurting blood over his jacket. He staggered and turned toward the attacker, who'd been sheltered behind a dune. This time the spade hit him full in the face, pulverizing his front teeth, smashing his nose and sending him sprawling. He tasted blood in his throat and tried to recall where he was. He heard the distant thunder of artillery. He was lying in a trench at the Somme, a ditch filled with dead and dying men. He struggled to recite four lines from Jeremiah, a prayer and a prophesy. How'd they go? He remembered now:

*I'll amputate his reveille*
*And stomp upon it heavily . . .*

The spade, especially sharpened for the purpose, descended with the force of an executioner's axe, four times in all, finally severing his head from his body.

Huber picked up Anderson's gun and threw away the spade. Sparks pulled a pistol from beneath his slicker and got in the car. Loben ran to the passenger side. A phalanx of towering waves crashed atop the dunes. Huber jumped on the running board and the car took off down the road. Dunne scrambled to his feet and ran in the same direction. He didn't hear a gun shot, but felt the hot, ugly whine of a bullet as it grazed his ear. He kept running. Sparks's car reached Roberta's sedan. She wasn't in it. The doors were locked. Sparks broke the window with the butt of his gun, opened the door, and released the brake. He and Loben went to the rear and started to push.

Huber had hopped off the car and was approaching. The acute, agonizing impact of a bullet in the back of his knee sent Dunne tumbling forward. His face struck the sand. He raised himself up on his other knee and wiped his eyes. Ahead, Sparks and Loben moved Roberta's car so there was space enough to squeeze past. They returned to their car. There was no sign of Roberta.

Dunne fumbled on the ground and wrapped his left hand around a piece of driftwood. His last chance was for Huber to come sufficiently close so that he could slam him with the wood. Ocean and sky were a single curtain of gray, devouring water. Huber stopped a few paces away, beyond where Dunne could reach him. As Dunne made a futile effort to stand, Huber staggered forward, dropped to his knees and collapsed face down on the sand. Roberta stood over him, her hair blowing across her face. She pushed it away and fired a single shot into the back of Huber's head, a coup de grace that finished the work of the other two bullets she had just put in his back. "I told you. Shoot first."

She knelt beside Dunne, put her arm under his shoulder, and helped him up. They stood on the knoll as the vast sea, a seamless fusion of water and wind, rushed over the dunes and trapped Sparks and Miss Loben. The roofs of their car and Roberta's sedan disappeared under the water's swift advance.

Dunne's weight and the force of the wind made it impossible for Roberta to move. She lowered Dunne onto the ground, removed the cloth belt from her jacket, tied it around his left wrist and her right. She lifted him back up as the water swept over the knoll and plunged them into the churning, unstoppable current. The debris of Sparks's cottage—shutters, doors, chairs, tables, and bedsteads—swirled around them.

His strength left him entirely. He tried to keep his head above water, but couldn't. He felt himself sinking and then the heavy tug of the cloth around his wrist. Roberta pulled him up. As the broken framework of a roof sailed by, she grabbed it and draped the belt over a protruding beam. She screamed at him to hold on. The rain pelted their faces. They swirled in circles. There was no east or west, nothing but water. He sank again, into the cold, enveloping silence of the sea. He closed his eyes. They were all there: Big Mike, his mother, Jack, Maura. All together again. Roberta dragged him up and shoved him across the beam. He gagged on the water he'd swallowed and struggled to breathe.

He remembered: Death by drowning could be quick and merciful. The secret is not to resist.

*Offer it up, Fin.*

November 1938

# 11

RAMPAGE IN GERMANY ENDS
JEWS ASK: 'WHERE ARE WE TO GO?"
by John Mayhew Taylor
Special to the *New York Standard*

BERLIN, Nov. 10—The havoc wreaked on Germany's Jewish population over the last two days represented a major escalation in the Nazi regime's anti-Semitic campaign. Estimates of the number of Jews arrested are as high as 30,000. Most were immediately shipped to concentration camps. Though there are as yet no official figures, it's thought at least 100 Jews lost their lives and thousands more were injured. While the police stood by, Germany's towns and cities reverberated with the sounds of shattering glass as Jewish businesses were looted and vandalized, and homes and apartments raided and pillaged. In Berlin and Munich, the major synagogues were put to the torch. A similar fate befell scores of other Jewish houses of worship throughout the country. In many instances, the crowds that gathered to watch quickly joined in, giving the violence the atmosphere of a street carnival. The event that ostensibly triggered this rampage was the assassination of the German Third Legation Secretary in Paris by a young Jew angry over the forced repatriation of Polish Jews, his family included. This expulsion, in turn, was a reaction to a recent decision by the Polish government to ban the return of its Jewish citizens living abroad. The almost universal refusal by other countries, including the U.S., to suspend entry controls and allow in more Jews has left many in a despondent state. In an apartment near the Kurfürstendam, with the smell of smoke from a nearby synagogue hanging in the air, a group of Jews were offered refuge by their gentile employer. The oldest, a well-dressed woman in her fifties, spoke for the rest when she asked, "Where are we to go? We must leave Germany but where can we go? Who will take us?"

"THE COLONEL WILL BE with you shortly." Colonel Donovan's secretary was businesslike without being impersonal. "If you'd like, the receptionist will bring you a cup of tea."

"I'll wait in the hallway," Dunne said.

He sat on the sill cattycornered to the elevator bank. He didn't feel like explaining about the trapped sensation that came from sitting too long, like being choked or drowned. The view out the window was the wall of the adjacent building, but the sliver of space was filled with cool, moist air. The sound of traffic wafted in from below, incessant honks, screeching brakes, impatient chorus of traffic choked in the narrow passageway of Wall Street.

Dunne picked his teeth with the edge of the matchbook he'd grabbed from his bureau. He hadn't noticed the logo until now: BEN MARDEN'S RIVERIA, FORT LEE, NEW JERSEY. He tore out a match, struck it, and held it to the tip of the cigarette in his mouth. As he sucked in the smoke, the flame shrank, flared as he exhaled.

He dropped the still-lit match out the window . . . *Looking for the light of a new love to brighten up the night, I have you love, and we can face the music together, dancing in the dark* . . . It spiraled downward, trailing a plumelet of smoke. Roberta Dee and Elba Corado had taken the train to Florida the week before. It was Roberta's idea. Though Wilfredo was quickly granted a new trial that resulted in his exoneration, she was sure that the taint of the Lynch case would remain and that before long the cops would turn their attention to her operation, either to bust it up or shake it down. She convinced Wilfredo to leave first.

Dunne escorted them to the train. "I promise I'll come," he said. "Soon as I've wrapped up some loose ends." He drew Roberta close. She pushed him away. "If you think you can interest anyone in what Anderson had to say about the grand schemes of Sparks and his Nazi friends, forget it. He couldn't convince anyone. Neither can you. People have to learn for themselves."

Elba waved distractedly at him from the window of the train.

She seemed neither pleased nor upset at the sight of the embrace. Dunne guessed that her mind was probably on other things: how confusing and complicated the triumph of good can be, the unexpected—even painful—truths it can reveal.

The train pulled out into the tunnel; its rear lights glowed, grew faint, then disappeared.

The rhythmic, deliberate tap-slap of footsteps, a military stride, signaled someone was coming down the marble hall, march time. Dunne stood in a civilian version of attention. Colonel Donovan stopped the instant he turned the corner. His eyes did a quick up-and-down. "I'm glad to see you, Dunne," he said. "I'm sorry about what happened." Walking slightly ahead of Dunne, he led the way past the receptionist and his secretary into his office.

"Please take a seat." He pulled his chair close to Dunne's. "Too bad about Anderson. I sent him to you because, well, I thought you could give him a hand." Donovan paused. "I'd no idea that he'd drag you out to Long Island and put you at mortal risk."

"I wasn't dragged."

"You got caught in that storm. Poor Anderson was lost."

Dunne opened his mouth, almost ready to say "was murdered," but stopped himself. "Colonel, would you mind if I stood by the window? I need a bit of air."

"Feel free." Donovan went to the window and raised it higher. It was a mild evening, wet with fog. "Would you care for water—or something stronger?"

"No, just some air, straight up."

"I heard you were pretty badly banged up. The Czech crisis was such a strong distraction that most people don't appreciate how vicious a storm it was. Towns and villages wrecked. Thousands of homes washed away. Over 2,300 people dead or seriously injured, yet the Weather Bureau never issued a single hurricane warning for Long Island or New England. Can you imagine if, instead of a storm, it had been an enemy fleet? Let's just hope naval intelligence doesn't have its head stuck in the same hole as the Weather Bureau."

"Anderson saw it coming," Dunne said.

"If I'd the slightest inkling of how it was all going to play out, I'd never have sent him to you. He was an intelligent, sensitive man, but the war left him a little addled. He'd been shell-shocked at the Somme, in 1916. After the war, he worked for British Intelligence, yet they maintain he'd gone on his own several years ago."

"He told me he worked for himself."

"He wouldn't have said whether or not he was an agent."

"Anderson didn't lie."

"He never would have been an intelligence agent if he didn't."

"Maybe that's why he left. He was telling truths most prefer not to hear."

"My first impression was that he'd become paranoid. But when he came to me looking for an introduction to someone in the prosecutor's office who was connected to that Grillo case, he seemed quite rational. I should have stuck with my initial impression."

Donovan's secretary knocked and entered. "Colonel," she said, "your car is waiting. Your dinner appointment is for six-thirty."

He nodded and went to his desk. He took a large manila envelope from the drawer and placed it next to that day's *New York Times*. He turned the paper so Dunne could see the banner headline:

GOV. LEHMAN RE-ELECTED:
BIG REPUBLICAN GAINS IN THE NATION

"I'm dining with the loser. He lost by only 64,000 votes. Lehman beat me in '32 by almost 900,000. If it hadn't been for the size of the Democratic pluralities in Albany and the Bronx, Dewey might have pulled off the upset of the century."

Donovan opened the envelope and spilled its contents on the desk: several pairs of cuff links, a set of gold shirt studs, and a gold watch and chain with a locket attached. "Unbeknown to me, Anderson made out a will and named me executor. He lived in a furnished room. I gave his clothes to the St. Vincent de Paul Society. He left his small savings to doctors, a married couple, who were friends of his. This is all that's left."

Dunne picked up the locket and pried it open with his thumbnail. Inside was an oval cut from a larger photograph: Mathilde Ignatz's face.

"I've no idea who she is," Donovan said. "Anderson had no family. I'm sure he'd be pleased if you kept it."

Dunne put the watch and locket in his pocket. "Maybe I can give it to someone who'd appreciate it."

Donovan took a letter from the same drawer as the manila envelope. "This was at his apartment. It's the only piece of personal correspondence that arrived after his disappearance. The postmark is Copenhagen but there's no name or return address. Can you make any sense of this?" He handed an index card to Dunne. On it was printed in large letters:

SS-AGENT GUSTAV HAUSSER (HUBER)/RENDEZVOUS: MONTAUK, 22.9.

"It seems as though he was planning some sort of rendevouz."

"He kept it."

"In Montauk?"

"Not far away." Dunne recalled a line of Roberta's, about love and the strange places it can take us, but kept it to himself.

Donovan didn't inquire further. He removed Anderson's card from the envelope. "This was in it, too." He turned it over so the four lines of verse on the back faced Dunne, who picked it up without reading it. Donovan gathered his papers. "I'll give you a ride uptown, if you'd like."

"Thanks. I'll walk. Need the exercise."

They rode the elevator down together. Wall Street was still clogged with traffic. "You'll probably beat me walking." It was refreshing, Donovan thought, to encounter somebody from the regiment who hadn't let himself go to seed. Although a little gaunt, Dunne seemed fit and trim. "Stay in touch, Dunne. I occasionally have use for a good detective. Never know when the need will arise." He shook Dunne's hand.

"I'd like that, Colonel." Dunne raised the collar of his trenchcoat. He decided to walk up Broadway to Duane, buy a pack of smokes at Liggetts before he went home and turned in early, be fresh and ready when the need arose.

March 1939

# 12

HITLER MARCHES ON CZECHS
RIPS UP MUNICH PACT BARELY
SIX MONTHS AFTER SIGNING IT

GERMANS ENTER PRAGUE
WITHOUT FIRING A SHOT:
ALLIES EXPRESS "SHOCK AND DISMAY"
BUT DO NOTHING
by John Mayhew Taylor
Special to the *New York Standard*

PRAGUE, March 15—The future arrived in Prague today. It rode in tanks and armored cars. It wore steel helmets and hobnail boots. It entered the city amid a blinding snow that did little to muffle the roar of bombers overhead or soften the echo of goose-stepping troops. The future stood at attention on the bridge across the Charles River. It raised its swastika standard atop the Hradschin Castle. It surveyed the latest fruits of its disregard for treaties and international agreements. It reiterated its contempt for physical weakness and intellectual dithering. It laughed aloud at the empty threats and hollow protests of its opponents. The future has no fear. It believes in its own destiny. "Who dares stop me?" it asks, and a death's-head sneer readily supplies the answer.

THE JURY ROOM COCKTAIL LOUNGE,
NEW YORK,

"NO, FOR THE LAST goddamn time, I do *not* want a drink," Doc Cropsey said.

"Tryin' to save you a trip, that's all." Corrigan started toward the bar.

"Then get me a club soda," Doc Cropsey shouted after him.

The Professor ignored the squabbling and opened a copy of the *Standard*. He commenced reading aloud a story about Fred Wistow, a dentist who'd wounded his wife and killed the man he suspected of being her lover. Wistow shot them on Fordham Road, in the middle of the afternoon, and tried to flee by commandeering a cab. The cab driver deliberately crashed into one of the iron pillars of the Jerome Avenue El, ending the escape.

"What a shame," the Professor said. "In normal times, an outrage such as Wistow's would have been front page. Today it ends up on page five without even a picture of a manacled perpetrator being taken away." He shook his head and returned to the headline, which he held up for his tablemates to see. The story, datelined Prague, was written by John Mayhew Taylor. The Professor read aloud the opening paragraph. "The boy can write," the Professor said.

Corrigan returned with three glasses tightly clasped in his hands. "Gotta give it to him. He got where he wanted, right in the middle of that foreign stew. Good luck to him. Still, you ask me, he's wastin' his time. People in this country are more determined than ever not to get snookered into another foreign foofaraw."

Doc Cropsey turned over his hands and examined his palms with the furrowed concentration of a fortune teller pondering the mottled fleshscape of lines and creases for a clue to the future. "What this country needs is somebody competent enough to predict the goddamn weather correctly."

The Professor folded the newspaper, put it aside, and claimed his drink. "Six months later and you're still lamenting the loss of that shack of yours?"

"Maybe it was a shack, but it was *my* goddamn shack, and it got wrecked because those idiots in the Weather Bureau never uttered so much as a peep about the approach of a storm the size of Texas."

"Warnin' or no warnin', been wrecked either way. Storm like that will level everthin' in its path," Corrigan said.

"Stick a sock in it, Corrigan," Doc Cropsey barked. "You're the last goddamn person I need to lecture me on the nature of hurricanes."

The young couple in the next booth looked over disapprovingly. The Professor recognized the man as Mike McCarthy, an up-and-coming assistant U.S. Attorney. The blonde he was with reached across and took his hand. They resumed talking.

"Pipe down," the Professor said. "You're distracting Romeo from his wooing."

"Those pipsqueaks want to moon over one another, they should find a soda fountain," Doc Cropsey said.

"If Mike McGloin were still alive, God rest his soul, he'd have seen to it that those two knew they weren't welcome." The Professor lifted his glass in tribute to the deceased barkeep, whom he'd discovered slumped over a newspaper one night in late September. Given the late hour, the Professor had assumed McGloin was asleep but, after trying several times to rouse him, realized he was dead. The Professor penned a tribute that ran on the *Standard's* obituary page. Since McGloin was a bachelor, without any close relatives, the Professor also arranged the funeral Mass at St. Agnes, on 43rd Street. Along with five other longtime patrons, he served as an honorary pallbearer.

The next afternoon, out of the blue, the Professor received a call from Fintan Dunne. He was in a hospital in Southampton. He'd been caught in the hurricane and was lucky to be alive. He asked the Professor to bring him some clothes from his apartment and cash stowed in his refrigerator. Hubert Dixon, the janitor at the Hackett Building, had a key and had already been told it was all right to give it to the Professor.

The train to Southampton halted at Riverhead. The track farther east was washed away in several places. A bus carried the handful of passengers the rest of the way, moving slowly through a wrecked countryside of uprooted elms and oaks. The leaves on the trees still standing had been turned brown by the salt-laced winds that had pushed the swollen ocean over the barrier dunes. Southampton had the stunned and battered look of a battle-scarred village. Dunne was sitting on the side of his bed, in a room in which four other patients were squeezed, his face drawn and gaunt. They went into the corridor for a smoke. The Professor noticed Dunne was limping. He offered no explanation of how or why he'd been caught in the hurricane.

That evening, in a restaurant off the main street, the Professor ran into Mayfield Close, an old colleague from the *Standard* who now worked for a New England newspaper and was writing a feature piece on the storm's impact on communities from Long Island to Vermont. Close told the Professor that town and county officials had published lists of the dead and missing, but he didn't put much store in them.

"This is like a country caught by a surprise attack," he said. "Confusion reigns." Off the record, a sergeant in the State Police had confided to Close that a number of corpses couldn't be accounted for. One was headless, another had been shot in the back several times.

Close believed that the storm, already enjoying notoriety as "The Hurricane of '38," was an embarrassment as well as a tragedy for the towns it struck. "The businessmen are afraid it will do to tourism what the Hindenburg explosion did to airship travel," he said. "The only blessing is that it happened off-season. Their aim now is to put the storm behind them and restore a degree of normality as quickly as possible."

The Professor inquired about Fintan Dunne. Close said that he'd tried to interview him but couldn't get much out of him. "He was found along with a woman. Lashed to a scrap of wood that served as a raft, they were washed up north of Montauk Highway, at the farthest point of the water's surge. The woman proved in better shape than Dunne, who'd been shot in the leg and lost a lot of blood. He claimed not to know how it happened. Any other time, the police would never settle for an answer like that, but in view of the present circumstances and what they have to deal with, they just hoped he'd leave as soon as possible and never come back."

"What about the woman?"

"She left before I got a chance to talk to her," Close said. "I bumped into Dunne a day or so later at the Westhampton school gym, which had been turned into a temporary morgue. He was looking for two people. I wrote down their names." Close took out his notebook and paged through it quickly. "Yes, here they are: Mr. Sparks and Miss Loben. Loben was found; that is, what was left of her after the gulls had a chance to feast on the corpse. But Sparks, no. He's apparently among the many who'll never be found. Dunne was mum about his interest in the pair. All he'd say was that 'they were acquaintances.'"

The Professor spent the night in a rooming house that was still without electricity. He walked to the hospital in the morning. Dunne was waiting in the reception area, dressed in the suit the Professor had brought him the previous day. He paid his bill. They boarded the bus to Riverhead, where they caught the train to Manhattan.

Dunne moved slowly, leaning heavily on a cane. His right hand, which he'd re-broken in a fall, was in a sling. He seemed in pain and sweated profusely on the short walk from the bus to the train. He hardly said a word on the trip back. The Professor recognized Dunne was still suffering from some form of shock from his ordeal and didn't press him with questions or ask for an account of what had occurred. Some things, the Professor knew from decades spent covering murder and mayhem, were best forgotten and left behind. The surest remedy for most tragedies and traumas was as simple as it was old: Get on with life and its everyday routines.

Six weeks after their return from Southampton, the day after a radio broadcast by *The Mercury Theatre of the Air* tricked half the country into believing that the Martians were taking over New Jersey, Dunne appeared in the Shack. News of the panic the broadcast caused was splashed all over the papers.

"I don't see what the fuss was about," the Professor said. "As far as I'm concerned, if the Martians want New Jersey, they can have it."

Dunne didn't smile. "The threat isn't from Mars. It's already here." He then inquired if the *Standard* had run any stories about an attack on two FBI agents at Camp Siegfried in September.

The Professor eventually sent some clips to Dunne that reported an assault on two G-men that took place during a search of the Bund's summer camp. Several Bund members were arrested for the crime and were awaiting trial in Brooklyn Federal Court. Although grateful for the information, Dunne never revealed the reason for his interest.

The Professor saw Dunne for the last time in February 1939, late on a winter's day, icy rain pelting from a formless sky. They met at Rostoff's for a cup of coffee. In a corner, by himself, was Tommy Hines. He sat scanning the newspaper accounts of the conviction Tom Dewey had won in his successful retrial of Tommy's uncle, Tammany leader Jimmy Hines.

For Dewey, it was a milestone in his crusade to clean up the city. Equally, it was sweet revenge for the narrow defeat he suffered in November at the hands of Governor Lehman. The D.A.'s name was back in the headlines. The national press took notice. From where Dunne and the Professor sat, they couldn't tell if Tommy Hines was weeping as he read the articles or the rain was dripping from his hair onto his face.

Dunne appeared to the Professor to be fully recovered. He said that he was leaving in a few days for Miami. He planned to stay with a lady friend whose daughter had opened a dress shop there. It was going to be an indefinite stay, he said. He'd given up his office in the Hackett Building and sublet his apartment to Doc Cropsey, who'd surrendered the lease to his own flat in expectation of retiring to Southold. (A plan he'd had to put off until his new cottage was built, this time at a good remove from the water.)

Dunne made no mention of the hurricane, which the Professor interpreted as a sign of psychological recovery. When they were about to leave, Dunne produced a business card with someone else's name on it and a biblical quote printed on the other side.

The Professor was puzzled. "Should I keep this for you until you come back?"

"It's for you. I thought a literary man like you might appreciate it."

Corrigan went back to the bar. He squinted at the price list of mixed cocktails posted by the cash register. The subdued light from the wall fixtures that had replaced the garish intensity of

McGloin's ceiling lamps made it difficult to see. The bartender wore a black bowtie and a short red jacket. His breast pocket was embossed with the symbol of a cocktail shaker and surrounded by the name the new owner had given McGloin's: THE JURY ROOM COCKTAIL LOUNGE.

"We have waitress service at the tables, sir," the bartender said.

"Tell that to the waitress," Corrigan replied. When he got back to the table with another round, the Professor and Doc Cropsey were engaged in an argument.

"The Nazi campaign against the Jews is no different from the pogroms and persecutions in the past," Doc Cropsey said. "The Germans will come to their senses. The Jews will keep their heads down until they do. That's the way it's always been."

The Professor shook his head. "You're wrong," he said. "The ancient bloodlust that's been with us since the time of Homer and before, the feverish desire for revenge and conquest, is being replaced by something more scientific and invidious."

"Here we go." Corrigan put down the drinks. "Yesterday, he went on for almost an hour about the fight 'tween Armageddon and Imogene."

"Their names were Agamemnon and Iphidamas," the Professor said. "My point is that we seem to be transgressing beyond the ordinary limits of face-to-face cruelty that our species has traditionally excelled in. The hope that human behavior and morality progress pari passu with the increasing power of our machines or the sophistication of our culture seems about to blow up in our faces."

The assistant U.S. attorney stood. He gave his hand to his companion as she shifted across her seat and exited the booth. They went to the jukebox and examined the selection of songs. The electric arch atop it bathed their faces in a rainbow glow. A coin dropped. The machine began to whirr.

"Anything should be blown up, it's that contraption." Doc Cropsey nodded toward the newly introduced music player—"the jukebox"—that began to play.

"Maybe somebody should put this to music," the Professor

said. In a voice strong enough to be heard over the music, he read
from a card in his hand:

*"We looked for peace,*
*But no good came:*
*For a time of healing,*
*But behold, terror."*


ABWEHR HEADQUARTERS, BERLIN


Oster maneuvered around the flanks of the bent, kneeling
washerwomen who kept scrubbing as he went down the hallway
they had just cleaned. He muttered an apology and quickened his
step, as if that might undo the damage. The offices were all closed.
The door to Canaris's office was opened but, seeing no light, Oster
continued past. Several doors down, he came upon Corporal
Gresser, who was working in the filing room. "What are you doing
here so late, Corporal?" Oster said.

"The Admiral is still in his office," Gresser said.

"Napping?"

"The last time I saw him he was looking out the window."
Gresser pushed the file drawer shut. "When I offered to order him
some dinner, he said only that he wished not to be disturbed. I
decided it would be wise if I remain until he leaves."

"The Admiral has his moods. We all know that. I'll see to it he
gets home."

Oster removed his overcoat and put it with his briefcase in the
closet behind Gresser's desk. He stepped over the threshold, into the
shadowy interior of Canaris's office, treading softly in case the
Admiral was asleep. The room was illuminated by ash-colored
moonlight. Canaris was near where Gresser had last seen him,
between the window and the desk, a one-dimensional cutout of
gray and black. He looked at Oster but did not speak.

"I was on my way home when I encountered Gresser. He told me
you were still here." Oster walked over and stood beside Canaris.

"I had a meeting with the Führer today," Canaris said softly, almost in a whisper. "I was summoned to report on the rearmament efforts of the British and French. In the middle of my presentation, he was informed the British had issued a non-negotiable guarantee of Poland's territorial integrity."

"At last they're showing some backbone. They've learned the hard way that the man's promises are utterly worthless." Oster was about to put a cigarette between his lips when Canaris suddenly shouted, "He's mad, Hans, mad beyond a doubt!"

Oster felt the hot, stale rush of his breath, the fine spray of his speech. The cigarette fell from Oster's mouth. He took a step back.

"I still can't take it all in!" Canaris said, his voice loud and anguished. "One minute he was talking calmly, the next ranting like the inmate of an insane asylum. He'll drown his enemies in their own blood, he said. Millions will die, but that's the price which must be paid if his destiny is to be fulfilled. He raved for so long that Ribbentrop had to fetch him a handkerchief to wipe the froth from his mouth."

Canaris bent down and retrieved Oster's cigarette. "I didn't mean to startle you," he said, regaining a measure of calm. "But the behavior I witnessed has left me shaken." Fetching the lighter from his desk, Canaris flicked the wheel. Oster concentrated on putting the cigarette in the middle of the trembling flame.

"Destiny, that's the word he keeps coming back to," Canaris said. "He believes he's its agent. The Czech crisis absolutely con firmed his belief. It's almost as if he knows that, as well as cowing the English and French, he exploded the hopes of those deluded enough to imagine they could depose him."

He recalled to himself a phrase that Heydrich had used: *Facts are paltry things in the face of destiny.* He realized for the first time that Heydrich had been undoubtedly quoting the Führer. The resolution of the Czech crisis, it seemed, had turned that wishful aphorism into actuality. Germany was under his sway now, completely. There were no more barriers. There would be no turning back.

Above, in what had become a nightly occurrence, a formation of army transport planes lumbered toward Templehof Airport. The heavy and familiar drone of their motors rattled against the windows. "They're returning from Prague, I suppose," Canaris said. "His supposed downfall turns out to be another bloodless triumph."

\* \* \*

Twice the conspirators are ready to carry out the coup. Their initial plans are derailed by Prime Minister Chamberlain's peace mission to the Führer's alpine retreat at Berchtesgarden. But, within a week, Hilter goes back on his promises. Meeting Chamberlain for a second time at Bad Godesburg, in the Rhineland, on September 22, he announces that he won't wait on plebiscites or timetables but will move on the Sudetenland immediately.

When it's clear that Hitler wants war and that no concessions will deter him, the conspiracy instantly revives. Oster oversees the preparation of the raiding party. Arms, ammunition, and hand grenades are distributed; maps of the interior of the Reich Chancellery studied and reviewed; the timing made certain. The moment the armed forces are mobilized, the Twenty-third division will move from Potsdam and, instead of heading south toward the Czech border, enter the capital and secure the government quarter. Himmler and Göbbels will be arrested.

Oster meets several times with Captain Friedrich Wilhelm Heinz, who's in charge of the main raiding party. They go over the plan. Heinz and his men are familiar to the sentries at 78 Wilhelmstrasse, the main entrance to the Reichchancellery, and will approach them as though on official business. Once the sentries are overpowered, the entrance will be secured and Heinz will lead a smaller group to take custody of the Führer. They know from careful observation that he is more lightly guarded than outsiders think.

The conspirators agree Hitler is be taken alive. The people will be told that he is mentally ill and being manipulated toward war by the likes of Himmler and Göbbels, who will be formally charged with criminal conspiracy and treason. Oster knows Heinz's intent is to revenge the murder of his friends in the SA and shoot Hitler on the spot. Let General Witzleben and the others come up with an explanation after the event. Oster is convinced it is better this way. Hitler is too dangerous alive.

The news of Mussolini's last-minute attempt to convene a four-party conference and defuse the crisis seems doomed to fail. General Witzleben is convinced that Hitler won't be swayed by the urgent pleas of his badly rattled friend. Oster, too, is sure that nothing can dissuade

*Hitler from his intent to attack the Czechs. He visits Heinz a last time on the afternoon of September 28. The captain's nervousness is obvious; Oster shares it. One way or another, the end is only hours away.*

*When he returns to Abwehr headquarters, Oster is instantly summoned by Canaris, who is seated at his desk, with the radio on. "Listen," he says, "a news flash from the BBC in London. Chamberlain has just announced to the House of Commons that Hitler has accepted Mussolini's proposal for a four-party conference in Munich and, on behalf on His Majesty's Government, so has he."*

*The announcer solemnly quotes the prime minister's words to parliament: "'We are all patriots, and there can be no honourable Member of the House who does not feel his heart leap that the crisis has been once more postponed to give us the opportunity to try what reason and good will and discussion will do to settle a problem which is already within the sight of settlement.'"*

*Shortly afterwards, without a word of greeting, General Witzleben enters Canaris's office, pours himself a glass of brandy and gulps it. Oster half-heartedly raises the possibility of still going forward with the coup. Witzleben dismisses the idea. "On what grounds?" he says. "That the Führer has brought Germany to the height of power without spilling a drop of German blood? It's obvious that if we try to do something now, history, and not just German history, will remember us only as a cabal of disgruntled reactionaries who refused to serve the greatest German at the very moment the whole world recognized his greatness."*

*Two days later, when Chamberlain returns to London waving the agreement he's reached with Hitler and declares that it represents "peace for our time," Canaris sits alone in silence and the dark. Outside, the noise of traffic, which had diminished during the crisis, is back to normal volume. A tram rings its bell continuously: a note not of warning, he realizes, but of celebration. A voice shouts, "Heil Hitler!" Other voices pick it up. The chorus echoes through the street.*

"They'll follow him over the cliff now," Canaris said. "They'll go wherever he wants them to go and take the rest of Europe with them."

"That remains to be seen. Perhaps we'll all have to pay for letting him get this far. Perhaps not. For the present, it's wise to keep our own counsel and be patient. Come, Wilhelm, I'll drop you home." Oster had thought for an instant that perhaps Canaris had fallen prey to the same outbursts as the Führer, as though his madness were contagious. It was a mistaken impression, he decided. The momentary slip of Canaris's mask, the glimpse of what lay behind his stoic, inexpressive demeanor revealed not rage, but fear, anticipation of the road ahead and where it led. The final destination. Oster went out and retrieved his coat and briefcase.

When he returned, Canaris was sitting at his desk with the lamp on. "I have work to do. I'll summon a driver to take me home."

"Suit yourself, but you won't do your country any good by working yourself to death," Oster said. As he turned to leave, he noticed the model of the *Dresden* on the mantel. It drew his mind to the sea, reminding him of a question he several times meant to ask but, in the confusion and despondency that followed the aborted coup, had forgotten. "Wilhelm," he said, "that submarine Heydrich dispatched to America, what happened to it?" He left unmentioned how Piekenbrock had told him about his trip to Copenhagen and his happy sense it was intended to foil the U-boat's mission.

Canaris put on his glasses and began to examine the stack of files on his desk. "There was a storm, a tremendous blow. The American weather service failed to detect that it was headed for the coast, but the captain of the U-boat was warned by a German merchant ship that had come through and barely survived. The captain asked permission to turn back, and it was granted."

"And those it was supposed to pick up?"

"God only knows. Either they drowned or found another escape route. If the SS knows, it's not telling."

"Well, then," Oster said, "there's cause for hope. The weather turned against them. Perhaps that's an omen of better days to come."

"Or of more bad weather."

"Always the pessimist."

Canaris bowed his head, as if to concentrate on the document in front of him. "I've learned that one is rarely disappointed when he expects the worst."

# April 1945

## EPILOGUE

After a man has experienced much and learned neither to hold fast, nor to go down, nor to die, but to stretch himself, to feel, not evade things, but to stand straight, with a steadfast soul, that is something.

—ALFRED DÖBLIN, *Berlin Alexanderplatz*

### FLOSSENBÜRG CONCENTRATION CAMP

*T*he sirens summon him from sleep. Instead of fleeing to the air-raid shelter beneath the building, he goes to the window and draws back the curtains. Searchlights move like clock hands across the darkness. In the distance, the flare of incendiary bombs lights up the horizon. The explosions draw nearer. The concussed ripples of the bombs rattle the window. He closes his eyes. The yellow flash penetrates his lids.

*"Come quickly, Admiral!"*

*A flashlight shines directly in his eyes. He puts up his hand to shield them.*

*"You must come to the shelter! The sirens are sounding! We have only a few minutes!"*

*He finally makes out who its: Gresser.*

*"Go ahead, I'll be down directly." He swings his feet onto the floor, rubs his eyes, and lights a cigarette. He goes to the window and draws back the curtains. The incendiary bombs are falling closer.*

*Somewhere on the canal, an oil barge is hit. Its contents catch fire and spill into the water, covering it with flames. A horde of rats scurries up the embankment until the street is hidden beneath a demented, heaving cover of gray-brown vermin. Fire trucks rush by, crushing them like grapes in a wine press. Their maddened squeaks and squeals grow into a single ear-splitting shriek.*

In these last minutes, he can't separate what he dreamed from what really occurred. Certainly, the air raids were no dream. Gresser and thousands of others died in them. Most of the casualties were civilians. But the rats? Did he dream them? He's not sure.

Canaris stares into the dark and waits to be summoned from his cell. Once the clock had been wound, its hands moved relentlessly and inexorably toward this moment.

The day the war begins, he knows where it will end. He tells a colleague, "This means the end of Germany."

For the next four years, he balances himself on the wire, a master of the tightrope, loyal to his nation and to its armed forces but an opponent of the regime, believing it is possible to separate the former from the latter, to serve one as a patriot and, where possible, resist the other.

He protests the liquidation of Soviet POWs.

Keitel replies on behalf of the Führer: "These objections accord with soldierly conceptions of a chivalrous war! What matters now is the destruction of an ideology. I therefore approve and endorse these measures."

The confirmation that Dr. Arnheim's fears were real, that mental patients are being murdered in the thousands as part of Operation T-4, no sooner arrives than an even more monstrous crime unfolds: the utter totality and finality of the solution that has been devised for the Jewish Question and is already being carried out.

He assists as many as he can to get away. He helps over five hundred escape from Holland at one time under the guise of being Abwehr agents en route to South America. At one point, Himmler's remark to the Führer about the Admiral's "strange regard for the Jews" results in a temporary suspension that leaves no doubt about the growing precariousness of his position.

He secretly meets with General Mengies of British Intelligence and General Donovan of the OSS in Santander, in Spain. They're accompanied by an aide, whom Donovan says is absolutely trust-worthy. "We served together in the last war," he says. "He saved my life." Mengies and Donovan implore Canaris to come over to the Allies. Germany is doomed and you know it, Donovan says.

Canaris proposes that if Hitler is removed, a cease-fire will be declared in the West and the new government of Germany, while dismantling the Nazi state, will be allowed to concentrate its resources on stopping the Soviet advance in the East.

The possibility of such deals died at Munich in 1938, Mengies says. Your choice, Admiral, is to come over to our side, to set an example for your countrymen, or to return and suffer the fate your nation has brought upon itself.

You must choose, Herr Admiral.

When the axe finally falls, when the SS raid the offices of the Abwehr and he's relieved of his command and put under house arrest, it almost comes as a relief. With Heydrich dead—assassinated by Czech partisans—Himmler himself takes control of a reorganized and consolidated intelligence operation. The war against the Reich's enemies, the Allies, the Jews, traitors, and spies, will be waged simul-taneously on all fronts.

He tells himself that he will soon be forgotten, relegated to some lowly, humiliating assignment, allowed to exist in quiet, protective oblivion. Even as he tells himself this, he knows it isn't true. In the old castle at Burg Lauenstein, where he is held under house arrest, there is a large Black Forest clock at the bottom of the stairway. He hears its ticking. In the middle of the night, at the quarter hour, its cuckoo emerges to sing a lyric especially for him: *The more familiar we become with National Socialist ideas, the more we'll discover they are truly soldierly ideas.*

Soon after the Allies land in France, a group of officers finally car-ries out an assassination attempt on the Führer. They fail, as he could have told them they would. It's too late to prevent what is in store for Germany. The crimes are too great. Fate will not allow it. Heaven demands it. The clock won't stop until it strikes the final hour.

All those suspected of opposing the regime are rounded up. On a warm, still July afternoon, a car comes for him. He is driven to Gestapo headquarters on Prinz-Albrecht Strasse, hustled from the car into an underground warren of stone corridors and steel doors.

He sees no visitors and is kept on a starvation diet. There is no light in the cell. He loses track of whether it is night or day. The screams and moans that filter in the hallway occur at all hours, around the clock. There seems to be no schedule.

Gruff and threatening as his interrogators are, they never touch him. Striking a superior officer is the last unnatural act left them. They grow exasperated with his insistent denials that he has ever betrayed his country—never—and with his name dropping and long, complex answers.

"Do you ever answer with a simple yes or no," one of them asked.

"That depends," he says.

He is six months in that dungeon before the roof caves in, and the dust and smoke choke jailers and prisoners alike. The Allied planes have made a special point of obliterating the Gestapo's home.

The prisoners are gathered in a yard. Canaris recognizes it as the place where he met Heydrich years before. He supposes he and the others are about to be shot.

Instead, they are put on a truck and driven away. Despite the warning not to, he peeks through the canvas and is awestruck at the smoldering wreckage of steel and bricks. The entire city seems to have been blown apart. Handcuffed and shackled, they travel what feels an interminable distance. The roads are packed with refugees who often seem oblivious to the furious, impatient honks that insist they get out of the way. Finally, they end their journey near the border that once divided Germany and Czechoslovakia, to the outskirts of Flossenbürg.

They descended from the truck onto a dirt yard. Rows of shabby, indistinguishable huts stretch off in every direction. A work squad of emaciated prisoners in tattered rags stumbles past as the guards kick and push them.

Ahead is a squat, bunkerlike structure, the camp's special detention center for prisoners to be kept in isolation. He is taken to a small cell and chained to the wall.

There is one last act: a mock trial that preserves the veneer of legality to which the SS continues to cling. There is no question of the outcome. The SS is now in possession of a secret trove of documents unearthed in the search of military headquarters. The treasonous conversation of 1938 and the plans for a coup are spelled out in them.

The nooses are made ready before the court convenes: verdict first, trial second.

He doesn't grovel, as they expect. He argues that the documents are inconclusive. His involvement was directed at keeping track of the conspirators, not at assisting them.

Oster is brought in. He is told what Canaris said. Their friendship had ruptured years before, when Canaris discovered Oster had leaked the plans for the blitzkrieg in the West to Dutch intelligence. In so doing, he'd proven himself a traitor to the nation. At the time, Oster defended himself by raising the issue of the message Canaris had sent in order to scuttle the rescue of an SS agent in America. Canaris scoffed at the comparison. It was one thing to resist the illegal maneuverings of Himmler and Heydrich, another to put the existence of the entire German army at risk. "That is our tragedy," Oster said. "There is no longer any difference."

Though Canaris never turns in Oster, neither does he forgive him.

Told of Canaris's denial of being an active member in the plot to overthrow the Führer, Oster says, "That's not true. He knew and was involved in every activity of the resistance."

The interrogators revel in the spectacle of the self-admitted traitor implicating the suspected one. The papers discovered in a raid on army headquarters is sufficient to convict both men of high treason. But they rephrase Oster's reply so the Admiral can throw the blame back on Oster and continue the game: "The prisoner is lying, is he not?"

They wait patiently for an answer. They let their silence speak for them: *Come, Admiral, grovel for your life. Listen to your fear, as you always have. It's too late for bravery. Convict Oster for us and perhaps we won't inflict on you the death you've so richly earned. Perhaps we'll throw you back in your cell, into the dark recesses where your type breeds. We'll let the Allies find you alive, shriveled, crawling on all fours away from the sunlight. But you'll be alive, our little Admiral. Alive.*

The only sound is the clock on the wall.

"No, he's telling the truth," Canaris says.

There is one final interrogation. They want more names. He won't give them. They break his nose. And there is a last message from him. He taps it on the wall of his cell, in code to the prisoner next door: *My time is up. Was not a traitor. Did my duty as a German. If you survive remember me to my wife.*

"Out you come!" The door of the cell opens. He joins a file of four other men and is put at its head. Oster is behind him. Behind Oster is Dietrich Bonhöffer, the minister and theologian who'd been sheltered within the Abwehr. Bonhöffer's father had been replaced in the chair of psychiatry at Berlin and Charite Hospital by Max de Crinis, who did his best to purge the profession of "Jewish influence."

Bonhöffer is praying aloud and is ordered to be quiet.

"Get undressed!" They are pushed into the bath cubicles at the end of the hall. Bonhöffer is the first to undress. He kneels beside the neat pile of his clothes.

Canaris is ordered out into the concrete yard. In its center is a gallows. A rope hangs from a hook. A stepladder is beneath.

He doesn't pray or feel the urge to. These are the final things he feels: cold morning air against the feverish warmth of his naked skin; wet tingle of the concrete beneath his feet; urgent loosening in his bowels.

His hands are tied behind him. He mounts the stepladder. It is almost dawn. The last sky he will ever see: black, blue, hint of violet. The rope is put around his neck and adjusted so that his toes will dangle just one or two agonizing, tantalizing inches above the floor.

He waits for the ladder to be kicked away. His executioners stand around as if they have all day.

His whole body trembles. *O Christ, don't let me shit on myself!*

He looks down: no rodent's claws, or rat's tail, just his ghost-white feet as the ladder sails away.

# OBITS

# 1941-1967

Oh, it's easy to say we're all human beings. If there's a God—not only do we differ before Him as regards our malevolence or kindness, we all have different natures and different lives, in kind, in origin, in future and destiny we are all different.     —ALFRED DÖBLIN, *Berlin Alexanderplatz*

## Suicide of German Exile
*(N. Y. Standard, June 25, 1941)*

The body of Dr. Franz Ignatz, age 56, was discovered in his Yorkville apartment yesterday. He hanged himself in the bathroom. Dr. Ignatz's wife passed away last year. Neighbors said the couple had fled Nazi Germany several years ago. They described Dr. Ignatz as distraught over his wife's death and the unbroken string of German military successes.

◆

## John Mayhew Taylor, Acclaimed Reporter, Killed in Plane Crash While Covering Progress of Allied Invasion
*(N.Y. World-Telegram, June 12, 1944)*

◆

## John Lockwood, 83, Dean of City's Crime Reporters, Dies/ 'End of an Era,' His Colleagues Say
*(Knickerbocker News, August 26, 1951)*

◆

## Wilfredo Grillo, patriota, exiliado e incansable luchador por una Cuba democrática, falleció repentinamente en su casa ayer por la manana de un paro cardiaco.
(Tampa, *El Libertador*, 21 de septiembre de 1958.)

*Residente de los Estados Unidos durante casi todos los ultimos 20 anos, a Grillo lo involucraron en una etapa de su vida en un homicidio, crimen por el cual fue injustamente convicto y luego absuelto. Despues de una breve estancia en Cuba, se radicó en Tampa pero viajó extensamente apoyando la opocisión en contra del regimen de*

*Batista en su patria natal. El obituario completo aparece en la página 8 de este periódico.*

[translation by Mia Carbonell: WILFREDO GRILLO, PATRIOT, EXILE AND TIRELESS ADVOCATE OF A DEMOCRATIC CUBA, died suddenly at home yesterday morning from a heart attack. A resident of the U.S. for most of the past 20 years, Grillo was at one time the center of a notorious murder case in New York, a crime for which he was unjustly convicted and subsequently exonerated. After a brief return to Cuba, he settled in Tampa yet traveled widely in support of the opposition to the Batista regime in his native land. A full obituary appears on p.8 of this newspaper. (Tampa, *The Liberator*, September 21, 1958)]

## Fintan Dunne, Former Detective and O.S.S. Agent, Succumbs to Cancer at Age 63
(*N.Y. Standard*, April 16, 1961)

Fintan Dunne, a former city police detective who was recruited by General William J. Donovan as an early member of the Office of Strategic Services (O.S.S.), died of lung cancer on March 31, at his winter residence in Palm Beach, Florida.

Mr. Dunne, who served under General Donovan in France during WWI, was recruited into the O.S.S. in its formative days. He was sent into the field on a variety of clandestine intelligence missions, which took him behind enemy lines in Italy and occupied France.

At war's end, Mr. Dunne, who held the rank of captain, joined the Allied Commission for the Investigation of War Crimes. He resigned in September 1946 after publicly alleging that the criminal complicity of German physicians in the infamous sterilization and euthanasia programs was not being adequately prosecuted.

He subsequently founded the All-American Detective Agency, a successful pioneer in providing security services to private business. He sold the agency to Intercontinental Service Industries in 1958. For the past several years, he spent his winters in Florida. As well as his wife, Roberta, Mr. Dunne is survived by a niece, Mrs. Elba Munoz, of Miami, and four grand nieces and nephews.

## Prudence Addison Babcock, Society Figure and Prison Reform Advocate, Dies at 63/ Jailed for Three Years in 'Lover's Triangle' Murder of her husband
(*N.Y. World-Journal-Tribune*, March 11, 1967)